# Death Stalks
# Mr. Blackthorne

A Kitsap Sheriff Detective Marcus Jefferson Novel

## PETER STOCKWELL

Peter Stockwell
PO Box 3847
Silverdale, WA 98383

home: 360 697-4099 - cell: 360 509-3651
stockwellpa@wavecable.com

Published by
Westridge Art
PO Box 3847
Silverdale, WA 98383

First Printing 2017
Copyright © by Peter Stockwell

20 17 7 6 5 4 3 2 1

ISBN-13: 978-0-9886471-5-2

Printed in the United States of America

Publisher's note

Cover Design by
Peter Stockwell
Images from Shutterstock.com

Interior Design by
Timothy L. Meikle - Kitsap Printing Poulsbo, Wa

Distributed by
Westridge Art
PO Box 3847
Silverdale, WA 98383

# OTHER WORKS BY PETER STOCKWELL

ADULT FICTION
**Motive series**

Motivations
Motive
Jerry's Motives

NONFICTION
Stormin' Norman – The Sermons of an Episcopal Priest

## DEDICATION

*To Sarah, David, Lara, TJ, and Michelle. Five of the best children a man could raise to become great adults and wonderful parents.*

*"WHERE THERE IS MYSTERY,*
*IT IS GENERALLY SUSPECTED*
*THERE MUST ALSO BE EVIL."*

———————————

LORD BYRON

# TABLE OF CONTENTS

# CHAPTER

# 1

The innocuous yellow fluid gleamed in the bottle with the light of the greenhouse grow lights. He figured an electricity bill was evidence of the type of plants growing in neat rows. The small amount of Marijuana, now legal for people to buy in Washington State, was his cover purchase. The person who contracted with him to act as an agent for the purchase of the fluid gave him a large stack of twenty, fifty, and hundred dollar bills, enough for the bottles and plenty in reserve to assure an up-grade of lifestyle. He didn't like smoking pot, so the small bundle would be exchanged with desperate people for additional up-grades.

He handed a manila envelope to the owner of the greenhouse and placed the bottle in a packet container as instructed by the woman at the old fire station refurbished as an upscale restaurant in Edmonds, Washington. She instructed him as to what to acquire.

"Is this the best stash you have?" he asked, not wanting to appear naive. "I only want the best, you know." The grower shrugged with indifference which irritated the young man. He turned and left the greenhouse with his prize. "Bitch," he whispered.

As he drove to Edmonds with the bottles in a car furnished by the person who contracted his services, he wondered about the person who added intrigue to his life. What was it that she had said to him? Something about the sweetness of revenge? About righting a wrong? It made little sense to him and he spaced out most of her words. The money was real, and a reboot of life was his aim. Now the container sat on the seat next to him, unassuming and bland.

The last few months on the streets of Edmonds left him without hope until he met her and her interest in his downfall from formalities of wealth because of an addiction to gambling. Nothing remained of the money inherited from his grandfather. A trust had provided a comfortable life until he turned 26 when all of the controls were removed, and the fund converted to his name and usability.

He underwent treatment with Gamblers Anonymous for a year and now, at the age of 31, he understood what he'd lost with his frivolous wantonness.

The woman was dark, Spanish-like and willing to help him trade his lifestyle of back alleys and doorways for a motel room and food, but it came with price tag. Resistance was futile.

After showering and shaving with new towels and toiletries, he had dressed in new clothing, consumed a meal at a local restaurant, and spent a comfortable night embracing his benefactor who educated him about sharing bodies properly. The liaison continued into a third week and his disbelief about this turn of luck faded with each passing day.

For acquiring her mysterious item, a prearranged meeting at the motel was another payday. Their interludes had diminished in the last few days as she demanded more of his talent for finding the right kind of contacts. She became more mysterious as the days turned into a week, a happening he regretted. The sex spurred him on as no other woman accomplished when he had wealth. Now he craved her companionship for a moment or an hour. Love was not part of the attraction, since he felt none for her and believed none existed from her. Physical satisfaction was all he wanted.

"Do you have it?" she asked as he opened the door to his temporary home. Her brown eyes expanded in anticipation. He observed the rising of her breasts as she inhaled and held out her left hand. He placed the carton in it and kissed her ruby lips not releasing her hand or her body which he caressed with his other hand. He understood she allowed such foolishness but only for a moment. He sat on the bed tossing the marijuana beside him.

"What's so important about those bottles? What is it?" His inquiry created a coolness as she hissed at him ignoring his questions. She placed the container on the dressing table and stripped out of her clothing. Standing in lace underwear which hid nothing but supported ample equipment for his hands to explore, she approached him.

"You have done well. Time for another reward, another lesson in how to sate the desires of a lust-filled lady." She pushed him until he lay flat on the bed. She unleashed the beast and consumed all of it. He placed hands on her head which needed no guidance. As the afternoon lesson continued, another person emerged from the bathroom unknown to the student whose naked body covered his Spanish senorita. A climax masked the needle's penetration.

His body slumped as the contents of the syringe instilled unconsciousness. She rolled him to one side and stood. The other woman asked, "Is it necessary for you to jump his bone each time he does what you want? Can't you just thank him?" A smile and a kiss quieted her question.

"I like sex." She placed a robe over her nakedness and continued. "You're the best sister a person could have. He is so into me that you could switch with me and he would never know. You might like what he has to offer." The twins hugged. The robed sibling headed for the bathroom and a shower; the other sat on the bed next to the unresponsive dupe, admiring his physique. Too bad they wouldn't be sharing him in the future. She enjoyed sex much like her sister, but his task was complete, and the role of boyfriend was over. Upon awaking in the next few hours, his head would hurt, and this dissolved partnership would break his heart. She fondled the limpness and thought of what her sister had said about switching places.

As she packed clothing and cleared the room of any trace of them, she wondered about their plans for another patsy. Their game had consequences which she worried could ruin life as they lived it.

Checking the floor around the bed, she looked at the victim of poverty so easily aroused to do whatever they wanted. The shower stopped, drawing attention to the bathroom door. After a few minutes her sister emerged, robed, with towel wrapped hair. "Oh, thank you for cleaning up." She dressed in clothes left out of the packing. "How's our boy doing?"

"He's done for the next couple of hours. Are we going to leave him as he lies, or should we put him inside the sheets?" She sat next to him and gazed.

"If you want to; you always are the better person when we leave someone behind." After clearing the bathroom of any girl items and traces of hair and skin which could derail plans, she placed a small vial near the coffee maker along with several nondescript tea bags. The two women left.

As predicted, he awoke to a throbbing, which blinded him for a moment and induced a vomit-like urge in his stomach. His clothing remained on the floor. His stash and money were on the side table. Looking around, he figured he had fallen asleep after making love to her. Was she in the bathroom? Wobbly legs struggled to reach the door which he despaired accomplishing. In the bathroom nothing remained of her cosmetics or clothing; no evidence of her existence. He sat on the toilet without needing to use it, confused and hurting. "What happened?"

Standing, shaky and unperceptive, he returned to the bedroom, found his clothing and dressed. Seeing the items on the shelf by the coffee machine, he grabbed the carafe and returned to the sink. With enough water for several cups he poured it into the drip box and placed the glass jar on the heating element. Coffee and filters eluded finding, so he opted for the teabags and flipped the switch. Collapsing on the bed, his legs dangled as he lay on the rumpled sheets.

"What time is it?" His whisper, aimed at no one, recalled the escapade from earlier in the day. The pot signaled the hot water was ready. Placing a bag in a cup, he poured hot water and stirred with a plastic spoon he tore from a small utensils bag. Picking up the small jar and tipping it, a slow stream joined the dark amber drink. Letting the steam rise, he found his watch. Checking it, he laughed. "I've lost three hours? What have I done? Where is she?" He picked up the cup and sipped it, trying not to burn his lips or tongue. The liquid tasted good and comforted his lost soul.

As he searched around the room, nothing indicated anyone else being present at any time. Since he still had his money and his stash of pot, he relaxed. Another couple of days in the motel was fine with him. He finished one cup and poured more water over the bag. Adding more sweetener from the small jar, he stirred the cup and drank with more gusto finishing the cup in a few seconds. "Food. I need food." He left for a restaurant next to the motel.

Returning to his room after consuming turkey, mashed potatoes with gravy, a side of mixed vegetables, some bread and several beers, he broke a sweat as if he'd run a marathon. His body twitched, and a feeling of nettles stung his skin. Cramps raced through his intestines as his chest burned with fire, intense and debilitating. His right hand reached for his left upper arm, rubbing it in a feeble attempt to quell the increasing tension his heart experienced. He crashed to the floor, crawling toward the bed, hoping for a night's rest to relieve his apparent food poisoning.

"Induce vomiting," he called aloud. He stood, moaning with each torturous step until he reached the bathroom. A finger in the throat to start the gag reflex failed to materialize, as he slumped on the cold linoleum, struggling to inhale air. His heart seemed to explode in his chest as a final farewell to poverty and a life changed by a beautiful brunette with ulterior motives. He closed his eyes and let the darkness consume his last attempt to live.

# CHAPTER

# 2

Kitsap Sheriff Detective Marcus Jefferson and his family boarded the Alaskan bound American Pacific cruise liner, Salish Sea, after clearing security and boarding protocols. They carried small bags of personal items with them, since their large suitcases were being handled by the crew.

Priority boarding, a luxury of the suites which were their homes for the next two weeks, afforded an extra easing of anxieties. The color of personalized key cards allowed Cruise director, Jarina Camacho, to recognize the occupants of the Elliot Bay suite. She smiled as people passed her station by the drawbridge. "Welcome aboard, Mr. And Mrs. Jefferson," she said, her pleasant Spanish-like visage providing the necessary attitude. The Jefferson clan stopped.

"I understand this is your first time traveling with us," she said. She continued her smile and Marc wondered how the young lady knew who they were. He dismissed it as a requirement of her job.

"Yes, my kids are excited, as are Joan and I."

Sarah asked, "How do we find our rooms?" She directed a young Southeast Asian man to come forward. The steward approached the family as Marc unfolded a map provided at the check-in desk.

"Follow me," he said. Sarah perked up, noticing his youthful face and foreign accent. He started for the elevators ascending to the next deck. "Let me take you on a tour of our ship." Checking the key cards, he said, "I see you are in the Elliot Bay Suite and one of the Puget Suites." He directed them to the elevators and pressed the button for the Navigation deck.

After climbing several levels to the suites which would house them for the trip's duration the steward led them to their destinations. "These are our finest accommodations. I'm sure you will be very comfortable here. Your luggage will be delivered soon. If there is anything else I can do for you, please contact the front desk." He winked at Sarah. He instructed them as to use of the key card and opened the Elliott Bay Suite door. He then proceeded to open the door to a Puget Suite door next to the Elliott Bay. Each suite appeared clean and orderly, ready for the family residing in them. The young steward then handed Marc the key cards he used to open the doors and turned to leave. He smiled at Sarah again, a blush crossing her face.

"Nice digs, Mrs. Jefferson." Marc bowed to Joan. Sarah's eyes turned upward and scanned the room.

"Thank you, Mr. Jefferson. I must call my parents to tell them again how much we appreciate them helping us to have time away from the grind of daily work." Joan's remark preceded Sarah's question about sleeping arrangements.

"So, where do I get to sleep? I don't see a bed other than the king in that separate room."

"As I remember," Marc said and moved to the large sofa, "there is a sleeper in this couch." He removed the cushions and pull out the queen bed folded into the seating. "This looks quite comfy." Sarah rolled her eyes again.

"Why do the boys get their own room and I have to share with you?"

Joan responded in as calm a voice an exacerbated parent could. "As we explained to you at home. This suite is large enough to accommodate the three of us and you are not willing to share with either of your brothers. So, you get to share with us."

"It's not fair. I should have my own room. I'm old enough and responsible enough. You've said so."

Joan's voice rose as her eyes glared at Sarah. "We are not wealthy people and are able to travel in this luxury because my parents, your grandparents, were generous enough to help. After what happened this spring with Uncle Jerry, Grandpa Ti, and your father, we needed to get away. Be happy you're here."

A long groan followed. "I get it. I just wish there were other girls aboard, so I don't get bored. I didn't see anyone in the boarding room who wasn't over thirty."

"I'm sure someone is aboard who meets your requirement for companionship." Sarah grimaced and tilted her head, resigned to suite confinement when not dining.

A commotion in the hallway attracted their attentions as they explored the suite. "Wait here," Marc cautioned. Joan frowned at his comment, but he missed it.

Outside the door an older man and two young women were entering another Puget Suite next to the boys' suite. Marc approached. "Good morning." One of the women turned and sneered as the man disappeared into the room. The other woman, who looked to be no more than 25 years old stuck out a hand for him to shake.

"Good morning to you," she said as he reciprocated with his own hand. Her grip was firm but gentle, warm and fit. "Are you in the Elliot Bay Suite?" Marc nodded. "Forgive my companions, we had hoped to be staying in it, but you booked before we did." Her face beamed a friendly smile and eyes glistened. "My name is Gabriella Montoya."

"Marcus Jefferson," he smiled intrigued by her beauty, youth, and overt personality. "Are you from around here? Seattle, I mean." Her head shook.

"We're from Phoenix, Arizona. Are you from this area?" Marc's head bobbed.

"Wendlesburg, actually. It's located across Puget Sound in Kitsap County." Before he could continue the conversation, a bellow distracted them.

"Excuse me. I must go. I'm sure my companions need me." She turned a skillful pirouette and waltzed into the room. Marc's head bent to his right as he studied the shapely body and form fitting pants. Joan sidled up beside him. As he became aware of her, he wheeled around with a warmth filling his face.

"Rather lovely, isn't she." Her face steeled against the possible jealousy burning in her heart. "A little young for you, don't you think?"

Marc chortled. "She hasn't anything on you. I was wondering

about the man in that room and his two companions. They have to be his daughters or he's Hugh Hefner in disguise." They turned and met three other pairs of eyes. Marc observed his eldest son craning to see the visage which had disappeared.

"Boys, let's see where you're staying." The room contained two beds and ample room for them to co-exist without conflict. "You should be comfortable here." They opened closets and cupboards and claimed a bed by landing on it with a jump.

"When does our luggage arrive?" James asked. A knock on the door fulfilled his query. A Filipino gentleman placed the bags on the luggage racks, accepted a tip from Joan and left to place other luggage in other rooms. Marcus and James unpacked, placing clothing in drawers and the closet. Joan rejoined Marc and Sarah who had departed to unpack their bags.

He approached and hugged her. She relaxed onto his shoulder and closed her eyes. Pressing her into his body, feeling her curves, expunged the memory of Ms. Montoya. Everything was well and criminal investigations could stay away for the two-week duration of the voyage. Sarah watched her parents as they flirted. Her eyes smiled even though a twinge of embarrassment reddened her face. She continued to unpack her bag as a distraction.

Joan said, "Marc, you can relax. Nothing will disrupt our vacation. Be happy. After all, you proved your uncle had not committed suicide. You destroyed an evil drug cartel, reunited family members, and made us safe. Now is our time for an escape from the rigors of our jobs." He squeezed her again as she whispered in his ear. "Make love to me." He glanced at his daughter, busy with clothing items.

"Sarah, why don't you and your brothers explore the boat and then be our guides," Marc expressed with a glint in his eyes." She rolled hers and left. A comment muttered as she left was not audible or intended to be heard.

Marc gazed at Joan as he said, "Do you think she knows what we intend?" He loosened clothing as he spoke. Joan stripped off her blouse, pondered his query and then continued disrobing.

"She's growing up and understands what people do the in the privacy of their own rooms." Marc placed the safety lock on after removing his pants.

# CHAPTER

## 3

The delivery van arrived as the passengers proceeded through the entry gates to the holding areas for the Salish Sea cruise ship. 'Flowers-to-go' advertised the contents with pictures of bouquets, baskets of fruit and smiling recipients, precious cargo to decorate suites and dining rooms on the ship. Boxes of fruit and wines and packages of various flowers would be used by the crew aboard to create baskets. Special orders ordered by family and friends were accepted and delivered after security measures occurred.

The Spanish-looking driver and her twin assistant loaded the ship's labeled carts, each delivery prescribed for refrigeration units in the storage holds of the ship. After they transferred carts to the scanning personnel, they returned to the van for the baskets destined for a particular suite or dining room. Jarina Camacho, as well as being the cruise director, oversaw the operation, checking the destination of each basket or bouquet. She thought it quaint that the delivery persons were twins who looked to be in their late twenties or early thirties. An emotional affinity to Spanish heritage because of her birth in Jamaica created the attraction which developed into a strange relationship months ago. The arrangement for one particular basket, sent from an unknown provider to a particular recipient, was not the usual procedure. Instructions from the more assertive twin were clear. The one particular basket was assigned for only one particular suite. The instructions made sense to Jarina, and the addition of a special envelope filled with new twenty-dollar bills would impel others aboard to do tasks to earn them.

After the crew scanned for illicit cargo, it was placed on a shelf for delivery to the assigned room marked on a card to assure proper delivery. Nothing suspicious appeared and the basket was cleared.

"Be sure to deliver these as soon as possible," she said to a young steward named Iskandar. He noted the baskets contained the usual wines and cheeses, crackers and breads. One basket contained an unlabeled bottle with a yellowish color, small and indistinct. He thought it was probably honey.

"Yes, ma'am." He picked up baskets and made his way to the suites, as the labels indicated. Jarina returned to sorting flowers and gifts, overseeing the members of the staff arranging the items for delivery. He smiled knowing the enjoyment awaiting the recipient.

Returning to the delivery center, another steward approached him. "Did you get that special package on site?" Iskandar nodded. "Then you can have anything you want on this cruise, money, girls, and in international water, you may gamble and drink alcohol." Eyes widened anticipating his entry into the dark world of cruise line employment.

Stories of adventure enticed him to delve into the mysterious events which occurred without knowledge of the command members of the crew or the passengers. His payments for completed tasks which were not listed on the manifest or advertised by the company, and the money, helped his family in Indonesia. Why shouldn't he enjoy the favors of others? He worked hard for his wages and wanted nothing more than to share the riches of this excess of living.

He had spotted a potential conquest as she entered the ship with other people who were probably family members. Her beauty excited in him a natural attraction, an urge to break protocol and speak with her. He had watched her and the others, accepting the time he had to wait for an opportunity. Had she seen him? Did she smile? His breathing increased. Iskandar wanted nothing more than acceptance as a trustworthy crewman. A twinge of anxiety flowed through him as easily as blood flushed his face. Another older steward handed him a twenty-dollar bill.

"Find out what you can about the young lady you admire. Her family is important to me. I want to know what happens to them without fail. There is more of this if you succeed and satisfy my interest without question." He nodded and stuffed the money in his right hip pocket.

As the family had finished checking in at the desk, his time arrived. The father appeared lost and worked a deck map without success. He jumped at the chance to help. "Follow me." His inquiry elicited a smile from the object of his quest. After checking their documents, he continued. "I see you are in the Elliot Bay Suite and one of the Puget Suites." He had guided the family of five to elevators which transported them to the proper deck.

Returning to the lower deck with anticipation for an interlude during the cruise, Iskandar spotted one special basket for deliver to the Elliot Bay Suite. Now, with all of the other prearranged gifts delivered, he asked for other assignments and accompanying bonuses. He scanned for the older steward but did not find him. He approached the cruise director and asked, "Is there anything I can do for you?"

Jarina pushed a cart toward him with several vases of flowers. "Deliver these to the Gold Rush dining room." He complied and left for an upper deck of the ship. He whistled as he waited for the service elevator. One of the Filipino room maids waited with him.

"You are happy today?" She grinned as she spoke. "I am finished with my room assignments if you want to meet when you are done." He returned her smile and thought about the last time he had spent his free time in her bed. He wagged his head, but thought of the young beauty in the Elliot Bay Suite. His practice with this girl would improve his attempt to share with the passenger.

"I will finish my shift with this delivery. Wait for me in your room. I will return." He pushed the button for the top deck and whistled an airy sound resembling a nondescript song from his home country. Life was better than he ever envisioned when he signed his contract for three years of sailing various parts of the world. The contract was complete when this sailing was finished. He wanted to stay in the northwest home of the cruise line, Seattle, Washington. An offer from a stranger who knew the older steward made staying a possibility. The stranger met him in Juneau, Alaska, on a previous seven-day trip out of Vancouver, British Columbia two years ago. The conversation was short and pointed. He needed to cooperate with the steward who set up the meeting. Iskandar agreed and received assurance that his family in Indonesia was safe and financially stable. All he had to do was carry certain packages he would receive in Vancouver to Seattle and deliver them to people who would meet him. For the last two years his mission was a success until a sudden and unexplained cessation of contacts in Vancouver.

He had been warned not to question the contents of the packages which resembled gifts and were easily brought aboard when he returned from land excursions. The crew member who checked him never questioned the packages. His instructions included returning only when certain people were working the scanners. But nothing had been available for the last few months. His family was still safe, but personal hush moneys dried up. Current moneys were a plus when he complied to instructions from the older steward.

Returning to the lower deck and his room, he washed his hands and face. He packed a pair of condoms in his pocket and left to find the young room maid and another lesson in sharing bodies. She had expressed an interest in a more permanent relationship which Iskandar dismissed as unacceptable. He was twenty-two. The girl had turned nineteen when she offered herself to him. He imagined she was a present for his unquestioning loyalty and cooperation.

Lying beside her as she slept, he studied her body. She was petite, pretty, with flawless skin and long black hair. She was not as smart as he liked, but her compliant nature excused her lack of knowledge. He figured this trip was the last he would see of her. Little did he realize the truth of his premonition.

# CHAPTER

# 4

James Blackthorne sat on the bed in the room which was his home for the next fourteen days. "This is not what I expected. Paula, how did this happen? I thought you booked our trip in plenty of time." His hands pounded the bed. "Who is the family in my suite? Find out and get them to switch rooms." He stood and moved toward the bathroom. "Get me answers. Now." Paula Merino and Gabriella Montoya left to fulfill his request.

After the door closed, he smiled. His editor, Gabrielle, improved his recent manuscripts into popular books which made him wealthier. He found her at a small publishing company and spirited her away with a promise of adventure and more money. Paula managed his life, both in private and in public, scheduling events, speeches and signings for more than ten years. This cruise came as a direct result of her inquiry to American Pacific Cruises. She was an asset which he was not willing to lose for any reason, but his complicated relationship with her drove a wedge between the young women until they discovered his delectations. Now each of them wanted more.

His third wife, Alana, had died because of complications from cirrhosis of the liver, drinking after her discovery of his penchant for his business manager. She had been the other woman which destroyed his second marriage. His first wife, Lenora, the love of his life, had been killed in an automobile accident, leaving him despondent and heartbroken. He grew more reclusive for several months, until a chance meeting at a book signing drew him out of his sheltered life. A man, whose sister accompanied him to meet James, dabbled in writing and engaged the author in conversation after the signing event.

Uncovering her single status, James asked her to dinner. When she accepted, he decided to stop hiding from life and embrace what it had to offer. They dated for several months and married, happy until her desire for children and an inability to procreate pushed them emotionally apart. James met and began his ill-advised tryst with Alana, who was an oasis in his emotional desert. Divorce cost him much of his accumulated wealth, but marriage to his tryst settled his mind but not his heart. When Paula came to work as his manager and his confidant, an affair began shortly after.

A knock reminded him he was alone and had to answer his own door. "Did you forget something?" Opening the door his eyes widened. "Oh, my luggage. Come in." He stepped aside holding the door as the steward entered with two large bags. "Just leave them." He tipped the man who closed the door as he left.

Opening one bag, he unpacked, placing some clothing in drawers and hanging suits and jackets in the closet. Placing the other bag on the bed, he unzipped the cover and flipped it back. Picking up a manila envelope, he cradled it for a moment before tossing it on the table behind him. Pulling out the next item, he smirked. The file folder contained the information he garnered from his contact in Seattle. No one was to see what he had gathered until he sent this most controversial book to his publisher. If anyone knew what he had, trouble could follow. One more piece of substantive information would complete the rough draft manuscript.

Looking around the room for a hiding place to keep the folder safe from prying eyes, he adopted the cliché "between the mattresses." Neither of his companions could know what the folder contained, but Gabby would edit it before he added the last material. His agent insisted.

He finished emptying his bag of writing utensils: a laptop, three books about character development, poisons, and a history of Seattle, and a small external hard drive. Opening the laptop, he logged in and plugged in the power supply. Attaching the hard drive, he set them on the table with the manila envelope.

A knock on the door interrupted his thinking. "Who is it?" His voice rose as he approached. "What do you want?"

"James, it's Gabby. I have answers." He opened the door. She strolled in with a sparkle in her eyes and a smile coursing her face. "The Jefferson's are unwilling to switch. Their daughter is with them and their two boys are in the room next to them. I'm sorry." She sat in a chair. The stateroom was large enough for a single person, a person who had little need or desire for opulence, except on this cruise ship. He was a star attraction for the early evening shows, who acquiesced to meeting an adoring readership and signing his latest best seller.

"I want to meet them and find out if they read my books, or any books. What does he do that he can afford such an expensive room?"

Gabby's brown eyes, flecked with green, explored the accommodations as she answered. "I don't know, but I'll ask for you."

"Where's Paula?" Blackthorne held out his hands for Gabby to hold as he pulled her to a standing position. "My god, you are beautiful." He pulled her closer without touching any part of her except the hands.

"Yes sir, as you have told me on numerous occasions. Paula is in our stateroom next door unpacking her suitcase. I need to attend to mine." She reached her mouth to his and kissed his lips. "I'll be back later. After your last show." Unhooking her hands from his, she left to attend to her suitcase and uncover the occupations of the Jefferson family.

Blackthorne clicked on the screen using a wireless mouse he retrieved from the bag on the bed. Opening the writing folder on the screen, he scrolled the numerous files until one cryptic name which he retrieved.

He made editorial corrections as he read the page on the screen. The manuscript read like many of his other books, built him a growing readership. "This next one will be greater than anything I've written before. I'll show those arrogant bastards in New York who controls my intellectual property."

The words appeared as magic fingers typed letter after letter without fail, constructing comprehensive sentences and paragraphs. Eyes glared at the screen and mouth filed a firm set with his brain. Opening the manila envelope, he removed the contents. Placing them next to his computer required a shift of the hard drive which contained the files of thirty-seven novels and business records. It acted as a backup for the files filling the 580 gigabyte internal drive. He had purchased the external drive to increase storage capacity. The next book was absent from both drives since the story was a deviation from his usual contracted books.

The expose' would finish the career of the one person he detested most. "Research be damned," he whispered. "He deserves this because of his callousness to my wants and desires." Fingers flew across the keyboard until a rap on the door interrupted his thoughts. He closed the laptop and placed the manuscript in the manilla envelope. "Coming," he said resigned to the lack of aloneness.

Opening the door, Gabby smiled and reported her findings as she walked into the room. "Mr. Jefferson is a sheriff's detective with Kitsap County here in Washington State and his wife is a nurse. I'm not aware of how they can afford the Elliot Bay Suite. They seem like nice people, though."

"Nice can be a pain in the ass." Pausing a moment, he continued, "Okay, we'll remain as we are, since everyone is settled. Lock the door and come here." She complied and wrapped her arms around his waist. His hands caressed her face, then held it as he pressed his lips to hers. "Is Paula next door?" She nodded. "Okay then let's make this quick before she needs me for something."

She released him and removed her clothing as he stepped out of his pants and folded them neatly before placing them on the chair. Gabby unbuttoned his shirt as he slid underwear to the floor.

"I love you," she said.

"I know."

# CHAPTER

# 5

The Steward checked the room to be sure he was correct. Elliot Bay Suite clearly showed on the tag of the gift basket. Instructed by his steward boss to be sure of a correct delivery, he read the envelope again. Although no name appeared on the card, he assured himself the delivery belonged in the room. Knocking he waited for an answer.

The door opened and the young lady who enthralled him appeared. Adrenaline boosted his heart rate when she smiled and said, "Come in." She stepped aside as he entered.

"I have a basket which is for you to enjoy as you travel." His English skills were improving with each voyage he made, speaking with American tourists, who had so much more than his family in Indonesia. He had promised to send money to support a mother and three younger siblings, which he accomplished with each passing month of work. The expense of money transfers through the organization he used was not as bad as other ways of transferring funds. The arrangement by unknown people for unidentified packages he carried to Seattle from Vancouver, B. C. included a small stipend. He asked no questions, and never refused requests of his services. Certain information he uncovered he kept to himself. Life presented a far improved environment from his home in Indonesia. The extra money he received from undisclosed sources augmented his salary with very few requirements.

So he waited, interested in the girl he had guided to these rooms, the beautiful teenager whose smile captivated his imagination. He waited for a word from her to encourage him to speak and ask her for one day of attention. She reciprocated.

"You're almost as young as I am, I think. Would you be willing to show me around the ship, if it isn't against the rules or something?"

"It would be an honor." His next statement was a simple lie which he figured was not atrocious. "I am eighteen years and three months." He hoped that was not too old for her. His mind raced with anticipation. His last voyage brought a quick no-strings-attached romance with an older woman of twenty-six years. She taught him about love-making and now he wanted to share his knowledge.

"I will be sixteen in two months." Sarah reached out her hand for him to hold which excited him, and her face flushed as she observed the change in him.

"I must get back to my chores. Can I see you in two hours? I will be free of any obligations until eight tonight. She nodded. "Meet me by the auditorium on the second floor." He left with a spring in his step. Although rules prohibited much fraternization between staff and guests, it happened and could be a lucrative increase in tax free pay, if played correctly.

Back in the bowels of the ship, he found his supervisor. "I met her, again. She is very pretty and asked me to show her around." His supervisor nodded and placed a twenty in his hand. Iskandar slipped it into his pocket.

"You did well. When are you meeting with her?"

"I asked her to go to the auditorium in two hours." He fidgeted knowing his next stop was the young Filipino maid.

"Go satisfy your hormones, but do not miss your assignment. Become her friend and I'll reward you well."

"After I become her friend, what then? Do I take her to my room?" Warmth spread in his face. He was not aware if his superior steward knew about his liaison with the other girl.

"I will let you know what I want you to do with her when the time arrives. Now is not the time for questions." The young steward turned and grinned as he departed. He felt taller and stronger than any of the other stewards as he returned to his room to gather his best clothes and meet the young maid. Each day brought another interesting experience. As he entered his room he thought about his family in Indonesia. A picture sat on the desk by his bed.

School had been a luxury for his siblings and himself. Now his two younger sisters were completing high school and his brother received a degree in computer systems integration. His father's health suffered from years of smoking, but medical science helped relieve the cravings. The money for helping his superiors accomplish unknown circumstances helped his family which helped him with confidence.

Hand raised in a fist to knock, he stalled by her door and thought about the girl in the Elliot Bay. "What am I doing?" His whisper was interrupted by the door opening. He stammered and dropped his fist. "Ah, hi. I was just about to knock." She stepped aside to let him in. Her room was as small as his but seemed neater, more orderly. His reluctance melted as the door closed.

Awakening after an exertion induced nap, Iskandar glanced at the flawless body next to him. She slept as peaceful as a kitten in a warm window. Picking up his watch, his eyes expanded. "Tae," he exclaimed with clenched teeth. His companion stirred and her eyes opened. As he dressed, she sat up dropping the sheet which covered her.

"What is the matter?" An innocent query raised his ire. She cringed.

"Nothing. I'm late to an appointment." He finished buttoning his shirt and tucked it into his pants. He gazed a moment longer than expected. Turning to the door, he said, "I must go."

As he approached the auditorium, he expected the girl would not be present. He feared what his boss would say if he failed his mission. He feared the loss of money for his family. He feared for their safety and for his own. Entering the balcony area, he scanned for her but saw nothing. He whirled to leave and knocked into his target. Hands from both of them connected to upper body areas. She dropped her hands from his chest, as he released her shoulders from his hands. "I do apologize." His voice wavered. She smiled.

"I thought you stood me up," she said, a blush brightening her cheeks. Her hands wrapped into each other behind her back. Her head tilted and eyes stared at the floor.

"I am sorry to be late. I was previously engaged in another affair." He offered a hand. "Shall we tour the ship?" Sarah unlocked her fingers and latched onto his hand. He led her around the auditorium and took her behind the stage to see where the shows started. A noise attracted their attention

Sarah whispered, "Should we be here?"

"It is okay. I think Ms. Jarina may be preparing for the next performance." He tugged her deeper into the waiting area of the stage. "Ms. Jarina, are you in here?" His voice echoed. Silence followed. His anxiety grew as measured steps drew them further into the darkness. Sarah pulled closer to him, hugging him for assurance. A loud click sounded and lights illuminated the backstage area.

"Welcome to my world, Iskandar." Jarina Camacho strolled to them. Sarah peaked around his shoulder. "Miss Jefferson, are you having a nice time on board?"

She nodded a slow acknowledgment to her question and stepped out from behind Iskandar. "Did you know we were coming?" she asked with a sheepish turn of her head. Sarah glanced at Iskandar and then at Jarina. She thought, "Am I in over my head?"

Jarina placed a hand on her shoulder. "I did not, but let me show you around. Back here is where everything gets started. Our entertainers have plenty of room in our green rooms and star dressing rooms to prepare. Have you met Mr. Blackthorne? I think he is in a suite near you."

"Yes, my parents have talked with him and his assistants. He seems like a nice person." Sarah squirmed as she spoke, remembering the argument between her father and the author. Iskandar held her hand again leading her toward the rear of the backstage. Jarina smiled as she watched the young couple. The plan to disrupt the family of Marcus Jefferson continued as designed by the twins. Her role was to insure the delivery of certain items and her personnel interacting with the family.

"I want to go," Sarah said to Iskandar. They cut through the curtain to the stage. Iskandar stopped and pulled Sarah to him. She suspired, anxiety rising as his lips caressed her cheek. "No, please." Her whisper halted his actions. His smiled disarmed her and she changed her mind. Cradling his face in her hands she placed her lips on his mouth. Arms wrapped her body tight to his. She realized the danger of being alone with him and didn't care anymore. Her life had contained no risk until this moment. His tongue traversed her gums and lips, a tingling traversing her body.

Panic set in with the feelings. She pushed his body away, though he resisted. He released his prey and said, "Let's go to my room where we can have some privacy." She hesitated to answer, curious but cautious. Her head rocked back and forth. Then she turned toward the stairs leading to the aisle and safety of her suite. Iskandar hurried after her to catch her before she attained a more public area. Grasping her arm and stopping her progress, he spun her to face him. "Please, accept my apology. I didn't mean to frighten you."

Sarah said nothing but tears rained down her cheeks. Wide eyes and an open mouth exploded on Iskandar's face. She ran from the hall to the  elevators. Pushing the button did not speed the call for a car. He arrived as the doors opened and stepped in with her. Trapped alone with him, her heart beat a faster pace and breathing slowed. "I can't. I can't fall for you. Not here." She pushed the button for the Navigation Deck and the Elliot Bay Suite. Silence held sway.

# CHAPTER

# 6

I can't believe the arrogance of the guy to think he should have this suite. I don't care if he is some famous writer." Marc stood on the veranda with Joan after their initiation of the bedroom. The ship's horn sounded to indicate departure for Alaskan waters. Family time had become a reality when Joan's parents gave them an early anniversary present which helped fund their elaborate cruise. Turning toward her, Marc grinned. "Nothing should interfere with our enjoying a relaxing, quiet voyage.

Joan wrapped her arm in his and said, "I wasn't sure this was happening when you undertook the investigation into your uncle's death." She laid her head on his chest and continued, "Thank you for being the best husband and companion a girl could want."

"Let's join the kids and head up top to watch the ship leave the dock." They entered the cabin to find Sarah sitting in a chair looking like a lost little girl. She looked up as they approached her. "How long have you been here? I thought you and the boys were exploring the boat. Is something wrong?"

"Dad, nothing's wrong. I just can't believe we're here in this cabin." He chuckled and suggested they find the boys.

On the Lido deck three intrepid explorers strolled decks with restaurants and pools, spas and fitness centers. James and Marcus ran up to them. "Let's get our suits on and swim for a while," James said. The boys left before any parental admonitions occurred. Sarah followed.

Clinging to Marc, Joan said, "I'm so happy we could do this." Marc smiled a crook grin and cocked an eyebrow. The stroll pace slowed when they approached the dockside railing and watched the last of the mooring ropes fall to the water as a tug pulled the bow out of the slip.

"Joan, we have nothing but smooth sailing ahead. Why don't we join the kids in the pool?" She nodded and they departed to retrace their steps to their elaborate accommodations. On the deck of their suite Gabrielle Montoya stood outside of the suite she shared with the other young lady.

"Hello, again, Mr. Jefferson, Mrs. Jefferson." Gabby remained polite which offered no cover as she fidgeted and set a straight jawline. A glance toward the cabin door caused Marc and Joan to stop.

"Is everything alright?" Marc asked. She turned her gaze to him, eyes widening and mouth opening to speak. Nothing came out. The door opened before another word could pass. She let her breath, held for a moment, respire as James Blackthorne exited the room. He paused, frowned and then spoke.

"Mr. Jefferson, I'm James Blackthorne, and I do wish you would reconsider a transfer of rooms. As a writer I desire certain privacies which are confounded by having two suites. My editor and manager are required of me for their skills and talents which are not easily accommodated by the present arrangement." He stuck forward a hand for shaking the verbal agreement he expected.

Marc's hand began an ascent and halted as Joan answered the query. "Mr. Blackthorne, I do appreciate the predicament which seems to be thwarting your convenience, but my husband and children are happy with our current situation which we have saved many years to enjoy. We'll stay where we are. It is a pleasure to meet you, though. I've read some of your work and do find it interesting.

"Thank you, I can sign any books you have with you, if you like." Marc figured his offer amounted to an incentive to reconsider exchanging suites. He turned to enter his room, but Joan stood her ground.

"Mr. Blackthorne, I don't have any books with me, though I would appreciate you signing one for me." Gabby disappeared into the suite. As the conversation lagged, Joan turned to follow Marc but hesitated. "Sir, I hope you have a pleasant voyage." His frown seemed painted on his face, a permanent addition. Gabby returned with his latest thriller. James grunted and pulled a thin tipped felt pen from his coat pocket. He signed his name only, not asking how to spell Joan. No message, no greeting, nothing more. He handed the book to her.

"What do I owe you?" She asked. He huffed and walked toward the elevators.

"I do apologize for my boss. He's under some pressure as a presenter. He's an introvert and crowds are not his forte." She backed away and turned to enter her suite. Facing Joan again, she continued, "As a nurse, do you think James is alright." She lowered her eyes. "He seems more distant than usual, as if he doesn't feel well. He won't say anything, though."

Joan stared at Gabby. "I didn't see anything out of the ordinary, but I wasn't evaluating him. Talk to Dr. Middlebury. He's ship's doctor for the cruise." She nodded and left Joan in the hallway. Entering their suite, she found Marc now in swimsuit, holding a towel. She gazed at her husband's body, trim and muscular, and thought about delaying the dip in the pool. Placing the book on the table, she scooted to him, place arms around his neck, and whispered her suggestion.

"What if the kids come back?" Joan place lips on his and his plan to join the children melted away.

Lying entwined on the king-sized bed after their escapade they relaxed. Joan unlocked and leaning on an elbow, faced Marc and said, "The young lady with that author asked me a strange question." Marc sat up. "She asked me if he was alright. She said he was more distant, like he wasn't well."

"What did you tell her?"

"What could I say? I didn't have any reference from which to draw any kind of conclusion." She left the bed and put on a robe. "That situation is odd. Two young women traveling with an older man doesn't seem right."

"It's none of our business what adults do in their own private lives." He rose from the bed and located his discarded swim shorts. Grabbing a towel, he continued, "They may have a strange arrangement, but it's their arrangement. Let's go swimming."

"I need a shower. You go and I'll join you." She entered the bathroom and closed the door. Marc followed.

"Are you okay? Did I do something wrong?" Her smile widened into a grin.

Oh no, you did nothing but please me. No, I was thinking about our neighbor's question. We need to keep an eye on them."

"We're on vacation. Leave them alone. I'm not playing detective, and you should not play medical expert."

"I know. Join me. I need my back washed." Leaving his shorts on, he stepped into the bathroom with her as she started the water. They shared the water and soap for the next few minutes, finished rinsing and once dry, prepared to join their children. The question lingered in her mind as if a mental virus invaded.

# CHAPTER

## 7

Marcus, Sarah, and James listened to the story related by Jarina Camacho. As cruise director she planned activities for all of the passengers. She contacted James Blackthorne about speaking on board after he applied for a position and was accepted. She had procured the dance team from Las Vegas which was contracted for three voyages from Seattle to Skagway and back and extended for the two weeks. This sailing was longer because Fairbanks, Alaska was included. Now she entertained the children of passengers so parents would attend shows in the auditorium or play casino style games in the card room.

"Each of you may have heard about the legendary Yeti of Nepal, but there is a larger and fiercer creature which exists here in the northwest. He is Sasquatch, and his name is feared by many. Others seek to find him so as to learn about him. But he is elusive and smart, living among the animals of the forests and plains. He observes us and stays away when we approach."

James interrupted, "But he doesn't exist. He's not real. My father has to deal with crazy people at home because of this fake beast." Although his last birthday made him a teenager, his attraction to her did not seem out of place to him. She was pretty, smart, and for unknown reasons, alluring.

"And your father is true to his cause of keeping you safe for another day. He is a brave person, but Sasquatch knows he has nothing to fear from your father." James shook his head. Marcus laughed and slapped his brother on the shoulder.

"You really know how to win a girl's heart." James sulked. "Sorry, Jarina. Maybe his crush is a good thing." Jarina feigned shock and surprise. Then she grinned and continued with the tale. Sarah rose and nodded to her brothers who rose and left with her.

"Gees, James, leave her alone. She's old enough to be your mother." Sarah mocked him.

"I think she's pretty. I wonder if she would go swimming with me?" Marcus laughed and grabbed his brother around the neck.

"Come on, Romeo, I'll show you some women your age so you can practice your pick up lines on them." They walked the corridor in silence until they reached the nearest staircase and elevators.

Sarah said, "Let's get our suits and go swimming." They agreed, descended the staircase to their level and separated into their suites. Sarah entered saying hello to her parents. She rummaged in a draw for one of her swimsuits and departed for the bathroom to change. Returning to the main room, she picked up her bag filled with what she deemed necessary. With the bright sky calling for sunburns, Joan intercepted her before she could leave. A knock on the door signaled the arrival of brothers. She opened it to let them in.

"Put this on if you are going topside in the sun. I don't want to nurse any of you for the next two weeks." She handed Sarah a tube of SPF 50 lotion. The two-piece suit reveal much of her body. "Sarah, is that the only suit you brought with you?"

"No, but it's the one which covers me the most." James and Marcus roared.

"Don't worry, Mom, she's too pretty for any of the old men on this boat. We'll keep her from running away with any rich guy." Marcus placed a reassuring hand on her shoulder. She shrugged it off.

"You take care of each of you. Be back by five to get ready for dinner. We are at the Captain's table. Dinner is at seven." Three sibling heads rocked in unison.

Marcus gazed at his sister. "I think Mom's right. There's not much to hide in that outfit." Sarah harrumphed.

"I'm not too worried about meeting anyone on this senior citizen tour. Let's just go swimming and enjoy the water." Her swimsuit cover flew behind her as she quickened her pace to the stairs and the Lido deck. Marcus decided she was right. He hadn't met any other young people his age. The children listening to Jarina were elementary aged. The closest in age to him was the narrator of the fanciful Sasquatch tales. He understood James' attraction to her. She had to be only a few years older than he, maybe the same age as the editor traveling with the writer. But he was not attracted to her. He wanted to meet someone who was as passionate about ending his personal humility as he was. He wanted to be with a girl his age who might be just as naive about such things.

On the Lido they claimed three chairs and a table with an umbrella. Other people were in the pool swimming laps. "Why do they just swim back and forth?" James asked.

"Old people are just trying to stay in shape and delay death another day." Marcus sounded wise, but Sarah still grinned at the absurdity of the words. She removed her cover and started for the pool. "Sarah, I'm not responsible for any old guys having a heart attack when they see you."

"Funny." She climbed into the bubbling hot tub, sitting next to a young lady who appeared as if her world collapsed. "Hi, I'm Sarah." She extended her hand and received a quick glance and no hand.

Her eyes exposed the hidden sadness and desperation. "I'm Gabrielle."

"Aren't you the lady traveling with that writer guy? Uh, Black something?"

"Blackthorne. Yes, I'm his editor." She lifted her body from the seat and stood a moment before rising out the tub. "Don't fall for a guy who cares only for his mistresses when it suits him." She stepped out and headed to the cocktail lounge. Marcus hopped into the tub.

"Wasn't that the girl with the writer?" Sarah nodded. "She's kind of cute." He sat across from her, watching the shapely form wriggle away, leaving a path of water droplets.

"She's in love with her boss."

"How would you know that?" James arrived and stepped in. The conversation lagged.

The warmth of the water lulled the three Jefferson children into a sense of leisure which captivated minds no longer worried about boredom. Sarah laid her head back on the edge of the pool thinking of her liaison in the auditorium. James splashed water by simulating depth charges exploding. Marcus watched other people and spied an unexpected pleasantry. He rose from the hot tub, moving toward the table and his towel, sandals, and shirt.

"Where are you going?" Sarah asked.

"Nowhere in particular." He scurried away as brother and sister watched, curiosity rising with each step.

James turned to Sarah. "What was that all about?"

Sarah scorned an answer. "He's probably bored and hates being with us."

James proffered a better solution. "Or he saw the girl I saw."

"What girl?" Sarah's eyes trailed after Marcus who entered into the buffet area and disappeared.

"Some girl about his age with dark hair."

"Are you kidding me? He's found someone on this boat who's his age and I'm stuck with you?" Sarah stood up to leave and spotted the young steward walking around the corner of the pool area. Her heart fluttered. She strutted to the table acting as though something was wrong or missing. Iskandar altered his progress and grinned.

"May I be of service to you?" His politeness, drilled into him by the incident in the auditorium, put her at ease.

"Why, yes. I do believe you can." She picked up her bag, said something, and then walked away with the young man.

James wondered about his siblings and their obsession with meeting other people, but his own mind conjured an image of the cruise director telling her Sasquatch story and his body mocked him. He sat in the water not interested in demonstrating the surge of energy he developed. The warm water aided his alteration as he developed wibbled fingers and toes. He decided a dash to the table and a towel to be his best defense. Rising out of the small pool, he placed hands strategically until he grabbed the towel and wrapped it around him midriff.

In the hallway outside of his suite, he spotted James Blackthorne talking to another passenger. As he passed, the writer snarled at him, or so he imagined. He pulled out the key card and slipped it into the slot. As the door unlocked and he opened it, he glanced back to find neither person still present. His predicament had subsided and he wondered what his parents were doing but decided not to interrupt them.

Lying on his bed. He thought about girls at his school and the lack of any interest in them other than as friends. It seemed to him that any girl he liked, didn't like him. And any girl who liked him was too ugly to pursue. He had several friends who were girls, but they were just that, friends. He slept and dreamed of Sasquatch, hunting with Jarina to find one.

# CHAPTER

## 8

Sarah said good-bye, giving Iskandar another kiss as a reminder. She watched him walk away and smiled as he pivoted and waved. As she closed the door, she questioned her meeting the handsome young man. She doubted her parents would be against her seeing an Asia person, but this guy was a steward. Would he remain nice or force her into an impossible situation?

She let loose of the door, drawn to the basket on the table which he had delivered. Pulling the card, she opened it and read the note. "Have a wonderful trip and may this be your last booking," she read aloud. "That's so weird," As she read, contemplating the cryptic message, the door opened and her parents entered. She looked that them still holding the note. Marc spied the basket behind her.

"Did we get a basket from your grandparents?" He moved toward it to inspect the goodies.

"I don't think so. Read this." Sarah handed her father the note.

The frown on his face concerned Joan, "What does it say? You look like it's something awful." A knock on the door diverted them. Sarah opened it. Marcus and James entered. Seeing the basket, James made a beeline for it.

"What's in the basket? Anything good to eat?"

"I don't think it's for us." Marc said as he handed the note to Joan. James pawed the cellophane wrap, trying to discover the contents without opening it. "James, leave it alone."

"This doesn't make much sense." Joan waved the paper. "Who would write such a note? There's no signature."

"It mentions a booking. I'm guessing this is for Mr. Blackthorne." Marc picked up the envelope Sarah had deposited on the table by the basket. He handed it to Joan who replaced the note and placed it with the gift. "I'll take this to the author's suite and see if anyone wants it." He left.

Joan's afternoon family arrangements for her children precipitated a disagreement with Sarah. "I have plans," she said attempting to be diplomatic.

"What sort of plans? Have you met someone and now want to hang out with him?" Joan hadn't raised her voice but the message was clear. Marcus turned away from his mother and signaled across his throat not to argue. Hazel eyes glared at Sarah. Their mother interrupted the exchange. "I suppose you want to meet with that young lady." Her voice remained calm while exasperation with crumbling tours and gaming opportunities destroyed family time again. Marc returned without the basket.

"Paula Merino was in her suite and took it off our hands." He glanced from person to person, confused about the meaning of the frustrated faces. "Is something wrong? Should I have kept the basket?"

Joan answered, "No dear. It wasn't ours, but two of our children are not willing to have a family outing with us. They prefer the company of strangers." Marc pondered the idea of losing his eldest to the girl introduced to them and wondered which of the others was the next defector.

"Well, then the remaining three will enjoy a raucous and rambunctious afternoon. James, are you leaving us, or Sarah, are you the culprit who wishes to escape?" She raised a guilty hand.

"Dad, I've met a boy who wants to show me around the ship. He's really nice and it would be fun to see parts we wouldn't otherwise be able to see." Marc understood. Joan folded her arms aware of the type of person who was to be her tour guide.

"Is he the steward who delivered the flowers?" Marc asked. Sarah furrowed her brow.

"How did you know that?"

He smiled at his only daughter, "I'm a detective and it is my job to know the motives of suspects even before they know. How old is he?"

"He's about my age. Don't you trust me?"

"I trust you," Joan said. "I don't know him to trust him. You can introduce us and then we can make a decision."

"You're so unfair. I'll be sixteen soon and I'm old enough to be on my own, doing what I want, without you butting in all the time." Marc cringed knowing he was next to intercede and halt the small battle raging within the family. He placed a hand on his wife's hip and stepped between the warring females.

"Sarah, your mother is right and she is only looking out for your own safety. We know nothing of this young man and stories abound of interaction of passengers and crew which have not worked out well. Let's meet him and then decide." Darkening eyes burned as he spoke. She stomped to her part of the suite, flinging herself onto the sofa with the sleeper in it.

"I'm not to be trusted and so I will remain a prisoner on this boat for the rest of this hateful trip." Marc grinned and could not stifle the laughter which came next. Joan rolled her eyes at the antics she witnessed. She sat next to Sarah.

"I want you to be free to decide things, but this is a place which can have unexpected consequences for rash actions of a moment. I'm not expecting you to do anything wrong or immoral. I just don't want you hurt. A broken heart heals. A broken body may not."

Sarah sat up. "I'm not going to have sex with him. I just wanted to be with someone my own age. Marc's not about to share his new girlfriend with me. So I chose the steward."

Marc finished the deal. "Let's meet him and then you can tour the boat with him. Okay?" Sarah acquiesced not revealing her recent sojourn. Joan reached for a hand which withdrew. Marc offered his as a substitute. Family time was for later, if ever. However, he wondered why an apparent mistaken basket delivery had occurred. It made little sense. Was the gift in reality for his family? And if so from whom?

# CHAPTER

# 9

The sun reflected off the waters of Puget Sound brightening the veranda of their suite. Marc and Joan sat in the deck chairs as Sarah stood next to the railing. "Dad, do you think we're destined to meet people who are famous? Mr. Blackthorne seems like a nice guy and all, but why did we get this suite instead of him? Isn't he supposed to be important?"

Joan spoke next, "Your father is important, but that doesn't make him famous. I do think without him you would not be here and several bad people who did nasty things would still be doing them." Sarah turned.

"I know. I was thinking about the people on board and what they might think about us because we're staying in the best room on the ship. I just wondered what they might be thinking."

Marc responded, "I wouldn't worry about it. Most people won't know we're here. Now, Mr. Blackthorne is a famous person who people will want to meet. You and Me? Not so much."

Sarah entered the suite and picked out one of the three swim suits she brought with her. Each of them was a two piece which Marcus stifled a comment against her wearing. He understood she was growing into a young woman and she attracted attention because of her figure and her looks. A father's fate was to lose his daughter to some other man but fifteen was too soon. Yet, he and

Joan had discussed the situation and decided to allow her room to explore with their cautions expressed. She assured them she was not about to get into trouble.

After changing she stepped onto the veranda and modeled. "I think this one is the best," she said. Marc bit his lower lip but admired the lady Sarah had become.

"I agree," her Mom responded. "Are you going to the pools on the Lido deck?" She nodded and turned to leave. "Get your brothers and don't forget to wear the outer jacket which goes with your suit."

"James and Marcus are already up on deck. And yes, I will hide my magnificent body from the lurid stares of old men." Marc's arms stretched as his mouth gaped. Joan laughed. She entered the suite and left after she placed the cover-up on her body.

"Our daughter is going to be a prize catch for somebody one day." Joan said.

"It doesn't have to be today." Marc stood. "Let's go up to the pool and lounge there."

"Spying? You don't seem the type." Joan hugged him and continued. "Trust her, Marc. She won't get into trouble." They entered the suite and changed into their swim suits. Joan wore a two piece which accented her body and awakened Marc's attention. He put arms around her from behind and pulled her tight. "Not now." She remarked.

On the Lido families and couples enjoyed the sun and music from a combo playing near the bar. Stewards attended to the requests for drinks and snacks. Joan and Marc placed their belongings on a table near the pool and sat for a moment. Marc surveyed the scene and found James playing shuffleboard with three other boys about his age. He did not see Sarah or Marcus, which raised his alertness.

"Come on," Joan said, "let's swim." She stripped the robe from her body and slipped into the pool. Before Marc could follow a young man swam to her and began a conversation which ended quickly. Marc hopped in beside her.

"I see you are making new friends. What did he want?"

"Are you jealous?"

Marc hesitated then said, "Ah, no. Just wondering."

"He asked if I wanted to play water polo. Nice opening line but not creative since I don't see a net." Marc kissed her more for the show in public than for the affection he felt. "I'm not interested in a shipboard romance unless it's with you."

"Good to know. I wish our children had the same idea." Marc looked up and spotted Marcus with a young girl hooked to his arm. "That didn't take long."

Joan followed his gaze and said, "She's pretty. We should invite her to have lunch with us." She waved at them but he appeared to ignore her.

The girl said something to Marcus who then looked at his parents and offered a waved. They came to the pool's side. "Mom, Dad, I'd like you to meet Delinda." She waved as she looked at them.

"Nice to meet you," Joan said. "Would you like to have lunch with us?" Marcus's face screwed up as he looked first at his mother and then at his dad.

"Thanks," Delinda answered, "but my Dad already invited Marcus to join us." Silence ruled for a moment as they began to walk away. She turned. "Would you like to meet him?"

"That's very thoughtful of you. Yes, I think we can do that." Joan hopped out of the pool as Marc stood in the water wondering what play had commenced. "Are you coming?" he heard and hopped out to accompany her to the lunch party.

Marcus and Delinda waited while they dried and robed. Marc whispered to Joan, "Should we get dressed first?" She rocked her head back and forth. He followed as she joined her son and his new acquaintance.

The young couple stayed a step or two ahead as if he hoped and prayed they would turn away and leave him alone. Delinda dragged to be polite and to end any curiosity about her.

"Mrs. Jefferson, my father is a delightful person. I think you'll really like him." Marc thought something was off. What teenager spoke well of parents? Keeping with his son now seemed smart. He caught up with the group and held on to Joan's hand for anchorage.

She responded to Delinda's comments. "What does he do for a living?" "Good," thought Marc, "dig deep and find out about him before we are disappointed."

"Dad's a cardiologist at St. Paul General in Minnesota. We came on the cruise as a result of one of his patients."

"Incredible. Was it a gift or payment of some sort?" Joan kept investigating as they walked to the restaurant at the aft of the deck.

Delinda smiled. "My dad had a patient who worked with the cruise line and suggested he try to be ship's doctor for a while." Sadness crossed her face. "Dad needed to have time away from the hospital."

Joan stopped the conversation as they approached a man in his early fifties sitting alone. He looked up as they neared.

"Hi, sweetheart. Hello Marcus." He stood with the arrival of two strangers. "You must be Marcus's parents. Randolph Middlebury." He offered his right hand to Marc, who accepted.

"Yes, I'm Marc Jefferson and this is my wife, Joan, his mother. Pleasure to meet you." They sat around the table, silent until Delinda spoke.

"Dad, I told them about you being the ship's doctor."

"Yes," he answered, "I came aboard for six months of cruising and nursing people back together."

Joan said, "I'm in medicine, as well. I work at a senior care center in Wendlesburg, Washington."

"And what do you do, Mr. Jefferson?"

Marc wanted anonymity about his profession, but answered, "I'm part of the sheriff's department in Kitsap County."

Joan scoffed at his answer. "He's being modest. He's the lead detective for the county.

"Dad just solved an important case in Washington which involved my uncle." Marcus said. "He proved Uncle Jerry didn't commit suicide and he destroyed a drug smuggling group."

Marc pursed his lips but remained silence. Randolph acted as if to say something but paused. Joan smiled. Delinda's eyes widened as she listened to Marcus. The waiter for their table approached, so they ordered lunch. After the waiter left, Dr. Middlebury asked, "Was it dangerous?"

Delinda placed a hand in Marcus's hand, waiting for a response. Marc answered the query. "My uncle is part of the Snohomish County Sheriff's office and was working a case involving a drug cartel in Everett. My father and I used evidence sequestered from the department by my uncle to uncover the culprits and end their business."

Delinda spoke, "Is your father a policeman, too?"

"He works for Seattle. Jerry is his younger brother."

Dr. Middlebury shifted in his chair. "So a family of police officers and medical personnel. Quite a family you found, Dee." She smiled at her father's comment and squeezed Marcus's hand. He glanced at her and reciprocated the squeeze.

Lunch arrived and conversation became mundane idle chatter about the ship and its amenities. Joan thought about his position as ship's doctor and imagined her being aboard as part of the medical staff of a cruise ship. Marc hoped the conversation about Jerry was completed.

As the sun heated the day to a comfortable and reasonable summer day for Alaskan waters, Dr. Middlebury excused himself when a call for medical assistance interrupted the lunch. The remaining group watched him disappear. Joan then asked a question which caused a gasp from Delinda.

"Is your mother traveling with you?"

"Mom," Marcus whispered, accenting the word.

"It's alright, Marcus." Delinda's eyes teared and she dabbed at them. "My mother died last year."

# CHAPTER

## 10

A loud pounding awakened Marc and Joan from a deep sleep after a night of listening to James Blackthorne and then dancing in the lounge. Arising from the bed, Marc said, "Stay here. I'll check on which of our boys is up so early." As he entered the main room, he saw Sarah at the door with Gabby, tears streaming from flooded eyes.

"I think he's dead." Her robe, tied hastily around her waist, revealed more than a man should see. "Come, quick, please."

"Sarah, get your mother and stay here." Sarah turned to find her mother coming into the room. Marc and Joan followed Gabby to Blackthorne's suite. Joan approached the tranquil body of the author. "Call security and get the medical staff here," he advised the young editor.

She adjusted her robe more securely and explained that Paula had called already.

Joan placed two fingers on his carotid artery and waited for a heartbeat. She felt no pulse and shook her head to Marc. She lifted an eyelid to observe any response to light changes. Nothing happened. "He's still warm, so he must have died within the last couple of hours."

Marc asked, "Do you think he had a heart attack? I don't see any wounds or blood." Turning to Gabby he inquired, "Were you here last night? With him?" Her eyes focused on the carpeting as she nodded.

"He was complaining he didn't feel well during his show and he came back as soon as he could. He skipped the book signing part which is not like him. I said I would stay with him."

Marc's frown preceded the next question. "Did you two engage in intercourse?" Gabby blushed which answered his query. Turning to Joan he said, "He may have over exerted himself. Could that have been why he died?"

"Possibly. Let's wait for the doctor to have a chance at evaluating him." Gabby started for the door but was halted by the security team and the medical staff.

"Who are you people?" Chief of Security, Dag Ingersoll, asked. He wore a rumpled brown suit which fit as though he had lost twenty pounds. Short, with graying dark brown hair, he entered "And why are you in here?" The doctor and a nurse attended to the late Mr. Blackthorne.

"My name is Marcus Jefferson. This is my wife, Joan. Gabrielle awakened us for help because of Mr. Blackthorne's apparent death. We're in the Elliot Bay Suite." He stepped aside as Ingersoll observed the doctor, Randolph Middlebury, who looked up and shook his head.

"It looks like he suffered a massive coronary fibrillation. I'll know more when we can autopsy the body at our next port stop. He reported to me he was not feeling well during his show last night."

Ingersoll looked at Marc and then Gabby. "What can you tell us about last night, Miss Montoya? Was he really not feeling well?" She pulled the robe closer around her shoulders and glanced at her former employer. Everything had changed in a fashion she had not imagined. Life centered around him and now he was gone. It had little meaning without him.

She blinked and said, "I asked him before the show if he was ready and he said he was. Just as he was to go on, he went into the toilet and threw up. He complained he thought he was coming down with the flu and cursed the air quality of the boat." She heaved a deep breath. "I asked him if he wanted to postpone the show, but he said he was going to go on, not disappoint his readers. I checked the crowd to see if was worth the effort. The auditorium was nearly full." She moved toward the door. "Can I go?" Ingersoll nodded.

Marc and Joan started toward the door. "Mr. Jefferson, what do you see as the reason for Mr. Blackthorne's death? After all, I understand you're a police detective."

"I am, but this is your ship, so I leave it up to you to make a final conclusion." They left for their room before another word was spoken. "Something bothering you, Joan? You were very quiet in there." She walked away to find Sarah sitting on the veranda. Comforted knowing her daughter was safe and not upset, she turned.

"Middlebury thought Blackthorne died for a natural reason. I'm not so sure he's right." Joan sat in a chair by the sliding glass door. Marc sat next to her and waited. "Marc, it needs to be investigated as a possible homicide."

"What? You think he was murdered?"

"His lips were a purple associated with poisoning, his eyes were discolored, and the drool from his mouth indicated a form of paralysis. He may have died from his heart stopping, but I think it was induced by something he may have eaten or drank. Remember the note? Something in that basket may have been poisoned."

Marc held her hands. "What reason would anyone on this boat have for killing a popular writer? A motive is needed. Who would have one?"

Joan peered into his eyes. "Isn't that what you do? Figure out a motive? Then you figure out who had one and uncover evidence to finish the job."

"It's not my responsibility to interfere with the security staff of this boat. If they're not concerned, why should I be?" She unhooked from him and stood. Looking out at Sarah as she watched the ocean, Marc continued. "I can talk with Mr. Ingersoll and determine what he thinks has happened. Don't get to hopped up on the idea a crime has been committed. He may have died from natural causes, just like the doctor said." A knock at the door interrupted any further debate for the merits of an investigation.

James and Marcus strolled in and asked, "What happened to Mr. Blackthorne?"

"He died this morning of an apparent heart attack." James sat on a chair near his mother.

Marcus asked, "Who found him?" Marc grimaced. "I mean does that girl need consoling?"

"You're a bit young for her, aren't you? And what about the young lady you were escorting and having lunch with yesterday? Would you mess with a ship board romance so cavalierly?"

Joan interrupted, "Marc, stop it." She turned to her son. "Marcus, you leave Miss Montoya alone. She's in mourning and will not be interested in a teenager. Stick to girls your own age." She smiled and mussed his hair. Yelling in the hallway disrupted their banter.

Marc stepped out to uncover the source of the voices. Paula Merino pushed at the ship's security person who was preventing her entry into Blackthorne's suite. "Let me in. I work for him." Gabby Montoya stood next to her attempting to distract her from the room.

"Paula, you have to let the doctor do his job. James died of a heart attack." Paula stopped struggling and turned to face her companion.

"You slept with him last night. He wasn't feeling well and you had sex with him and caused a heart attack. Admit it. You killed him." Tears accumulated in her eyes as they did in Gabby's spilling down the cheeks of both women.

"I didn't think he was so sick. He wanted me and ..." Her hands hid the shame blushing her face. Marc approached them offering a handkerchief to either of them.

"Why don't we come over to my suite. I have some questions which might help clear up what happened last night." Gabby took the handkerchief and daubed her tears. Marc placed a hand on each of their shoulders and steered a course to the Elliot Bay Suite.

For a large room a tangle of people made it feel like a crowd had formed. Gabby inadvertently rewarded Marcus by sitting next to him, her robe loosening at her shoulders. He placed an arm above her on the back of the sofa. Paula remained on her feet. James opened the sliding glass door and joined his sister on the veranda.

"What sort of questions would clear up how James died?" Paula grunted. "He and that tart had sex and the exertion caused a heart attack. Nothing more need be said."

Marc looked at her and asked, "Did you and Miss Montoya share affections with him? Are you jealous of her being with him last night?" He watched for a tell which could corrupt her answers.

"That's none of your business. Gabby and I get along just fine." She glanced at her companion and supposed friend. Her eyes grew wider with rage. Blackthorne and Paula had never thought of marriage as a proper contract, but he promised to take care of her and twenty-years difference was not an obstacle to the arrangement. She shared him with Gabrielle because he liked the youthful exuberance which carried to her, as well. Her friendship expanded as the two women learned to care about each other and promised to keep their own personal concord secret from their writer.

"Do you know of anyone who may have had a vendetta or score to settle with Mr. Blackthorne?" Marc flitted between the two pairs of eyes which glared at each other. He sensed a friendship strained under the pressure of an uncertain future.

Paula responded first. "No one wanted to harm him. He wrote with a zeal for perfecting his craft and entertaining an adoring readership."

"Paula, remember that letter he got last year from a disgruntled fan who called him an ineffective hack. Maybe that person wanted to kill him."

"Gabby, you were with him all night. How could someone get in and poison him?"

Marc found it interesting that she mentioned poisoning and interjected, "I understand he wasn't well before his show. Joan and I were present but he seemed alright to us at that time." Joan nodded agreeing with the assessment. "What did he have just before he went on? When he got sick and threw up?" The women pondered for a moment.

Gabby answered, "He had a glass of wine, but he did that before every show."

"Was it a new bottle or one which was open?" Marc asked, thinking of the contents of the basket in his room.

Paula spoke, "I opened one from the basket in his stateroom for him. We took it with us."

"What did he have before that?"

"We went to dinner with the captain. He ate a steak and potatoes with mixed vegetables. Do you think someone in the kitchen poisoned him?"

"I don't know if he was poisoned or not. I do find it interesting, Miss Merino, that you think he was poisoned. Did you do it?" Teeth clenched and air seethed from her mouth.

"I would never kill him. He and I were close. I loved him." She strode toward the door but turned. "He was a man of few friends and even fewer enemies."

Marc picked up the innuendo. "But enemies none the less. Someone may have wanted him dead. I suggest you be cooperative with the ship's security staff. It wouldn't look good for you to be obstructive." She departed without retort. Marc turned attention to the other suspect. He noticed a compassionate arm draped on her shoulder and her head resting on his son's upper chest. Marcus grimaced as if to say, "Just trying to be helpful." The glass door slid open and James and Sarah walked in, a shiver coursing their bodies. A breeze chilled the air for the time the door exposed the interior to the outside temperature.

Gabby straightened from her repose and Marcus removed his arm. Their hands touched and she slid fingers into his. Marc watched the interplay but remained silent. He figured any game she played would be revealed, or she simply besought comfort a broken heart.

"Miss Montoya, have you ever seen Miss Merino do something to any of Mr. Blackthorne's foods or drinks?" He watched her eyes, the conduit to a person's soul. Hands detached and adjusted her robe hiding more of her tawny flesh. He sensed her unease at the question. Whether she hesitated for her own guilt or her suspicion of a colleague, he knew not, so he waited. Waited for a response to incriminate or exonerate. Waited, as did a young son, whose education into the wiles of feminine charm may have begun.

"Mr. Jefferson, neither of us wanted anything to happen to him. I loved him, even though I know he didn't feel the same toward me."

"What relationship did he and Miss Merino have. Was she in love with him?" Marc stared at her for signs of jealousy or anger. Tears cascaded down her cheeks. Marcus placed an arm around her again, pulling her toward him. She reciprocated by hugging him, her body taunting his innocence. "Did you burn with rage enough to contaminate his food or drink?" The drama played on as Joan watched her son's face switch from interest to concern.

She sat up again but held a hand for comfort. "I didn't do anything to him. And neither did Paula. We both adored him and no competition existed between us for affection."

"Was there more to your relationship with Miss Merino than you are telling us?" Eyes widened, a short inhale exposed a hidden truth.

"We worked together to make his books better and to be sure he had the largest readership possible. What are you implying? That we cared more for each other than James? That we wanted to get him out of the way for us to be together? That's financial suicide."

"Explain." Marc leaned toward her and signaled his son to release his catch. "Explain why it would be financially disadvantageous to you and Miss Merino?" Marcus stood and nodded to James to follow him. He whispered to his mother that they were going to their room since the conversation had become more serious.

Gabby stood and adjusted her robe revealing a hint to the lack of much clothing underneath. "I needed this job. I don't have any other source of income and James was generous with his money. I edited his work and no one else. With his death I have to find another way to make an income." Tears, real or fake, returned.

"What about Miss Merino? Was this her only source of income?" Gabby rocked her head up and down. "Were there any insurance policies on Mr. Blackthorne's life? Did he have a registered will? Does he have any family who stand to inherit his estate?" Gabby sat again an inside thigh exposed. Joan shook her head and guided Sarah away from the interrogation and to the veranda.

"I know he had a will and his daughter and son were his beneficiaries. His second wife was to receive a portion as part of the divorce agreement, but I don't know how much. As for life insurance, you'll have to ask Paula."

Marc rose from the chair he occupied, his view of the young beauty before him modified to observing a cleavage meant to distract him from the questions. Or so he thought. "Thank you, Miss Montoya, you have been most helpful. I suggest our conversation remain between us for the time being. As it stands, Mr. Blackthorne died from a heart attack and nothing points to murder." He extended a hand for her to use to rise from the couch. He averted eyes as her robe separated but the tawny skin glowed as light reflected on her.

"If someone did kill him, how did they do it? I was there all night."

Marc did not answer but holding her forearm he led her to the door, opened it for her to leave and shook her hand. She hesitated. A pleading face gazed at him before she retraced steps to her suite shared with Merino.

Joan approached him as he watched a dejected woman disappear into her suite. His inquiry to his highly competent wife was clear. "Did the doctor think something may have induced a cardiac arrest?" As they stood in the hall, she looked toward the room which held her suspicions of a homicide.

"He said he'd have to wait for an autopsy." Marc followed her gaze noticing the security staff had failed to secure the room. His doubts about any follow through mounted. He decided to check the basket to see what had been consumed besides the bottle of wine. As he approached the doorway, Ingersoll returned.

"Did you need something, else, Detective?" Dag asked.

Marc weighed investigating the basket but arrested further interference. "No, I don't need anything, but please, let me know what you find out. As a detective, I question actions until I'm sure I know what transpired." Ingersoll frowned.

"Any information I uncover is privileged. We have protocols and procedures in place to handle situations such as this." He removed the wedge holding the door open and checked to assure the lock had latched. He regarded Marcus's presence and then walked away to catch his doctor's attention before privilege could be compromised.

Joan smiled as Marc pivoted to their suite. "He's not going to be much help in an investigation."

"As I said before, this is not my jurisdiction. I'll let him handle it." He moved around her and entered the suite.

She followed. "That never seemed to stop you in the past." He thought about the basket and how to retrieve it.

# CHAPTER

## 11

Sarah hear a door open and blushed when she saw her brother come into the hallway with Delinda. Immediately, she realized Marcus had a girl with him and James was absent. Had he? She didn't want the thought in her head, but the idea of his being with the Middlebury girl pushed her closer to giving the steward what she was sure he wanted but doubted she did. If he could be active, then so could she. Her mind raced as he came out of the room.

"Hi, Sarah. Delinda and I are going for a swim. Come on and join us. Bring your friend." They disappeared from view as if a dream had ended when the alarm clock rang. "Iskandar, are allowed to swim with us?"

"I cannot use the pool during a cruise. I can meet with people and show them around. That is all, but I wanted to be with you, alone. You are the most beautiful creature I ever met." He tugged her toward the suite. "We can be alone and I'll be gentle and kind. You will see. We can please each other." Sarah realized her mistake and pulled her hand from his.

"Iski, I can't." Her thoughts convinced her. Marcus was older. If he wanted to be with someone, he had the right. "Thank you for showing me the ship. Maybe I'll see you later, and we can hang out." Iskandar, shook his head, turned away, and left her standing alone. She wanted to ask Marcus about what it was like. Then she would decide.

The door of the suite next to author's room opened and Gabrielle Montoya entered the hallway. They stared at each other a moment which seemed an eternity. "Hi, Sarah." Her brow furrowed. "Is something wrong?"

A flood cascaded from her eyes. "Gabby, am I an idiot for wanting to be with a guy I just met?" Two arms embraced the shaking body.

"No. We all wish things to work out and they don't. Want to talk about it?" Sarah figured anyone who lived more years than she would know what to think. They entered the Elliot Bay Suite.

"What's it like? You know, having..." She blushed. Gabbie smiled as they sat in chairs around the table.

"When you find someone you like; you think about it. Just wanting to do it, can leave you wondering. You're young. You have plenty of time."

Sarah gazed around the room, and then connects eyes with Gabbie. "Did you love him? Mr. Blackthorne?"

"I guess."

"Did he love you?" Sarah leaned in, placing elbows on the table.

"Probably not. But he was a good man and treated me well."

Sarah scrunched her brows. "Did he and Paula ...?" She narrowed her eyes unable to comprehend a person sharing partners.

"He and Paula had been together for a few years before he hired me as his editor. They weren't in love as much as they just wanted each other." Her faced dropped to her chest. Sarah remained silent, waiting. "He told me I was beautiful and I thought him exciting and alluring. I didn't care about the age difference. He paid attention to me and I craved it." Her eyes met Sarah's and the glint supported pleasant memories.

"Were you jealous of Paula's relationship with Mr. Blackthorne?"

"No. Maybe a little. We talked about it." Gabbie stood and stared out the window to the Pacific Ocean. Turning to face Sarah. "I wanted her gone, not him. I don't know what I'm going to do now."

"Can't you get another job as an editor?" Sarah grinned, not sure of what to ask next.

"Probably, but it can be difficult to freelance and publishers aren't hiring." She walked toward the door. "I've got to go." After a hesitation, she opened the door and departed.

Sarah thought about her steward and what she avoided. Age didn't matter, according to Gabrielle, but thirty years seemed grotesque. A shower to cleanse her soul and mind seemed appropriate. As the warm water cascaded across her body, she imagined another type of person with her, someone who was as different from the steward as a dog from a cat. Water cascaded from her eyes as the water thumped her head. Did Marcus? Should she?

After drying and dressing in tan shorts and a scarlet blouse, she opened the door of the suite to find her family, and attain safety in numbers. In the hallway she spotted her steward entering James Blackthorne's suite. What was he doing? The room had been declared a no entry area by the security director, Mr. Ingersoll. She crossed the hall and knocked on the suite next to Blackthorne's. No one answered. She glanced at the other room's door expecting discovery by Iskandar. She pounded again as the door opened and Paula appeared. She scooted into the room.

"Close the door. Close it." Gabrielle lay on one of the beds covered by a sheet. Sarah regarded her and then Paula, wondering because of the lack of clothing under her robe.

"What do you want?" Paula's voice grizzled.

"I saw a steward entering Mr. Blackthorne's suite. Isn't it supposed to be locked?"

Gabrielle rose from the bed, the sheet dropping away, exposing an incredible shape. She slipped on a robe and tied it shut. Sarah's mind wandered to the situation demonstrated by the lack of clothing. Paula redirected her attention, "Supposed to be. Maybe we should check it out."

CHAPTER

12

James had watched the medical staff carry the body of Blackthorne away from the suite. He had scanned the scene, watching his parents as they spoke with people. His hunger for the contents of the basket motivated him to enter the room and grab what he wanted or could possess before the door would close and opportunity was lost. He spied Paula Merino and Gabby Montoya disappear into their suite and with caution moved toward the vacated room.

He scanned again the hallway of the two suites, one occupied by him and his brother, the other by a writer described to him by his parents as famous. Looking around, he hustled to the room and remarked by nodding his head at how much the place was like his. The basket remained on a side table, open and tempting. Rummaging through the remaining items he read the coffee packets, tossing them back into the basket. He picked up a jar of something yellow and sweet. Honey. He smiled and pocketed the bottle. A package of deli style rye bread was his next victim. Snacks for later when he wanted something and had not stocked up at the food bar. Spying a package of summer sausage, he was about to grab it when a noise outside raised adrenalin levels. With open eyes and fast heart, it was flight or fight reasoning. He chose flight.

"James." The voice halted progress in the hall. "What are you doing?" He turned to face his brother, pushing the contraband jar into his pocket. He dropped the loaf of deli rye behind the doorway. "What'd you throw back into the room?" James shrugged and slipped past hoping to hide his treasure. Marc peered into the writer's room and retrieved the bread.

In his suite James pulled the jar from his pocket and surveyed a hiding place. "My suitcase," he whispered and unzipped the top compartment. He put the case back where it was.

Marcus entered the room. "Stealing bread from a dead man? Are you crazy?" He threw the package at his brother who caught it and smiled.

"Snacks, bro. I might not make it to the buffet again. Besides, it was the only good thing left, except a summer sausage you made me miss. That old man ate the whole basket."

"You're a dork." James put the bread on the table beside his bed.

"Thanks for getting it. I wasn't sure if I was going to get back to it."

"What else did you take?"

"Nothing." His ire rose as his brother pawed him for the secret stash. "Leave me alone, or I'll tell Mom you beat me up again." Marcus put hands on shoulders and pushed. James fell back onto the bed and off to the floor. An unexpected loud thwack was rose from behind the bed. "Shit," was the response from the floor.

"Crap, are you alright?" Marcus found his brother rubbing his head, blood trickling between his fingers. "Oh no." He retreated to the bathroom and grabbed a towel. "Here put this on your head."

"Leave me alone. I'm fine." He tussled the towel from Marcus's grasp and pressed the cut. "I need ice."

Marcus left with a bucket to ask his parents for ice from their refrigerator. James examined the towel and then his head in the mirror. The shallow cut bled, but his experience from last winter's head trauma told him he was fine. "Head wounds bleed a lot." He recalled from his memory about sports injuries. He decided to reward his hunger with a honey and rye sandwich. Searching the drawers, he found the flatware used by occupants of the room. Pulling out a knife, he opened the suitcase compartment and grabbed the bottle. No label explained the ingredients or the nutritional value, but he cared little. Taking two slices of bread, he lathered the honey on one slice and folded it over. He repeated the process and bit into the tasty morsels. While chewing he recapped the bottle and tied the loaf bag tight. He slowed and made a face.

"That is not the best honey I've ever had, but it'll do." He crammed the remaining half sandwich in his mouth. Looking out the door, he surveyed the scene again, hoping to make a dash for the sausage. Marcus came around a corner carrying ice. James ducked back into the room and jammed his other half sandwich into the pocket of his jacket hanging on a chair by his bed. He swallowed what remained in his mouth as Marcus entered.

"Here. I found ice on the Lido deck." Marcus folded some into the wet clean towel and gave it his brother. "Put it on your head. It'll keep the swelling down." James did so. "What are you eating?"

James cleared his throat, "Some of the rye. It's really good." Marcus rocked his head.

"Maybe I should scrounge up the salami so you can make a sandwich." Marcus sneered.

"Would you?" James removed the towel which had less blood on it. "Please."

"No. And you're so busted. If you step out of line, I'll tell Mom and Dad."

"Yeah, and how will you explain cracking my head open?" Marcus stayed quiet. "So, it's a draw. Okay? Here, have some bread." He picked up the bag but Marcus declined. James put it down again.

"I mean it. I want you to have a nice leisurely walk around the boat and leave me alone for an hour or two." The grin on James face revealed his understanding. He stood tossing the towel into the bathroom.

"I hope she's worth it, because if you say anything about the bread..." With a slow stroll to the door, he turned and pricked one more sore spot. "Maybe this time the girl won't be so unhappy about doing it with you." He was out with door closed as a crashing sound followed. "That was close."

Knocking on the Elliot Bay Suite door, he waited for an answer. No one came. Turning to ascend the stairs to the next deck and open air, he spied Delinda approaching.

"Hi, is your brother here." James looked her over, creating a disgusted face from her. "What are you, a pervert? Take a long look because you ain't getting any of this." Her hands outlined her body. James had to admire his brother's ability to get classy girls. Her raven hair, cut short but stylish, and her green eyes, accentuated her ruby lips and rouged cheeks. She had come to have some fun. He imagined touching the mounds in front of him held in by a bikini top under a sheer sun dress.

"Do you have a sister?" Delinda snorted and faced the door to knock. He grinned as he observed the rear view of the other half of the swim wear. Silence alerted him to see her facing him.

"Don't say anything to anyone about me being here. If I have a younger sister, she'd be old enough to play dolls with you. So get lost." She rapped twice on the door. Marcus opened it and smiled. Seeing James, his smile turned upside down. James winked and walked away. He'd keep quiet for now, but an ace in the hole is a good thing to possess. And he had two.

# CHAPTER

# 13

Marcus heard two raps beyond the door and opened it. Delinda Middlebury's appearance brought a smile to his face. James' appearance brought a frown. His brother winked and walked away. "Are you going to ask me in?" His heart swelled at the sound of her voice as he stepped aside. Her bathing suit cover hid nothing. James became a distant memory. He closed the door and leaned against it.

"You look great." He moved toward her.

"That's because I'm the only girl on board who pays any attention to you." She removed the cover. Her swim suit provided the merest of modesty. Marcus realized a growth and turned away to hide his embarrassment. Deciding nothing was to be lost, he turned and faced her.

"You're the only girl my age on this ship. And you are the most beautiful person I've ever met." His right hand reached for her left hand and fingers entwined. Green eyes glistened and a smile coursed her face as he spoke.

"Do you have anything to drink?" She dragged him toward one of the beds where they sat on the edge.

"Like a soda? Or something stronger?" He released her hand to check the refrigerator for sodas. Remembering his brother's obsession with the basket down the hall, he thought about wine bottles, but dismissed the idea of leaving her. He retrieved two cans which had been stocked by the staff. He handed one to her and snapped open his can. "I'm sorry there's nothing stronger." He began to draw out the liquid only to weaken when she smiled. Close to drowning himself, he stopped.

Snapping her can open, she swigged a long draw, much as a spokesperson for any popular refreshment, swallowed and flipped her raven hair. "You ever been with anyone before?" Her eyes sparkled, awakening his mind to what awaited. His head rolled a slow arc, not a 'no' but the question was answered to her satisfaction.

Marc steadied his head and peered into her eyes. "Have you... uh... been...?" She grinned and then laughed.

"What a pair." Putting her drink on the table, she stood and approached him, placed her hands on his cheeks and kissed his lips. He placed the can on the counter and then slid up her bare skin arousing the beast caged inside him. He pulled her to him crushing her breasts into his chest. "Be gentle," she whispered.

"I've never given myself to anyone." Marc pressed his lips to hers, tongues explored and blood rushed through their anatomies. His hand reached the draw string of her swimsuit bra. A slight tug and the knot disengaged. He released his hold of her body to allow the clothing to slide off her shoulders. Her bare skin drew his eyes to the exposed orbs, blood left his head as it focused in his loins.

"Are you sure?" he said, placing a hand on her left nipple which firmed to his touch. "I want to, but I'm kind of new to this, also." Her hand gripped his shorts. A groan mocked his sense of rationality. Doubt surged upward to his brain and convinced his hand to relinquish its prize. Her captured prey escaped as he moved away.

Her frown attested to her surprise only to be replaced by something he couldn't understand. Her eyes seemed to gleam as her mouth curled open highlighting the dimples of her cheeks.

"It's okay," she purred. "I didn't know until right now what a big deal this is. I want to but, I'm scared." She picked up the fallen article. "Would you help into this?" He tied the strings after she replaced it on her chest. "Your parents raised you well." She covered her body with the sun dress. "We can wait. We should wait." He moved toward her. She reached for his hand and placed it on the same breast which held it before. "But the cruise will not end without..." She ended her affirmation.

"Can I walk you to your cabin?"

"If you've recovered enough to not show the blessing down there, we can go swimming. Afterward you can walk me to my room." He grabbed a towel and key card, then held her hand as he opened the door. This closeness to potential intimacy had made him aware, but the experience of a lifetime rumbled through his brain. He had fallen in love. Opening the door, he almost missed seeing the other couple approaching the Elliot Bay.

Outside the suite, Sarah and the young steward stopped and she stared at them. Her blush reminded Marc of his situation and he wondered if she was about to experience what he corralled a moment ago. "Hi, sis." She stopped her march toward the suite as if to contradict his speculation. He grimaced as he tallied the moment to embarrass her. "Don't do anything I didn't do."

Glaring darts spewed from angered eyes to attack him. He turned and walked away with his prize and his pride.

"What was that for?" Delinda remarked.

"A cautionary rebuke, I guess. Mom and Dad weren't too keen on her seeing that guy. I know he looks young, but who knows?"

"Do you think he wants to take advantage of her?" She wrapped her arm in his and continued. "Like you wanted to do to me?" As he attempted to escape her hold, she flexed her muscles gripping him in an inescapable vise.

"That's not fair. You wanted it as much as I did. Maybe even more." Acquiescing to her grip of his arm, he said, "I think I love you." Her body leaned to his.

"I love you, too."

They approached the elevators and released from each other aware of others looking at them. A ding sounded and a door opened. Several people emptied out and Delinda moved to enter. "That's going down," Marc said.

"Come on. I need to go to my room and get something." He followed her into the car. No one else seemed to want to descend and the doors closed. Her lips covered his, her eyes closed, hands caressing his back. Oblivious of the movement to lower decks they locked together arousing earlier passions. The car ceased its descent and doors opened. A throat clearing noise sounding alerted them to other human presence. Delinda sucked in air. Her father faced the opening, his right eyebrow rising above the other.

"Mr. Jefferson, are your intentions honorable or do I need to be worried?" Delinda's lids expanded exposing unfounded guilt.

"Dr. Middlebury, Dee and I have done nothing wrong and my intentions are most honorable. I like your daughter. A lot." Delinda exited and hugged her dad.

"Don't worry so much, Dad. I'm old enough to take care of myself."

He returned the hug. "I worry since your mother died. You and I haven't had much time together. I don't want you disappointed because of some irrational decision. You're so young." An ugly utterance like a choler rising as bile in an irritated bowel issued from her. She separated from her father.

"Mom's death has nothing to do with how I feel about being a prisoner aboard a ship you chose to escape to instead of facing the truth about her illness." She stamped away leaving the two men to duke out the lingering debate of a father and a daughter.

"Sir, we are not ready to engage in activity which might strain a future together. We both realize the gravity, as my mother, who is a nurse, reminds me continually about my actions having unexpected consequences."

Turning to Marc, ignoring his retreating offspring, he asked, "Have you seen your mother? I would like to talk with her about a medical situation I've encountered."

Marcus ears picked up the nuance of the question. "You mean Mr. Blackthorne?" Middlebury shrugged.

"Careful what you say. Dead bodies can be a problem aboard a ship. It is not wise to speak of this matter in a public arena. One has no idea who may be listening." Marcus squinted.

"I'll let her know when I see her." He turned to follow Delinda and retrieve information about her mother and the disease which claimed her life. But his curiosity about the death of the author rose because of the enciphered message in the simple request for a nurse's opinion. Something had happened which made suspicion his wary companion.

# CHAPTER

## 14

"Wait up, Dee." Marcus scurried after her as she turned a corner in the hallway. Delinda returned a look toward him and then opened the door to the room housing herself and her father. She slipped in and waited. He clutched the frame and stared at her. "What was that all about?"

Walking further in she released the door which closed a slow traverse to his fingers. His hand caught the door. He pushed it away and followed her. She remained mute.

"Talk to me, please. What happened back there?" Hands interlaced as tears rained from critical emerald eyes. He pulled her body close to his. Her hands escaping his, wrapped arms around his neck and sobbed. He held steady as her body quivered. Waiting for a calm, he whispered, "I do think I love you, no matter what happened in the past." The quivering slowed after seconds which seemed like minutes.

Delinda stepped back from Marcus and sat on her bed. He sat next to her. "My father's been unhappy for a year." Marcus remained quiet, a trait of his father. Listening produced more evidence than asking. "Mom got sick about three years ago and the cancer spread quickly." She stood up. Walked to the port window and stared. "We knew Mom was dying. We prepared for a memorial. We, or better, my Dad planned time for us to get away for a while." She faced

Marcus. "Are your parents happy?" He smiled.

"There are times when Dad is called to an investigation and Mom gets mad. But most of the time they're fine. Why?" He stood and closed the distance between them.

"My Dad worked lots of hours at the hospital and Mom wasn't happy. I wonder if her cancer wasn't a blessing for her. She didn't need to think about us anymore." Her eyes swagged and trickled. He held her hands, his attention meant as an assurance to calm her emotions.

"I want you." She kissed his mouth before he could contend with her request. She dragged him to her bed and pushed him onto it. Setting the safety lock to keep parental interruptions out, she removed her cover and swimsuit. Marcus acquiesced.

><del>⊃⊂</del><

Lying quiet and sated next to her, he thought of the earlier encounter in the suite upstairs and his worry that it was too soon. No regrets, though. He did enjoy her intelligence and company. Her beauty had no equal. No regrets. Delinda slept, her emotions tranquil for a moment.

Standing, he retrieved swimsuit and sandals. Looking at her, she stirred. Covering her with the sheet, he turned and opened the door. Riding the elevator to the Lido deck, he searched for his mother to relay the message from Dr. Middlebury.

He pulled out his cell and punched his Mom's preset. As the ringing continued, he thought of Delinda and his time with her. Had he ruined a young woman's future or her relationship with her father? Had he taken advantage of her because of emotions? His mind was staggered by a voice. "Hello, Mom. Where are you? I have a message for you from Dr. Middlebury." He listened and nodded as if she saw it. "Okay, I'll be right there." He clicked off and headed for the library area of the observation lounge. He wanted to return to Delinda without fail before she questioned his hit and run actions.

Entering the lounge, he scanned and located his parents. "Mom, Dad, glad I found you." He sat down in a chair next to the sofa they occupied. The Pacific Ocean gleamed in the sunlight.

"Well, you said Dr. Middlebury wanted to see me." Joan leaned toward her son and continued, "Did he say what he wanted from me?"

"Something about a medical problem. I asked him if it was about Mr. Blackthorne and he said something about being careful when talking in public areas about dead bodies. What's going on? Dad, is Mr. Blackthorne's death suspicious?"

Marc gazed at his oldest child. "Don't think anything bad happened. We have no evidence of any wrongdoing. The doctor is just being thorough."

"I've got to go," Marcus said. He rose, as did his parents, whom he embraced before leaving. "Keep us safe, please." He left to assuage Delinda's supposed anger for abandoning her.

"Marc, if our son suspects events aren't as advertised, then you need to contact someone about it. I know I've been harsh about investigations in the past, but he didn't die naturally." Her eyes locked on his, imploring an answer. His head wriggled imperceptive to others. "Are you coming with me?" Another nod.

"Where do you think we can find him?" Marc asked.

Joan grinned. "As a detective you are the best. For everyday thinking, I wonder." She locked arms with him as they left the observatory. "He's probably in the infirmary. Or someone there will know where he may be." They stood by the elevators saying nothing. Another investigation and danger looming. Would there ever be a time without intrusions into family life?

The doors opened and they entered along with a family of five. Marc wondered about the complement of people aboard and any harm possible. If someone did murder Blackthorne, that person was still aboard and dangerous. And if more than one existed, the problem became more intense. The elevator stopped allowing the family to leave. No one waited and the car continued its descent to the main deck. Silenced reigned.

As the first deck arrived and doors opened, Joan spoke, "What were you thinking? You're quiet and I know it means you're thinking." They exchanged glances and proceeded to the ship's office.

Marc inquired of the concierge behind the counter about the infirmary and the whereabouts of Dr. Middlebury. "Is there a medical problem?" the lady asked.

"No, my wife is a nurse and wanted to see where people get help.

Just a curiosity." The Indonesian woman asked them to wait. Marc scanned the room. Only a few people were present. He whispered to Joan, "I was thinking that if he was killed, the person or persons responsible are still aboard. We have only until Juneau to uncover motive and method." The woman returned.

"Dr. Middlebury is in his office in the infirmary which is located one deck down. Use the stairs over there or the elevator to floor L." Joan and Marc thanked her and descended the stairs. At the medical station a nurse was wrapping a bandage on the arm of a young girl while another lady watched. She presumed the person was the mother.

"Have a seat. I'll be right with you." They sat in the leather sofa which was firm and fairly new. The nurse finished her work and the patient and mother left. "You're the Jefferson's, aren't you? I remember you in the suite with the author when we were called about his death. What do you want?"

"I came to see Dr. Middlebury," Joan said. "He asked to see me."

"About Mr. Blackthorne?"

"I'll leave that to the good doctor to answer. I don't know what he wants." Her ire piqued with the question. Marc placed a hand on her thigh, attempting to quell the storm.

Dr. Middlebury entered. "Ah, good. Your son conveyed my message. Come, see where I work. That's all for today, Mrs. Pendragon." The nurse eyed Joan with a loathing which crawled through her like ice water. They followed him to back rooms with tables for examinations and other medical procedures. A locked, well-stocked drug room and a surgical facility completed the tour.

"Marcus said you wanted to see me about a medical question." Joan offered no information about her son's interest in the request.

"Yes, but I need to show you something first." He left to lock the infirmary door, placing a 'will return' sign in a frame on the hallway wall. "What did you think of Mr. Blackthorne when you saw him. I do want an honest assessment."

Marc spoke first, "Do you suspect his death was not a heart attack?"

"Oh, no. He died of heart failure. I'm interested in what your wife thought may have caused it."

Joan touched Marc's arm. "His lips indicated some kind of

poisoning as did his eyes. The drool seemed to indicate a paralytic event before his heart stopped, probably for the same reason. He consumed something which predicated his demise. Is that what you wanted to hear?"

Dr. Middlebury wagged an index finger for them to follow him. He unlocked a door which emitted a cool air when opened. Six lockers in two rows of three and a table were all that the room contained. "It's a simple exam room for forensic work, but it fits the bill most of the time." He walked to number 1 and opened the metal access. He pulled out a tray which contained the black body bag of deceased human remains.

"Mr. Blackthorne, I presume," Marc said.

"Yes, we don't often have need to place bodies on hold while cruising, but every ship has a morgue in case someone dies. This is the first time I've used it." He unzipped the bag and pulled the halves apart. "Please, use your judgment and expertise." He handed her latex gloves, then asked, "I assume you are not allergic." Her head rocked from side to side. She opened his lids one at a time, checked his mouth and felt around his stomach and chest.

Pulling off the gloves and wrapping one within the other with outside enfolded, she asked. "Have you taken samples of blood, saliva, tissues, stomach contents?"

"I've not had an opportunity to do an autopsy, as that usually is done by an expert pathologist while we are in port."

"I think it might be best to have samples taken so they can be examined as soon as possible when we dock. Marc has acquaintances in Seattle who are the best M.E.'s anywhere. We can send the samples to them, as well as, having the local M.E. do an autopsy. If someone wanted him dead, they may be aware of your doubt about why he died."

Marc continued, "If he was murdered, we have little time to uncover motive and method. One or more people aboard may be involved. You need to be careful who you talk with about this and trust no one."

"It seems to me," Middlebury said, "we've a criminal among us."

# CHAPTER

## 15

In the Elliot Bay Marc and Joan sat at the table holding hands. "Marc, are we in any danger?"

"I don't think so, but I'm wondering if the basket really was misplaced or were we the intended targets." He heeded her inquiry as a possible outcome. Enemies abounded in a policeman's job. Which case was coming back to haunt him? How could he keep Joan and the kids safe without any evidence of a perpetrator. The steward who delivered the basket was a good start. Sarah knew who he was. But putting her in harm's way made no sense. The basket may have contained the poison which killed the author. How ironic. A writer of thrillers and mysteries was now the subject of his own story.

"We have to keep the children safe with us without raising alarm."

"I know. At the same time, we have to act as though nothing is suspicious. Only a few people are involved and I doubt they are serial killers out to do in a ship load of families and oldsters." The door opened with Sarah entering alone.

"Hi. Am I intruding?" She acted oblivious to any seriousness from her parents. "James and Marcus are not in their room. Have you seen them?"

"We saw Marcus in the observatory about an hour ago. James wasn't with him. Are you concerned about them?" Joan rose to hug her daughter. "What have you been up to?"

"Nothing. I thought the guy I met wanted to show me around, but he got called to duty."

Marc asked in a curt tone, "Do you know where he is?"

"No. Why? You sound like you want to hurt him. He didn't do anything wrong. He didn't hurt me."

"I want to talk with him about the basket he delivered to us. I feel bad about giving it away when your grandparents may have sent it to us, a bon voyage gift."

Sarah sat on her couch/bed. "Am I ugly?"

Joan sat with her. "No. You are beautiful and smart. Why? Did he say something to you?" Sarah wagged her head.

Marc stepped to her side. "I still want to talk with him." Her eyes tilted upward to meet his. Her head wagged again.

"I don't know where he is." A tear formed in her right eye and trailed down her face below her ear. Marc moved away to the veranda door, staring at the scenery. "Dad, what's wrong? Is he in trouble?" A silence prompted another question. "Are we in trouble?"

"No, we're not in trouble, and neither is he." Marc held her hand as he spoke. "I need to know if the basket was meant for us."

"But the card? It said something about books. Did the basket have something in it that harmed the writer?"

"I don't think Mr. Blackthorne was harmed by anything in the basket." He looked at Joan and back to his daughter. "As to the card, it said 'booking' and since I book suspects, we may have been a bit rash in sending the basket to him." She separated and said goodbye. Leaving her parents to their own thoughts, she left.

Joan followed Sarah's departure, then turned to Marc. "She is intuitive. Can we uncover the truth before others are harmed? We need to find the boys."

"I agree."

⚬

Marcus paced the floor next to the elevators, impatience building a wall of frustration. Deciding to descend by the stairs, he turned as elevator 1 dinged its arrival. Several people emptied from the car.

He entered alone and pushed the button for the lower deck. Each floor claimed a stop. As people entered and departed, he claimed a corner away from the myriad passengers. On deck one the last of them left him to ride alone to the lower floor.

In the hallway he passed a young Filipino girl who smiled and swayed hips as she passed. Another time, another place, he may have been interested. Delinda was primary for now. At her room he raised a fist poised to knock. His brain argued to avoid a confrontation. His heart pushed to finish the action. The door opened

Delinda smiled, looked at his face, and saw his raised arm. "Where did you go? I thought you abandoned me. Use me and leave me. Another conquest to brag about to friends. But I guess I'm wrong." With a gentle motion she lowered his arm and clasped his folded fingers, leading him into the room. She asked again, "Where were you?"

"Your dad asked me to contact my mother about a medical case. I asked if it had anything to do with the death of that author on our deck. He was cryptic, cautioning me about dead bodies on ships and people listening. He's spooked about something." They sat on her bed and he realized she wore a robe untied and open.

"My father imagines conspiracies with little evidence to back his claims." She closed her robe and tied the cord. "He wants life to be fair and predictable, and it's not. You resisted me in your suite and I appreciated your control. Why did you break here?" She laid a hand on his bare leg at the seam of his swimsuit, high on the thigh. "I'm not complaining. Just wondering."

He turned his face away from her, hiding a rosy hue which warmed him. "I don't know. Being with you was the most incredible thing I've ever done." He realized a change near her hand and blushed more.

"Do you want to do it again? My dad isn't expected for another hour or so. He keeps away from me for most of the day." Delinda untied and removed the robe. His predicament interfered with mental control. Her body begged another trip to Eden and the tree of knowledge. Her hand moved to his predicament, and she grinned.

As Marc and Joan searched for James and Marcus, Dag Ingersoll approached them. "Mr. Jefferson," he ignored Joan, "may I have a word with you?" His rumpled suit draped across him in comic fashion.

Marc looked at Joan and said, "My wife and I are looking for our sons. Have you seen them?" Ingersoll flushed, frustrated by the question.

"No, I haven't. I was hoping to speak with you about your neighbor. You're a detective and I am asking for you to ignore anything about what happened this morning. This a maritime issue and none of your business."

"I have no intention of interfering with any investigation you or this ship's crew may pursue. We are on vacation and nothing about Mr. Blackthorne is suspicious. Correct?"

Ingersoll stammered, "Ah, yes, you are correct. I can expect your cooperation?" Marc nodded and the security chief trundled off. Marc eyed him until he entered a door and faded from the scene.

"That was certainly odd." Joan said as she caressed his arm. "You think he knows we've studied the body? That Middlebury asked for help?"

"I don't know, but his request raises my suspicions. Let's find the boys and get Sarah before something happens to ruin this trip." The need to obtain tissue samples and stomach contents before the body was removed from the ship increased as a result of Ingersoll's admonition. Two days until Juneau left little time for speculation.

James sat in the game room of the ship battling another younger adversary in a test of wits. Joan and Marc watched for a few seconds. Marc spoke first. "Go to the infirmary and ask Middlebury for the whereabouts of his daughter. I'll call Sarah and direct James to continue playing until his sister is here. Bring Marcus when you find them."

"Keep us safe." Her rejoinder dug deep into his heart. A simple vacation and now chaos, imminent and potentially harmful. She set off on her mission.

Marc watched his son as he removed his cell from a jacket pocket and punched the preset. Listening to the ringing he thought of the mistake he made which cost a person his life. What was in the basket which caused James Blackthorne to die? How could he expose the motive and the person or persons responsible? When Sarah answered, he asked her to come to the game room. He did not hear her as he watched James collapse from the chair to the floor. His phone dropped to the carpet as he reached for his fallen son.

Checking for heartbeats and breathing, both were shallow. He yelled for help as others crowded around. Recovering his phone, he asked for Sarah to speak, proving she was still connected. "Get the doctor and your mother. James is sick. I'll meet you in the infirmary." He clicked off, picked up the limp body and ran the corridors and stairs, shouting for clearance as he encountered other passengers and crew. James eyes rolled back in their sockets. "Don't you dare die on me." Tears formed obscuring sight. He blinked them away and raced to the help he needed.

# CHAPTER

# <u>16</u>

Randolph closed the cap containing the sample of blood from the distinguished author. He had extracted stomach contents, skin and muscle tissue samples, and digestive juices from the intestines. All he needed was a chance to get these pieces of evidence to proper medical examination labs. Blackthorne died from something other than natural reasons, that he knew. Joan Jefferson believed the same, that he also knew. How could he team with her husband, Detective Marcus Jefferson, to uncover the person or persons responsible?

A knock on his door, locked against disruption and discovery, interrupted his thinking. Placing the materials in lockers in the morgue, he rose to find who disturbed his work. A patient? Ingersoll? He knew not. A bead of sweat rolled down his cheek. He breathed deep and slow. He wiped away the droplet and walked to the door. Joan Jefferson raised a hand to repeat the wrapping. He waved as she dropped her hand.

"Mrs. Jefferson, how nice of you to drop by. May I help you?" He stood aside to allow her entry into the infirmary.

"Marc asked me to come. We're looking for our son. Is he nearby with your daughter?"

Randolph scrunched his face. "I haven't seen them." Eyes widened, "I wonder if they're in my cabin? We share it and I haven't been there in some time." Joan widened eyes, as well.

"They aren't..." Finishing her words seemed foolish. She understood what had transpired. A man instead of a boy. "Take me there."

He nodded. Before they rounded the corner to the hallway, Marcus and Delinda approached. Fingers interlaced and smiles beamed from each of them. Parents exchanged knowing looks. "Delinda, I do hope you and Marcus are enjoying the ship." Blushing faces exposed a secret.

"Your father wants you up in the observatory. Now." Marcus frowned and unhooked from Delinda.

"I'll go find out what he wants and come back for you." He stepped to the elevator and pushed the button. As he waited he glanced back at her. A father's arm across her shoulder directed her into the infirmary. The doors opened and he entered. As they closed, a commotion drew his attention.

"Dr. Middlebury," yelled Marc. "Doc, my son. I need your help." Randolph saw the limp body and signaled Marc to follow him. Joan gasped as hands covered her mouth. She guided Marc and James into the exam room as Middlebury scrubbed hands and gloved them.

"Put him on the table." Middlebury opened eyelids, one then the other. Listening to a heartbeat, he pursed lips. "What has he had to eat?" A noise stopped any answer to his query. Sarah entered the room, breathless. Another sound indicated Marcus came back from his elevator ride. Middlebury repeated the question. Each family member looked at each other awaiting a response.

As the silence degenerated into despair, Marcus spoke. "When I last saw him, he ate some bread from the basket in Mr. Blackthorne's room."

"I've got to pump his stomach. First, we've got to stabilize him. Joan, hand me that bottle of epinephrine. He needs stimulation of his nervous system. There's a syringe on the top shelf of that cabinet." She retrieved it. After the injection, he monitored James' heart rate and other vital signs. The young son remained unconscious but breathing became steady and his heart beat stronger.

Joan asked, "Where are your supplies for clearing his stomach." Mothering instincts became secondary to medical instincts for patient survival. Marc directed Sarah away from the work they did on James. Marcus followed, finding Delinda in the waiting area.

"Dad, is he going to be okay?" Sarah's voice quivered.

"I don't know, but your mother is an excellent nurse. She'll see to it that Dr. Middlebury does his best." The basket. His brain pictured the contents, but he couldn't remember seeing bread. What else was there?

"Dad. Dad." Hearing his parental name, his brain defogged from its journey. "Mom wants you." He nodded, leaving his oldest children. Delinda curled into Marcus's body while Sarah paced a short linear path.

Inside the exam room his son blinked, staring blindly as moisture dripped from his mouth. His head was turned to one side to allow for the drainage. A tube trailed from it leading to a glass collection beaker which contained a yellowish brown fluid with mushy pieces of unidentifiable solids.

Joan approached and whispered, "Dr. Middlebury believes he was poisoned. It may be the same material which struck down Blackthorne. He's going to test it against the samples he has from the author." Marc stared at James. "Marc, if the basket was meant for us, then someone may want you dead."

He looked at her, the fear glistened in the tears puddling on her lids. "I know. Or someone wants to exact revenge by harming you or the children. I must get that basket." He wrapped arms around her for assurance. For her as well as for him. An idea germinated in his mind, small and insignificant. He did not want to think it possible and relaying the notion to Joan would ricochet old experiences.

"Doc, is James going to be alright?" A simple question, ambivalent and uneasy.

"I think so. He has some of the same symptoms indicated in Mr. Blackthorne's body. You brought him here in plenty of time. Whatever transpired in that suite, James somehow experienced. That's what puzzles me. The only commonality is food. What has he eaten lately?" Marcus responded to Middlebury's question.

"He may have eaten some bread from a basket delivered to Mr. Blackthorne." Marc pondered Marcus's words.

"How did he get a hold of the bread?" Marc asked. Silence reigned a brief moment.

Joan responded, "You're the detective. I guess you'll go and detect." Marc frowned, unappreciative of the attempt at humor. As Marc left the room, she followed. "Be careful."

Three pairs of eyes greeted them as they entered the waiting area of the infirmary. A grieving daughter besought the arms of her mother, while a concerned son hugged a dark-haired beauty who did not understand the seriousness of being a policeman's child. Marc signaled for the three offspring to sit. After they did, he sat across from them with Joan at his side.

"James is very sick. He's going to need our help to find out what caused his illness. Marcus, explain about the bread he ate." Marcus looked at his father, then his mother, and back to his father.

"He snuck into the dead man's suite. I caught him with the bread. He threw it down, so I retrieved it and gave it to him."

"Did he take anything else?"

"I don't know. I didn't see anything." Marcus fidgeted, guilt rising in his throat. "Did I do something bad?"

"No, but we need to search your room to find anything he may have taken before you spotted him." Marcus wagged his head in agreement. "Sarah, Joan, stay with James. We're going to find that basket and find what else James took."

The two eldest males left two distraught women to discover the whereabouts of any other contents of a basket and gain access to a secured suite. On the elevator Marcus again asked, "Is this my fault?" A furrowed brow and slack jaw accompanied the question.

"No, it is not anyone's fault except the person who placed the poison in the basket. I can't see it being the bread, so something else was in there and James got it." The bing alerted them to a floor being accessed. They were not near their destination. Marc pressed the Navigation deck button several times. Three women entered the car to ride up with them. Silence ruled. A muteness required by the unfamiliarity of the other people. Another bing and the car stopped on the promenade. Two more interlopers joined the throng of quiet strangers.

When the car stopped on the navigation level, Marc and Marcus left five people to introduce themselves to each other and finish a ride to the Lido for a refreshing drink or a dip in the pool. "Let's start in your room." Marcus pulled out his key card and headed to his door. Marc stopped and knocked with authority on the suite shared by two overwrought females, possibly capable of accessing their employer's suite. What was in the room which led another person to want him dead? Or was there nothing incriminating?

The door opened to reveal a blurry-eyed young editor, dressed in sweatpants and t-shirt. She stepped aside accepting the incursion as inevitable. She was alone in a room mussed by clothing and towels. As the door trapped him with her she asked, "What do you want from me?" He realized she wore no other items of clothing than the pants and shirt.

"Do you have a key for your boss's room?" She stared a moment at him as if the query was wrong. Then she shuffled through stuff on the shelf and produced the card. She held it out, then her hand retreated.

"Why?"

"I need to look in the gift basket." His eyes squeezed together and a fist formed of his right hand.

"I need you to promise me something." Marc waited, his fist tightening. "Promise me you'll find out why James died. Promise me and you can have this key. Promise." Relaxing, he realized her loss and the guilt eating at her.

"I cannot promise I will uncover a motive for why he died, but I will uncover what caused it." She handed the card to him, slipped on loafers and followed him next door.

In the hallway, Marcus emerged from his suite holding a small jar. He displayed it to his father and Gabby, a prize for diligent investigating. "Dad, this was in his suitcase." Marc relieved his son of the bottle of obscure material. He removed the lid and waving the fragrance of the contents to his nose, he sampled the air. Brows knit together and head cocked to one side.

"Was this all you found?" Marcus bobbed his head looking from father to editor and then to the jar. "Come with me to the infirmary, Miss Montoya. I want you to see something." Three people left and one suspected another may have inadvertently caused a death.

# CHAPTER

## <u>17</u>

Joan entered the exam room to check on James who remained comatose. "Mrs. Jefferson, I think we can move your son to a more comfortable setting." They picked him up between them and carried him to one of the infirmary beds. He checked vitals again and nodded. "He's stable. I think he'll be fine."

"Doctor, what connection is there to Blackthorne? James exhibited several of the symptoms I saw in the author." She sat in a chair nearby, waiting for a response. He pulled up a chair next to her.

"I saw the same thing. I imagine that Blackthorne, being an older and less healthy person may have had an adverse reaction to whatever he ingested. James, being young and healthy, did not experience a fatal reaction. I'll watch him over the next few hours. You get some rest. If I need you, I'll be in contact." He rose from the chair and offered a hand to her. She accepted and rose as well.

"Dr. Middlebury, do you think Mr. Blackthorne was murdered?"

"Call me Randolph, or Randy, if you prefer. I'm not a medical examiner, but the signs point to a poisoning. I just don't have a lab which can diagnose. I'll get my evidence to shore at Juneau when we dock. If he died because he had an enemy, we are obligated to report to any suspicious deaths to the FBI. Ingersoll was clear. He didn't want me to say a word. Do you think your husband can figure this out before we dock in two days?"

"He's not sure he should be involved, but that hasn't stopped him from investigating cases which are not his venue. He's creative about getting the truth out. I asked him about it earlier, and now that James is a victim, I don't think anyone will stop him." Joan departed to gather her son and daughter.

Randolph followed to keep his daughter from leaving with her new found companion. Sure of the activity within the cabin before this interruption, he wanted to discuss life and responsibilities, a condition ignored since her mother's death. He couldn't ignore the subject of sex any longer.

"Delinda, do you like this new guy, Marcus?" Placing a secure, assuring hand on her shoulder. She dipped to avoid contact. He let it go.

"He's really nice and smart and I like him." She weaved a path away from her father. He traced her path but remained behind her. A sudden turn caused a near collision. "Dad, I'm old enough to know what I'm doing. Trust me." A quick embrace gave no assurance for a distraught father.

"He does seem like a nice person. His family is friendly and talented. If he is anything like either of his parents, I get the attraction. But honey, please be careful. Today's actions can have future consequences."

"Geez, Dad, Mom and I had this conversation years ago. If I want to have sex with someone, I get to choose who and when. Not you." Delinda raced from the room, leaving her father alone with an unfounded accusation which had a modicum of truth. It was not important to confront her or deal with parents unaware of their son's activities with his daughter.

He closed the door and locked intruders out. He sat at his desk, clicked on his computer and typed a summary of his findings regarding James Blackthorne. James Jefferson was another story. Another file and another summary of a young man's fight for survival. Finishing, he saved each to a folder on a thumb drive, ejected the drive from the computer system and removed it. Placing it in his coat pocket, he closed the computer and left for his room.

Entering the small cabin, shared with a freewheeling young girl, now a woman, he sat on his bed, alone. Sadness raised its ugly head. He lost his love to a nasty disease. Now he understood this trip may have cost him a daughter. Loneliness was not part of his plan. He had started this adventure with high hopes and aspirations. But his fog remained, obscuring any idea of happiness.

A knock interrupted his pity party. He wiped an errant tear from his cheek and stood to open the door. No one awaited his response but an envelope had been placed in the message rack. Lifting it from the case, he opened it and read. Words jumped from the page. His body clashed with the wall by the door, as the paper floated softly to the carpet. His brain raced for an answer to the contents. Instincts railed as he concluded the author of the note meant to destroy his career and family. An imprudent decision scraped through his brain.

Picking up the note, he placed it in the envelope which conveyed the message and embarked on a hunt for help. Marcus Jefferson could be a reason for the message. His father was a detective. He had to find either of them. Panic mastered the art of deceit and he could not let it win.

In the hallway outside his room he searched for anybody who might have sent it. It stared at him with empty ends and empty threats. The note burned in his pocket like a misplaced pilfered cigarette. He quit the day after her death and fought urges to return to the habit. He pushed the up button, then changed his mind and traced the steps to the main deck. Searching each floor consumed precious time. Delinda was priority one. Finding the coward who wrote the note lived at another level of his brain. Joan Jefferson recognized the truth. Was she to be a victim? Marc Jefferson solved cases others thought improbable. Was he going to be a victim?

An absent Delinda impelled him to search another deck, but it contained only rooms for passengers of lesser means. He skipped and raced stairs to another more probable place. "James," his thoughts betrayed him. "I left him alone in the infirmary." Making a reversal of direction, he returned to the lower deck to assure himself of the safety of his only patient. "Get one of the nurses' aides to man the desk." Thoughts clouded judgment. What if one of these people was part of the problem?

James rested. One of the nurses had arrived for her shift and was checking on him. "Doctor, there's no chart for this patient." Yes, one existed, but no one must see it.

"I think it's on my desk. Just check vitals every hour. I'll get the chart later. I'm off to find my daughter." Another time his nurse would question no chart. Today, simple and with sweetness, she did not press for information.

Continuing his search, he left and ascended to the observation level, planning to work his way down, deck by deck. He rued the dismissal of her plea for a cell phone. On the navigation deck he visited the conflicted, ambivalent author's suite. The suite next to it contained his pair of women. What was their involvement? Turning to leave, he decided to knock on the Jefferson's residence at sea. Lack of an answer disappointed him. He needed help. Delinda was missing as far as he was concerned. A detective seemed a right person to contact.

Where next to search? He headed to where people tended to gather.

# CHAPTER

# 18

Joan discovered Marc with Marcus and Gabby Montoya in the Lido deck restaurant. "Have you seen Sarah? Uh, That's a dumb question. She's not here." As she spoke Marc and Marcus grinned at each other. "What aren't you telling me?"

Marc answered her question, "Marcus found something in James' suitcase which may be from the basket. We're on the way to the infirmary with it."

"Where's Sarah?"

"We left her with you." Marc screwed his face, confused.

Joan answered, "She said she was heading back to the room."

"We need to get her a phone when we get home, so we can keep track of her."

"Oh, so that's why I get a phone. Not for communications, but for keeping track of me," Marcus said with a laugh.

"Marcus, go find your sister and bring her back to the infirmary. If she's not in the suite, you get to the infirmary." Marcus nodded agreement to his dad's request and left.

Turning to Joan he said, "Let's get this jar to the lab and uncover what is in it, which may be causing illness in James and may have contributed to Blackthorne's death." Holding Gabby by the elbow, he guided her as they moved toward the elevators. "You may know more than you remember, Miss Montoya. By the way, where is your roommate?"

"She's spending time in one of the lounges, drinking. Too much."

A bing indicated the arrival of a car with an up arrow. Several passengers got out, leaving the car empty. As they waited for another, Joan saw Middlebury. "What's the doctor doing up here? Who's with James?" She indicated she was going to get answers. Marc watched his wife with admiration of her anger control. Abandoning James was not a wise choice.

Middlebury disappeared into the hall at the other end of the restaurant. She followed. Another car arrived going the right direction. Marc and Gabby stepped aboard and rode to the lower deck. Because of the absence of medical staff, he would check on his son. Gabby did not resist, but wrapped an arm around his.

"I do hope your son will be alright." Marc gazed into her eyes, pools which could mesmerize Jason and his Argonauts.

"Doc says he'll recover." Quiet became the norm for the few seconds the ride took.

⎯⎯◦◦⎯⎯

Joan scanned the hallway but did not see her quarry. Why was he not with James? She stepped through the doorway to scan the pool area. Nothing. Returning to the hallway, she pressed the button for a down elevator and waited. A tall steward waited with her. He was older than most of the stewards who worked the floors, restaurants and lounges. His uniform possessed the adornments of a managing member of the crew.

"I do hope your experience with us has been joyful." He smiled, but Joan thought it insincere. Who was this person. From where had he come? Her mind conjured conspiracy where none existed.

"I have enjoyed this cruise. Your people are polite, well trained, efficient, and friendly." The elevator arrived as she spoke. Holding the door for her, the steward again formed his insincere smile. She entered and turned. A sneer coursed his face.

"I do hope nothing happens to you or your family during the remainder of your voyage. Unfortunate accidents have occurred. Do be careful. What you do can have such serious consequences. Choose carefully so nothing surprising takes place." He released the door, watching until it closed. Her heart pounded in her chest as breathing shallowed and quickened. This cryptic threat left no question in her mind that he knew about the death of Mr. Blackthorne. The car stopped on the next floor for an older couple.

The lady stared and asked, "Are you alright. You look seasick."

"Thank you for asking. No, I'm fine. Just thinking about how wonderful this trip is for me."

She asked, "Is this your first time?     Herman and I are on our fourteenth trip with American Pacific. We've been around the Caribbean, through the Panama Canal, Mexico, South America, and Hawaii. This marks our seventh trip to Alaska." A proud face returned Joan's smile and nod. She wanted out of the car. A bing granted her an escape.

As the door opened, the couple preceded her, waving a genteel good-bye. She stayed put. Two more entered to ride down to oblivion. Another conversation, not wanted, broke forth leaving her uninvolved. As the last floor lit on the panel arrived, her escape seemed imminent. Thoughts of the admonition from the steward swarmed her mind. James was an unwitting victim of an assault on the author. Or was Marc correct and the basket was theirs from the beginning. A swirl of ideas scrambled around with nothing abating her moment of insanity.

Alone for the first time since his nefarious communication, she raced to the infirmary. Her mind reeled from the haunting words. Marc would know what to do. James survived, but were the women traveling with the author out of danger? Was their family the real target? The steward's words left little question of the danger.

At the office the nurse checked James vitals a second time. She wrote the results on a post-it. Joan crashed through the doors creating a ruckus which frightened the nurse. "I am so sorry for scaring you. Is the doctor here?"

"No, and who are you?"

"My son James is here recovering from an illness." She passed the woman to find her son and assess his condition. "How is he?" She placed a hand on his head.

"He's resting comfortably. His vital signs are stable and strong."

Joan grasped her hand. "Thank you for taking good care of him." A noise halted any other conversation, and Marcus appeared in the doorway. "Oh, good. Is Dad on his way? And did you find your sister?"

"I thought I'd find him here," Marcus said. "Sarah was not in the suite." He peered at his brother's passive body.

"Explain what you found in James' suitcase."

"It was a jar of honey." Holding up a bag, "I brought the bread, as long as I was up at our room."

"Good." Another sound alerted them to others arriving. Marc and Gabby entered the room. The nurse gazed from person to person.

"Who are you people?" No one answered, but Joan signaled Marc to follow her. She retreated to the exam room. He followed.

"What's up?" he asked.

"Marc, one of the stewards confronted me upstairs. What he said sounded like a threat." Relating the conversation as calm as she could, Joan's eyes filled.

Marc held her close. "If he was threatening us, then you were correct to say Mr. Blackthorne's death was not natural." Her tears spilled onto his shoulder. "We need to be diligent about who we talk to and who we interact with."

"Why would anyone want to attack us? We're on vacation."

Marcus interrupted. "I couldn't help overhearing. Are we in danger?"

Joan and Marc separated, and his father responded. "Marcus, we need to be careful, but I don't think we are in any danger." He closed the distance. "Find your sister and get her to stay in the suite for now. If she is with the steward, be kind but get her to our room." Marcus said nothing but frowned and turned and left the infirmary.

Marc walked back to the room where James rested. "Miss, ah... I don't your name."

She squirmed a bit. "Olivia. Olivia Breckenridge. Why?"

"Miss Breckenridge, my son is important to me. So I'm happy to know he's in good hands. Tell me about Doctor Middlebury. How long have you and he been aboard?"

She turned away. "I came aboard in Seattle for this trip. He was already here. His previous nurse had completed her term. Why are you asking me questions? I feel like I'm on trial for something."

"I merely want to be sure my son will recover." He smiled a relaxed, closed mouth smile. Put them at ease he always thought.

Put them at ease. "How long do you get to enjoy the travels of American Pacific?"

She sat in folding chair set near James. "I signed up for six months. I haven't ever been on a cruise before, but they had a need for nursing assistance and I was next on the list."

"So you haven't had much contact with Middlebury." Marc crossed arms.

"No, your son is our first passenger." Hands clamped the sides of the chair and arms locked. Marc dropped his arms and leaned against the wall.

"Have you had any contact with any of the crew?"

"Not since our initial meetings. We have to evaluate new hires." Marc stood straight. "How many new hires did you see?" Olivia's arms relaxed and hands released the chair.

Marc took one step toward her but stopped. She leaned back into the chair. "We met with three."

"That seems to say that turn over isn't very high."

"We didn't get any of the transfers." Marc came closer. "They can ask for one ship or another while they have a contract. The company makes the final decisions." He held out his hand to shake hers. She accepted. After he stroked his son's hair, kissed his forehead, he joined Joan who stood in the doorway. It seemed to him someone aboard the ship manipulated events and personnel. What was Middlebury's role in it?

# CHAPTER

# 19

Sarah wandered the upper deck in the warm air and bright sunshine. Her mind played with her feelings as she scanned for any sight of Iskandar. She wanted to know it was alright to not sleep with him and he would still care about her. No one at school attracted as much attention to her emotions, a rational reasoning she did not comprehend. He was exotic, handsome, older, and interested in her. "Mom's right," she thought, "all men want is sex." Now she wanted the experience. Maybe he was not to be the first. Did it matter? She figured anyone could be the lucky guy. But what was the rationale for waiting for number one? That love was what brought out the exhilaration of the physical act, as Mom had explained? Her mind dismissed the relationship.

"I've been looking for you." Sarah's heart raced in anticipation. She turned to face the voice.

"Oh, it's you." Marcus scrunched his face.

"And you were expecting someone else? Maybe that steward you're hot for? He only wants to sack you and leave you when our trip is finished." Marcus smirked as his words drove home in Sarah's brain the thought of sex with Iskandar.

"So what, I'm old enough to do what I want. I suppose you and that girl are as chaste as ever." Sarcasm dripped as molasses in January. Marcus blushed. Her eyes expanded. "You and she did it, didn't you?" Turning away and facing him again, she continued. "Do Mom and Dad know?"

"I don't know. They were in the infirmary when Dee and I came in. And you better be quiet."

"What's it like? Does it hurt? Can you really get pregnant the first time?"

"I don't know if it hurt her. It didn't for me. And I hope she's not pregnant." He placed hands on her shoulders. "But none of this is important. Mom and Dad want us in the suite as soon as possible. Something scared Mom. I overheard her say she felt like she was being threatened." Releasing her body, he started for the elevators and a short descent to their floor. She followed, but stopped when she saw her quarry on the other side of the ship.

Marcus pushed a down button, then saw that Sarah had not followed. She ran up to him. "I saw him. Isakandar. He's over on the other side of the ship." Marcus's head wagged for her to stay.

"We have to get to the suite. I'll help you later to find him." They left the steward for another time. On the elevator with other passengers, questions waited. On the Navigation deck they vacated the box to the others and hurried to the Elliot Bay Suite. Sarah opened the door with her key card and they entered. As the door closed, they searched for parents. Finding no one else with them, they sat.

Sarah spoke first. "Is James okay? And explain what you meant by Mom felt threatened."

"James is fine, I guess. He was sleeping when I saw him. As for Mom, she and Dad were talking alone when I walked in. She said a steward had threatened her and our family with an accident or worse. Dad brushed it off, but I think he said that for my sake. Blackthorne may have died at the hands of someone on board. And if that's the case James is sick because he took some honey and bread from the basket that we sent over. What if the basket was meant for us?"

Sarah's eyes filled with tears. As they spilled over her lids, she asked, "Who wants to hurt us?" Marcus pulled her to him and held her close as she shivered with fear. A door opened and thier parents entered.

Marc screwed his eyebrows together. "What's the matter?" Joan followed him to their children.

Marcus peered up "I told Sarah what I heard you say about Blackthorne. And what Mom had said about being threatened." He and Sarah separated. "Dad, what's going on? Is someone trying to hurt us? You said we aren't in any danger, but it seems like we might be interfering with someone's plans."

Marc grimaced and looked at Joan. Her head bobbed an imperceptive assent. He connected with his son. "As your Mother waited for the elevator, an older steward approached and made what could be interpreted as threatening words about our investigating the death of James Blackthorne."

"Are you?" Marcus asked.

"Am I what?"

"Are you investigating Mr. Blackthorne's death as a murder?"

Joan broke in to answer his question. "When I observed Mr. Blackthorne in his suite, I noticed a few signs of his being poisoned. So when Dr. Middlebury contacted me about the death and asked for my evaluation, I figured he understood something was wrong. Your father is gathering evidence to show the security staff. James getting sick seemed to add to the intrigue as he exhibited the same traits as the author. Fortunately, your father got him to Middlebury in a timely manner." Marcus turned to look at Sarah.

"Was the basket meant for us," he asked.

Marc finished the inquiry, "I don't know, but if it was, then someone, somewhere, wanted us harmed. It could be related to a case in my history. So we are going to be diligent and stay together more as it will be safer for us."

The atmosphere thickened as they exchanged glances. What security was going to be saving them from an unknown enemy?

⨾⊶⊷⨿

Iskandar glanced at her as she talked with her brother. She was young, smart, and beautiful. The steward said she was his target for this voyage. He came so close to satisfying his lust with her. He averted his eyes as she glanced his way. The time for another encounter would come, he believed his abilities to be infallible. Sure she was watching, he walked into the storage room behind the bar.

Upon returning, she was gone. He smiled.

As he completed each of his assigned duties, thoughts of the young woman encouraged his aims. He whistled a tune from his childhood in Indonesia. So much had changed from the poverty he escaped. He finished the last of his clean-up on the Lido deck and returned to the stewards' meeting room on the lowest deck of the ship. He found his supervisor, the older steward, and reported his assignments completed. "Do you need me for anything else?"

"Iskandar, when you delivered the gift baskets to the suites, are you sure each one was in the proper room?" He spoke without raising eyes to meet the young man.

"Yes sir, each card had a room number and I placed each basket in the proper room. Why" Has someone complained?"

His head raised so eyes met eyes. The narrowness of the older steward's eyes became mere slits. Iskandar stood taller as his own eye sockets widened. He had not witnessed wrath from his boss and mentor in many months. "The basket for the Elliot Bay Suite, was it placed in the room as the card stated?" His mouth formed a line across his face.

"Yes, remember I told you the young lady was there. You said I did well, and you gave me money. She asked me to show her the ship. Why? What's wrong?" Breathing slowed. Palms moistened. His mouth dried.

"It is nothing. It seems to me you are trying your best." He reached for a small jar and gave it to Iskandar. "For your troubles. I did not mean to frighten you. Here is some tea to go with your sweetener." He waved a hand, dismissing his charge. Taking the prizes, he backed out of the room and walked with a spring in his step. The young beauty was his next goal. He realized his thoughts provoked an increase of blood to his abdomen. He slipped quiet as a mouse into his room. Placing the tea by a small coffee maker on a ledge, he examined the jar. Removing the lid, he dipped a finger into it and licked. It was as good as any he had tasted. Filling the carafe and turning on the power, he retrieved a mug from a shelf and placed a tea bag in it.

When the water was hot, he poured it into the mug along with a generous amount of the sweetener. He changed clothes while the water cooled. His brain conjured a picture of the girl lying on his bed wearing the swim suit which hid nothing from any observer. He cradled his privates in his left hand, picked up the mug and drank the warm liquid. The sensation of the warm fluid relaxed his mind. He dismissed the words of the steward and watched his imaginary companion remove the two pieces of clothing. Shaking his head, the image vanished as a mist in the heat of the day. He finished the tea and departed to find a young lady to make real the dream in his room.

Riding an elevator to the Navigation deck, he worked to blend with the passengers. Approaching the Elliot Bay, a bit of angst rose with each step. Her parents were nice enough, but if they were unsure of his intentions, he might not be able to escort his lady around the ship again. Willingness to accomplish his mission overrode his fears.

He knocked on the door. A twinge swerved through him as the door opened. Four sets of eyes gazed at him. The twinge subsided. "May I come in?" Marc stepped to one side and held the door. Iskandar stepped past him and walked toward Sarah. "I wish to continue your tour of our fine ship." Turning to Marc, he continued, "If it is acceptable to your parents." He smiled.

The door closed as Marc approached him. "Do you know of an older steward aboard?"

Iskandar scrunched his brow. He scanned each face a few seconds before answering. "We have several older stewards who are the supervisors for each of the crew assignments. Is there a problem?"

"No, no problem. Is one of them your supervisor?" The questions unnerved him for a moment.

"My supervisor is a nice person. I can seek him for you." Iskandar offered but preferred to leave with Sarah. Time had become a valuable commodity and he sought to have as much of it with her. Alone. The twinge returned, a reminder of his anxiety about sharing a bed with her. Something filled his body with an uneasiness. "I can get him for you, but I need to leave. I forgot a chore I promised an older couple. We can continue the tour when I am done." He bid a humble good-bye and left. Breathing was his forgotten chore as his stomach cramped and churned. A pain ran through his muscles.

He hastened to his lower deck and the security of his room. His mind concocted an evil spirit battling him for supremacy of his body. His heart roared in his chest. His feet clumped as if concrete replaced toes and flesh. In his room he tumbled to the bed, where no imagination interrupted his sudden sickness. Pain swirled inside his body and air in lungs despaired of entry. A hand grasped a chest now wracked with an unfamiliar torture. He closed his eyes concentrating on figuring his next breath. Nothing came as his structure froze, paralysis flowing free as a river. Darkness of closed lids morphed into the darkness of eternity.

# CHAPTER

# <u>20</u>

Middlebury scurried around the upper deck, his stomach twisting in a knot no antacid could uncurl. Slowing his pace, hands knitting a protective invisible web, he scanned the area and people hoping for a miracle. The note left no doubt someone wanted no interference an investigation aboard might install. Had the culprit nabbed the only good thing left to him? He envisioned her alone, twisting bindings in a futile attempt at escaping, confused and fearing for her future. A voice stabbed his mentality, unfamiliar, far from reality.

"Dr. Middlebury, "the voice echoed in his skull. "Can you look at my toe?" Toe? Who has time for a toe? Delinda's lost whereabouts shuddered to a stop. He gazed at the embodiment of the sounds rattling the air.

"Yes. What? Your toe. Yes. What happened?" The purple of the enlarged digit answered the question. "I do believe you should get that x-rayed when we land in Juneau. I don't have a machine on board, but it appears to be broken." The woman's head bobbed as he spoke. "Elevate the foot and place ice on it to hinder any more swelling." He pivoted from her presence and continued his search. He hadn't wanted to upset his daughter, but believing she had engaged in the age old action that fathers dreaded, unsettled his life.

Now a note left no question about the danger of investigating the suspicious death of Blackthorne. He wandered into the lounge and found a staggering Paula Merino. As gravity waved an unsteadying wand, Randolph caught her and guided her to a bench seat and table. She spoke indiscernible sentences. "What am I going to do? He was my only client, my friend, companion, and that slut killed him." Her head clamored to make intelligent thought but failed.

Another interruption to his hunt. He closed eyes for an indefinite moment, then said, "You need to return to your suite and rest. His death was an accident." Comforting words with little solace ingested by Merino. The business manager would conduct no more conversations this day. Signaling a member of the ship's crew, he left instructions for someone to escort her to her suite as soon as she was able.

Rising from the bench, he gazed a while at the young woman. "Too bad," he thought. "She's a smart and talented person." His mind rummaged around for the right ideas of approaching her later for a dinner engagement. Delinda popped into his head. Leaving the lounge, another scan of the pool area imposed another frustration. His pace slowed when he spied a young woman wearing the outfit last seen on his daughter.

Standing above the figure, her back confronting him, he sat on the edge of the chaise. "I am so sorry. I should trust your judgment." She rolled over and glared at him. Redness in her eyes relayed the message. "Can you please forgive me?"

"I want to believe you mean what you say, Dad, but I am eighteen, conscripted to a voyage I preferred not to take, and yet, I have found someone to love who loves me. You had Mom and she'd gone. I miss her as much as you do, but we both need to get on with living."

"Living is the most important thing right now. I want you to return with me to the infirmary."

"Is that a request or command?" Her breathing halted for an answer.

"A request, but with a caveat. I need to show you something which I prefer not to do here." He stood to allow her room for maneuvering.

Delinda leaned on an elbow, declining movement. "What is it,

Dad? Another attempt to embarrass me in front of Marcus? Is he waiting for my return?" Inertia remained static.

"I received a note which I want you to read but not here, please." His plight encouraged a willingness to accompany, if only for the curiosity of an unknown letter.

As they arrived at an elevator Marc and Joan joined them. Marc spoke. "We want to check on James and see if he's making progress." Marc curled eyebrows together and asked, "Who's with him?"

"One of my nurses is there." Delinda absorbed the question as apparent danger. But danger to whom? A mysterious note? James sick with an undiagnosed illness? Unusual anger from a distraught father? She remained quiet, but attentive.

The bing of an arriving car focused attention to the descent. Nothing vocal entertained them. Each concerned with a personal affect wringing beads of moisture from brows and chasing deep breathing into the shallows of life.

No other passengers or crew accompanied them. At the last floor the car crawled to a halt and doors expanded their world. Middlebury led them to the room housing James, who sat up and ate ice chips fed to him by the nurse.

"I see our patient has recovered." Middlebury pressed a finger onto his neck and found a strong beat. "Can you stand?" James placed his feet over the edge of the bed with the aid of Nurse Breckenridge. Wobbly legs prompted a return to the bed. "You relax, young man. Plenty of time for you to try walking."

Joan held out a hand for James to grasp, but most of the effort was hers. Salty water welled up in the eyes of a mother who understood the medical implications, but feared for a life uninvolved in the escapade awaiting them.

Randolph placed his hand on Marc's shoulder. "I need to speak to you in private." Marc followed him to the office area along with Delinda who accompanied her father.

"What's wrong, Doctor? I assume it involves your daughter."

"I received a note, anonymously." He produced the paper from the envelope and thrust it toward Marc. "Please read it and tell me what you think I should do." He wrapped an arm around Delinda as tears formed. Marc read and returned it. Randolph handed it to his daughter. A timorous shrill accompanied her release of the note.

Marc reached for the cascading document and caught it midway in flight. "I trust this is the first time Delinda has read this." Randolph nodded. Her hands encased her mouth, breathing became shallow and rapid. "Someone aboard this vessel is signaling an impending war. The question remains whether the thrust of the war is to keep secret the reason for an author's death or to target the unsuspecting quarry of the true reason for the poison." He peered around the corner of the door frame to signal Joan to come into the office. As she entered, he pushed the paper to her. She read the words. "Dr. Middlebury, as a sensible person it behooves you to acquaint yourself with the protocols of reporting a death aboard our ship. If you feel a need to be diligent and contact stateside authorities to report a suspicious death, then be aware of the risk your lovely daughter may find herself in. Do follow instructions to have the death of Mr. Blackthorne remain one of natural causes. One hates losing another family member to an insidious cancer." No signature ended the note.

"As I see this, Dr. Middlebury, the cancer is in the ship's crew and capable of spreading to other parts and causing irreparable harm. If Delinda is a target, then Marcus may get caught in the crossfire."

Delinda squeaked, "No. He can't be in danger. He can't be. What's going on? Why would somebody want to hurt me?" She buried her face in her father's shoulder.

Joan spoke, "She's right. Someone knows about your suspicions and wants silence. Blackmailing you with the threat to Delinda is an insurance policy. Marc, what can we do?"

Marc set teeth together, then answered, "I'll contact my father in Seattle. He has friends everywhere. Maybe we can get his help and keep it under wraps. Meanwhile, Doc, act according to this note. I doubt anyone would move on her if she was accompanied by people every minute of the day. I suggest she stay with us."

"No, I want her with me. She's all I have left." His gripped tightened.

"Alright, but she should not be alone. Anywhere."

Facing her guardians, she offered, "Marcus can stay with me." Joan stepped forward, but Marc halted her progress.

He said, "Yes, yes he can. I'll speak with him about being with you from morning through evening," Guiding Joan to the door, he turned before leaving. "Delinda, I advise you not to leave unless Marcus arrives or your father delivers you." Delinda nodded. Life had taken an irritating turn and twisted a wonder-filled vacation into an odyssey of survival. Marc and Joan departed to find their other children and safety. James remained until the effects of his poisoning ameliorated. He was safe. Or so Marc wanted to believe. His son was not a target as much as an innocent victim of a vicious act against an unsuspecting writer. If James Blackthorne was also an unintended victim, then the threat aboard remained and might strike again at the original target, himself.

# CHAPTER

# 21

Sarah and Marcus sat on the veranda watching the coastline pass. The rural forests broke for an occasional house or cabin. Although the scenery probably engaged the attention of other people, the conversation echoed the cautions of parents concerned with a troubling scenario, the basket was meant for them.

"I don't believe he meant to harm us. He's a nice young man and only wanted to show me the ship." Sarah sat with her hands clenched and foot rocking her leg in vertical gyrations.

Marcus said, "He probably wanted more. But I agree with you. He was doing his job when he delivered that basket."

Her foot stopped. "By more, what do you mean? That he wanted to do to me what you and Delinda did?"

He tilted his head and reached out a hand to her elbow. "I don't know for sure, but you do attract attention."

Freeing hands from the exertion of squeezing fingers together, she stood and walked to the railing. "He hasn't contacted me about finishing our tour. If he wants to have more, then maybe he'll get lucky." The conversation served to distract her fears of having killed an author because she questioned the card accompanying the basket.

Marcus joined her. "He doesn't need to get lucky with you. You have lots of time and better prospects than some guy from an unknown area of the world who is lucky enough already to be on this ship."

Fear manifested its ugly head. "I killed him. I thought the gift was meant for him. And now we may be in danger because the wrong person died." Before he could say an encouraging word, the door from the suite opened and Marc and Joan came out.

Sarah embraced her father, burying her head into his shoulder. He reciprocated, but said, "I'm glad you two are here. We need to talk about what's happening."

A muffled voice asked, "Did I kill him?"

Joan asked, "Kill who? James? No, he's resting and will return to us as soon as he is able." Sarah unhitched her clasp and turned to her mother.

"I meant the author, Mr. Blackthorne. I thought the basket was his. That's why Dad took it to him."

Marc spoke, "You did nothing wrong and we all thought the same as you. Who wanted to give us a present?" Hands grasped shoulders. "We are not sure who the intended recipient was. So for now, we will act as though we're on vacation."

"Act? Dad, that sounds like we're in some kind danger?"

"Your mother and I are just being cautious. James getting sick was an accident which could have been worse if the basket had stayed with us." He signaled Marcus to follow him into the suite. To Sarah, he said, "You stay with your mother. I have to speak with your brother about his girlfriend."

Inside Marcus asked, "Has something happened to Dee?" He reached out to his father's arm. "Is she okay?"

"She's fine, but a note was given to her father which sounded like a threat to her to keep him in line."

"In line? Why? What's he done?" Marc tapped his son's hand as it lay on his arm.

"Dr. Middlebury suspected, as did you mother, that Mr. Blackthorne's death may have been induced. As such, someone on this ship may still want to do harm."

"And Delinda's the next target?"

"Only to keep her father from pressing for an autopsy and a ruling of homicide. Your mother and I are thinking that I may have been the intended victim and that the person or persons responsible will try again. What I want you to do is go to the infirmary and escort Delinda up here, where we can keep an eye on her while her father does his medical job on the ship."

"Dad, who would want to hurt you?"

"That's the big question. I have enemies. And they may want to seek revenge, but how they know about us being aboard, is a mystery to me. You get Delinda and be cautious. Stay in public areas and be watchful. I'm going to contact your grandfather, Tiberius." Marcus left to seek his new love and protect her as best he could. Marc clicked the speed dial for his father.

As the phone connected and started ringing, Joan and Sarah entered the suite. Marc pointed a finger upward and cast eyes downward as he listened. They shut the door and watched. The phone went to message, which prompted a note to call as soon as possible.

"Was that Tiberius?" Joan asked. Marc nodded and placed his cell back in his pocket. Sarah sat on her sofa-bed, an attempt to ignore the obvious situation. People aboard the ship wanted her father dead.

"I left a message. He'll get back to me as soon as he can. Marcus left to get Delinda." They sat in the chairs at the dining table of the suite. Holding hands, he continued the conversation. "What indication was there that a poison was in the honey?"

"Blackthorne and James showed signs of paralysis which is consistent with some kind of poison. An analysis of the jar should uncover what kind. I'm interested in how someone knew about Dr. Middlebury asking for our help."

"Good point. Who had any contact with him or us? The only people who would know anything are Merino, Gonzales, Ingersoll and his assistant, the nurse who came with Middlebury, and the two stewards who hauled out the body. Any one of them may have assisted the person who wanted to poison me or the author. A motive would be nice to have, as then it would offer some direction for an investigation." Sarah approached from her lair.

"Dad, since Iskandar delivered the basket, he may know who wanted you dead." She turned to reposition back to her solitude.

"Oh my god, of course. Thank you, Sarah. That is a brilliant idea. How do we get a hold of him?" Marc followed her as he spoke. "He must have a room aboard and certainly has a supervisor. We need to get a message to him." An idea floated to the top of his scheming. "Sarah, go to the main desk and ask if Iskandar is available. If you find him, tell him I want to talk with him." She left to fulfill the assignment.

Mission Impossible music sounded. "Marc pulled out his phone and clicked the receive button. "Hi, Dad, glad you called back." He listened as his father asked how the vacation was going. "That's why I called you. We have a problem initiated by the death of a person aboard who was a famous author. Joan suspects he was poisoned."

"Who died?"

"His name was James Blackthorne, but that's not the real problem. Someone aboard this ship had to have been involved to get the poison onto the ship. Someone whose true target may have been me." He explained the rationale for his speculation. "And James exhibiting the same symptoms as the author after eating some of the contents of the gift basket makes my suspicions even greater." Explaining how James got the honey and bread led to the next question. "Have there been any curious deaths in Seattle or King County?"

"Other than the usual gunshots and accidents, I can't think of any off hand. Let me check with the coroner. I can get back to you tomorrow. Are you sure of this, that someone is after you? How does anyone even know you're on vacation aboard a cruise ship?"

"Good question. I'll await your call tomorrow. We dock in Juneau in another day, so be sure to let me know as soon as possible, or someone may escape." He clicked off.

Joan was sitting where Sarah had been unsure of an appearance that life was safe. Marc joined her. The door clicked open and Marcus and Delinda entered holding hands in an embrace which exceeded romance. Glancing out in the hallway for followers, they closed the door.

Four unflinching souls stared at each other as thoughts of the gravity of the problems mounted. When Sarah returned, they might have an answer to the question of who provided the material which was wreaking havoc with the lives of two families and two young women who may have been more involved. Marc decided another round of questions for the editor and business manager was in order. He stood and moved to the door to continue an investigation of a case with no reason for existing.

Knocking on their suite's door, he formulated some questions. No one answered the inquiry. He turned away to return to the Elliot Bay Suite, as the door opened. "Mr. Jefferson?" He faced the voice. Paula Merino looked as if a truck had run into her. Blurry eyes glanced around the hallway and back at him. He retraced his steps to meet her gaze.

"I wanted to ask you a few questions, if I may." She stepped back into the room expecting him to follow. Inside he found Gabby lying in the bed asleep. "Are you alright?" he asked.

"I'm hung over. They brought me back to my room an hour ago. Gabby and I have made a pact to help each other. Do you want her answering questions, too?" She rubbed her temples, closing her eyes and sighing. Gabby awoke from her slumber.

"Oh, we have a guest." Marc realized she wore few clothing items or nothing at all as she sat up holding the sheet around her. He looked away allowing her to robe her body. "You're a gentleman." She accommodated him. "You may turn around now." Her body fitted the robe, leaving little to the imagination.

"I have some questions for the two of you."

"Are you investigating us," Gabby asked. "Are we under suspicion of killing our boss?"

# CHAPTER

## 22

Sarah waited by the elevator tapping her foot again. Was Dad right? He was the object of someone's retaliation and the family was in the sights of people on board? Iskandar had answers. Her foot stopped as the bing announced a car arriving. The door opened and an older steward she recognized as a manager and a person who knew Iski stood in front of her. She smiled. He could help her.

"Sir," she gleamed as she spoke. "You're Iskandar's supervisor, aren't you?" He gazed at her as he stepped from the elevator. The door closed before she entered. "Do you know where he is? He promised a tour of the ship and we haven't finished it."

Tilting his head to his left, he kept his eyes on her. "He is in his cabin, as far as I know. He is resting before coming back on duty." A grin crossed his face. "May I be of help to you?"

She rocked her head. "Thank you, but no. If I can go to his cabin, I can ask him if he wants to show me the ship."

"I'm afraid that is not possible. Unless you are escorted by one of the staff, the crew quarters are off limits. I would help you but must report for my duties." He waited for her to leave, but she pushed the button for an elevator. "I recommend you enjoy the pool or the game area."

Her smile faded as eyes darkened. "Thank you for your advice."

The bing caught her attention. As the door opened and a family existed, she placed herself between them and the steward, entering the car and pushing the button for the main deck and the concierge desk. Her breathing began to slow as she blew out a deep inhale. Another time her intuition might have abandoned her, but her father's warning stayed with her. Trust no one. The car descended without interruption, an oddity. As the numbers on the screen closed in on 1, her foot started tapping. A bing on 3 stopped the action and a quick grimace and set teeth showed.

The door opened to expose two young men who grinned when the view for them improved. They entered with eyes glued to the beauty riding down with them. The silence, as the doors closed, thickened the atmosphere. They stood on either side of her. Sarah folded her arms over her chest and stared at the door. Her mind raced as she imagined them touching her. She swallowed and breathed in hard. The number on the screen changed to 1 and respite slid apart, opening her rescue.

The guys left her walking backward as they gawked. She ignored them and approached the main desk. "May I help you?" A young Indonesian woman smiled at Sarah. Her mind refocused and forgot the two lechers.

"Yes, I want to speak with one of your stewards. His name is Iskandar. I think he's in his cabin right now." The young woman grinned and clicked on her keyboard. Sarah scanned the room for any person who might be a threat.

"He is off duty." Sarah stared at the young woman whose smile seemed painted on her face.

"I know. Can you contact him for me?"

"Just a minute, please." She left the desk, entering a room behind her. Sarah breathed in and held it for a moment. She saw the two guys again, but they ignored her as they came to the desk and spoke with another of the agents. She turned away from them, her back acting as a shield. She tapped a hand on the counter. The door opened and the young lady returned. Sarah faced her. "I called his room, but there was no answer. He may be in another part of the ship, or asleep."

"Can you send someone to check on him?" Her foot resumed its activity. She placed both hands on the counter and glared at the woman who repainted her expression.

"I am sorry, but we are not usually allowed to interact with passengers, except in an official duty."

"This is official. He has been showing me the ship and we need to finish the tour." Sarah squared her shoulders and repeated her question. "Can you please send someone to check on him for me?" She looked at the woman's name tag. "Mara."

Mara picked up her phone and clicked some numbers. Her conversation was short and pointed. "Someone is going to see if he is in his room. I can leave him a message that you are trying to connect with him about the tour."

Sarah hissed, "Fine. If he is not there, then leave him a message. I am in the Elliot Bay Suite on the Navigation Deck."

"And whom shall I say is contacting him?"

"I'm Sarah Jefferson."

"May I see some identification, please." Sarah showed her the key card. "Thank you." Mara wrote a message and left the desk to place it somewhere for Iskandar to retrieve. Sarah waited for a response to the inquest of his presence in his cabin. The young woman returned and stated that no one answered the knock on his cabin door. Sarah nodded and returned to the elevator area. She had no idea which deck or cabin was his, and attempting to find him was a needle and haystack situation. An idea crept into her brain as she waited. The stairs were around the corner and one deck below was the infirmary.

As she descended the steps, Delinda came to mind and she wondered if her brother had found her and escorted her to the suite. The trip was only two days old and intrigue had screwed with family plans for rest and relaxation. At the doctor's office she found her brother, James, standing by the desk with Dr. Middlebury and another person who appeared to be a nurse. They looked at her as she entered.

"Oh, good." Dr. Middlebury's words were reassuring and soft. "James is ready to go back upstairs to his suite. He must not exert himself for another twelve to fifteen hours. Are you here to take him?" She changed her plans and agreed with a nod.

"Did Marcus find Delinda?" Sarah blurted out the question. The nurse squeezed her eyebrows as the doctor finished paperwork.

He spoke as he placed his pen on the desk. "Yes, he came about half an hour ago. They should be up in your parents' suite by now." She and James walked from the infirmary and headed to the elevators.

"Are you feeling better?" Her inquiry filled the vacuum between them. He nodded. "Why did you take that honey?"

"I don't know. It was just there and nobody was going to use it."

"Mom and Dad think someone tampered with it, that it was poisoned. You could have died." James did not acknowledge her comment. He knew he had a close call with death. If death remained aboard, other people were being stalked, just like Mr. Blackthorne. He was scared.

The door opened and the tall, older steward stepped out and looked at Sarah and then James. He walked away without turning again. They entered and she pushed the button for the Navigation deck and their rooms.

When they arrived at the suite, Marcus and Delinda were entering the boys' suite. James followed. Sarah used her key card to enter her room and relate her investigation of Iskandar.

"I couldn't find him. He was off duty but not in his room. I left a message at the main desk for him to contact me." She sat on her couch/bed and waited for an answer to the question remaining unstated and beckoning. What did he know about the basket?

Marc sat next to his daughter. "Thank you for trying. We need to get James, now."

"I stopped by the infirmary and got him. He's next door with Marcus and Delinda."

"Good. That means we are all safe for now. We should stick together." The suite phone rang and Joan picked up the receiver. She listened for a moment and replaced the instrument. "That was Dr. Middlebury. They found Iskandar in his cabin." She looked at Sarah. "He seems to have died of natural causes, a heart failure of some sort." Sarah inhaled quick and shallow. Marc glared at the floor.

He spoke, "They're covering their tracks." Standing, he joined Joan by the phone. "We should talk with Middlebury and see what he thinks."

"Won't our coming to him so soon raise suspicions?" Joan locked her arm in Marc's arm. Sarah buried her head in her hands. "We have to tell the boys and explain the situation to Delinda." Marc rocked his head in agreement. Someone was killing anyone who might know the truth. He figured Ingersoll had to know the deaths were not accidental. Time was approaching for his reinforcement unless he was part of the conspiracy.

# CHAPTER

# 23

The supervising steward let himself into the room where Iskandar rested for eternity. He picked up the jar and the remaining teabags before calling for assistance. Ingersoll was the logical first call, but convincing Middlebury that death aboard a cruise ship did not involve homicide was best for his small cadre of people. The collapse of the trade between Vancouver and Edmonds curtailed a lucrative income stream. The party responsible for its demise had slipped the noose. Suspicions mounted with each death and threats had not deterred conversations among various passengers and crew.

A quick investigation of the young steward's personal effects uncovered no damaging evidence. He clicked his radio and called for Middlebury to come to the room for an examination of a body. Picking up the cabin phone, he dialed a number for a certain crew member. "It's done." He listened a moment, "Yes, Middlebury is coming soon." Another listening moment. "Ingersoll's an idiot. He'll want to keep it under wraps, which helps, but information will slip out if he's contacted by anyone investigating these deaths." He listened to the name given. "Yes, Jefferson." He hung up the receiver.

A knock interrupted his thoughts. Opening the door, Middlebury filled the doorway. "Where's the body?" The steward flicked a finger toward the bed. Middlebury entered, followed by two young men and a gurney. A cursory examination ensued, after which the body was placed on the gurney for transport down the hall to the infirmary and morgue. "Well, he seems a bit young for a heart attack, but an autopsy will fill in the blanks."

"Doctor, are you sure about his death being a natural event?" Middlebury nodded. "I'll do a more thorough investigation in the infirmary. If you have any information which can explain his death, I'd appreciate it. I'll pull his file and check his medical records." He turned and followed Iskandar's body. The steward curled lips downward and set his jaw.

In the infirmary Middlebury and his nurse watched the two young men place the corpse on an examining table. They departed as soon as they completed the task. Middlebury placed a surgical gown over his clothing and mask on face, as did the nurse. After gloving hands, he tested arm and leg flexibility for rigor mortis. Inserting a body temperature gauge into the liver revealed a 93 degree reading. The nurse extracted a blood sample and tissue samples.

"Check his stomach contents." Nurse Breckenridge opened Iskandar's mouth and inserted a long tube which she worked down his esophagus until she entered the stomach. Using a suction devise, gastric juices collected in a jar attached to the end of the tube.

Middlebury wrote notes on a chart. "I have the stomach contents. Do you think he ate something which disagreed with his metabolism and physical functions?" Randolph stopped writing and looked up.

Frowning, he asked, "You mean poisoning? What makes you ask that? I can speculate but would rather collect evidence so as to make a rational decision."

"This is the third case of a person coming to the infirmary with the same symptoms. Is there a problem on this ship?" Olivia gazed at him awaiting clarity to her question. He continued writing without responding. She placed the samples in proper containers with labels and seals, and then refrigerated them. "He seems awfully young to have had a heart condition. That's why I asked about ingesting an unsavory substance." Middlebury looked up from the chart. "Are we in any danger?"

"I don't know, but I'm sure of one thing. These two deaths and the illness of young Mr. Jefferson all point to a common cause. When we get to Juneau, I want to have the samples sent to the M.E. for analysis. We'll keep the bodies in our morgue until we return to Seattle."

"May there be no more deaths or this morgue is going to need expansion." Middlebury dropped the chart on his desk and picked up his phone. His call was short and coded about a death being natural causes. "Was that security? I think security should be informed."

"I called someone who needed to be informed of this young man's demise." A commotion in the waiting area alerted them to another presence. Dag Ingersoll, wearing another of his rumpled suits entered. Nurse Breckenridge sat at a second desk and wrote notes for the report file. "What do you want?" Dag shuffled into the office area with Middlebury chasing after him. "What do you want?" he repeated with a crescendo in his voice.

Ingersoll whirled to face the doctor. "I understand you have another body in here. One of our stewards has died?" One eyebrow rose.

"Yes, but how did you find out? Who told you?"

"I know everything that's going on aboard this ship." Smug as he sounded, Middlebury doubted it. "Explain what you know about young Iskandar."

"He was found by his supervisor about half an hour ago. He called to let me know and we came and got the body. He's lying in the exam room." Ingersoll leaned over until he could peer around the corner of the doorway and observe. His balance failed and he tumbled onto the floor. Middlebury stifled a snicker. Breckenridge bolted in to see what had happened. He popped up and attempted to smooth an impossible wrinkle out of the suit.

"Are you alright?" Olivia asked. The supervisor of security shook his head up and down, shaking his placid body as he did.

"Now, about this young man. Middlebury, I want you to keep quiet about these deaths. We needn't attract attention to our ship and interrupt the passengers as they travel."

"What are talking about? These deaths need to be investigated to understand what caused three people to have the same symptoms after ingesting something which may have been tainted." Middlebury faced Ingersoll, hands on hips.

"If we allow for the forensics to be done later in Seattle, I don't see what the problem is." Ingersoll folded his arms, stretching his height to match the doctor as best he could.

"Forensics needs to be done as soon as possible to prevent the deterioration of evidence." Middlebury snorted. "Are you a cop or not so much?"

"My history is nothing to you. If we contact the authorities in Juneau, then this voyage will be in jeopardy."

"Better the trip be in jeopardy, then more passengers end up dying."

"Are you saying there may be a possible contamination of our food stores?"

"How did you ever get a job as a detective? No, someone is harming people. Deliberately." Ingersoll dropped his arms, understanding the seriousness of what Middlebury had said.

Breckenridge slipped away as they argued. They took no notice. Their conversation had illuminated the danger present on board.

Ingersoll asked, "Did someone murder Blackthorne and the steward?"

"I can't be sure, but my nurse... Where is she?" He probed each room but Breckenridge was gone. "Well, she's suspicious of these deaths and the illness of a young boy who had the same symptoms. And the boy's mother is a nurse in Kitsap County in Washington State. She thinks the author's death was suspect."

"I have to inform the FBI then, unless we can investigate this ourselves. How about that detective who's on board?" Ingersoll leaned toward Middlebury.

"He's already on it. I called them to ask for their help. You should talk with him, too."

"I'll take the lead on this. After all, I am the security on this voyage."

Middlebury scorned the boast. "Don't let your ego interfere with a conclusive end."

"Keep this within the confines of this ship. Keep Captain Dalgaard out of the loop or he'll press for informing the FBI.

"That's not going to be easy. The author is no longer on the entertainment schedule and one of the crew is off shift. He'll know."

"Then we have to uncover the culprits before we dock in another day."

"Go see Mr. And Mrs. Jefferson in the Elliot Bay Suite. They can be a great deal of help. By the way, someone threatened my daughter earlier today. You might want to investigate that as well." Furrowed brows and a slack jaw caused Middlebury to sigh. He pulled out the letter from his pocket and shoved it at his security chief.

After reading the note, still encased in a plastic bag, he said, "We need to be careful."

"Obviously."

Ingersoll returned the letter and left the doctor alone to finish his forensic work. Someone was killing people and he knew not the next victim.

Middlebury picked up the receiver and dialed the Elliot Bay again. Caution had evaporated like steam in the spa. "Ingersoll just left. He doesn't want to inform the captain or the FBI. Did my daughter get up to you?" He listened and smiled. "Good. Can we meet? Soon?" Another answer. "Good. I'll be done here in the next half hour and will meet you in the Lido lounge." He hung up the phone as Breckenridge entered with the supervising steward. His heart paced a bit faster and he breathed in deep and held it a moment longer.

"Who were you talking to?" she asked.

"Nobody in particular. Let's finish with our work here and plant Mr. Iskandar in a drawer." His path to the exam room was blocked by the steward.

"Don't get too hasty to come up with a conclusion of murder." The steward stood firm and resolute. "We don't want any trouble on this voyage." Middlebury blinked.

"Ingersoll wanted the same thing. I guess we can wait until we get back to Seattle," he lied. "Now let us get on with the rest of the job we're here to do." He and Breckenridge entered the exam room while the steward stood and watched. Middlebury's focus was not where he wanted it to be. Another threat? At least Delinda was safe. He hoped.

# CHAPTER

# 24

Middlebury sat in the Lido Lounge, a cup of coffee wafting steam puffs into the air. Marc said to Joan, "There he is." They surveyed the people in the area and joined him. "This certainly has been a busy day," Marc said as he sat. Joan signaled to a waiter for two coffees. She sat next to Marc.

Randolph sipped from his cup and responded, "Too busy, if you ask me. I wanted to meet with you because the steward who died had the same evidence as Blackthorne and your son. I think someone tainted the food here and its killing people."

"I doubt the food is the problem. Was there any honey in his room?"

"I didn't see any, but I wasn't there long. So you think the honey your son stole is the source?" Middlebury placed his forearms on the table.

"More likely something in the honey. Someone knew I was traveling aboard this ship and sent me a basket of wines, cheeses, bread and honey. We mistook it as a gift for the author and sent it to him. He may have died as a result of a mistake I made. Sarah, my daughter is devastated because she was the first one to suggest it belonged to Blackthorne."

Joan cut in. "Did you sample the stomach contents of the steward who died?"

"Yes, Olivia, my nurse, extracted the contents when we gathered samples. But I have another idea which just came to me." Two pairs of eyes glued to his. "What if the honey, itself, is the poison?"

Marc frowned but kept listening. Joan sat back in her chair.

"It's known by most people in the northwest not to feed rhododendrons to people or animals as the flowers and stems, as well as the leaves are toxic to humans and domestic pets. What if the honey is the product of a deviant mind?"

Marc tilted his head to the right and then said, "I know they make you sick, but we're talking about killing people. Doesn't that make the potency of the flower greater than anything we grow in the northwest?"

"If Blackthorne had any heart problems, it would exacerbate his condition. Your son was young and healthy, and you got him to me in a very short period of time. Iskandar's death would point to a potency which speaks to a horticultural expert in exotic rhodies. There's a story of a Greek legion in Turkey which was decimated after consuming a gift of honey from the local people and becoming so sick, the Turks crushed them the next day. What if someone has created a hybrid so powerful as to be a murder weapon?"

"Could that be applied to the leaves? I mean, drying and crushing them and mixing them with tea could add to the ability of the toxic substance to be lethal. What is in rhododendrons which makes them toxic?" Marc asked.

"I don't remember the exact name, but I have a library of poisons in my cabin. I'll let you know what I find out."

Joan's mouth formed an 'O'. "Did you say the name of the steward was Iskandar?"

"Yes, he was about finished with his contract, this was his last cruise, He was going home to Indonesia from Seattle." Marc studied Joan and then Randolph.

Snapping his fingers, he said, "Sure, he escorted us to our suites the day we sailed out of Seattle. Sarah met him for a tour of the ship. This will be quite unsettling to her. I don't believe in coincidence. What if he was a spy for whomever is aboard and trying to kill us. What if he contacted Sarah deliberately to keep a close connection with us, especially after the author's death?"

"That would mean he was part of a cadre of people who commit nefarious acts while acting as if they are here to serve." Middlebury rolled his head as he spoke, his hands parting as if asking questions.

"I called my father in Seattle to look into any deaths which are curious but attributed to natural causes. He's a Seattle police officer with connections in the King County Medical Examiner's office. Do you know of any way of testing the honey to determine the flower source?"

"No."

"Then I'll get back to him and have him find out from the medical examiner if there is any way. I also have a contact in Kitsap County. She is a beekeeper and honey producer. She should know.

Joan interjected a thought. "No more tea or honey while aboard this ship." Marc attempted a smile while Randolph sat motionless.

"Let me call Tiberius so he has more information with which to work. Do you want me to escort Delinda to you? It's getting late, and we haven't eaten. We can have her eat with us and then Marcus and I will come to the infirmary." Middlebury agreed. They parted ways. Before returning to their suite, Marc placed a call to his father, fully expecting to leave a message.

"Hello, son." Tiberius answered.

"Oh, Dad. I wasn't expecting to connect with you."

"I haven't found out anything in King County, yet, but a body came in from Edmonds which appears to match what happened aboard your ship. Funny thing about it was a puncture wound on his buttocks and remnants of a fast acting sedative. M.E. doesn't think it had anything to with his death."

"Have the M.E. check for any honey ingestion. We think there may be a strong strain of honey made from rhododendrons. I don't know how, but I have a contact in Kitsap which might be able to help find an answer."

"Honey? I know rhodies can make you sick, but bees pollinate from many sources. You're talking about isolating what pollen the bees can accumulate. That may be like finding a needle in a haystack."

"The doctor aboard the ship came up with this hypothesis, so we have not established it as a fact. When we dock tomorrow in Juneau, he plans on sending some samples to the M.E. for testing. We may be in the midst of a group of people who have been using the ship for something other than cruising passengers. If the target turns out to be me as is speculated, then some case I investigated involved these people or others related to them. I'll attempt to get personnel records and match them to my cases."

"Shouldn't the FBI be informed?" Tiberius asked.

"Since I trust no one working on board, including the doctor, I'll let you contact your friend in the Seattle office. I'm out of my jurisdiction, but the doctor wants my help. So trust or not, I'll work with him until he's cleared or implicated. The security person, Dag Ingersoll, seems a bit over his head. He's a former cop, however."

"Alright, I'll step back on the FBI until you can get more information as to whether these two bodies are victims of assault and murder." They ended the call.

Joan asked, "What'd he find out?" She reached for his hand which he accepted.

"A body from Edmonds had oddities. He needs to have the M.E. test for honey in his foods."

"Do you believe it possible for honey to have enough potency to be lethal? I've never heard of anyone getting seriously sick from honey. A couple of cases of children sick from eating the petals is known, but being lethal is unknown to me." They strolled on toward their suites and their children.

Marc stopped at the elevators and pushed the button. Safety was paramount, now. "I've not heard of anything about rhododendrons being poisonous. We grew them in the yard when we were growing up, but we never had interaction with them. My parents had us do yard work, including plucking exhausted flowers from the stems. We didn't imagine eating them.

The elevator binged and they entered after several other people vacated the car. Joan squeezed his hand and asked, "If someone still wants us harmed or worse you dead, what prevents them from using more force? Kidnapping one of the children or a frontal attack? A knife in the stomach can be fatal. A slash of the throat." Her skin flushed as she spoke and tears puddled in her lids.

"I know." The ride was short and the bing stilted more conversation. The door opened and they stepped out and walked a brisk pace to the suite. Paula Merino was at her suite door but halted entering.

"Mr. Jefferson, could I speak with you?" The author's suite door opened and Gabby Montoya came out with a large suitcase and a bag slung over her shoulder. Marc left Joan to finish the journey to the Elliot Bay.

"What can I do for you?"

"I want to apologize for my behavior this morning. James death struck me hard. Gabby and I have decided to get off in Juneau and fly home. We have no reason to continue this trip without James."

"I understand, but until we dock questions as to your involvement with him may need clarification." Informing them of the misplacement of the basket was not part of his plan but changed his mind. "You and Miss Montoya are victims of a cruel miscarriage, since his death may have been a mistake."

"A mistake? I don't understand. How is a heart attack a mistake?"

"We are fairly certain his heart attack may have been induced by the honey in the basket we sent to you. The gift, more than likely, was for my family and contained a poison intended to cause harm to me directly or indirectly to my family. Someone on board may be seeking revenge for something I did in one of my cases."

Gabby spoke next. "Is your son, James, okay?"

"Yes, he's in his suite. But another person died today, possibly from the same substance which caused Mr. Blackthorne's death. James had the same symptoms.

"I thought you said honey. How does honey induce heart problems?"

"I'm not yet fully aware of the reasoning, but rhododendrons contain a toxic material which is harmful to humans and many animals. If the honey is a by-product of bees collecting the pollen from this bush, then it may be the culprit."

"I didn't see any honey in the basket."

"My son, James, took it this morning and ate some of it. Enough to make him sick, but we caught it in time for him to recover." Gabby placed the bag on the floor of the deck.

"Are we in any danger?" she asked.

"I don't think so."

Paula asked, "Who was the other person who died?"

"One of the stewards, the one who delivered us to our suites and then brought the basket to us."

"The one interested in your daughter?"

"I guess. He was showing her the ship."

The two young women thanked him for the information and entered their suite. Before the door closed, he caught it and opened it. "Gabby, you have a card for his suite?" She nodded. "I would like to look inside for any evidence I can use to flush out the responsible persons." He followed her and entered when she opened the door. A quick scan revealed nothing more than the fateful basket with one bottle of water, some crackers and an unopened cheese. Marc stirred around the materials discovering one teabag under the crackers. He picked it out and placed it in a plastic bag he had decided to carry, if needed. "What was he working on for his next book?"

"Another of his thrillers. He hadn't yet shown me the manuscript, but I have it in the bag next door. I packed up all of his things so we can return to Arizona." Marc observed the bed, still rumpled from the occupants who engaged in a personal endeavor before sleep. One corner of the bedding was tucked differently than the other.

"Could you get me that manuscript. Maybe it contains something which could prove my original theory was correct." She left to fill his request. As the door closed, he lifted the corner which revealed the secret folder. Marc pulled it out and hid it under his shirt. Gabby returned with the other manuscript. "I'll get this back to you before you leave."

Inside the Elliot Bay he placed the manuscript on the table and pulled the folder from under his shirt. "What are these?" Joan asked.

# CHAPTER

# 25

As Breckenridge and Middlebury concluded gathering samples and other evidence from Iskandar, the steward remained in the doorway until the body was inducted in a morgue drawer. As he walked away, Olivia asked, "What did he want?"

"I don't know, but I know someone who will find out." Randolph clicked open his cell phone and dialed a number he had written on an index card. "Marc, Dr. Middlebury, I need to speak with you about an incident here in the infirmary." He clicked off. "Let's clean up and get out of here."

With the lab clean and no one invading with hypochondriac illnesses, they ambled out of the infirmary. The doctor locked the door. Olivia watched the action, a gentle biting of her lip, staring at him. He turned to find her leaning toward him. "What?" he asked.

"Uh, I wondered if you might want to have dinner with me." She straightened as she spoke.

"I was planning on getting my daughter and taking her to dinner. Would you like to join us?" Their eyes locked a moment longer than they usually did. She was about the same age, as he recalled from her file. A woman with three children in the care of family while she fulfilled a contract with the cruise line. Delinda had not commented about her to him and he wondered if the time was right to pursue any kind of relationship. He came with baggage, but so did most of the females he might find interesting. Breckenridge was no different.

"Thank you, I would love to." Checking her watch, she finished, "I can meet you in about an hour."

"Alright then, we have a table in the Mount Tahoma Dining Room. We'll see you there." They parted ways. Randolph stepped to the elevators and pushed the up button. As he waited, the supervising steward walked past. Although no interchange of comments happened, Middlebury's neck hairs tightened. What was his beef? One of his staff members was dead and he exhibited little or no regard for him.

The elevator chimed its usual bing and Middlebury stepped in to hide from his oppressor. Randolph wondered about any connection between the two deaths. He hoped Ingersoll and Jefferson could uncover what was happening on this fateful voyage.

As he walked toward the Elliot Bay Suite, he paused to view the Puget Suite which history would record as the end of a career. Was death stalking Mr. Blackthorne? Or Marcus Jefferson. Or someone who was yet to be revealed. The door of the suite next to the author's opened and Gabrielle Montoya appeared.

"Hello, Dr. Middlebury." Her buoyancy caught him off guard. With what happened, how was she able to hold emotions in check and exude happiness?

"How are you doing?"

"Okay, I guess. Today's been a terrible shock." She approached and probed. "Did someone kill my boss?" He stared a moment before she continued. "How did it happen?"

"I don't know if anyone was after Mr. Blackthorne. We are sending samples to the lab in Anchorage for analysis. We should know something when we arrive in another week."

"Paula and I are leaving when we dock. We have no reason to stay." He nodded and turned away. "Please, let me know what happened to him. Please." Her last word, a whimper, had no buoyancy or verve. A young woman whose life received a cruel twist of fate. She left him wondering about the cruel twist of his own past. No god should be so uninvolved as to destroy a person by eliminating another. And yet Delinda had mastered the technique of recovery. Now a credible suitor crossed her path of life. The full implications of his decisions about her after losing her mother to cancer eluded him.

He knocked on the door to the suite, turning to watch the young editor sway toward the elevators. As it opened, Marc said, "Doc, what's up?" Randolph faced the voice. Marc leaned out to follow the view. "Quite an attractive young woman." He stepped back and held the door for Middlebury.

"Do you know the steward who supervised the young man in the morgue? He found the body and then stayed with me while samples were gathered for the M.E. in Anchorage." He sat with Marc and Joan at the dining table.

Joan spoke next. "I had an encounter with an older steward earlier today. What he said sounded like a veiled threat against Marc and me. Do you think he has something to do with the young man's death?"

Middlebury answered, "His supervisor is a cold person. I've not been impressed with his personality. What if he is the one who orchestrated the death of the author and the young steward?"

"Possibly, but my concern deals with the real idea; I was the target." Marc placed a hand in Joan's hand, but could he reassure her of their safety without knowing who to trust? Even Middlebury remained a question. If he designed the note about Delinda, what possibility existed that he put a mark on the Jefferson family?

"Mr. Jefferson, if you are the true target of the people on this ship, what do you propose to do to protect your family? I ran into Miss Montoya outside and she stated they were leaving in Juneau. I have no reservations in joining the exodus with Delinda. I will protect her as best I can."

A knock and door opening alerted them to children entering. Sarah was first, followed by Delinda, James, and Marcus. Randolph rose to hug his daughter. Marcus spoke. "Mom, Dad, we've decided to confront our foes. We aren't sure what to do, but nobody is going to threaten Dee or you and get away with it." Marc grinned. Joan unhooked from Marc.

"We are not under any threat," she said. "But I do think it wise to be aware of surroundings and people. Remember, most passengers are not cognizant of any intrigue or this ship would be chaos."

Another knock on the door drew several sets of eyes. Marc stood and walked to the door. Opening it, he discovered Dag Ingersoll and another younger version of him. "May we enter?"

Marc stepped aside to allow them in. "What do want?" His voice was curt and respectful.

"Oh, good, Dr. Middlebury, I'm glad you're here." He waited for the door's closure and handed a note to Marc. As he read it, eyes glanced to Ingersoll and back to the note.

"Thanks for stopping by. Your interest in police work in the United States is intriguing. We can discuss this at dinner, tonight. We all were just about to leave." A finger to his mouth halted any protests. He handed the note to Joan, who gave it to Randolph. Curious children gathered behind the doctor to read over his shoulder. It read: This room may be bugged.

"Delinda, we have a dinner guest, tonight." He stood and placed a hand on her shoulder. "We will see you later," he said to Marc.

"Good idea. I'm hungry. Let's go now before the crowd arrives." They exited the room. The group strolled to the elevators, but in the hall Marc pulled Dag aside and asked, "Ingersoll, what makes you think our room is bugged?"

"I have been investigating, as quietly as possible, a few members of the crew who may be involved in the transport of contraband drugs from Vancouver to Seattle. By the way, this is my son, Jorgen. He's with Royal Canadian Mounted Police in North Vancouver. He came aboard six months ago to assist me with ferreting out the culprits. We identified the senior supervising steward as a person of interest. Now one of his charges is dead. Something happened in the United States and Vancouver which dried up the flow. My sources indicated that the person responsible is you." Marc remained silent. "Jorgen works with Regina McDonald and they are in communication regularly. As a result, she contacted him as soon as your investigation cleared the cartel from Everett and cleared your uncle of any wrong doing. You have a few enemies who are on this ship."

"How did these people know we were sailing on this particular cruise?" Marc's question was interrupted when Joan joined the conversation as the others entered an elevator.

"What are you talking about?" she asked.

Marc said, "Mr. Ingersoll and his son, Jorgen, are investigating the same cartel we destroyed in Everett. It looks like we are the focus of people aboard. Let's join our children and finish this after dinner."

"We'll catch up with you later, Mr. Jefferson," said Dag.

After they had descended by way of the stair case, Joan asked, "An explanation please?"

"He's not the bumbling idiot he portrays." His son works with Regina McDonald in the North Vancouver division of the RCMP. They are in contact with each other." She locked an arm in his and they left the passageway to join their children and enjoy a quiet dinner. Marc figured a sweep of the suite could wait. Since they had booked this cruise several months ago, someone other than the steward was the head of the snake.

# CHAPTER

# 26

The steward arrived at the stage in the Pacific Auditorium and surveyed the area. "Jarina?" His voice echoed in the emptiness. He descended the aisle. As he stepped up the stairs to the stage, Jarina appeared from behind the left side.

"You have botched this assignment. All your team had to do was deliver the basket and let the actions take care of it. Now we have a dead body and suspicious people." She folded arms together and continued. "I think you need to clean this up before we reach Juneau."

"I have begun correcting everything. Young Iskandar is no longer a problem." Her eyes closed and arms dropped to hips.

"What happened to him? Another accidental death?"

"He sleeps with the author."

Jarina turned away from him and flipped her arm over her shoulder. He obeyed and followed. Behind the curtain she entered one of the green rooms and sat at a desk. Flipping open the laptop, she waited for the screen to shine. "Who have you spoken with regarding the author? I supposed the letter to the doctor has had little or no effect. Has that detective contacted him?"

"Yes, ma'am. I spoke with Mrs. Jefferson about having a safe trip. As to the note about his daughter, I have not observed them together. I did watch as the nurse and Middlebury took sample tissue and fluids from Iskandar. I think he wants to send them to a lab for testing." The steward stood as stiff as a statue awaiting his next command.

"Let him. We'll be gone before any results can be returned. Is Breckenridge cooperating?" Jarina began typing.

"She has informed me of his actions. I know the doctor and the detective have met, but I do not know the content of their conversations. The youngest member of the Jefferson's was in the infirmary as a patient. He was sick and observed until he was well enough to leave."

She halted her work on the computer and looked up at the steward. "What caused his illness?"

"Breckenridge didn't know. No chart was available for reading." He squirmed, shifting from one leg to the other. Camacho had demonstrated her displeasure with failure and he was unwilling to receive proof of her emotional state.

"I suppose that idiot, Ingersoll, has spoken with Jefferson."

"I do not know to what extent he has communicated. He did have a rather intense argument with Middlebury about informing the FBI. Breckenridge told me that."

"He went to the Elliot bay a few moments ago. I heard them talking. See to it that Jefferson is not able to interfere or you just may become a victim yourself."

"I do not need a lecture from you or to be threatened. Remember, you came to me about getting the materials into the United States. All I have done for you can just as easily be undone. As long as our pipeline is connected, we can find other material and start it flowing again."

"I don't understand why the basket ended up in the author's suite."

"According to Iskandar, the daughter believed it had been misplaced. As a result, Jefferson gave it to him and his assistants." Jarina rose to her full height which loomed several inches above the steward.

"I just sent a message to the twins to meet us in Juneau. I have an idea as to how to compromise the doctor and eliminate that pesky detective." She opened the door for him to leave. "And get your scanner people ready. They're resupplying our stocks. I'll be sure they have proper credentials for boarding the ship."

The steward nodded and left. Mumbling about her as he walked off the stage, he formulated a plan to quiet Jefferson. The lost revenue from the organization in Vancouver cut into his retirement plans. He had amassed nearly half a million dollars and thought it best to leave when the ship docked in Seattle. Acquiring American citizenship with his alias afforded a nice protective layer for an escape from the cartel and Camacho.

In the dining room, he oversaw his staff working the tables and bars of the Mt. Baker Dining Room. The two floors in the aft of the ship provided wonderful views of the waters of the Pacific Ocean and the coast of Alaska. By one of the windows he noticed the Jefferson family with Dag Ingersoll and his son, Jorgen. "Orang yg buruk sekali." They were in communication as Camacho had said. His plan involved another person carrying out the assault, but he decided to do the job himself and leave no doubt about the success.

At another table he saw Randolph and Delinda Middlebury dining with Olivia Breckenridge. What was she doing with them? Keeping close watch on the good doctor? Or was she a threat to the organization? His note had not incurred the proper respect. He formulated another plan to convince the good doctor to ignore any further investigation. How had such a simple plan gone so badly?

As dinner wound to a conclusion families vacated Mt. Baker. Paula Merino and Gabriella Montoya stopped by the Jefferson's table. He wondered about the conversation but dismissed it as inconsequential interaction. His concern focused on Middlebury and Breckenridge. What was she doing with him outside of her professional role as a nurse?

"They look good together." He jumped and gasped at the remark. Turning, he found Jarina Camacho standing behind him with arms folded across her chest. Her eyes aligned on the same target as his eyes. "Do you suppose our nurse has turned to the other side?"

"I don't know. Probably not. She has instructions to stay close to him to find out what he's up to. What better way than to become a confidante." His racing heart slowed its beat. The cruise director sneaked around the ship like a ghost.

Stepping away, she said, "I'll find out." He watched as she approached the table with Middlebury and Breckenridge. After shaking hands and a short interlude, she left and strode to the Jefferson's and Ingersoll. Laughter invaded his ears from across the room. He felt assurance her probe had accomplished what she wanted. She left the dining room by the doors on the other side of the room. Checking his watch reminded him of her need to emcee the evening show.

When all the passengers had departed the dining area and the staff had cleared the tables and set up for the morning, the steward returned to his room for a rest before executing his plans. He signaled the young maid who satisfied Iskandar's lust to join him in his room. She complied with the request. The money she accumulated for sating their hunger prosecuted her goal of independence from a squalid life in the Philippines.

Awaking in the morning with the maid still beside him, he grunted. He needed to be alone. "Get up." His gruff voice affected no answer or fear. She stepped out of his sheets and stood. Her body elicited a reaction he knew would delay his thinking time to plan. She crawled across the bed to his side and fondled his abdomen, awaking the desire for more. "Not now, you cow. Get away from me or there will be no more financial reward on this ship." She snorted a snide reply, dressed, and departed.

A quick shower to erase remaining traces of the maid, cleared his head for executing a plan to rid his world of the entanglements of Mr. Jefferson. The detective effected a damaging attack which crushed several income streams. Revenge would be sweet. He did not like eliminating people but when the need arose, it was just business.

Arranging for one of the crew to sacrifice freedom for family financial security and safety at home worked miracles. Much of the contraband drugs came from the Indonesian cartels, which used bribery of government officials and crushed opposition. Detective Marcus Jefferson had survived the first round. The young son had sickened for an unknown reason. A reason similar to the author. A reason for which detection was now plausible.

He dressed and departed to supervise staff and arrange for the right person to distract Jefferson so a more direct assault could occur.

# CHAPTER

# 27

Marc and Joan had prepared for sleep without much conversation except to sound like tourists. A sweep of the room uncovered three devises, one in their bedroom, one in the main suite area, and one on the veranda. Marc suspected the room had been bugged from the first day they arrived. After dinner with Ingersoll and his son, he and Joan made a pact with them to continue the search for the culprit or culprits risking unsuspecting passengers in a gambit for revenge. Jarina Camacho's interception of their dinner time roused little attention, but no crew member was beyond reproach. The revelation that Dag Ingersoll was an agent of the investigation wing of American Pacific Cruises and not a washed up police officer was uplifting.

As they prepared for the next day, conversations with Sarah remained about sightseeing in Juneau and possible excursions for the family. Iskandar became a memory. Sarah suffered the effects of guilt for suggesting the author was the true recipient of the fateful basket. Marc and Joan consoled her, pleading for her to believe the mistake was not hers but carelessness of the note.

In the hallway talk became more concentrated to the investigation. A sweep of the Puget Suite the boys occupied uncovered no bugs. Marc said, "Marcus, as soon as you can, accompany Delinda Middlebury. We need to do some things with her father and I want her safe from any interference. Sarah and James will stay with you, as well."

"Dad, I can take care of her without babysitters."

"This is not about keeping you from interacting with her. It is about the idea of safety in a crowd. We dock tomorrow and the time for ending this investigation is coming to an end."

Marcus bobbed his head. Yesterday's magic could wait another day.

James lost his usual smiling affection and carefree attitude. His nearness to death sobered his demeanor. Sarah rolled her eyes at the mention of babysitters but wanted the closeness of her brothers. She liked Delinda, so the day was not a bust for her.

Joan said, "Stay near the Lido deck so we can find you as quickly as needed. We'll join you for lunch there." She and Marc left the suite, heading for their arranged meeting with Ingersoll, Middlebury, and Capt. Lars Dalgaard in the Mt. Baker Dining Room. Breakfast was a cover for colligating actions of the various people cleansing the ship of nefarious characters. Ingersoll had been the security liaison aboard the ship for over a year and a half. His observation of the actions aboard increased his awareness that something was not right. Without the knowledge or permission of Dalgaard he began his probe to find what the misdeeds were and the people involved. Trust was an issue until a conversation with Dalgaard regarding concerns by the captain about activity aboard the ship which compromised the integrity of his command and the company's reputation. He explained finding an unsavory operation aboard which pointed to drug running and his not having enough material to make a solid case.

As they entered the dining area, the supervising steward glowered at them. A well-dressed Filipino waitress directed them to the Captain's Table. They found Dag and Jorgen already seated and drinking coffee. "Good morning, Mr. and Mrs. Jefferson. I do hope you slept well."

"We did," Marc said. When the waitress finished pouring coffee and left, he continued. "I found three bugs in our suite, none in our boys' room, and I want to wipe this organization from the face of the earth. The tentacles of this octopus keep growing back." Dag smiled.

Jorgen spoke next, "I have communicated with Miss McDonald regarding our progress. She has some information for us regarding the suppliers. Indonesian for the most part."

Dag retorted, "Makes sense with the population of service personnel on this ship." Captain Dalgaard approached with one of his senior officers. Marc and Joan rose to shake hands.

"Mr. And Mrs. Jefferson, it is a pleasure to meet you. I do hope your voyage has been pleasant for the most part." They all sat. "This is my first officer, Cayde Thorsen. He is privy to our program and to be trusted."

The waitress returned to take breakfast orders and the conversation stopped. After each stated preference for food and drinks, she left. Dag took up the conversation. "I informed the captain of my suspicions about a month ago and we formed an alliance to continue the search for the culprits and root out the operation."

"Capt. Dalgaard," Marc asked, "Are you aware of the two deaths aboard your ship in a single day and the illness of my son? All three cases have similar symptomatic evidence of the use of a poison. My wife is a geriatric care nurse in Washington State who recognized them as soon as she saw Mr. Blackthorne's body in his suite. We are leaning to the idea that the original target was me. We had received a gift basket and sent it to the author's suite after misreading the intent of the accompanying card."

"Dag informed me last night. I have placed Officer Thorsen in charge of gathering the evidence we need to crush the group aboard which is undermining the integrity of Pacific American Cruises and my authority as captain." The wait staff returned to replenish juices and coffees. The chief steward approached.

"How is everyone today?" Looking at Marc he said, "I do hope nothing will impede a superb day. Enjoy your breakfasts." Marc locked eyes with him as if to say, "you're dead." The steward smiled and returned to the entry of the dining room. Joan placed a reassuring hand on her husband's lap.

"That guy has a severe price to pay for messing with my family."

Ingersoll intoned, "But he is only an underling. I do not have evidence enough to show complicity. And he is not the boss. Someone is directing him."

"Captain Dalgaard, my brother in Seattle is a police officer who is checking for any strange deaths in King and Snohomish Counties. He found a recent one in Edmonds at a motel. A man in his thirties was discovered to have died ostensibly from heart failure, although questions arose as to why. A connection there may lead us to the culprits here."

Looking at his senior officer, Dalgaard said, "Cayde, be sure to include Mr. And Mrs. Jefferson in your investigation." Turning to Marc he said, "Dag stated you and the Snohomish County sheriff department crushed the group in Everett which was supplying drugs to the area. You may have stirred the hornets' nest." Marc firmed his mouth and nodded. Breakfast arrived and the conversation struck a modest tone of ship operations and histories of the officers and crew.

The meal concluded with laughter for the sake of anyone inferring another reason for the gathering of these people. Marc and Joan strolled past the Steward and each smiled as cordial as a passenger about to embark on an adventure.

In the hallway a young man approached and asked if they needed any assistance. He handed them a brochure for excursions in Juneau. Marc noticed the lack of other people, took the brochure and hurried away from the young man. "Are you alright," Joan asked as they found other passengers with which to mingle.

"Too convenient for an assault." She understood his paranoia. "Let's find the kids and contact Middlebury." They rode a packed elevator to the Lido deck and spied their obedient children and the one guest invited by Marc to entertain Marcus. They were eating waffles and eggs with bacon, sausage, and potatoes. The buffet was in full swing and the crowd was large. Marc understood the emptiness of the Mt. Baker Dining Room. He relaxed and sat with his family. Joan asked a waiter for two coffees. When asked about any sweeteners or creams, she responded, "Just cream, please."

Marcus asked, "How was breakfast with the Captain?"

"Informative." Was there any more to say? Marc wished for any other outcome but the danger remained. "Delinda, it is a pleasure to see you. I hope Marcus has been a true gentleman."

"Yes sir. He is the most kind and caring person I've ever met. My father thinks you are one of the finest he has interacted with."

"He has much to be thankful for, despite what he is dealing

with. Take good care of him." Marc touched her hand, one father commiserating about a fellow father.

"Dad, I heard that Gabby and Paula are getting off the boat in Juneau. Maybe we should think about leaving."

"Possibly, but I want whomever feels like harming us out of service."

Joan sat with two steaming cups. "What are we plotting?" The lilt in her voice gave sway to the serious visages of two men she adored. "I guess our antagonists weigh upon us as great as a hod of bricks."

"Marcus pressed the idea of our departing the voyage in Juneau. I am not of a mind to do so, but it makes sense for you and the children to leave."

Joan tilted her head to her right and said, "That may draw suspicion for them to realize we are involved in ferreting out the bad guys." Marc bobbed his head. Delinda scooted her chair closer to Marcus and reached for his hand.

"I don't want you to leave. I'd miss you." Her plea held more as her eyes begged for acceptance of her case. She squeezed his hand. He reciprocated.

"We'll stay, Dad. Who can resist that?"

"Joan, we need to be sure of what we know and contact Dad as soon as we dock in Juneau. He may have more information regarding the man in Edmonds." Marcus lowered his head and leaned to his father.

"Another person met the same fate as the author?"

"Looks like it." A waiter approached to clear dishes and replenish drinks. When he departed, Marc continued. "The M.E. found the death was not consistent with the health of the victim. No heart disease or structural malformations, no reason for anything bad to happen. A drug screen is not yet back from the lab." He leaned back in his chair. "Delinda, that's why it is critical for your Dad to get the tissue samples to the M.E. when we dock." He leaned forward and said, "No, someone will be watching. I'll get them and take them myself, if he agrees. We can go as a family on an excursion and just drop by the lab."

Olivia Breckenridge entered the Lido Deck from the aft doorway and walked toward the Jefferson clan. Marc had come to believe she was more than a nurse. Her curiosity about events was not in line with her duties. "Mr. Jefferson, I would like a word with you and your wife." He stood, as did Joan, and moved away from the family to an isolated cabana.

"What's up?" he asked.

"The infirmary was broken into last night and the samples taken from Mr. Blackthorne and the young steward are missing." An eyebrow rose on Marc's face. "I need to tell you something which is in the strictest confidence." They straightened bodies and focused their vision on her.

"Something bad is happening aboard the ship. I fear the good doctor may be in trouble. You've become a friend of his. Can you help him?"

"By strictest confidence, is that it? We know something is up." Placing arms on the table, he said, "Doctor Middlebury and I have worked together on the author's death. Someone in this ship is killing people. James was an accidental poisoning because of his stealing from the basket. We suspect the honey was tainted."

"That explains what happened. Whoever broke in wanted to make sure no one could prove what killed them." Olivia walked away. Marc and Joan gazed after her.

"That was weird." Marc shook his head. "She never explained her strictest confidence comment." They returned to their children. Something about that woman was missing in the scheme of things. As a nurse she appeared competent, as a person, an enigma.

# CHAPTER

# 28

"S ir, I did as you asked and approached him with information regarding excursions in Juneau. He seemed in a hurry." The young man, one of the few Caucasian men who worked as a steward, stood with his supervisor in the Mt. Baker Dining Room.

The supervisor grilled him. "Were other people nearby? What did you say to him? Did you spook him?"

"No sir, the hallway was empty. All I did was hand them a brochure and ask if they needed any help. He took it and they hurried off. I came to you as soon as I could."

"You are relieved of duty. Go find a nice Filipino girl and have fun." The man left. The steward glanced at the podium and picked up the carving knife from the shelf below the podium top. He replaced it as a couple entered the room for a late breakfast.

"Would you please follow me," he said in a cordial manner. At a window seat which displayed the wake of the ship as it plied the waters of the Pacific Ocean, he pulled out the chair for the woman.

"Your waiter will be with you shortly." He returned to the host podium, picked up the knife which he wrapped in a napkin, signaled one of the other crew members to replace him.

In the hallway outside of the dining room he stepped to the elevators and pushed the down button. A change of clothing to a more relaxed outfit would assist in disguising him as a crew member.

Tourists dressed in many manners. His would be similar. On the lower deck near his cabin, he saw a member of his small secret crew and signaled him to follow. Inside the cabin he said, "I need you to get that detective to follow you to an isolated part of the ship. He has to be eliminated before we dock, tomorrow."

"Won't another death raise more problems for us?" he asked.

"This operation is dead. We need to vacate and split up. No one knows who we are and it needs to stay that way."

Not satisfied, the underling pursued his question. "If you kill him, and we leave the ship, I don't see how you aren't tracked down until captured."

"I have resources to make my escape. You stay, if you want. I'll disappear before anyone knows I'm gone."

The arrangement made, the other man left to locate Marc Jefferson and lure him to a prearranged spot in the lower holds of the ship. Intrigue was the game and the steward believed the proper message was enough for a detective to investigate. His cohort was to played the part of a concerned member of the crew, leading the detective to a clue about the deaths of two people. Curiosity killed the cat, so why not let it extinguish a cop?

He arranged with two of the scan operators to line a large crate with plastic for hiding the body, which then could be off loaded as waste material to be sent to a landfill. They would discharge him from the ship in Juneau, leaving no record of his departure and failure to return. Everything was ready. Now to execute both man and plan.

Marc and Joan returned to the suite for a change of clothing. Turning on the shower to distract would be listeners, they whispered in the bathroom. Marc said, "We need to speak with Middlebury about the break-in. He may have evidence which can lead us to whomever was stupid enough to pull that off."

"I'll stay with the kids while you do that. Are you going to call your dad?"

"Yeah, as soon as I see what happened downstairs." Turning off the water their conversation reverted to clothing and lunch plans and excursions in Juneau. "I'll see you on the Lido," he said as he left her alone for Act II of the charade.

At the elevators he waited for the car to arrive for him to descend to the deck with the infirmary. A young steward approached. "Mr. Jefferson, may I have a word about something which I think you can help me solve?" The bing interrupted his script. Marc entered the car and the man followed.

Marc pushed the Main Deck button. "What needs solving?"

"I understand you are a police officer. I am concerned about activities aboard this ship which are not legal. What can I do?"

"Can you give me any more information?" Marc's hairs prickled on his neck. Adrenalin pumped in his veins.

"I can show you what I mean. In one of the holds is a cargo which I think is illegal." The bing sounded again as the car stopped to pick up passengers. The steward stood like a statue when three elderly women entered. Marc shifted to the back of the car away from the other man. The women acknowledged the presence of a fine looking passenger, ignoring the crew member. Marc smiled and cocked his head in response, but his vision remained planted on the other male aboard the elevator.

They rode to the main deck and all exited. The steward walked away but handed Marc a piece of paper. It read, "Meet me in the auditorium in half an hour." Assured the man was gone, Marc descended the stairs to the lower deck and after a quick glance about the hallway, he entered the infirmary. Noises in the examination room directed him to the doctor.

"I heard you had a break-in and that your tissue samples are missing."

"It seems so. Olivia came in first to find this mess. Why do people have to destroy other stuff when they steal what they want?" The glass on the floor appeared to be for show. The refrigerator had no glass.

"Have you contacted Ingersoll?'

"Yes, he said to leave it until he could take pictures. He should be here any minute." At that moment the door opened. Randolph went into the office to see who needed medical assistance. Dag and Jorgen walked to him. Jorgen held a camera in his right hand.

"Where is the break-in?" Ingersoll asked. Randolph flipped a hand over his shoulder as he turned to lead him. In the exam room the security chief said, "Oh, Marc, good that you're here. I believe our rivals are getting nervous."

Marc scrunched his brows. "Should we exterminate any bugs which may invade this place?"

"I've already checked. Nothing here. So doctor, you said they grabbed the samples for the lab. Anything else missing?" Jorgen shot pictures of the area of the breakage.

"No. Just the samples. A few unimportant over the counter medicines. Nothing else."

Dag watched his son, diligent and deliberate. Marc remained quiet. He then said, "I'm going to the captain with this, as he needs to understand the need for us to be able to work without interference from off-ship investigative personnel."

Marc smirked, "You mean FBI." Dag chortled.

"We do have the RCMP, a sheriff's office, ship security, and medical already working the case. Others would have to be read in and the culprits would dry up faster than a puddle on a summer day in Arizona."

Olivia Breckenridge appeared as if from thin air. "Do we have all we need for finding out who is killing people?" She strolled over to Randolph and smiled. "Thanks for dining with me last night." Her demeanor recorded little or no concern of the mess in the room nor the missing materials. "Randolph, I have a confession to make." The atmosphere of the room thickened among the gentlemen. "I want to get to know you better."

"What?" His response mirrored the emotions of confusion from the other men. "We have a problem here and all you can say is you want to get to know me better?"

"I have another confession." Her feet shifted positions. She clasped her hands together. Her eyes glanced at the wall to her left, away from the men.

Marc reacted to the suppressed complaints. "Ms. Breckenridge, you are hindering the furthering of our investigation by your coy interplay for Dr. Middlebury's affects. What do you have to confess?"

"I took the samples." Faces gaped, mouths dropped open, gasps raced forth.

# CHAPTER

# 29

The supervisor waited for the remaining scanner operators under his command to memorize the list of items coming aboard in Juneau. Each of them reviewed the list and confirmed their readiness. "It's important to get this right. Our operation is under attack and we need to clean up this mess."

The man assigned to lure Jefferson to the cargo hold returned and reported he had left a note with him, but he failed to show. "Dammit. He is a pain in the neck. Alright, plan B. Get one of his children or his wife to think something has happened and they need to get to him. We can then use that to get him to the cargo hold."

"Yes sir, I'll get on it right away." The man left. The supervisor called other people in his charge, not affiliated with the cartel, and assigned them their daily tasks. Alone for the moment his thinking came out in his words. "I'm going to have to do this myself before Camacho has me terminated.

"You were saying?" Jarina Camacho leaned on the doorway. She uncrossed her legs and straightened her body from the frame. "Is our detective giving you trouble?"

"Nothing I can't handle."

"That's what Pepper said, and he ended up with a bullet in his head." She approached him. "Don't underestimate him. Our detective is wily and resourceful. Get rid of him or we all end up losing." She turned to depart but stopped. "The twins are coming aboard. See to their needs." Her head crossed her right shoulder without seeing him. "I'll assign their tasks." She walked out the door, leaving him wondering if he was to be one of the tasks. All of the successful history diminished with the collapse of the organization in Vancouver and the dismantling of Andrew Pepper and his gang in Everett. Jefferson and his family of cops had pricked too deeply, creating a festering personnel casualty in his life. An infection running rampant through his ship. Ingersoll and Dalgaard were like puppets to manipulate. But maybe, just maybe they were under-appreciated.

Seven men remained part of the group which worked the smuggling. Everybody was trusted only as far as they did their jobs correctly. Camacho oversaw the operation for Pepper and his death meant she was the boss. Could she rebuild what they had or was the end of operations soon to arrive? Breckenridge had a reputation as a ruthless person, coming aboard in Seattle, a recommendation of another member of the Pepper organization who survived the assault on the warehouse. The plan had been simple. Each person doing what was needed to instill the poisonous honey into that infernal family and watch them die. The note was written by Camacho, so recognizing the error, he wanted to execute her.

He decided to go topside and find the family. Helping escort one of the children shouldn't be a problem.

⤛⚬⤜

"You what?" Ingersoll screamed the words. Marc placed a hand on his shoulder. Then he asked a reasonable question, "Why would you take the samples?"

"I knew they were coming to get them. By the way, this damage is not from me. I suspect whoever was here exhibited a bit of frustration. The missing items are not important medicines. The narcotics are safe and securely locked up." The men just listened. "I overheard a conversation I wasn't supposed to hear and took measures to prevent any loss of evidence." Her grin exuded a pleasure for her cleverness.

Middlebury asked, "Are the samples in a proper environment?"

She nodded. "Well, I suppose we're still in business."

"Doc, I have a request of you," Marc said. "I think it wise for me to take the samples into Juneau instead of you. Whoever is working this gig is probably waiting for you to go there. I can take them and get them to the proper authorities without any problems." To Breckenridge he asked, "As for you overhearing something, who said they were coming to get the tissue samples?"

"Someone you already suspect, the supervising steward. I was entering in the crew lounge when I heard him ask two of his wards to get the materials out of the infirmary. I assumed he meant the tissue samples, so I came back here directly and took them." Pairs of eyes bounced from person to person. "I'll have the tissues ready for you in the morning when we dock." She left them wondering about who she was.

Marc pulled Dag aside, "I got a note from one of the crew about meeting him in a cargo hold. He said he had concerns about illicit cargo. I blew it off as a possible threat to me surviving this day. However, if he was on the up and up, maybe I should go with him. I need backup. Can you send your son with me? He can tail behind and punch in if things go sour."

"Sure, he'll keep an eye out for anyone moving after you get there. You think they want to get rid of you when we dock?"

Marc shrugged shoulders and grimaced. "Keep an eye on my family, as well. Kidnapping is hard incentive to make one comply, although most end up with a dead hostage."

Using the note as a guide and Jorgen as a free pass to the lower parts of the ship, he made his way to the locale. Studying the area, full of crates and shelves of food stuffs and supplies for the ships marketplace, nothing looked odd or illegal. He cracked a couple of boxes open but nothing contraband was found. Another large box, lined with plastic caught his attention. Empty. A perfect hiding place for a body. But whose? "Mine," he thought. Aloud he called for Jorgen. No one responded.

Instinct caught him reaching for a missing .38 caliber revolver. He began a careful trek to the hatchway. A body appeared which was not Jorgen. "Oh good, you came. I thought maybe you'd ignore me as a crackpot. Did you find the stuff?"

Marc paced closer to the young man. "No, please, show me."

As the man led the way back to the large empty crate, heart beats ticked higher and pupils widened. He watched for hands to reach under the jacket for a weapon. By the box the man gazed into it and inhaled a quick breath. Without turning, he waved at Marc to join him.

"It's supposed to be here. In this box. But it's empty."

Fists clenched, Marc asked, "What is supposed to be in the box?"

A whirl of his body revealed a small caliber pistol. "You are." He raised the weapon as Marc jumped toward him, hitting his arm as the gun discharged. Fists pounded the assailant who toppled back toward the crate. Raising the gun to aim, eyes blurred with blood, his next shot whizzed past Marc, echoing off the hull.

A can of yams became a weapon for Marc as he picked it up and tossed it toward the would-be assassin, who ducked as it cracked a box on a shelf behind him. A second can made a better sound against the man's head. The gun fell to the floor as the man toppled into the shelves. Rushing his attacker, Marc corralled an arm and twisted it so the man flipped over onto his face. A knee in the back of the neck immobilized him. Kicking the gun out of reach, Marc pulled a disposable plastic riot cuff from his pocket for wrists and another for ankles. Restrained and semi-conscious the man groaned, and Marc searched pockets for additional tools and reloading clips. Clearing him of the added material, including a master key card, he picked him up and threw him into the awaiting crate. Now armed and calming, Marc realized a pain on the side of his head. The bullet had been closer than he imagined. A trickle rolled down his ear and dropped onto his shirt, scarlet and wet.

Head throbs started interfering with thinking. He had to find Jorgen and get medical help from Middlebury or Joan. In the hallway leading to the hold, a crumpled body sat in a doorway in a pool of blood. Jorgen still had the knife embedded in his back. Marc checked for signs of life. A heart beat and breathing reassured him, but getting help was not going to be easy.

# CHAPTER

# 30

Dag Ingersoll approached Joan and the children as they sat by the pool on the Lido deck. "May I have a word with you?" he said to her. They trailed away from prying ears of four young people. "Your husband and my son are in the infirmary. I don't mean to alarm you, but there was an altercation in one of the holds. We have the attacker in custody."

"What happened?" Her cool resolve impressed the security chief.

"Jorgen received a knife wound and is in serious trouble. Middlebury says he needs blood. Marc was nicked in the side of his head by a bullet. He'll recover, although he has a new part in his hair." Joan returned to the children. Stoicism had grown in her the longer she remained married to Marc. His wounds throughout his career left marks on his body and in her soul, but she concluded after the last investigation of his Uncle Jerry that he was indestructible and usually correct in assessing situations.

"Kids, stay here in this crowd. Go nowhere with anyone you do not know or trust. I am going to see Dr. Middlebury." She and Ingersoll left them for the elevators and a descent to discovering why people were attacking her family. The crowds of families and couples, oblivious to the added adventure occurring around them, created a difficult opportunity to speak. They entered a car without other passengers and Dag used a key card to express the elevator the infirmary deck.

"Is the captain aware of this latest breech aboard his ship?"

"Yes, I contacted him after finding our two men in the lower gangway outside the hold. I had two of my most trusted subordinates with me. They got Middlebury and Breckenridge who stabilized my son and tended to the wound of your husband. Marc was conscious enough to tell me of the steward in a crate in the hold."

The bing announced arrival of the proper deck. Joan rushed out leaving Dag to trail her into the medical facility. Finding Randolph and Olivia tending to the knife wound, she gloved her hands to assist. Middlebury asked, "Don't you want to see Marc?" She nodded.

"Instincts kick in, I guess," she said. He pointed her to the recovery area where she found him lying peacefully, his eyes closed. She picked up one hand, saying nothing as tears formed and dripped down her cheeks.

"Just another day at the office." His attempt at humor engendered a smile from her. He opened his lids and looked at her. "I am so sorry for all this."

"Tell me what happened. I feel like it's all my fault. After all, I asked you to investigate."

"I went to the hold to see what the steward considered contraband. He entered as I was looking around. He pulled a pistol and took a couple of shots at me. The second one grazed my head. He's in custody, though, and I need to get to him as soon as Middlebury gets back in here." He sat up and wobbled.

"You lie down, mister." She unwrapped the bandage and examined him. "This is deep. Your hard head and the angle of the bullet are the only things keeping you alive. You may have a cracked skull and a concussion." She re-wrapped the bandage. He lay on the bed and closed his eyes. Middlebury entered the room pulling latex gloves from his hands. "How is Jorgen?" she asked.

"Not good. He needs blood and we are out of his type. The knife nicked his Hepatic artery and lacerated his liver. I was able to close the nick but blood loss is his next challenge. His liver will recover. We stapled it together so it can regenerate." If he survives, she thought. "As for Marc, if you looked at him, I'm sure you see the structural damage to the skull. Concussion is evident, as well."

"Yes, he needs to stay here until we dock in Juneau. What is

Jorgen's blood type?"

"He's AB negative."

"I'm no help, then. Can we do a blood drive?"

"I suppose, but that might raise suspicions in the passengers if they discover why he lost some much blood."

Joan persisted "Do you have any records of crew blood types? We could get them involved and leave the passengers out of it."

Middlebury mused the idea and said, "We have medical histories since they need immunizations and other checks before hire. That might work." Dag entered, glanced at Marc and turned to Randolph.

"He's in bad shape, isn't he?"

"He needs blood. Are you AB negative?"

"Yes, he can have all of it if needed for survival."

"You don't need to be dramatic, but a couple of pints will help. Joan thought that we may have crew who are Rh Negative and we could get them to donate. I'll check the records and find out who matches. It's not going to be easy, though." Middlebury turned to Joan. "Go see if Olivia wants any help." She looked at Marc who appeared to sleep.

When she was gone, Marc said, "We don't yet know which crew members are crooked. Let me interview our prisoner before someone gets to him." He sat up again and tried standing. Dag reached him before he toppled to the floor.

As he helped Marc sit, he said, "I have two of the best watching our guest. He's in no danger and you can have at him when we are in Juneau. As for the use of the crew to find blood, start with me, and then we'll evaluate the situation." Middlebury nodded and then attended to his patient.

"Marc, I think you should transfer to the hospital in Juneau. This wound may have complications from hemorrhaging within the cranial cavity which can be serious. It can possibly lead to paralysis or death."

"You worry about Jorgen; I have my own medical staff to look out for me."

"You can't even stand, so stay right here until we dock and then we'll get you off the ship and into the hospital."

Marc waved off the comments. "Dag, bring that bastard to me so I can wrench the truth out of his wretched body. I need to know who all of the combatants are so they can be taken off the ship and incarcerated in Juneau."

"I don't think that's a good idea. He's protected where he is and transporting him here may lead to someone attacking him so he won't rat out the others."

"Alright, Randolph, get me a wheel chair. I'm going to him and spill his guts if he doesn't spill them first." Joan heard the conversation as she entered from cleaning up the operating area.

"Marc, please stay here and get better. You are in no condition to move." Her face scrunched and hands waved. She knew, however, the fruitlessness of halting his interrogation of the prisoner.

"Well, either I get a chair or someone needs to go with me so I can walk." Marc stood again less coggled and more determined. A wheel chair entered, pushed by Breckenridge.

In the brig area of the ship. Marc observed his adversary with a smile. "So, young man, I suppose the other members of this gang are searching for you as we speak. I wonder if they want to keep you around since you failed your boss whoever that person is." He leaned forward. "I imagine you'll end up like Iskandar, just another body as part of doing business. Maybe we'll let you go and spread the word that you gave them all up. We'll find them when they eliminate you from the crew."

Dag stepped toward the jail. "Are they holding your family hostage in Indonesia?" The prisoner flitted eyes between the two interrogators. "That's what happens when you agree to work with these types. They send word to others to wipe out your family, unless you cooperate. Or is the money you send home the incentive?"

Silence reigned as the two officers watched beads of sweat accumulate and his tongue wet his lips. His mouth opened but no words escaped. He turned away from them. They waited.

As he faced them again he plead for the safety of his family. "You must get them away from these people. My mother and father do not know the danger. My little sister will be sold as a sex slave and my brother will be killed. Please, help."

Marc placed hands on the arms of the chair and raised up to stand. "I am less sympathetic to your cause because of what you have done to me and to Mr. Ingersoll's son. That being the case, I am willing to see that you get what you want if you are cooperative.

Tell me who ordered the hit. Tell me who wants me dead. Tell me who on this ship aids and abets this criminal activity. Or you and your family can rot in hell." One of the security men handed Dag a folder. As he read, he glanced at the man in the cage and back to the words on the page. He handed the folder to Marc.

"Normally, we await Federal authorities to come and get you," he said as Marc read the file. "This situation is different in that you have attacked a fellow law enforcement officer. What is his crime? A vacation aboard our ship is not a reason to attack a passenger. Has he offended you in any way?"

"I can't tell you what I don't know. I can say our operations in Vancouver and Seattle ended. We used the ship to transport drugs from Vancouver to Seattle. Bypassing customs was easy since our people controlled the check points." Marc closed the folder.

"Thank you. You answered the one question my Uncle Jerry didn't solve. He will be pleased to know." The man stared blank as a sheet of paper. Looking at Dag, he said, "This ship is part of the operation we destroyed earlier this year. He is a small member, but he can lead us to the others." Turning to meet the eyes of a cornered rabbit, he said, "You can, can't you."

# CHAPTER

# 31

The steward found Jarina in her office on the aft part of the ship. "One of my crew is in custody for attacking Jefferson and Jorgen Ingersoll. We will be next."

She scoffed at his statement. "We are not all part of any round up. Do you have access to your man?" He shook his head. "You will go with security if they come for you. If you implement me in any way, you will not see tomorrow and your family will be history. Do I make myself clear?" She returned to her work on the desk at which she sat. "Get out of here before you're seen. Any of your crew speak out, and their families will be dead before morning. As long as some of us are in the clear, we can get the rest of you out of the country and to safety." He nodded and left without her looking up at him.

Her time aboard the ship was at an end. One more chance at avenging her father's death at the hands of the Jefferson family remained. The twins would be aboard in the morning and could work their magic while sailing to Skagway. She had to stay and act as if nothing was wrong. No one, except the steward, knew of her involvement. A visit to the infirmary to give sympathy could bolster her position as a concerned cruise director. Nothing happened without her knowing about it.

She picked up her phone and dialed the number of her last call.

"Hi. It's me again." She listened and continued. "The crew is lost to us. You need to be careful when you come aboard. I have your documents waiting at the entry portal." Another listen. "The fools botched an attempt to rid us of our adversary and are being collected." Her head shook as she listened again. "They don't have anything on me and you will be new and therefore clean. Is the material coming aboard with you or as cargo?" She finished the conversation and clicked off.

Completing the schedule updates for the evening shows, she forwarded them to the announcement center. Leaving her office, she decided to visit the medical facility immediately instead of waiting. As she walked down the stairs to the lower deck, her mind raced through a myriad of scenarios which might leave her vulnerable to detection. With confidence she entered to look for Middlebury, noticing a security man sitting in the waiting room. As she passed the examination room she saw Dag Ingersoll with a tube in his arm and blood draining into a bag. Joan Jefferson monitored.

"I didn't realize we were having a blood drawing today. Is this just for crew or should we announce it to the passengers. They may want to become part of it." Randolph monitored the operation and looked up at her.

"No, we need a particular type for one of our own. No announcement to the passengers."

"What happened?" Her voice rose with the words.

Not wanting to alarm her he lied. "There was an accident and Jorgen Ingersoll was injured and lost blood. Fortunately, his father is a match." Olivia Breckenridge entered as he spoke. She carried a second pouch and a bottle of saline.

"Hello, Jarina." The lilt in her voice meant to relax their visitor. Jarina smiled, but the sight of red fluid raised a vulgar taste in her mouth.

"Excuse me." She departed and crossed the reception area to the recovery room. Jorgen lay on his side, a massive bandage covering his lower back. Marc Jefferson sat in a wheelchair with white gauze wrapping his head. "What happened to you?" Her breathing deepened as she suppressed the rage in her.

"Hi, Jarina. I bumped my head on one of the bulkheads." She sat on the bed next to his seat. "My kids enjoyed your story time to other day. I think my son James has a crush on you. According to my daughter."

"Innocence," she thought. She missed having any growing up in her father's California home. He abandoned them when she was fifteen, old enough to know what he did and who he was. She followed him as soon as she finished high school, ending up in Seattle. Close to where he started his business in Everett, but out of the way of the expansion his operations.

Now her empire was crumpling and the cause sat next to her.

"I do hope you recover quickly. Vacations are not for injuries or illnesses. How are the rest of your family?" A sparkle in her eyes and a calming emotion posed a resolve for a later date with Mr. Jefferson. A stronger potion was arriving with the twins.

"Thanks. I feel kind of stupid for what I did."

She rose from the bed and shook hands with him. Thinking about Breckenridge, the nurse needed educating about her role in the company. Olivia was an asset still undiscovered and free to assist with eliminating Jefferson. But was she to be trusted. The twins would know.

⚬

"That's enough, Dag." Randolph handed the second bag to Olivia who returned to Jorgen's bedside to instill the blood into his veins. His vital signs had stabilized with the infusion of the first pint. He remained unconscious which made his chances to survive better.

"Can I see him?"

"You need to remain quiet for a few minutes. He's not going to leave. Wait 30 and then we'll let you in."

"How's Marc doing?"

"He's fine. Motion steadiness is returning. He should be able to return to his cabin for the evening." Randolph had not seen his daughter since early in the morning when Marcus arrived to escort her to the Jefferson family. He missed her, but safety was paramount. "Stay here. I'll be right back. By the way, are the rest of the perps being rounded up?"

"Yes, Dalgaard had Thorsen oversee my men as they left to escort the named persons to the detention area. All hush, hush, so as not to alarm passengers. I hope it works." Dag lay on the exam table eating an orange provided by Breckenridge.

Randolph realized he had not eaten since breakfast. Checking the time, the afternoon was half finished. "Olivia, watch our guests while I go and get some food for us. Have you had anything to eat, lately?"

"Thank you, doctor. I appreciate the thoughtfulness." He left the room and nodded at the security guard assigned by Dag to watch the facility. Riding an elevator to the Lido deck where food was available most of the day and evening, he gathered hamburgers and fries to go and bottles of water. He saw the Jefferson clan sitting by the pool. His daughter, seated close to Marcus, held his hand, her head resting on his shoulder. They were cute together, his mind raged with the idea of their youth trapping them before accessing an unknown future.

He strolled to them and said, "Hi." Delinda raised her head but kept hold of the hand. He furrowed his brow but said nothing more.

"How's my dad doing? Mom told us about his accident." Marcus stood up.

"He's fine. I'm getting him some food. I'll cut him loose in about an hour." Delinda stood by Marcus.

She said, "Do you need some help with your treasure? I haven't seen you all day." Her code, meant for a desperate father, had been instituted before the first journey aboard the ship. His response let her know if all was well in his world.

"Thanks, Dee, but I have the treasure collected and safe." He turned to Marcus. "Where's your mother? She left the infirmary just before me."

Sarah answered, "We haven't see her since she left us." Sarah winced. "Is she in trouble?"

"I don't think so. She seems quite capable of taking care of herself." He turned away as he said, "I'll look for her in your suite or through the Lido buffet area. Stay here." He bit his lip as he walked toward the doors.

Looking for Joan was not his priority. Returning to the infirmary to deliver food to Olivia made more sense. She flirted with him. She had dinner with him. Her nursing skills were superb. Delinda liked her. What was the problem?

"Good," she said as he entered the medical waiting area. "Food. You are the best guy on this ship." She grabbed a box and departed for the office. He followed.

"Olivia, where are we going? I thought you were a nurse wanting adventure. Do you want something more from me?"

"Randolph, you are a wonderful man, conflicted about so many things. Just ride out this voyage and see where this leads. I do like you for more reasons than your medical abilities. When we land in Juneau, I suggest we tour the city together."

"And my daughter?"

"She seems well taken care of by that Jefferson lad." Olivia sat at her desk. Middlebury stood a moment and then sat at his desk. They ate in silence, his mind musing the tale just told. This journey had twisted into a radical conundrum of unexpected highs and miserable lows. Had the end come? To being insecure about Delinda's future? To his misery because of his wife's death? To people affected by the criminals infecting the ship?

"Let's check on our patients." Change subject, his brain told him. Having finished the meal, he stood, checking whether she followed him, and left the room. In the recovery area Marc sat on the edge of his bed rubbing his head bandage. "Please stop that. I don't want to have to surgically tie you together."

Placing hands on the bed, he said, "Sorry, the pain meds are wearing off. Can I go soon?"

"Olivia, take his vitals, and if he's okay, cut him loose." He checked the inert body on the next bed and glanced at Dag who sat by his son. "How are you feeling?"

Dag answered, "I'm fine. How is my son?" Eyes scanned from Middlebury to Jorgen.

"He needs a hospital to fully recover."

Dag nodded. "I'll get a team together for protection. Do you want to take the samples with you when you escort my son?" Middlebury's brows furrowed.

"I'm sending the samples with Marc Jefferson. We could act as decoy in case you don't have all of the perps in custody."

"We have the ones on the list. They will be escorted by Alaskan State Patrol when we dock. I've arranged with them to keep the FBI out of this for now."

"How did you arrange for that?" Marc stood next to the doctor.

Dag answered, "The head of the department owes me a favor. And I'm letting him have some of the credit." He smirked.

Randolph asked, "Olivia, is Marc okay to go?"

"He's fine." Marc gathered his materials from a collection bag, waved good-bye and left without another word to anyone. "He seems in a hurry."

"Let's get everything set for tomorrow," Dag said. "We have much to do." Checking his watch, he continued, "The afternoon is soon to end and the evening may still have surprises for us."

# CHAPTER

# 32

Joan stood on the veranda in the early dawn watching the ship slide into the pier. Marc tossed and turned most of the night. Captain Lars Dalgaard and Cayde Thorsen visited the suite after they returned from dinner with Randolph Middlebury. Everything about this trip had fallen into an abyss from which no one was to escape.

The door opened. She turned to see a beautiful reflection of her face, young and naive. "Hi. Did you sleep well?" Sarah leaned on the railing and gazed at the water.

"I guess. I heard Dad most of the night. Is he okay?"

"His head hurts and he refuses any pain killers. I am sorry for all of this. I figured a vacation away from his work was best for us."

"But it followed us." Joan placed an arm around her pulling her close. She had nothing to say which could answer her. The last of the pier lines shot to the land crew. "I guess it's time for our subterfuge." Dag had the listening devises removed while his team rounded up the group. Words were safe again.

Joan faced Sarah, "Such a big word. I don't want you part of any of this." She moved toward the suite and stopped. "We have to save your father from harm. He has a big target on his back and more bad guys are out there. You and Marcus need to be strong and help James through this." Entering the suite, she glanced at

Marc, still asleep, and figured he needed it. She walked to the door, waited for Sarah to follow, and finished her instructions. "Let's get your brothers and start this play."

Marcus answered the door after a couple of knocks. "Hi, Mom, what's up?" Sarah pushed past to find James. Four detectives ready for a mission none wanted. Ready to face an unknown enemy. Ready to end the war. Joan joined her daughter. "Mom, I need to get Dee before we go to breakfast."

"Do that, and meet us in the Lido restaurant." He left to accomplish the one goal he enjoyed the most. "James, get dressed. We're going to breakfast."

Sarah and James left to eat. Joan returned to the suite to get Marc. He sat on the edge of the King bed rubbing the bandage concealing his new hairline part. "Can I take this off. I look ridiculous."

"Okay, but you need something on your head to protect that wound." She pulled a scarf from a drawer and displayed it. A slow wag discouraged that idea.

"All I need is a hat." He placed a ball cap on and winced. "The bandage takes up too much space."

"You're such a baby." Joan pulled scissors from her makeup bag and sliced the gauze on the side opposite his crease. Removing the material revealed dried blood. "You realize that two head wounds within such a short period of time is not good for your brain."

"Pepper smacked me over three months ago. I'm fine. How does it look?" Joan held a mirror up. "I guess I'll change hair styles. Longer hair like Marcus." He placed the cap on his head. "Much better."

"When are you meeting Breckenridge for the samples?" Joan cupped his hand in hers.

"Just before the gangway is laid and the doors open." They left to join their children.

As they scanned the port side of the ship for a table with three offspring and a guest, Jarina Camacho approached.

"Good morning, Mr. And Mrs. Jefferson. Do you have any plans for the city?" Her cordiality seemed to never waver. She smiled as she spoke but her eyes did not match. Marc pressed the memory button in his head. They exchanged handshakes.

"Not much." Marc worked a smile of his own. "We'll walk around town, maybe take the tram up to the park. Joan wants me to stop by the hospital and get an x-ray, just to be sure my head is still in one piece. How about you? Anything spectacular planned for passengers remaining aboard?"

"We don't entertain until this evening when the ship departs for Glacier Bay and Skagway." She strolled toward an exit.

"Something about her." Marc watched as she turned her head to espy them before leaving the room.

"Don't let your paranoia cloud judgment." Joan slipped an arm in his. "There are two of our charges." Joining them, they noticed the plates of food. "Starting before we got here, I see."

"Oh, hi, Mom." James' words were muffled by the challenge of coursing around a mouth full of pancakes.

Marc asked, "Where's your brother?"

"Right here." The voice materialized from thin air. Marcus and Delinda had little daylight between them. "I'm starving." He and Delinda wandered off to find their own pancakes.

"May I be of service to you?" A steward approached with a coffee carafe in hand.

"Thank you, coffee will be fine and some orange juice." Marc asked in a polite voice as he figured a couple of the usual service staff were missing. He and Joan sat as the steward poured two cups. He retreated to get the juices. Marc removed his hat and pain shot through his head.

"You need to leave that on as it is applying pressure to keep swelling under control." He replaced it. Marcus and Delinda returned with more food than either of them should be allowed to eat.

He said, "Here, we brought you some, as well." A family in turmoil sat quiet as church attendees, avoiding conversation about a secret mission.

⋙⟜⟞⋘

Jarina watched the deck crew run the ramps to the ship's gangway door. Her pacing interfered occasionally but no one complained. She observed the activity on the dock where people milled around waiting to accost passengers with deals to see eagles and whales. Two people were more familiar. The twins had fulfilled her request.

Now they would fulfill a greater need for the business. Her pacing halted as the twins faced the ship, gesturing a small wave of opposite hands. A complete person in two bodies. Ironic.

"We're ready." The crewman said. The scanners had been placed for the people boarding to enjoy the remainder of the voyage. Three of the regular scan members were soon to leave for the state detention center. Jefferson created this mess and now would pay the ultimate price. Family members were not exempt.

"Thanks. I'll make an announcement in five minutes." Passengers lined the hallway in front of the elevators and stairs. "We'll be ready in about three minutes," Several people nodded. Others left to wait elsewhere. She skipped up the stairs to the main desk and broadcast room. She picked up the package the head steward prepared as his last project. Opening it, she perused the documents and grinned. Bypassing regular channels made life so much easier. Time for an announcement.

Back at the gangway, she informed the entry people to allow the twins access. She handed the identity cards and entry documents to them as the girls walked up the ramp. Their beauty attracted attention. "Welcome aboard. If you will come with me, I will get you set up in your suite." With documents in hand, their bags were scanned for contraband. The boxes they carried were opened and jars of yellowish fluid were inspected. Nothing suspicious.

In her office behind the stage three women sat and discussed their plan of action. "We need to be careful. Our security chief has lost his son and we are short of staff to run operations."

Kerrine and Kaliana listened, each grinning, eyes locked on one another. Kerrine asked, "Is the security guy a problem?

"I don't know, exactly, but Middlebury took tissue samples from the author and one of the stewards who died. Their bodies are in the morgue and the good doctor is sending the samples to the medical examiner's office. If they figure out what killed them, it could mean trouble.

"I'm sure the doctor can be stopped. I have a power of persuasion," she said as she swept hands from beasts to abdomen, "which will occupy him. What happened to the security chief's son?" Kaliana cocked her head to the right. Her dark hair cascaded around her brown shoulder. Jarina recognized the jasmine shampoo from her meeting a year ago. The power was real and Middlebury was vulnerable.

"Dr. Middlebury hasn't released much information, but he lost enough blood that his father donated a couple of pints."

Kerrine spoke next, "Must be a knife wound. Probably cut an artery. He'll need a hospital."

Kaliana answered, "Was there a fight?"

Jarina started to speak and stopped. The twins' Cheshire grins contrasted their tan skin. She admired their ability to extract actions from mindless men simply because of their beauty and attentive nature. "I'm not sure about a fight, but our crew is incarcerated, and Jefferson is still alive."

"We are here as you requested to remedy the malady," Kerrine's smirk belied her cold heart. "Leave him to us."

# CHAPTER

# 33

Captain Lars Dalgaard and Cayde Thorsen addressed the Jefferson clan as breakfast finished. "Good morning, detective. I do hope your head is better." Marc stood and extended a hand.

"Thank you, Captain, I am much improved. We are ready to embark on our mission. I need to see Breckenridge for the materials, then depart for the city, and drop them at the proper place." He rubbed his hat, a gentle and small gesture. "When are the prisoners heading to shore?"

"State patrol is coming aboard around ten. Cayde is overseeing the transfer. I have contacts at the state patrol office in Juneau who will see that the samples are sent directly to the Medical Examiner's office in Anchorage. When we arrive there in four days, they should have some results for us."

Marc smiled. "Thanks for all you have done."

"I understand the author's young ladies are leaving to go home to Arizona. I assume you are staying aboard to help us ferret out any remaining rascals, although, I am certain we have them all."

Marc signaled his family to follow him. "We're staying aboard. After all, this is a vacation." They left the captain and his officer and headed for the prearranged pick-up.

When he saw Breckenridge, he asked the four young people to

wait away from any conversation. "Olivia, good to see you. Are we ready?" She handed him a small hand-held cooler. He handed it to Joan. "How's Jorgen?"

Eyes dropped and her head rolled left. "He's not doing well. Randolph sent for an ambulance to transfer him to Bartlett Regional. Dag's going with him."

Marc froze. "We can send the samples with him. Anyone suspecting either me or Middlebury, or even you, might not follow a grieving father." Joan pushed the cooler forward across the table.

"Maybe, but what if all of the rats are not yet off the ship?"

"Dalgaard hinted at others rats. What do you mean?" Marc placed a hand on the cooler. "Who's left?"

"I don't know. I'm not the detective."

"Are there any more of these coolers? We could send one with each group of people leaving the ship to distract anyone who might be watching." Marc glanced at Joan knowing an edgy emotional dread lurked within her. His injury conjured other close calls and they now gambled with fire which had a potential for losing containment.

"I'll find one for Randolph when he takes Jorgen to Bartlett."

Marc signaled for his children and Delinda to rejoin parents. "Thorsen is assisting the state patrol when they come for our guests." Her knowing the details was not a concern to him. She had proved her worth. Breckenridge departed to obtain another cooler.

"Shall we go Juneau?" The strain in his voice cast doubt about his accomplishing an undertaking fraught with possible danger. They flashed the key cards which recorded their departure from the ship. As he walked the gangway to the shore a body familiar in shape and out of uniform stood near the entry of the dock facility. He waved. Joan followed his visage and saw her father-in-law, Tiberius Jefferson and another family member thought to have died and now resurrected because of Marc's doggedness in cracking truth out of buried lies. Jeremais Jefferson accompanied his older brother to finish the hunt started over two years ago.

Tiberius spoke first, "Welcome to Alaska."

"I wasn't expecting to see you, Dad. Or you either, Uncle Jerry. What are you doing here?" Hugs by family members allowed a break in giving an answer.

He followed with a simple explanation, "We have some

information for you and I think you'll be wise to listen. By the way, I see you have another young lady in your entourage. Hi, I'm Tiberius Jefferson, Marc's father. And this is Jerry Jefferson, his uncle."

Marc finished the introductions. "Delinda Middlebury, my family. Her father is the doctor aboard the ship." Tiberius scanned the hands held tight and surmised the relationship.

"Marcus, I do hope you are treating her with Jefferson personal protocol."

"Grandpa, you needn't worry." Smiles mixed with Marc's furrowed brow and slitted eyes.

"Back to why you're here." Marc deflected the love fest. "What have you found that makes you fly here when you could easily have just called and told me?"

"We had some vacation time and convinced your mother and Aunt Lydia to come for a get-away. We're staying at the Aspen Suites out by the airport. By the way, what happened to your head?" A drop of red fluid trailed down past his ear to his cheek. He felt the stream with his fingers and pulled a tissue from his pocket.

"We've had some excitement on this journey. The security chief's son was stabbed and almost killed. He and I were investigating a lead and were attacked."

"And you?" Jerry asked.

Joan intercepted the answer. "Someone aboard the ship shot him. The only thing saving him was his hard Jefferson head." Marc pulled off the hat which had scratched the scabbing free. He daubed at the trickle with the tissue.

"Wow, that's some valley. Joan, are you heading to the hospital for an x-ray?" Jerry asked.

"Yes, your nephew probably has a concussion as well as the gunshot wound. Will you boys please stop playing in dangerous games? I can't handle the idea of any of you dying. I already endured your death and resurrection. I don't want another one."

"Come on then, we can drive you to the hospital. Jerry and I rented a Jeep Cherokee for the week."

As they piled into the car which held only four, the children were left to fend for themselves. A promise to meet for lunch at the Hanger on the Wharf assuaged young stomachs.

"Alright, we're alone. What did you bring me? Us?" Marc asked.

Joan clamped her hands on the cooler. "Oh, we need to stop at the state patrol office and have this cooler sent to Anchorage to the state medical examiner. Then I can get my head examined."

"Okay, lead the way, son." He gave the address which was punched into the car's GPS. As Tiberius backed out of the space, Marc noticed two strikingly beautiful women who looked so much alike, he figured they played games with men they met. The Hispanic or more correctly, Mexican, heritage was evident. The long cascade of shimmering brunette hair and bodily figures invited leers from other men standing nearby and quick ogles of husbands and sons coming down the gangway. They ignored all lechery as they had a vision they focused on. They were non-attentive to any leering which followed any movement they made. He watched the track of their eyes. He wanted Joan to know nothing about them. A sense of foreboding roused his brain to a mental note for later. Their focus was clear. They were looking at him.

# CHAPTER

# 34

Three intrepid law enforcers approached the state patrol office, scanning for other people who might follow them. "Do you want us wait outside for your girl friends?"

"Very funny, Dad. I don't know who they are. I haven't seen them aboard before today." He opened the front door and entered. Father and Uncle joined him. Good to his word, Captain Dalgaard had arranged with his connections for the transport of the samples to Anchorage. A report would await their arrival in four days.

Uncle Jerry said, "Now to the hospital. I promised Joan we'd return to have you checked out." She had Tiberius drive her to see about Jorgen Ingersoll.

"Why hasn't the FBI been called in to assist with what happened to the author, you, and the security chief's son?" Jerry asked. "I thought the protocol for any unexplained death was to contact them."

Marc adjusted his hat as he winced. "Captain Dalgaard knew someone in the crew was complicit with transporting illicit contraband but had no tangible proof. My traveling on vacation alerted the gang of a chance to eliminate me for breaking up the cartel in Everett. Unfortunately, I thought a gift basket sent to our room was actually meant for an author, James Blackthorne. It wasn't. Something in the honey caused a paralytic reaction which killed him, threatened James with death, and killed one of the crew, probably because he was the one who delivered the basket. Now that we have intercepted the six members of the crew who were responsible for the drug trafficking, things should be better aboard the ship. American Pacific does not want negative publicity which I don't think they can avoid."

"So who else aboard the love boat do you suspect of nefarious activities?" Tiberius chortled as he spoke. "Maybe those twins should be investigated. Closely."

"Uncle Jerry, can't you control your brother?"

"Ha. Sure."

Tiberius parked the car in a slot near the entry to the hospital. As they walked to the doors another car entered, drove by and departed the lot. The driver wore dark glasses, had dark hair wrapped in a scarf, and never looked at the three men. But the person was familiar. From the ship? From Seattle? Kitsap? Marc's hackles rose as the vehicle vanished.

"Are you alright?" Tiberius asked. "You look like you saw a ghost."

"That car which just passed, I think the lady driving was someone I knew."

Uncle Jerry offered an observation which made some sense. "Maybe that head of yours is more seriously damaged than you think. Are you seeing things that are not there?"

Marc pushed his way past his uncle without answering. A shrug of elder shoulders went unobserved by the younger member of the family. At the main desk Marc asked, "Where can I find a patient brought in earlier today from a cruise ship?" He flashed his sheriff's badge as incentive to answer his inquest.

"Do you know the name of the person?" A curt request from a stoic nurse.

"Jorgen Ingersoll. His father, Dag Ingersoll, came with him."

"He's in the emergency care department downstairs. I can page his father for you, if you wish."

"Thank you. Also, my wife, Joan Jefferson, is here somewhere. Please page her, as well."

The stoicism evaporated with his request. "Oh, Mr. Jefferson, you are to report to diagnostic imaging for an MRI. We had an opening and your wife scheduled it for you as soon as she arrived.

You should report to them," she checked the clock, "in about an hour."

Tiberius and Jerry chortled. His uncle said, "Joan is a no nonsense person. You need a head shot; she gets you a head shot." Marc curled a lip at Jerry.

Tiberius asked before his son could disappear, "And which way is diagnostic imaging?" The nurse pointed to the elevator.

"It's on the floor below us. When you get off the elevator, turn right and it is the second door on the left. I'll have your party meet you there." She smiled, not a painted fake, but a genuine concerned face. The three men entered the car and descended the one floor.

"I hope the MRI is conclusive that you are okay, son." Marc grimaced and cocked his head. As the doors opened, Joan passed by without looking in. Her pace suggested an emergency. They vacated and called to her.

"Oh, Marc, glad you're here, but Dag just called. Jorgen's critical. He's taken a turn for the worse. Follow me." They hurried to keep with her as she disappeared through a pair of swinging doors.

"That woman can move." Jerry's statement, meant as a compliment irked his nephew. She flicked a finger at them as they neared the bed with Jorgen. Monitors flashed the vital information about a simple stabbing gone awry. Randolph had done his best and two pints from a grieving father may have saved his life. More blood streamed from a bag hanging next to a glucose solution.

"Dag, look who I found wandering the hospital." Joan's upbeat tone masked the heaviness of the atmosphere around the bed. "I would like you to meet my father-in-law, Sergeant Tiberius Jefferson, a Seattle officer and his brother, Jeremais Jefferson, a Snohomish County deputy. He was recently promoted to lieutenant after completing a three-year investigation of the very group which received drugs from the crew aboard our ship." They shook hands and exchanged pleasantries. Dag's mind was occupied by the body on the bed.

"Now, Mr. Jefferson," Joan said, a bit of medical authority expressed, "time for you to get a picture of your head." Marcus followed her as she rotated and headed for another set of doors marked radiology. Like third wheels, Tiberius and Jerry scurried to stay part of the entourage. Joan acted as if this facility was no different than the senior care unit in Wendlesburg. Hospital personnel reacted with favorable attitude as she commanded respect with an aura of leadership.

Marc received a change of clothing, less flattering and more exposing than he wanted. As he lay on the MRI bed and waited for all of the images to be recorded, he thought of the car in the parking lot. Was he paranoid? Had the wound and concussion elevated his awareness to a fantasy level? Did he now suspect innocent people before knowing them? The twin Hispanic women at the ship were an example of his now exposed fantasy paranoia. His desire to shake his head and dismiss the dreaming was thwarted by the restraints on his skull. The whirring, clicking, and banging noises chased any boredom. As time passed at a snail's pace, he concocted responses to the queries about newfound fears and anxieties. Who were the beauties now aboard his ship? Not his but the vacation ship. He was going to miss the young editor, Gabby, and wondered if she was as talented in the book errata construction as he speculated her talents for satisfying an elder author.

The author's death had been a mistake. Now Marc lay strapped to a table being examined because an unknown enemy stalked him and his family to eradicate the perpetrator of disaster for the demon scum infesting Everett and other parts of the northwest. He regretted the misjudgment of the gift card and the awful loss to a literate world of thriller readers. He regretted Jorgen lying on death's door, fighting to live. He regretted James near tragic illness and the loss of the young steward. These bastards exacted a heavy toll. He did not regret their losses or incarceration.

The technician pushed a button and the bed moved freeing him from the brain drain. Joan stood next to him as the straps were loosened, freeing him from his own incarceration. "Mr. Jefferson, you are finished and may get dressed." Marc nodded. Joan aided his standing. The throb in his skull thundered with the minor altitude adjustment. Gritting teeth and seething a breath in, then out, he closed eyes and snapped at Joan.

"The bastards must pay. If there are any more rats aboard, they must pay." He completed clothing his body. Joan wise with experience waited for his rant to end.

"They will," she said. "They will."

"How soon do I get results?" Marc leaned against the door frame. "We should find the kids. They're probably wondering if we still exist."

Tiberius answered him. "I'll go get Gabby and Lydia and bring them back here. Jerry, call the kids and get them up to date. I'm guessing they have eaten lunch without us." He checked the clock on the wall which glared in red numerals, 2:27." He left for the hotel. Jerry wandered to a quiet area for his call. Joan spoke with the technician about the results for which he could not comment. He showed her the images. She worked through the dozens of slices and noticed a slight coloring near the wound. A narrow line delineated the crack in his cranium. She figured the coloring was blood in the meninges and needed monitoring for any swelling. She thanked the tech who stated he had contacted the radiologist.

Jerry made a second call for a taxi to ferry Marc and Joan back to the ship. "Marc, Joan, we'll take care of the kids and see they return before final boarding."

Marc growled, "I'm fine. I want to see the kids and be sure they're alright. Something is wrong on the Salish Sea and with Dag here with his son, security aboard the ship is diminished. I'm sure Captain Dalgaard wouldn't mind a stand-in." Marc still leaned on the frame. "We'll wait for results unless the time gets late. They can send the diagnosis to the ship. I have the best medical staff right in my suite."

When Tiberius returned with mother and aunt, a reunion fraught with tears and hugs, kisses and reprimands, eased Marc's emotional state. True to his word, the radiologist returned by three and checked the images. "The skull is cracked but not serious enough for any surgery. The discoloring is blood which fed through the wound. I don't see it as a problem as no swelling has occurred. You must keep calm and avoid any more damage to your head. I noticed an older injury just above where the bullet grazed your head. What happened?"

"Occupational hazard. I was clubbed with a pistol by a bad guy who now lies with the worms." Marc shrugged shoulders and waited for Joan to reprimand him. He was handed the slides.

"Take these with you and see your local physician when you return home. He should follow up with another scan to see what progress is made in the next month or two."

"Thank you, doctor," Joan said. "I will see to it."

As the four readied to leave, Dag entered. Eyes were blotchy and wet. He breathed deep and steady, holding for a moment before saying, "He woke up. The doctor says he's going to make a full recovery. They'll keep him here to heal and then transfer him to a facility for therapy. Marc, I contacted Lars to inform him of my leave of absence and asked him to allow you to act in my place. It's highly irregular, but he agreed. Get the rest of them, if there are any. Stay safe." He left to be with his only offspring.

As the intrepid group checked out of the hospital, Marc wondered what he could do aboard a ship with compromised crew members lurking about and a health report which required rest. When the cab arrived for he and Joan, Tiberius, Jerry, Gabrielle, and Lydia left to meet the children and find a nice place for dinner. Joan sat in the back seat while Marc observed the same automobile from the morning arrival parked away from other cars. Two women sat in the front seats and studied him as he stood at the car door.

CHAPTER

# 35

You're playing with fire." Olivia Breckenridge sat with Randolph Middlebury on the Lido Deck drinking coffee and watching passengers frolic in the pool. "Delinda is a beautiful young woman and keeping her penned up aboard this ship is wrong. She's moved on. You need the chance to move on."

Middlebury sipped tea and stared across the deck. "I know you're right. My wife's death hit me harder than I realized. Dee has found a friend but it's not the right time for me, I guess." He looked at her. She was pretty, not young nor old. She had a matronly look. He didn't need a mother, nor a savior. "So. Just sex." She laughed.

"You are a funny man. I'm not one to jump into bed with anyone, but you may be an exception." They laughed a quiet understanding of aloneness.

Olivia stood. "Since we have no passenger crises at the moment, I am going to my cabin and take a nap. I would enjoy having a fine meal with you this evening." Randolph agreed with a wink and a nod. Leaving the Lido deck, she descended the aft staircase until she stood in front of the entry to the auditorium. Walking the aisle to the stage, she stopped and listened. Jarina and she had few conversations, but the camaraderie stemmed from an earlier encounter at Andrew Pepper's warehouse in Everett, Washington, when introductions were made. Jarina had been a companion to

Pepper and ran his operations until her move to the ship. Olivia had been hired to nurse any minor injuries and wounds so as to avoid hospitals, doctor clinics, and unwanted questions.

The collapse of Pepper's cartel required a move to the ship, as well. Connections helped get her aboard. Everything was working well and the Jefferson family vacation played right into her plans. The addition of crew members was an expected move. The loss of six cohorts was not. She had been part of Jarina's play and clarified in her mind the reasoning for removing the tissue samples from the ship before anyone suspected her. Playing double agent was not her forte', but she kept information from each side of the battle. A noise alerted her to another presence.

"Olivia," Jarina said. "What are doing here?"

"We need to talk."

"That's never a good thing. About what?"

"Let's go to a more secure place." Jarina led her to the office back stage. "Are the bugs still operational in the Jefferson suite?"

"No. They must have suspected something was wrong after the incident in the cargo hold. Why?"

Olivia sat on the sofa next to the desk. "Middlebury sent the tissue samples of the author and steward to the medical examiner in Anchorage. He expects a report when the ship docks there in five days."

Jarina sat in the chair at her desk. "So what. Does he expect to find poison or something? Nothing points to us and nothing will be found that is lethal."

"Still, someone slipped up when the basket went to the wrong cabin."

"Iskandar delivered it correctly and they gave it to the author. You know that. Now we have to adjust and change tactics. Too bad that head wound didn't kill him."

"Are you so upset that you'll make a mistake?"

"I don't make mistakes, and it would be wise for you to do what you're told." Olivia stood and fronted Jarina.

"My job is to monitor what happens aboard this ship. Contrived illnesses can raise suspicions, so I'll make sure you are not exposed to inquiry. No mistakes by either of us. For now, I suggest we leave the Jefferson clan alone so they think the threats are done. Catching them unaware will be best for us." Jarina said nothing as Olivia left.

Descending the stairs to the crews' quarters, she walked to her cabin and entered. Removing her blouse and pants, she lay on her bed and closed her eyes. A knock interrupted an attempt at sleep. Rising she slipped on her robe and opened the door. "What do you want?"

"We should have a conversation about what is happening aboard this ship." She stepped aside and allowed the visitor to enter.

"Well?" she asked.

"Operations are finished for now. Any further actions which threaten any passenger or crew must stop. We can rebuild at a future time when we replace crew members."

"I understand your concern, but you're not in charge of what happens. You have been well compensated for allowing the transport of our cargo without suspicions. Your captain thinks something is rotten. Keep an eye on him and we'll finish what needs to be done." Her visitor breathed a deep inhale, held it moment, and released.

"Okay, but if anything else goes wrong, we'll have to vacate the operations permanently." He turned to leave. At the door he said, "If she can't get it together, she's next to go." He departed.

Latching the door, she lay on the bed. Sleep eluded her, but the calm and quiet restored her energies. After an hour she rose from her slumber, dressed, and left for the medical facility. No page came in from Randolph, but she felt the need to assure herself that no one was in crisis. He was a good doctor and she was attracted to him. Could he accept her occupation as a nurse and never find out about her other job? Or should she be truthful and let him in on her secret life? Their relationship was strictly professional with short dalliances over dinner. They had known each other for only four days; a ship board romance was not her goal. Still her life remained empty of companionship because of the need for flexibility. Changes happened as quick as a northwest rainstorm.

The clinic was empty of anyone needing assistance. Something was wrong. A cupboard door was ajar. She checked the contents and found nothing missing. Closing it, she scanned the room for other anomalies. She then checked the locked drug cabinet and discovered the padlock on the cage door was reversed from her last closure. Had Randolph opened it? She unlocked the door and flipped the combination dial on the cabinet door. Opening it and checking the inventory log against the contents, she found a vial of morphine missing. Only four people knew the combination. Only three had a key to the padlock. Only two names were fixed on the log.

She knew she was innocent. That left Middlebury. A discreet inquiry at dinner might answer the question of why he took one vial of morphine. It was not enough to harm anyone, unless a medical condition existed or an allergic reaction might happen. Another death on the ship would be hard to explain to authorities. She showered and prepared for an evening of relaxation. Dressing in a dark navy cocktail ensemble, she wanted a chance to impress him with her ability to be coy and sexy. Heels and a faux pearl necklace completed the illusion.

In the dining room she sat at a rear table awaiting her companion. Questions flooded her mind. Morphine? Middlebury? Jorgen Ingersoll's condition? Jarina? The Jefferson clan? Had her employer trusted her reasoning for this task? Randolph arrived as her brain roiled with ideas.

"Good evening," he said as he sniffed of air. "I don't recognize the fragrance? It's delightful on you. And I must say, you look smashing tonight. May I join you? Or are you awaiting the arrival of another rival?"

"Funny. Have a seat. Yes, I am rather smashing this evening and the fragrance is Tabu, which I plan to not be." He seated himself across from her and gazed at the necklace which lay in her cleavage. "Are you impressed with the necklace or where it lies?"

"Pardon me? I was thinking about a pearl necklace my wife gave to Delinda before she died. We left it home because of the value. You look stunning in yours."

"Thank you. Continue to be courteous and gentlemanly and I may reward you." A large group of people approached the table. Marcus and Delinda still had little space between them. James and Sarah lagged behind Mom and Dad.

Marc spoke first, "Good evening, Olivia, Randolph. Mission accomplished."

"Great to hear," Randolph said. "I must say, your son seems to care for my daughter more than I imagined." He stood to shake

Marc's hand and then offered it to Joan. "Dee, please return to the cabin before eleven. I want to be sure you are secure."

Her eyes rolled a slight up and down motion. "Yes, Daddy. Marcus will make sure I am home in at a reasonable time." The young people left to find seats at a table reserved for them. Sarah and James followed.

Randolph asked, "How is Jorgen doing?"

Joan answered, "He is stable but not out of the woods yet." Marc reached for her arm. "Marc's head is fine, but he needs to rest and not get hit or shot again for the rest of his life." The crescendo of her voice emphasized her concern for his health.

Marc gently held her arm as he began to leave, but Randolph asked another question. "Is Dag staying with him?"

"Yes, and he asked me to kind of keep an eye on things until he joins us in Skagway. He called the captain this afternoon." Randolph nodded approval though he had little control.

Marc and Joan joined the children. As they awaited a server to take drink orders, a pair of women entered the room and sat on the opposite side but within view. Marc's hackles rose. The beautiful twins paid no attention to him, but he suspected they were stalking their next prey. Why? Who were they? What might be their intentions? When would they make their move on him?

# CHAPTER

# 36

The waiter delivered drinks to the twins. Kerrine sipped her chardonnay while Kaliana tasted a vodka martini. "What shall we do this evening after dinner?" Kaliana asked. "He acts so like we are not here." She glanced at Marc as she placed her glass on the table.

"He will remember us until he can't." Kerrine took another sip. "We will leave him alone this evening and attend the show in the auditorium. When Jarina is finished we can institute our plan to eliminate Mr. Jefferson."

"I suppose you want to compromise his marriage before we remove him from life." Kaliana sneered. "I'm not sure how you could execute a physical liaison without some kind of incentive."

Kerrine gazed out the window watching the wake of the ship. "We establish a nice little incarceration of his wife and children. Or better, we let her watch. She can be tied up with a knife at her throat. A small cut to give him the idea we mean business. He will need to be confined so he does not resist much. We can take turns cutting the bitch and riding the bastard. After we're done, sated, and ready to finish them off, we can force them to drink our elixir. As they sleep, we will place them together on the bed. No one will suspect foul play until we are long gone."

"What about their children? They'll want to see them."

"True, but they will get to suffer for the sins of their parents." Dinner consisted of Alaskan salmon on a bed of wild rice and asparagus, a green salad, and assorted rolls. Dessert was a slice of apple pie with vanilla ice cream. They ate and ignored their adversary, glancing on short occasions to remind him to be watchful. The game was more exciting when the prey was aware and nervous.

Sated for the evening, they sipped warm brandy to complete their meal. A quick peek at the Jefferson clan revealed an empty table. Kerrine smiled. "I do hope they get some sleep tonight." Kaliana paid no attention to her sister. She stared at the man standing behind Kerrine.

"I certainly plan to get sleep tonight," Marc said. "I would like to introduce myself so that we can be better acquainted and neither of you need stalk me or my family. You are both lovely women in search of a quarry. For what gain?"

Kerrine turned to face him. "Mr. Jefferson, I do apologize for not knowing of what you speak."

"Knowing my name means you have an advantage over me." He pulled chair from another table and sat between them. "May I know your names since we are on a course of convergence for which one of us is going to pay a hefty price?"

Kaliana answered, "I am Kaliana, and this is my sister Kerrine. We came aboard today in Juneau to continue the trip north to Anchorage. I'm sure we have nothing for which any of us will regret meeting."

Kerrine spoke next. "We were attracted to your lovely family. I do not think we were stalking you as much as Juneau is a small city and we crossed paths." Her eyes glistened much as the witch in Snow White. "Would you be interested in sharing an evening cocktail with us before we retire? I am curious as to what you do in life which affords you taking a family on a cruise. Are you a rich businessman or Internet entrepreneur?"

Kaliana repeated the request. "I think an after dinner nightcap might be just the thing for us to be better acquainted."

"While I appreciate your interest in an older man, I am happily married and not interested in spreading my charm as much as you seem willing. Thank you." He stood and replaced the chair. As he left them, to wonder how much he understood their future role in his life, they reveled with hands held left and right and walked out of the dining area.

"This will be fun and our best caper yet. He may think he is immune, but a taste of our charms and he will melt with the first touch." Kerrine skipped a step as she spoke. "His son is cute and not much younger than we are. Maybe he would like to replace his girlfriend for two older and more experienced women. We can teach him how to please the doctor's daughter in ways he doesn't know. Or we can teach her how to pleasure a man."

"Your crazed affections astonish me at times. Although, I wouldn't be unhappy sharing time with either of them."

They headed for the final show in the auditorium and a backstage meeting with Jarina. All of the players needed to be revealed so that no hitches cropped up. The batch of honey they brought aboard was the best of the crop. A small taste would do no harm, even if Jarina guarded it like a gold ingot.

They commented about her talent as a master of ceremonies. She ran a tight ship and an even tighter syndicate. Act after act performed with flawless precision. After an hour of entertainment, the final singer, dancer, comedian left with raucous applause. Kerrine and Kaliana stayed seated as families and couples departed. An older gentleman, alone and investigative, stopped to speak with them.

"I hope you enjoyed the performances this evening. I manage the band which performed second." The group consisted of three young men and a woman. "I thought maybe you would like to meet the band and celebrate with them. This is their first long term engagement."

Kerrine responded that they were meeting someone but might be interested in attending the party as soon as they could. The gentleman handed a card with the necessary information to her and left. "I do believe he just propositioned us to be companions for part of the band. Do you think the girl is a partner of one of the guys? Or are they all gay and the girl needs companionship?"

"Everything with you is sex, isn't it?" Kaliana grinned.

"Why sister, I do believe you want to party. Consider it practice for our conquest of Mr. Jefferson. Let's find Jarina." They vacated the seats and worked their way to the stage. One of the stage crew asked if they needed any help. "If Jarina is free, we would like to see her." He motioned for them to follow him.

In her office Jarina completed her log of the shows and the size of the audience for statistical records. The importance of these records for future bookings helped keep the entertainment of each cruise as satisfying as possible for passengers. The twins sat quiet as church mice waiting for her to complete work.

At last she looked at them and asked, "What do you want?" Each smiled at her testing her limits of endurance and patience. "Well?"

Kerrine said softly and gentle. "We want to test the caliber of product tonight on one of your acts, the band of three guys and one girl."

Kaliana continued, "We have been invited to a party by their manager. If our test is successful, we can use it against Mr. Jefferson and any others in his party who mean to stop us."

Jarina remained silent. She stood, hesitated, and then walked to the cabinet holding the jars and bags of specially designed tea. Removing a small container of tea bags and one jar, she faced them.

"Please be judicious with these. We do not need any references to our operation by Ingersoll, Jefferson, or Middlebury. The captain is already suspicious of the activities ongoing aboard his ship."

"Who can we trust?" asked Kerrine. "Who still works for you and the remaining members of the cartel? Who will assist in carrying out our plans?"

"The loss of the supervising steward, his assistant, and four members of the scanning crew has damaged our ability to function effectively." Jarina withheld the requested items. "You both are the newest to be brought here. We have one other person high in the ranks and not known to anyone other than me. A nurse came aboard for this cruise who worked for Pepper before his collapse. She is assisting the doctor who has seen two deaths, the youngest Jefferson boy get sick, and three injuries as a result of a failed assassination attempt on Jefferson. He is quite capable but definitely not on our side.

"He does have a daughter who may be vulnerable to coercion and can be leveraged to get his cooperation. The nurse is acting in alliance with the security and medical people but had reported activities to the steward before his loss. I have not yet contacted her, although we are acquainted with each other." Her lie was small in her thinking but meant to keep the twins from overstepping their role in the rebuilding process. Olivia and the twins were not familiar with each other as far as Jarina knew.

"So may we have our test product and see if it produces the desired results?" Kerrine held out her hand to receive her request. Jarina placed the items in a bag and gave it to her.

"Be careful with these. A little goes a long way. And I don't need the band members sick on the way to Skagway."

"Will the manager be needed since he doesn't perform?" Kaliana asked.

"Get out of here." Jarina sat at her desk and fiddled with the keyboard of the computer.

In the auditorium they made a plan to slip the honey into drinks which call for it and watch the results. At the band's after party in the Veranda Tahoma Lounge, they found the manager and asked him about the band members and their relationships to each other. Each twin took an arm so he could not escape. Encouraged by the attention, he relaxed and chatted as to how the members formed an incredible musical group about six months ago.

"Wayne and Layana are related, brother and sister. Greg, the drummer, is dating Layana. Joaquin is the loner of the group. They advertised for a bassist and chose him from a group of players who responded in Seattle. Are you interested in getting to know them?"

Kerrine squeezed his arm. "I may be more interested in knowing the man who put them together and booked them on this cruise." His face flushed.

Kaliana continued the ploy. "We both have an affinity for strong older men who know what they want and how to get it." A warmth rose from his neck to the crown of his head. His heart beat a bit faster. She asked the next question to help institute the test. "Have you ever tried a Bee's Kiss?"

Curiosity cooled his head. "I don't drink much. It gets in the way of my brain. But to answer your question, no, I haven't. What is it?"

Kerrine guided him to the bar. "Mr. Bartender, do you know how to fix a Bee's Kiss?"

"I don't know that drink."

"Do you have white rum and half and half?" She fingered the jar in her pocket.

He checked the shelf, found a bottle of Tanduay Silver, and placed it on the bar. He opened the refrigerator and placed a carton of half and half beside the rum. "What else?" She lifted the jar from her pocket and added it to the small collection.

"2 ounces of rum, a teaspoon of cream, and a teaspoon of honey. Shake vigorously with ice and strain over ice cubes into a glass." He followed her instructions exactly as given. Handing the cocktail to her, she transferred it to her prey, who sipped it and declared the drink to be a masterpiece. Asking for another, she placed a finger on his lips. "Not so fast. I want you sober for later when we are alone." The warmth returned to the unsuspecting victim.

The bartender asked, "May I keep the jar?" Kaliana picked it up and pursed her lips.

"The price for this is higher than you might want to pay. Are you free later when the party ends?"

Eyes widened. "Yes."

Two fingers graced her lips and then touched his mouth. She walked away without saying another word. The manager introduced the band members to Kerrine and Kaliana. The party was small. Four bandies, two roadies, the manager, and a couple who were the parents of Wayne and Layana. When the twins had met everyone, they decided to chat with the lone wolf bass player. He looked to be in his early twenties with long dark hair hanging around his face like a mask.

Handsome enough to attract their interest, his introverted personality slowed the progress of familiarizing themselves to him. Kaliana whispered in his ear that she wanted to see the suite which was his for the voyage. Taking the tea bags with her they left to become more acquainted. Kerrine stayed to finish her testing of the manager. Another Bee's Kiss and she suggested a showing of his room might be rewarding to him. The evening finished with his failure to consummate any liaison as his heart and muscles failed to operate properly when they arrived at his cabin.

Her test was a success. He remained alone complaining of pains and paralysis as she left to ostensibly find the doctor.

# CHAPTER

# 37

Middlebury received a post-midnight call for assistance on the Upper Veranda in a Puget Suite occupied by the manager of one the bands playing aboard the Salish Seas. He called Olivia to join him. The ship had departed Juneau at 8:00 pm as scheduled and the evening shows had ended around eleven. The manager had contacted one of his band members to get the doctor.

"He complained of heart problems and like not being able to use his legs and arms, like they were paralyzed," he had said over the phone. Randolph sent Olivia to monitor the man while he stopped by the Elliot Bay Suite to waken Marc and Joan about another possible poisoning.

Inside the suite Marc asked, "Who's this person? Does he have any connection to anyone aboard the ship?" Joan sat with Sarah who awaken when pounding disturbed the room. Sarah had answered the door.

"He's the manager of the one of music groups. They were having an after performance party. He left with a young lady and then contacted the lead singer soon after." Marc dressed and accompanied Randolph to the upper level Puget Suite.

Olivia intercepted them before Middlebury examined the victim. "He's showing similar signs as the other three. I administered a stimulant as you suggested."

"Good. Let's see how he's doing." Marc followed to observe the actions of the manager and the members of the band who had gathered. Someone had knowledge of the evening's activities before the fateful event.

"How's he doing, Doc?" The question came from the bassist, Joaquin, and attracted Marc's attention.

Randolph listened through his stethoscope, checked responses at proper points, and then asked, "What have you had to eat this evening?" The manager remained conscious from the first moment he noticed his failing health.

"We ate dinner before the show in the Lido Restaurant. I ate a burger and fries and a cup of green tea."

"Did you put anything in the tea?" Middlebury asked.

"Some lemon."

"Anything else you consumed before coming to your suite?" Marc inquired.

"I had a couple of drinks at the party. A young woman I invited to attend suggested it. A Bee's knees, no, kiss, a Bee's Kiss. Quite delicious. I had two."

Marc probed deeper. "The young lady, can you describe her? And second, what's in a Bee's Kiss?" Marc's mind pictured bees and a honey comb. Was this a connection?

The manager rolled eyes and rotated his head. "She was young, about the age of the band members, which was why I asked her and her sister to join us. Dark hair and eyes, tawny skin tone with Spanish features." The twins. Marc's brain conjured her sneaking some drug into the drink when he wasn't watching. What motivation existed to attack this person? "The drink had rum, cream, and honey."

"Her sister. Did she have the same features?"

"Yeah, they were identical. Hard to tell 'em apart. One talked with Joaquin. I came back here with the other and then I felt like my body was failing me. She departed and I went to bed, but called Wayne to come help me. By the way, who are you?"

"Thank you. I'm Marcus Jefferson, a guest on vacation." The manager closed his eyes, ending the interview. Marc touched Randolph's arm and led him to the veranda.

"Doc, I saw those two earlier, yesterday, and at dinner last night. According to one of them, they came aboard in Juneau to travel to Anchorage. We have more of Pepper's crew active aboard this ship."

"This can't go on. An innocent person's going to get hurt. I'll leave it to you to figure out what's going on."

"I'm asking the bassist more about his adventure with the other sister. Maybe he has some insight for us." Randolph nodded and returned to check his patient's progress. Marc signaled Joaquin to join him on the veranda. Wayne came with him.

"Who are you? My manager asked and you said you're a guest. So why should we talk to you?" He crossed his arms and stood in front of Joaquin.

"Fair enough. Wayne, right?" A nod affirmed his inquiry. "I'm a detective in Kitsap County, which is in Washington State. I'm helping the security chief while he stays in Juneau with his son who is recovering from an injury. He'll rejoin us in Skagway." He stepped around Wayne. "Joaquin, did you spend time with the other girl?"

With eyes cast to the decking he said, "She asked to see my room. I figured we might ... you know, ..." He cleared his throat. "She fixed some tea and we talked a moment. Then she kissed me. We made out until Layana banged on the door."

"Did you drink any of the tea?" With Marc's question Wayne screwed his face. "Do you have any of it?"

Joaquin tapped his fellow band member. "No, I didn't drink any of it."

"Will you see her again?" Marc squared his feet.

"Nah, she seems too old for me."

Marc wanted the tea. "Can you take me to your room?"

"Sure. Is something, like, bad happening, man?"

Marc shook his head. "There's nothing for you to be concerned." After acquiring the sample, he returned to Randolph. "How do we find out what's in this tea?"

"I guess we send it to Anchorage. Why the tea? I still think the honey is tainted with a strong agent which induces paralysis."

Marc pulled him aside, away from any of the others. "A theory. What if the ingredient or ingredients can be pulverized and added to the tea? What if these two young ladies are aboard to extract revenge for the actions which occurred the other day? My question remains. Who contacted them and how did they get credentials for boarding?"

"Someone other than the steward must run the organization on this ship. Someone who has the ability and authority to allow people on board."

Marc squared his shoulders, "Any idea who might have that authority, other than Captain Dalgaard?"

"If someone can get in the system, they can make whatever is needed. A couple of other people might have that authority. I don't. Maybe Thorsen, Camacho, the supervisory steward?"

"So two people who still operate aboard and could be the key to all of these attacks. Our young rat may not have known all of the people who were part of the cartel. We need to watch for anyone who is acting out of the normal mode of operations." Marc departed for his suite taking the sample with him. He trusted few people because of the last three days. Someone wanted him dead.

Entering the Elliot Bay, he found his daughter, Sarah, asleep and Joan in bed waiting for his return. "What was that all about?" Her question yielded a smile. He placed the tea on the counter by the window.

"Another person experienced a non-lethal dose of "we're out to get you. I don't know why this person was targeted, but the fact remains. Someone is out to do harm. Those two young ladies who came aboard yesterday are vixens with venomous intentions."

Joan asked, "The twins you saw? Why? How are they involved?"

"One of them was with the patient Middlebury's working on. The other was with a player in the band. That is some tea she fixed for him."

"And you think the tea is tainted?"

Marc nodded, climbed into bed, and kissed Joan. The next few hours before daylight were fraught with imagery of two women coaxing Marc to betray a trust and enticing Joan to join them. Young Marcus was not immune to the allure within his mind. Sleep was not restful.

At breakfast the family sat in the Lido Restaurant watching the ship sail into Glacier Bay. Other cruise ships had the same destination. As they ate, Marc noticed the band members gathered in a corner area accompanied by the manager who appeared recovered from the early morning medical crisis.

Marcus watched his father and said. "Do you know them. They're one of the hot new groups out of Seattle."

"Not really." Inconclusive evasion seemed the best action for the moment. Delinda and Randolph approached from the other side of the ship.

"Good morning," Randolph said with a lilt in his voice. "I hope you got enough sleep." Delinda unhooked her arm from her father and sat in a chair she pulled from an empty table and sat next to Marcus.

"Marc, you have a sec?"

"Sure." He stood and walked a short distance away from any piercing ears. "The manager is recovering because I don't think he received a heavy enough dose of the poison. It makes little sense to me. Why him?"

"I don't know. It may have been an opportune moment to test the potency of a new batch of poison. These girls came aboard yesterday. They may have brought it with them. How's Delinda holding up? Is she curious about the late night antics?"

"She slept through it." He looked at her, now tightly holding onto Marcus. "Will your son let her down gently when this trip is over?"

"I don't think he wants to let go. He's made comments which indicate there may be more to their relationship than a ship board romance." They gazed at the couple both thinking they were too young for anything serious.

Marc observed Jarina Camacho approach the band and speak to the manager. He couldn't make out any words, but it appeared she showed concerns for his health problem. They shook hands and she walked away. Another pair of beauties also met with the members of the band. Joaquin stood and spoke with one of the twins, while the manager asked for the other to sit with him. Ironic, Marc thought. These ladies are intent on destruction but make friendly with the objects of their late night prank.

Randolph interrupted his machinations. "Do you think they meant no harm? Maybe we're wrong about them. He did invite them to the party." Marc faced him.

"Maybe, but caution is the better part of valor. Let's join our families."

As they sat and finished eating, the twins rose from the tables where the band sat. Joaquin followed one of them, bidding farewell to his cohorts. The other twin walked by Marc and surveyed his family as she approached. She then eyed Marc and pursed her lips. He stared as she walked to the other side of the ship. Sarah asked, "Who's that?"

Marc admired his daughter, "Just another passenger." He looked toward the vixen's route, but she was gone. Joan frowned. "Let's go out on the observation deck and watch the glaciers. Maybe it will calve for us." His ire was mounting and a distraction might help.

As the children separated from their parents, Marc, Joan, and Randolph hung together by the railing. A thunderous cracking alerted them to ice slipping from the face. The three looked to see the water whirling where the calf had dropped. "Is she a threat?" Joan asked. Marc remained focused on the Margerie Glacier and Grand Pacific Glacier. He had no answer.

After a reflective moment he said, "I don't know. Randolph and I encountered the results of her activities last night, but there's no evidence of any foul play." He placed an arm around her shoulders. She laid her head on his chest. A large berg separated from the face of Margerie creating a large wave. The crackling followed. Was his life as fragile as the ice? Enough pressure and it collapses?

# CHAPTER

# 38

The four family members looked back at the two engine Cessna which had flown them from Juneau, Alaska to Skagway. "Man, this is some vacation we're on." Tiberius slapped his brother, Jeremais, on the back as they led their wives away from the mail carrier.

Gabrielle whispered to Lydia, "These boys are losing touch with reality."

"What'd you say?" Jerry asked. The men turned and walked backward, grinning from ear to ear. "Do you think we have gone crazy?" A man pushing a cart passed them. Three mail bags, five large corrugated boxes, and four suitcases occupied it. "We are on an adventure."

Lydia answered, "I put up with your insane idea of killing yourself. I have witnessed my family members get shot and beaten severely. I have lived in fear of one or more of you dying. So, yes, Gabby is ᵗ You are losing touch with reality."

ᵗʰ̣ey know we are meeting them when the ship arrives Gabby asked.

ᵈded, "I left Marc a message when we finished ᵗted the information of our coming here and to veryone. You both agreed to this investigation us to disguise our true intent. Please, don't be mad."

Jerry spoke next. "Sometimes investigations aren't exactly by the book. So let's have some fun while we await the next part of our trip. We'll retrieve the files which should have arrived in one of those mail bags." He laced fingers in Lydia's hand. Gabby locked her arm in Tiberius's arm. The remainder of the stroll to the baggage claim area, such as it was, was quiet.

A college aged girl stood next to a Buick Skylark from another era of auto history. "Needing a ride to your hotel or cabin rental? I'm the only taxi in town." Her raven locks twirled about her face and cascaded across her back and chest. Flecks of golden thread-like hairs interlaced the darker tresses. Emerald eyes, peering at the foursome, glistened in the summer sun. She towered above the roof of the car with a fit frame. The rich red of her lips and the gilt tone of her cheeks contrasted the plaid shirt and cargo pants of her outfit. Hiking boots finished the odd ensemble.

The four adventurers braved the unusual manner and explained their need to head for the Westmark Inn, home for the next couple of days. "Where y'all from?" She volunteered an answer before anyone else. "I'm from Tennessee. Come up here in the summer to make money for college. I attend Sewanee. I'm studying environmental science and anthropology as it relates to native populations. Oh, but where are my manners. I asked where you hail from." A grin exposed teeth like snow and neatly ordered because of orthodontia.

Tiberius answered, "We hail from Washington State."

"That's a beautiful state. I visit there when I finish here. My brother works for Microsoft and his wife is a doctor at Eastside General." The car ended its trip in front the of a rustic building. "We're here." She removed the bags from the spacious trunk and held out a hand. Tiberius and Jeremais retrieved them and headed for the front entrance. Gabby and Lydia shrugged and handed her an appropriate amount for travel and tip. "Let me know when you need a ride." She slipped into the driver side and disappeared to find another mark.

As they checked into the two rooms they reserved, Tibe asked the clerk, "How soon does mail get delivered after it a by plane?"

"Are you expecting something? We usually receive the morning flight by late this afternoon. Did you fly with it? If so, I can watch for anything which is addressed for you."

"Another perky young lady in town for the summer," thought Tiberius. She had a swagger which seemed a part of the history of the 1898 Klondike Gold Rush jumping off spot.

"Yes, thanks. I'll check back with you." The four of them followed the direction to the rooms which were neat, clean, and surprisingly roomy. "I guess this will do." Alone for the first time in many hours, he grabbed Gabby and crushed her into his body. "I love you for going along with this. I promise nothing bad will happen."

She kissed his cheek and pushed away from him. "It has already. Our son has a new part in his hairline and our grandson was nearly poisoned to death. So don't promise what you can't deliver."

"Fair enough. But Jerry and I must finish this, for good. We've sacrificed enough time and energy, as well as, bodily injury to let any of these people succeed in rebuilding."

A knock interrupted them. Gabby opened the door. "You ready for some adventure?" Jerry had changed clothes into western attire. Lydia remained in her traveling clothes. They left to walk the downtown of Skagway and find out about the Chilkoot Trail, Soapy Smith, and the gold rush. Time was an asset for them.

◦◦◦◦◦◦◦

Cayde Thorsen stepped across the stage and knocked on Jarina's office door. "Hello," she purred, and signaled for him to enter. She closed the door and latched it from intruders. "What may I do for you?" He wrapped an arm around her waist, pulling her to him.

When finished with the tryst, they dressed. As he readied to leave, he said, "Keep those two friends of yours under control. They were dangerously close to tipping their hands last night with the members of one of the bands."

"They are very good at what they do. If they are taunting Mr. Jefferson, their intentions are sound. I will remind them who is in charge, and you need to remember, as well."

He nodded and left her to formulate the next assault of the antagonists to rebuilding the cartel and locating it somewhere other than Snohomish County. He didn't appreciate being threatened, but his compromise with her satisfied him. His family was safe from retribution and retirement from sailing was closer than before. She fulfilled the physical desires he missed while at sea.

Arriving on the bridge in time for his shift, he oversaw the sailing out of Glacier Bay and toward Lynn Canal and Skagway. His morning interlude relaxed his mind except his concerns about the twins. He had been instrumental in their boarding when the steward approached him about the request. He fulfilled his part of the bargain and Jarina rewarded him with a night together. Now he concentrated on piloting the ship from bay to the head of the fjord.

The day warmed as the ship plied the cold waters of Alaska. The pilot navigated with skill from years of following the same course. He flipped the twins from his brain; Jarina was responsible for them. His main concern was Dalgaard.

Marcus and Delinda wandered the aft recreation area hoping to lose James and Sarah. Alone time had not happened since the suite treat. "I feel bad leaving them behind," Marcus said, "but I want to be alone with you."

"As long as those bad guys are gone, Sarah and James will be okay." Delinda squeezed his hand as they squirreled around to the staircase. Three flights later Marcus stopped and clasp his raven-haired beauty around her waist. They locked lips. When he opened his eyes two young women smiled at him. They were exotic and alike. He returned the smile. Delinda turned to discover why Marcus was smiling. They smiled again at her.

After another flight of stairs and he slammed on the brakes. "Those girls looked familiar."

"What? Did you find them attractive? I mean, like, they smiled because they saw us kissing."

"Yeah, probably. Let's go to my room." Walking a few paces faster than needed, he kept thinking where he had seen them. Dad's paranoia about people was rubbing off.

Flashing his key card on the lock, he pushed open the door and stepped aside for Delinda to enter. Letting the door close, he stood attentive to other thoughts than making love to Dee. "Are you alright," she asked. "Are we going to do it or not?"

"I remember where I saw them." He closed distance and placed hands on her shoulders. "They were at breakfast this morning. One of them passed our table and I saw her blow a kiss to Dad." He dropped his arms. "Sarah asked who she was. Dad was evasive."

"Was that when our dads didn't want us to hear what they were saying?"

He turned toward his veranda and back to Dee. "He knew who she was, and he doesn't want us to know." He slapped his hands against his thighs. "He's involved with her somehow."

"You mean, like, having an affair?" Delinda's eyes widened and hands splayed.

"What? No. Dad's as faithful as a dog. No, I mean she's not here to be his friend; she's here to harm him. I don't know why, but with what has happened, it seems reasonable."

"Marcus, are you crazy? I know someone attacked him and all, but the bad guys are in jail." She clasped his head in her hands. "I came with you to make love and now you're scaring me." She kissed him, but his return had little passion in it. His family was in trouble.

# CHAPTER

# 39

Standing on the veranda of their Elliot Bay suite, Joan and Marc marveled at the beauty of the Lynn Canal leading into one of the starting points for the Klondike miners. Without changing focus on the landscape or what he had to reveal, he said, "I have a surprise for you." Joan faced him, but he kept concentrating on the view.

"I don't want any more surprises. I asked you to look into Blackthorne's death, but what has happened goes beyond allowing for another surprise."

"Dad's in Skagway." He watched the wake pass. Joan bopped in on the shoulder.

"Quit scaring me." A grin crept his face.

"Mom, Uncle Jerry, and Aunt Lydia are here, too." His facial crease broke open to expose teeth. "They flew up yesterday when we were in Glacier Bay. He left me a note about it but asked me to say nothing."

"Does he have any information to help finish the last of the investigation?"

Facing her he said, "I don't know. It depends on whether he received any mail from Seattle." His smile faded as he gazed at her. "I love you." A clatter inside alerted them to Sarah's return. They entered to greet her and James.

"Mom, Dad, Marcus and Dee ditched us." James stood behind her not caring about being abandoned.

"Where did they go?" Mom asked an empty question. Abandonment sent shivers through her. Any attack was not what she wanted. Marc was better, but the wound left a horrid scar on his head and in her heart.

"I don't know," Sarah whispered. The knock on the door interrupted them. Marc opened it and found their missing son.

"Dad, those twins, we saw them." He dragged Delinda into the room. "They were smiling at us like we were part of their next scam."

"What are you talking about?"

"Dad, I remember her at breakfast. She blew you a kiss. I figured you knew she was out to get you, since you wouldn't dare step out on Mom." A snicker snorted from Marc's nose. "Come on, Dad, they shot you and poisoned the author and James. The security guy's son almost died."

"Someone's imagination is running wild." Joan planted a hand on his free arm since Delinda occupied the other. "Marcus, your father is the detective in this family."

"But I know what I saw. She sent you a message."

Marc said, "Are you sure a pretty woman is not attracted to an older man?"

A chorus of "eww" erupted from younger people. Laugher trailed from parents.

"Dee, is your father available in the infirmary?" Marc fronted her despite his son's interference. She shrugged.

"I've been with Marcus, Sarah, and James all day."

"Alright, stay here while I check something out with him." He left.

Joan asked, "Marcus, Delinda, when you were ditching Sarah and James, where did you go and when did you see those girls?"

"We were in the rear and had gone down a couple flights. They were there and just smiled at us."

"I want you to stay together. We aren't finished with our trip and need to be on the lookout for any problems."

"Gees, Mom, are we in trouble? You said we weren't and now you want us to look out for trouble. I can take care of Dee and me."

Olivia greeted Marc as he entered, "Good to see you, Mr. Jefferson."

Marc smiled. "Good to see you, as well. Is Randolph in?"

"He left a few minutes ago to meet with Dalgaard." Marc nodded and turned to leave. "By the way, I have a question for you."

He faced her and waited for her to speak. She closed the distance.

"Well? What's your question?" She leaned toward him, swiveled her head right, then left.

"Do you suspect any other members of the crew?"

"Like who?"

"That's the problem. I don't know. You're the detective."

"So I hear. I think we have a couple of ladies who came aboard in Juneau who might be involved. Nothing I can pin on them."

"The girls from last night? With the band?" Marc rocked his head. "Who are they?'

"They don't seem to be part of the crew. But if the truth includes the fact they brought tainted honey with them, then my family is not safe. And I'm not sure Middlebury or his daughter is either." Another swivel of her head and she cleared a path for Marc to leave. "Let him know I'm looking for him, if I don't find him soon." He left.

Marc rode an elevator to the upper levels of the ship. Finding one of the officers, he asked about the captain. "Can you escort me to his whereabouts?"

"Sir, I have no authority to allow you in navigation or on the bridge, since you are a passenger." He left Marc wondering. Was he another member of the cartel? Was anyone not part of the cartel? Middlebury seemed a key to solving the mysteries aboard. Where to look?

Jarina approached from behind him. "Hello, detective." An ugly sound escaped his throat. "Oh. I'm sorry. I didn't mean to scare you."

A sigh followed. "That's alright." His heart calmed and irises contracted. "Have you seen Dr. Middlebury?" Watching her chest rise as she inhaled and held her breath, and then fall when she released. Her head rose and tilted right with eyes rolling upward.

"I think I saw him with Captain Dalgaard in the dining area." Her voice squeaked as she continued, "Are you okay? Do you need medical help?" A twinkle gleamed as she focused on his face. She glanced at his wound. "Does that hurt?" She pointed as if she wanted to touch it. He winced.

"No, but don't touch, please." Brushing her hand away from his head, he asked, "Do you have any pull getting new passengers on board, or know who does?" He watched for a tell as skilled as any poker player. She remained steady.

"Do we have new passengers? I usually know who comes on board, but no one was scheduled for entry in Juneau. That doesn't mean someone wasn't accepted. I can check."

"Thanks. I'd appreciate it." He walked away from her without looking at her. She lied to him. Dag was to return to the ship in Skagway. He would know the procedure.

At the dining room Marc scanned for anyone sitting at a table. The room was empty on the first floor. He ascended the stairs to the second deck and found his targets. Approaching them he formulated a question for the captain. Who, besides him, had the authority?

"Gentlemen, am I glad to find you." He sat in the chair next to Middlebury. "Captain, we have two ladies who came aboard in Juneau. Who, other than you, has authority to grant them access, if they had not prearranged to join this journey?"

Dalgaard scrunched his forehead. "If I understand you, two passengers are aboard and I have no information about them? I get the manifest for each city we visit and new passengers do come aboard. As far as I know, no one came aboard in Juneau. I'll ask Cayde if he accepted new passengers, but he should have informed me for final say."

Middlebury spoke next. "Twin girls in their late twenties. We had an incident with the manager of one of the music acts getting sick very much like Blackthorne and the steward, Iskandar. These twins, invited to an after party, were there when he fell ill. They followed Marc around Juneau. We need to understand who they are and more important, why they're here."

Marc leaned toward Dalgaard, "When did you suspect something was wrong aboard your ship?" He sat back in his chair.

"About a year ago a new crew included some people who were

new to cruise work. Their training in Seattle seemed right but soon after the first voyage north, I noticed some anomalies in operations. Things didn't seem right, but I had no evidence of any sort. When we returned to Seattle, I approached corporate and relayed my concerns. They assigned a federal person to travel with us the next trip. He found nothing. So corporate removed him and asked me to keep looking. I asked an old friend to be my security chief and Dag said yes. We formulated a plan and began collecting information. He's played the incompetent inspector well. This trip his son traveled with us as a favor." Dalgaard placed arms on the table and watched for reactions from Marc and his doctor.

Remaining back in his seat, Marc's comment seemed obvious. "Well, something is certainly wrong." His next surprised the two members of the crew. "Which of you is part of the problem? I don't mean that you are part of the group undermining the integrity of the American Pacific Cruise Line. However, if you are correct and this has been going on for a year, who on the crew did you suspect? A new person or one of your regulars?"

Dalgaard picked up his arms. "I asked my second in command to collect work schedules and compare anomalies to their work. Cayde Thorsen found a few things which amounted to nothing. Until the death of Mr. Blackthorne and the attacks on you and Jorgen, we have had a hard time proving anything. Your presence aboard has changed the dynamics."

"Since the dismissal of six members of the crew, has anyone stuck out to you?" Marc leaned forward. "Do you trust your top officers?" Dalgaard remained silent. Which of his command could be corrupt?

# CHAPTER

# 40

With the last line tied to the pier, and the gangway placed, passengers departed for investigations of the 1898 Klondike Gold Rush jump off point. Train rides, eagle observation tours, stories of Soapy Smith, and Frank Reid killing the notorious con man, and salmon barbecues awaited them. Jarina bid goodbye to each individual or family as they checked out through the security gate.

Kerrine and Kaliana passed by without acknowledging her, a request to keep their relationship anonymous. As others departed, she wondered when the Jefferson clan might leave. The plan was in place. All that was needed was for the participants to show. Thorsen and Dalgaard had met, according to Cayde, and discussed the twin's arrival. He assured the captain he would investigate and resolve the enigma.

She did not want another cataclysmic disaster. Her escape plan remained ready if anything happened. Jefferson was more of a challenge than she anticipated. Eliminating him was a priority but such an act would raise snakes she didn't want to kill.

Delinda and Marcus arrived at the gangway. "Good morning. Are you off to an adventure?"

"We're going to look around town and meet my parents for lunch." Marcus held Delinda's hand for assurance, his as well as hers. "They should be here shortly." After scanning their key cards, they descended the walkway and strolled to the town which had been home to thousands of eager adventurers over a century earlier.

Jarina excused herself and left the checkpoint. An idea entered her brain to elicit assistance from Olivia Breckenridge. Her loyalty to the cartel was shaky in Jarina's mind, but no evidence or action had compromised their concordance. Now was a good time to use her relationship with Middlebury to distract him. The plan made sense with him under control.

"Olivia, where is Middlebury?" Jarina stood in the infirmary. "I need you to keep him occupied."

Olivia guffawed, "What are you talking about? He has his duties as doctor. He'll be in as soon as Delinda's gone with that Jefferson kid."

"They just left. The rest of the Jefferson brood is still aboard, so I need to be assured you stay with our doctor."

"Will do." She returned to some paperwork she was completing when interrupted by the cruise director. "By the way, who do we connect with aboard this ship when you are busy? Who else is part of our small group?"

Jarina scowled and harrumphed. "We are the last of our group. The six who left in Juneau were the main contingent. The process has been severed. We will regroup and rebuild. Are you with me?"

"I guess. I just wasn't sure what you wanted from me. Keeping Randolph company is a pleasure, but what is the end result?"

"You needn't concern yourself about what end result occurs. Do as I ask." She turned to leave but then faced Olivia. "This phase of the operation may be finished. One more task to accomplish and then we can leave this hell hole and find another place to live and work."

"An honest endeavor?" Olivia gazed at Jarina. "I kind of like what I'm doing."

"Whatever, I want more than this and I have prospects. You can stay as long as you want." She left Olivia snickering. Her temper rising.

Returning to the gangway, she checked the registry. Jefferson and clan had departed. Time to replace the cameras in the suite. Compromising videos would control him and his meddling wife. The twins promised their wiles were irresistible. They could prove their worth on the way to Anchorage. Personal honey and bee honey made a perfect match.

⤞⬿◉⬾⤝

"Dee, let me get your picture in front of the train. Then we can go to the visitor center over there." He pointed. She posed and he clicked a couple of pictures. An older man volunteered to take a picture of them both in front of the engine. Marcus adored the idea of having a beautiful girlfriend and the comments by the man and his companion, which he figured was the man's wife, reinforced his commitment to staying in contact when the voyage ended. He did not want to lose her. He started school in the fall at Olympic College in Wendlesburg but had not uncovered her plans once school began in September.

They walked to the small museum and visitor center. Watching the movie was not easy as the darkness of the room encouraged his desire to kiss her. She played coy but reciprocated. After the movie they wandered to the White Pass and Yukon Railroad station and purchased tickets to ride up to the Canadian border. The pass had an afternoon time stamped on it. Leaving the station, he bumped into a remarkably attractive young woman who smiled and apologized. He thought little of it and continued toward the main part of Skagway. When he and Delinda stopped in at a shop, he realized his wallet was missing. The attractive brunette had picked his pocket.

"Damn it." His expletive surprised Delinda.

"What's the matter?"

"That lady I bumped into at the train station stole my wallet."

"Did you lose anything valuable?"

"Not much, my pride. I'm the son of a cop. I should have known better. I think I remember what she looks like. I'll keep an eye out for her. I won't be her only mark today."

Dee hugged his left arm and placed her head on his shoulder. "Guess I need to protect you from wanton women. Skagway has a reputation for loose morals and looser women." She kissed him. "I'm the only loose woman you can take advantage of. Clear?" He kissed her.

As they walked the streets of the small burg at the end of Lynn Canal, another person approached and stopped to talk. "I saw what that woman did to you at the train depot. I think I know where she is, if you want what she took from you returned."

The red hair, an obvious dye worn by many teenagers, and dark glasses to fight the glare, muted her looks. Marcus, eager for retribution, agreed to accompany the attractive woman. Dee pulled him aside. "I don't trust her. She may be working in concert with the other one."

"I know. Let's check out what she has and we'll be careful." Delinda bobbed her head, and the venture to find the perpetrator began. The three people moved from the main area of town to a small house on the east side near the train repair facility. Nearing the building they spotted their target entering the front door.

Marcus followed and approached the door. Delinda pulled on his arm. "I'm scared. Let's call the police. They can handle this." He detached from her and knocked.

The face which came to the door had a familiarity from the ship. She was blond, but the features were Hispanic and clothing hid nothing of the shapeliness of her body. He turned and saw Delinda slumped in the arms of the other woman whose features matched. The prick in his neck ended his search.

<hr />

Marc and Joan directed their two children to accompany them to the hotel where Tiberius and Jerry resided with Gabby and Lydia. "Glad you made it," Tiberius said. "I have some information from Seattle which I had sent to us. Very interesting information." They sat in the Sweet Tooth Cafe awaiting the arrival of Marcus and Delinda. An envelope lay on the table, the contents spread out for Marc to peruse.

Tiberius continued. "So we have a report from the delivery company which is contracted by American Pacific to transport flowers and baskets to the ship, that one of the trucks was hijacked by two women. The men, who were scheduled to drive the truck from the Seattle warehouse to the dock, were found drugged or more possibly poisoned in a motel on Aurora Avenue. Neither will be telling tales. Witnesses say they arrived with two women and only the women left later in the day. The two men must have picked up the women or more likely they were seduced before making their delivery."

"Was any evidence of the women found at the scene?" Marc asked.

"That's the queer part of this. There were no signs or traces of any evidence of females in the room. Yet, the manager had them on his security recording arriving and leaving."

Joan interjected, "Marc, I'm worried about Marcus and Delinda. They should have met us here by now."

"They'll be fine. Not much can happen in a town this size. It's hard to get lost."

"We'll keep an eye out for them," Uncle Jerry responded. They'll be back on the ship before it leaves. They probably got tickets to ride the train to the Canadian border and forgot about meeting you."

Joan winced, "You better be right. If something happened to Marcus, I couldn't handle it."

"I don't think Randolph would handle losing his only child." Marc expressed.

"We're staying here tonight. If they miss the boat, we'll put them on a flight to Anchorage with us."

"Thanks, Dad." Marc placed a reassuring hand on Joan's arm. She wriggled and frowned.

"Ti, they don't know how to find you and I have no idea where they are. I called his cell phone; it went to voice."

Jerry reassured his niece, "You've raised a fine young man. He has a level head and can solve intricate problems. We'll find him and his girlfriend."

Joan stood and moved away from them. Sarah joined her. "Mom, is Marcus in trouble?" Tears flooded her mother's eyes. Arms embraced her. Tears streamed from her, as well. Marc encircled his girls. Crisis after crisis. When would an end embrace all of them?

# CHAPTER

# 41

"Kaliana, take these back to the ship and give them to Jarina. I'll stay here and entertain our guests." Kerrine handed her the key cards for Marcus and Delinda. "If she is working the scanner, be sure to get them done. If not, hold them until you can deliver them to her. We have our instructions. Let's finish the clean-up as Jarina asked."

"Kerrine, don't do anything foolish like letting them go." A smirk crossed her face. "After you finish with him, please let me know how much he begged to be released. How much he begged for you to leave his tramp alone. I'll let you know what it was like to seduce my target and compromise his life."

They hugged and had one last look at Marcus and Delinda lying next to each other on a queen bed, unconscious. The straps from one arm and one ankle each tied to the bed frame secured them from escaping. Their other arms and ankles were tied to each other and then to the frame.

"They look so peaceful," Kerrine said. "He is a beautiful specimen of a boy. I can see why she's attracted to him." Clothing had been removed from the victims.

"Will you play with her?" Kaliana stroked Delinda's hair and then kissed her nipples.

"I may, but I do want to have him. You should enjoy a wonderful time with his father, if he is anything like his son." She caressed him as she spoke. "Now get out of here."

Kaliana left for the ship, still sporting red hair and dark glasses. She had changed clothing to appear more touristy in case a member of the Jefferson family spotted her. Kerrine checked the bindings to be sure no one was departing before her fun was complete. A groan escaped from Marcus as she checked the last strap on Delinda's ankle. His eyes blinked as consciousness returned. He jerked at the confinement shifting Delinda.

"Welcome back, Mr. Jefferson. I wasn't sure when you would awaken. I do hope your head doesn't hurt very much. It was a strong sedative and does have a nasty habit of leaving you with a migraine for a while. If you behave, I'll give you some nice strong tea and honey to help alleviate it."

He glanced at the straps and his naked body. "What do you want?" He rolled his head to find Dee and the bindings on his arm and ankle. She lay still and naked. "I guess you're one of the twins."

"Oh, you are a smart boy, aren't you? I suppose I should expect nothing less. Now as to your question, I want to enjoy an afternoon with you and your friend. Then we'll engage in an early evening party of tea and crumpets. What do you say to that?"

Marcus attempted to bend his right leg but the strap to the bed post prevented it. "What do you mean, you want to have some fun? Where are my clothes?"

"You won't be needing those until later. As a matter of proper decorum, I should remove mine. That way we'll all be able to enjoy the fun in a more natural environment." She unbuttoned her shirt and removed it. "Do you like what you see?" Marcus closed his eyes.

She unhooked her belt, sliding it out of the loops. Dangling the buckle above his abdomen, she dipped it to touch him, then lifted it. "I can use this to convince you to cooperate or maybe you can watch her as I use it on her." Her smile faded. She placed the belt on a chair and undid the buttons of her jeans. She folded and put them on the same chair. He stared at her, daggers flying as he tensed muscles.

"You want to see more?" He turned his head when a moan alerted them to another awakening. Delinda tightened and screamed, thrashing to no avail. "You mustn't make any noise, or you'll miss the fun." Kerrine walked to her side and covered her mouth with a folded towel. "I can hold this until you are quiet of your own accord or you simply stop breathing." Placing a hand around Delinda's neck, she said. "Please be a dear and relax, so nobody hurts you. You might enjoy the festivities I have planned." The begging subsided.

As silence filled the room, Kerrine removed the last articles of clothing. "There, now we are all set to play a game of who wants to have me first. I do believe, Mr. Jefferson, that you should be first." She climbed on the bed and straddled his abdomen. She placed a finger on his lips and said, "Make no sound or I'll use my belt on her. And I will bite your little friend if you fight me." Delinda filled her lungs with air and held it. Her eyes closed.

"Please be kind enough to watch. I will teach you how to benefit from these lessons." Her hand reached for the warm skin between Delinda's thighs. "I do believe I feel an expansion beneath me."

Marcus spoke, "Do what you want but don't hurt her. It's me you want to humiliate, to get back at my father. I don't even know what he's done to you."

"Your father is a pariah. He acts so high and mighty. Once he has his lesson in humility with my sister, no one in your family will live in respect. He destroyed my family. Now I get to destroy yours. But I want some fun first." She removed herself from atop him. He lay still, rage burning in his soul as she did what she wanted to his body. Useless to resist he sent his mind to other places and fought the physical reaction she initiated. When she was satisfied with her results, she placed her body on his and moved until he could not hold any longer.

"Thank you," she said. "Now, Delinda, I am going to release your hand. I want you to take him with your mouth. Do it or I will remove it from him." Kerrine untied the binding from the post and pulled the strap across the bed until Delinda's head was in the same place Kerrine's body had been. "Take it. Now."

Grabbing a fist of hair, Kerrine forced her head up and down. She choked, a gag reflex to her head being manipulated. "Keep going until he finishes."

"Stop it. I don't have any more to give."

Kerrine held Delinda's head down suffocating her as she struggled to breathe. "Well, I guess she stops now and dies." She let the head up as coughing replaced gagging.

"Alright, you've had your fun. Let her off me."

"Oh, Marcus, we're not finished yet. I want to watch you and her."

"You're sadistic."

"No, sadistic would have me dismember you and force it into her body. That would be a waste." She forced Delinda's head down again but the game was over. Holding the strap, she let Delinda's head up and moved to other side of the bed and untied her ankle from the post. Pulling both straps across the bed, she fitted the ankle knot over Marcus's ankle strap and pulled it tight. Delinda's body caressed Marcus's lower abdomen. Kerrine tied the wrist strap to the post holding Marcus's wrist. Her body covered his. Kerrine planted a kiss on each buttock and then slapped them.

"Do enjoy each other for now. I am going to make some tea and when I return we will have another party." She robed herself and left the bedroom.

Tears dropped on Marcus's face. "Dee, we'll get out of this. She has to free us so we can drink her tea." Tears continued cascading on his cheeks.

"She's going to kill us, isn't she?"

"I don't think so. She needs us for some reason. I haven't figured it out, yet. We'll play along and when an opportunity arises I'll make my move." Dee lay her head on Marcus. He sensed her breathing become more steady. The sobbing halted. The touch of her breasts roused remembrance of their first encounter. Time was not a benefit for him as he thought of an escape. If they were to die, he wanted a fight.

A whistling kettle alerted his ears that only a few minutes remained before their captor would return. Delinda raised a little. "Now? Incredible." He maneuvered his body to be free from beneath her pelvis.

Kerrine returned with a tray containing two mugs steaming with hot tea and a pot containing more. Crackers on a plate and a jar of yellow fluid completed the ensemble. Placing the tray on a side table, she noticed the predicament of her captive couple. "On my, this simply will not do. How are you to enjoy a last tryst if you can't conjoin bodies. Let me fix that for you." Her hands teased them for a moment. "Now move and when finished, I'll free you for our tea party." She sat in the chair and watched.

Delinda whispered, "It's okay. Just do it so we can get out of here."

"I don't want her to have the satisfaction."

"Please, I want to return to the ship." He completed the task to the glee of his Hispanic sentry. She stood and loosened Delinda's wrist strap from the post.

"You will remain calm while I remove your ankle and retie it." She held a knife in her hand. "If you try anything, he's going to bleed to death when I cut it off." Delinda cooperated. "Now for the party. I do believe you two need to regain some strength. Please feed him a cracker and have him drink some tea. I sweetened it with some special honey I brought with me." She handed Delinda a cracker which was placed in his mouth. The honey lacing it had a bitter-sweet taste. He swallowed. One mug of tea followed after Kerrine poured some honey into it. Delinda placed it on his mouth and tilted the cup. He sipped the hot liquid and winced.

"I'm sorry," Kerrine pined, "is it too hot?" She pushed the cup against his lips. "Drink it all." Tears formed as he burned his throat with each gulp. When the mug was empty, she handed the other to Delinda and said, "Drink it all or he bleeds." She wielded the knife close to his body. Delinda drank all of the liquid which burned her throat. After another two cups each, Kerrine dressed and left them tied to the bed posts.

"Enjoy your last moments together. I will be returning to the ship now."

Marcus complained, "You can't just leave us here." She smiled.

"You won't have to worry for very long. I doubt anyone will find you before the end comes. I'll greet your parents for you when I see them." She stayed another hour to watch the effects of the party creep through them. As sweat broke out, cramping and heart arrhythmias wracked their bodies. She left them to suffer a fate Marcus recognized when James fell ill.

# CHAPTER

## 42

Kaliana ascended the ramp to the scanners looking for Jarina. One of the crew sat at the machine as she held her key for the red laser to record her return. She said nothing as she handed Jarina an envelope containing the key cards of Marcus and Delinda. A conversation later would update the fate of two offspring. She returned to her room to clean the dye from her hair and change clothing. She expected her sister within the next couple of hours.

The warm shower water cascaded through her hair and refreshed her body. As she shampooed, the red dye ran as blood down the drain. She remembered the carnage she witnessed in Everett when the Snohomish Sheriff office coordinated with Everett police, raided the warehouses of Andrew Pepper. She and two other women had hidden from the hail of bullets which penetrated walls and windows.

Jefferson had been one of the officers. She remembered the face of the man, clear as a washed window. He wouldn't remember her nor care about the loss she suffered. He would remember after the night was over. He would care about the loss he was to suffer. Life compromised with another woman. Divorce. Children abandoning him. Death would be a welcome exchange for his humiliation.

As she dressed in a summer ensemble designed to entice men to ogle, her motif was to approach Jefferson and hand him the note. Wait for his response and meet him in her suite. He had to come to discover what happened to his son. He had to succumb to her and love it. Not just like it. Then Kerrine would join and feed him his last supper.

The two days sailing to Anchorage would be tense. The loss of a passenger was hard to explain, but Middlebury, compromised by his daughter's kidnapping, would support a report of death from natural causes.

How to separate Jefferson from his family was the challenge. The note stated Marcus and Delinda had been kidnapped. She was to act as intermediary to resolve the conditions for their return. Seduction was one of the conditions. If he cared for his family and their safety, he would accede to a tryst. Then the other twin would arrive with the location of the missing children. After some tea and honey, he could send for them. The video would be the instrumentation to force him to accept whatever the kidnappers wanted.

The plan was simple. Read the note. Follow the directions. Believe the safety of children was guaranteed. Die.

Kaliana returned to the gangway to watch Jarina signal whether her target had returned. As she descended in the elevator, her mind slipped into imagining her sister and the Jefferson boy. His death would not come as easily as the man in the Edmonds hotel or the two drivers they seduced. He was more physically fit than they were. Delinda was not petite, but her death should be more sure and painful. The bing awakened her attention to the present. The doors opened and she departed. Jarina looked her way and swayed her head from side to side. Turning, she decided to ascend the stairs and ride the elevator on the next floor to the lounge on the Lido deck. Time was an ally.

With a Mai Tai to sooth any anxiety and sunshine affectively calming her, she sat embracing the actions soon to commence. Her mind recalled the scene in the warehouse, rearing its ugly head as she remembered his voice committing them to safety, away from danger. She recalled the calming, but cold words, when silence signaled the end of the hostilities. He was doing his job, she enjoined with a sneer. He had no empathy for the drastic alteration of her life in the near fatal attack. Heat rose, not from any sun, but from a roiling anger implanted on that day. She had learned her uncle was lost to her and Pepper was reportedly dead. Her wounds were internal, despisal for the end of much of her family and fear of discovery of her true position in the cartel.

When Kerrine proposed nearly six years ago they use their identical beauty to eliminate antagonists of Andrew Pepper, she balked. Their first unfortunate person tested the integrity of Pepper's business interests and the order was given for an intervention. Finding their weapon of choice aroused her competitive sisterly love. Participation demonstrated an exhilaration she missed from days in high school disrupting other students' romantic liaisons.

As the investigation ground to a halt involving the unfortunate older gentleman's demise, she observed the effectiveness of using an unexpected and unusual weapon. After six successful operations she adopted Kerrine's new employment plan. The next target was hers alone. A man who should not be underestimated. A family which could undermine her plan.

Jarina walked by and dropped a small envelope on the table. Kaliana picked it up and removed the contents, two key cards. One gave her entry to a doctor. The other to a younger brother.

Marc, Tiberius, and Jerry searched the streets of Skagway, while Joan and the children returned to the ship. Gabrielle and Lydia checked tourist spots for any trace of the two young lovers. All evidence pointed to nothing bad happening, but a mother's instinct kicked Joan into action. She wanted assurance they were not aboard the ship. Sarah and James stayed in the suite, while she went to Middlebury to find out if Delinda had returned.

"I haven't seen her since she left with Marcus. Let me contact the office and find out if they returned. The key cards will tell us." Middlebury picked up the com-phone. After some time, he nodded his head and hung up. "Their cards were scanned about two hours ago. Supposedly, they're aboard."

"Then where are they?" Joan shrieked. Middlebury sat down and dropped his head. He pulled a paper from his jacket pocket and handed it to her. As she read, eyes expanded and jaw fell. "Really, someone wants you to follow directions because they kidnapped Delinda? That means they have Marcus, too. I've got to contact

Marc."

"I'm going with you, if you leave the ship. Olivia can take care of the infirmary."

Worried parents departed for the gangway, as time was short. As the afternoon crept on to evening and a ship departure, finding lost offspring consumed their energies.

"Delinda's kidnapping may be a hoax. Someone playing a cruel joke." Randolph mused. "I can't lose her. My heart has little affinity left for misdeeds of anyone who harms our children. I've come to understand her feelings for Marcus. She has a full heart and will fight through any adversity. I can do no less."

Joan smiled, remembering how resourceful her son had been in less stressful situations. "Marcus is not one to fail himself or your daughter. He's smart and creative. If they are in a compromising situation, he has the ability to figure a way out." A frown replaced her grin. "As long as nothing has happened to him." A growl escaped her. "I will kill anyone who harms my children."

Middlebury placed a hand on her shoulder. "We'll get them back."

At the departure portal, Jarina Camacho greeted them with a smile. "Remember, we leave port at eight pm. Please be back aboard by seven."

They checked through the scanners and exited. Clicking her speed dial, Joan walked as she listened for an answer from Marc. She halted at the base of the gangway. "Have you found them?" after to short conversation she closed out the call. "Nothing yet."

⋯⟨◦⟩⋯

Marcus fought pain and paralysis, staying alert as he evaluated the challenge he and Delinda encountered. The twin was confident and evil, but she made one small mistake. The cord stretched as he pulled with what strength remained. The tightening knot left enough of a gap for his hand to slip from the loop. Pain raged, as thumb displaced when he extracted it from the cord.

Breathing hurt and nothing bodily functioned well. Working his other hand closer to his chest dragged a limp, unconscious Delinda closer. He checked for breathing and a pulse. Faint.

His thumb throbbed as he worked the knot on his left wrist. Tears raced down his cheeks. As the cord loosened, resolve to save Delinda pressed him on. Half the knot unraveled. A moan alerted an awakening partner.

"I hurt," she mumbled. Marcus stroked her face. Another moan.

"Lie still while I work the knots loose." With his other hand free, he worked the cords holding her hands until she was untied. Freeing ankles drained of his energies. They rolled together, entwined, warming each other's naked bodies.

"Stay here. I'm going to get help," Marcus slurred. He crawled off the bed and found clothes piled in a corner. Pulling on pants and shirt took an eternity. Sweat drizzled his forehead. "I've got to find help. Stay here," he repeated. Covering her body, he kissed her.

"Don't leave me," she pleaded. He kissed her again and stumbled to the door only to discover it locked. Collapsing to the floor, his breathing labored, consciousness waning, he felt a pang in his left pectoral muscle. He rubbed the area and rolled over.

Pulling a failing body to standing, he fell toward a window and crashed through it to the outside ground. Blood trickled from hands, face, and feet. Creeping around the building to the street, Marcus scanned for people. A car approached and stopped as the driver observed Marcus straining to move toward the road.

"Help me." The young, tall, dark headed woman exited a classic Skylark and ran to him.

"What happened to you?" She reached him as he collapsed.

"Get help. Girlfriend inside. Poisoned." Words came in quiet slurs.

"Let me help you into my car." She picked him up and started toward her car.

Marcus resisted. "Inside house. Another person. Poisoned. Dying. Get her." He crawled into the back seat, as the Tennessee college student raced up the front porch and attempted to open the door. Finding it locked, she kicked in the window framing the doorway. Reaching in she unlatched the lock and entered. After a quick search in the living area and kitchen, she found Delinda, naked and unconscious after kicking in the bedroom door. Cutting the remaining cords with a knife she carried as protection, she rolled the blanket around Dee and carried her out to the car.

Racing to the Skagway's Dahl Memorial Clinic, the Tennessee student hoped to find it open and occupied. Marcus squirmed in the backseat holding tight to Delinda, encouraging her to breathe. He was not much better off as his heart beat a sluggish rate and cramping wracked his body. Screeching to a halt at the Dahl Memorial, the student hopped out and opened the door to retrieve Delinda. Marcus struggled to follow, but collapsed on the pavement by the walkway. Two nurse practitioners collected him into a wheelchair and took him inside.

The lone doctor on duty asked him, "Can you tell me what happened? What kind of poison?"

Marcus's answer was not clear. "Atropine." The doctor stared at him, and then his nurse.

"Get it," he said to her. She opened a locked cupboard and handed syringes and bottle to the doctor, who administered a shot to each patient. His head swiveled as he bit his lower lip, Delinda's heart beat barely discernible. After repeating the process with Marcus, he nodded.

They were moved to the clinic's recovery room and monitored, their survival questionable.

# CHAPTER

# 43

Joan pulled her cell phone from her pocket and called Marc. She paced the dock as she waited for him to answer. "Come one. Come on. Pick up." Leaving a message, she turned to Randolph. "No answer. Where is the hospital?"

"If I remember correctly, it's on 14th between State and Broadway. I worked there a couple of months last year. Why?"

Striding in the direction of town with Middlebury scurrying to catch her, she said, "If anyone is injured or sick, they may be there."

"The police are closer on State. We can be there sooner and get their help." He pointed across a vacant lot which made the trek shorter. They headed in the direction he indicated.

Entering the front door of the modest building, a clerk sat behind a counter typing on a computer keyboard. As she looked at them, she asked, "May I help you?"

Joan spoke first. "Yes, I need to get to the hospital."

"Are you injured?"

"No. I'm looking for my son. We're from the Salish Sea which came in this morning. I'm Joan Jefferson and this is Dr. Middlebury. My son is not aboard nor his daughter, but the ship records say they are. Someone is playing a dangerous game. Please, can someone help?"

"Let me call the officer on deck." She turned away and activated the radio. Joan and Randolph could not hear what she said because of her whisper.

Randolph interrupted, "Miss, I'm a medical doctor and need to get to the hospital as quickly as I can. Will someone please take us or call us a cab." She glanced at them and returned to the radio.

Finished, she said, "An officer will be with you soon. Have a seat." She returned to the keyboard.

"This isn't getting us anywhere." The front door opened and a tall beauty strolled in. Her hair reflected light from the golden strands lacing her brunette tresses.

"I want to report a suspicious ... I don't know ... crime?" The clerk picked up a clipboard and handed it to her.

"Fill this out and we'll follow-up on your report."

"Okay, but these two kids are in the hospital and one of them claims they were poisoned." Joan jumped from her seat.

"Boy and girl? About 18? Boy has sandy hair. Girl has dark hair."

"Yeah, I found them at a house near the rail repair yard. Do you know them?" The girl placed the clipboard on the counter as a door opened and a man with a Skagway police uniform joined them.

"Somebody requested assistance to the hospital?" Joan was surprising in that he was not tall or robust. Young and good-looking, he seemed to be just out of high school. "Hi, Tashika." The young lady flipped her head and grinned.

"Can either of you please take us to your hospital?" Joan folded arms across her chest and cocked her head. Middlebury started for the front door and clasped the handle.

"I'll take you," Tashika said. Three people climbed into a Buick Skylark for a drive to uncover whether children were alive or dead.

⸺◈⸺

Tiberius and Jerry watched as Marc slapped at a bug buzzing his head. "Damn it."

"We'll find them." Tiberius put an arm around his son's shoulder. "They can't be far. This town is too small to hide in."

Marc growled, "All I ever wanted was to be a good cop and take bad people off the street. They're not supposed to be following me and causing havoc for my family." Another buzz caught his attention.

He retrieved his cell from his pocket. "I missed a called from Joan." He activated the voice mail app and put it on speaker.

"Marc, call me when you get this. The kids have been scanned by security and are supposed to be aboard; they're nowhere to be found. Randolph and I are going to check the hospital."

Jerry responded, "That's a good call. Let me get a hold of Gabby and Lydia. Is there a cab company here?" He pressed his preset for his wife's phone. She answered.

"Marc, any problems on board are not going to resolve unless you get back and find out who is still operating there. Your security guy should be here on the late afternoon flight from Juneau. When I spoke with him, he said he was enlisting additional help to replace his son, who, by the way, is going to recover." Tiberius released Marc as he spoke.

"Our wives are at the hotel. They have not found any trace of them in town other than they purchased rail tickets and did not redeem them. I say we head there and find out where this hospital is located." Jerry slipped his phone into his rear pocket.

At the hotel Marc approached the main desk and the college-aged girl working it. "Where is your hospital located and is there a car service which can get us to it, if it isn't nearby?"

"Yes sir, Mr. Jefferson; Dahl Memorial is on fourteenth. I'll call our driver and have her pick you up. She may be on another run and it could take some time before she gets here."

"Do it." Marc turned to his father. "This place is as backward as any place can be."

Jerry asked, "Is there a taxi service? Or car rental place?"

"No taxi, as you might expect, but Tashika, the young lady who drove you here, works for us. As for a car rental, Avis is located by the airport. I can call them."

"How about the police? You do have a police station, don't you?" Jerry asked.

"Yes sir."

"Call them and tell them it's an emergency. That someone needs transport to the hospital."

"Sir, that would be the fire department."

"Call your girl, then." Marc pulled his phone out and punched in Joan's number. No answer. He left a brief message.

The desk clerk punched in the number and waited. "Tee, where are you? I have passengers who want to go to the hospital." Amazement coursed her face. After disconnecting, she said, "She's heading there right now."

Marc punched Joan's number again. When she answered, he asked, "Are you heading to the hospital? I'm at the hotel with my parents and uncle and aunt." He listened. "Alright, send her to us as soon as you get there."

Clicking off, he related the information to the others. Patience is a virtue best left to those not in a hurry; but Marc wore a path in the carpeting of the lobby. Other patrons stared but left him alone. Every few seconds he peered out the doorway hoping to see the Buick pull up. Time passed like a slug slithering across a walkway at home in Wendlesburg. Tiberius and Jerry stepped outside to leave him to ponder his next move aboard.

"Your son is wound tight. That Tennessee girl better show soon."

"He'll be fine. He gets this way whenever he needs to accomplish a task and is trapped. As soon as he knows how Marcus is, he'll proffer a plan and bring us in on it. Go get Lydia and Gabby so we are ready to leave as soon as she arrives."

"Getting pretty bossy there for an older brother." Jerry said and cracked a smile. He entered the hotel and heard the phone ring at the desk. The girl answered and signaled for one of the Jefferson's. Tiberius approached.

"Tee is on her way."

"Great. She's deserving of a nice tip along with her fee."

"She'll be glad to hear that. She needs a ton of money to finish her degree."

Tiberius acknowledged the comment and turned to Marc. "Let's wait outside. She's on her way. Four family members joined the fifth one on the walkway in front of the hotel. Within a couple of minutes, the Skylark rounded the corner and parked for them to enter.

"Mr. Jefferson, your wife and Dr. Middlebury are at the hospital. I'm sorry your son and his girlfriend are so bad off. I found him and took them to clinic. I was heading to the police station to report it when I ran into them in the station." She drove as she spoke, watching the road and breaking the rules of speed with abandon.

Within three minutes they arrived.

Jerry handed her two twenties and asked her to wait. He explained more was available, if she did. She killed the engine and followed them into clinic.

"Where are the young man and girl brought in this hour?" Marc asked the nurse behind the desk. "My wife and a Dr. Middlebury just arrived, as well."

"Yes, they're in recovery." She pointed to a door. The crowd moved toward it and stopped when she asked, "Are you all family? There's not a lot of room in there."

Tiberius said, "Marc, you go. Find out what you can and report back to us. We'll wait."

Marc pushed the door open and disappeared into the inner area of the clinic. He searched until he found Joan and Randolph by the beds occupied with their children.

"Oh Marc, they were abducted and held prisoner. Then Marcus said they were poisoned like Mr. Blackthorne and James." Tears trickled down Joan's face.

"Are they going to be alright?" Marc squeezed her hand, gentle but firm. "Do they know who did it?" Her head rocked back and forth.

"Delinda is in bad shape. Marcus is in an induced sleep to rest his body. All he said was they were tricked into going to a house, tied together, and poisoned."

A young man in scrubs entered. "Dr. Middlebury, may I have a word with you?" Randolph signaled for Marc to follow. In the hallway he continued, "You mentioned something about this happening aboard the cruise ship on which you work. Explain."

Randolph glanced at Marc. "We had a death after the first night which I thought to be suspicious. Mrs. Jefferson also suspected his death was not from natural causes. She's a certified nurse in Washington state and this man's wife. That's their son in there. My daughter and he met aboard and have been hard to separate ever since. Soon after the first death Detective Jefferson's other son became ill with similar symptoms, as did a steward who was found dead in his cabin. All of this is related, and an investigation by our ship's security personnel with Mr. Jefferson's help uncovered a plot to kill him because of his police work in Washington. We have sent tissue and blood samples to Anchorage for analysis with a plan to have the results when the ship docks in three days."

Marc interjected his concerns. "We need you to keep an airtight lid on this so we can finish ferreting out the culprits who are responsible. I want it reported that these two have perished. That will keep the criminal element aboard the ship from thinking they failed in their attempt."

"That's highly unusual. I have to report deaths to the coroner and the police, and I can't guarantee one or both won't die this evening. Do you have any idea what kind of poison was used?" He placed his hands on his hips and scrunched his brows.

"No, but we think it is mixed in with honey and maybe tea." Marc pointed to the doors. "My father and uncle are out there. They are both peace officers and are not aboard the Salish Sea. I'm returning to the ship with Dr. Middlebury. If you agree to have our children remain here, my mother and aunt can stay and be of help to you. Joan and I need to act a play for which we have not a script.

Joan joined the trio of men discussing the dilemma. "Marc, I need to get to the ship and check on Sarah and James. They're supposed to stay in the suite, but there's no guarantee. I doubt anyone would harm them if they were in public areas, but enticing them with false information could work."

"You go. I'll join you as soon as we formulate plans for tomorrow and when we arrive in Anchorage." She left to find Tashika and a ride to the ship.

Turning to Randolph, Marc asked, "When Ingersoll arrives, how will he get this second person aboard the ship?"

"I suppose he has privileges or he's prearranged it with Dalgaard. I'm not sure I can perform this play you're proposing for us. I can't leave Delinda here without knowing whether she makes a full recovery."

The young doctor responded, "You're experience with Mr. Jefferson's younger son gave us the needed information to prescribe a plan of action to help your daughter survive. We'll keep monitoring them through the night. You can contact us in the morning."

Reluctance fought to control staying, but he acquiesced to accompanying Joan to the ship. Finding out his daughter's survival would have to await.

# CHAPTER

# 44

As the small plane descended, Dag chatted with his son's replacement. Jorgen remained in Juneau recovering from his knife wound. "I understand we are surprising people who haven't seen you in months."

"Yes, it'll be wonderful to see them again." The young Mountie, dressed in civilian clothes, smiled. "I was sorry to hear about Jorgen's unfortunate situation. I've enjoyed working with him in Vancouver. He's a talented officer."

"Thank you. He has high praise for you, as well."

The pilot announced their approach to Skagway, and touchdown occurred within a few minutes. After the plane taxied to a stop, doors opened and two passengers touched the tarmac. A tall brunette with golden strands stepped up. "Are you Dag Ingersoll," she asked.

"Yes. And you are?"

"My name is Tashika Kelso. I will be your driver to take you to meet your compatriots. They sent me to fetch you to the hospital."

"Hospital?" Dag's voice rose. "Another attack on a member of the Jefferson family?"

"I'm not at liberty to say." They gathered bags and sat in the back seat of the Skylark. The short drive to Dahl Memorial was silent, until arrival. "Leave your travel bags and I'll take you to the ship after they inform you of what has happened." Glancing at each other, Dag and his travel companion complied.

Inside the clinic Marc, Tiberius, and Jerry set strategy for the next two days before arrival in Anchorage. Marc looked up to see Dag and Regina McDonald. "Well, my goodness." He stood and hugged the Royal Canadian Mountie, who returned the affection. "I wasn't expecting to see you." Tiberius and Jerry exchanged pleasantries with her before Marc turned to Dag. "Nice to see you, too." They shook hands. "How's Jorgen?"

"He'll be fine. He's returning to Vancouver when he's released. He suggested I ask Regina to replace him. Her duties allowed for this to happen. She said you would be surprised."

"I am. Just sorry my nephew's not here. I'm sure JJ would like to see her again."

"So what's happened? Why are we at Dahl?"

"Someone kidnapped my son and Middlebury's daughter and poisoned them. They're here recovering from the same stuff that killed the author and that steward." Marc turned toward the room containing Marcus and Delinda. "Someone has escalated the battle. And that someone needs to pay for all that has happened."

"What are you planning?"

Marc rubbed his chin. "Dad thinks we need to secure our knowledge of what the truth is about our kids. We report them missing and open a police record. The doctor will report them as deceased. Hopefully, those aboard the ship will screw up and we can close down the last of the perps." He sighed and splayed hands, palms up. "By the way, how does one get on board without proper credentials?"

Dag chuckled. "Remember your question about those twins? Someone on board arranged for the papers and key cards. Don't you think a head of security would have that knowledge and the clearance to do the same? I called Seattle and set it up. Since we stop in Vancouver on our way to Alaska, authorization was prime." He glanced at Regina and nodded.

"I can only imagine what our competition will think when they meet her." Marc turned to speak with her. "Regina, what part are you portraying in this play we're staging?"

"I am coming aboard as a replacement for Jorgen. Makes sense since he's incapacitated."

"And what background do you have to be a guard aboard a cruise ship?"

"Ah, the detective comes out. I have worked in private security for a pharmaceutical company. Good enough for you?" A firm jaw and a crooked closed mouth answered her.

"Well, let's add my father and uncle to this conspiracy we are instigating."

"How's JJ?" she asked.

"Last I heard, he's doing well. As a result of his involvement with our raid, he was promoted."

"I know. He told me when he came north to see me."

"You and JJ?" She smiled as her eyes reflected her glee.

"He wanted to keep it under wraps for a while, but I told him I was coming north to see you and his dad. He said I should let you know. Sorry for pulling your chain, a bit."

"It's okay." The remaining time before needing to return to the ship was dedicated to finalizing each task and formulating contingencies.

⊶⊷

Kerrine scanned her card at the gangway, smiled at the gentlemen manning the equipment and Jarina, and proceeded to her cabin and sister. Everything was ready.

Finding the room empty, she went topside to the Lido deck and examined the small crowd until she saw Kaliana seated by the pool. "Have any of the Jefferson's returned?" She sat across from her sister.

"I haven't seen them nor has Jarina contacted me. Did your afternoon soiree end well?"

Kerrine bared teeth and growled. "We shall have no trouble from them and will command Middlebury and Jefferson as we wish. Do you have the ransom note with you?" Kaliana handed it over. After reading it, she continued, "We may not be able to use this as is. A contingency note should spell out that other family members might meet the same fate if they do not acquiesce." She folded the paper and placed in a breast pocket. "I'll take care of it. Find out if any of the Jefferson clan is aboard. I'll check on the good doctor."

Kaliana left to find Jarina. Kerrine returned to their cabin and created the alternate note. She daubed a jasmine cologne behind ears, an enticement for the good doctor. She collected a small bottle of honey and a box of herbal tea. A slight whistle accompanied her stride to an elevator for a ride to the proper floor for her visit to the infirmary.

Opening the door, she saw Olivia Breckenridge sitting at a desk writing on a pad of paper. Looking up, she asked, "May I help you?"

"Yes, I was hoping to see the doctor about an issue of a personal nature." Olivia examined the young beauty before her. She had heard about her from Randolph and Marc. Now she stood before her, sleek and emitting a hint of jasmine. She held her hands together against her abdomen, one foot slightly in front of the other.

"He's returning from a trek into Skagway to meet with his daughter. I may be able to help you, if I can ask a few questions about any medical challenge you have."

"Thank you, but it's not a medical issue. I have some information for him, given to me by a friend of his from Seattle." Her hands shifted to behind her back. A smile crossed her chin.

"He should be here shortly, if you wish to wait."

"Thank you. I will return this evening after the ship sails."

"May I have your name so I can let him know who wants to see him?" Olivia handed her a piece of paper and a pencil. Kerrine hesitated, then changed her mind and wrote "a friend has information about your daughter. Find me in the Lido Lounge" Folding it and sealing it with a staple, she placed it on the desk.

As she made her way to the lounge to wait, her instincts about people initiated doubt about leaving the note. She turned to retrieve it but saw Joan Jefferson and Middlebury waiting at an elevator. She halted. After they shook hands and separated, she approached Randolph to introduce herself and tell him about the note. The elevator binged and doors opened to swallow him before she could interact.

"I guess I'll wait for him in the lounge." She gasped and jumped when tapped on her shoulder. Turning to see her sister, she asked, "Did you see that bitch and the doctor?"

"Yes, I was at the gangway when they came in. I followed them here until I saw you."

"How cozy were they?"

"Is that all you think about? They were friendly without any sensuality or hint of impropriety. You can have him eating out of your hand by midnight. Our detective is still ashore."

"What time is it? I don't have my phone with me."

Kaliana clicked her phone." It's nearly five, why?"

"He needs to return by seven or our plans will need revision. Where are the two other evil spawn?"

"I saw them in the banquet room getting food about an hour ago. I followed them to the Jefferson suite. They're still there. I did use the key card to investigate the boys' room. Nothing of any importance."

"Give me the key to Middlebury's room. I might as well have it. I can say the kidnappers told me to use it."

"Are you going to feed him our special treat?" Kalaina licked her lips. "I could join you if Jefferson doesn't show."

"If he doesn't show, we have to devise another way to get to him. I want him dead." Kerrine balled her fists and flung them to her sides. "Dead."

Kaliana said, "Maybe we should play our chameleon game."

"Of course. You really are a smart one."

# CHAPTER

## 45

D ad, Mom and Aunt Lydia agreed to stay with Marcus and Delinda. Dag and I are returning to the ship and taking Regina with us. Are you going to meet us in Anchorage in two days?" They were seated around a table in the lounge area of the clinic. Tashika had made a pizza run to assuage a missed restaurant dinner, and time was running out for boarding.

"We're staying another day before leaving to meet up again. Your mother and Aunt Lydia want to return to Seattle, but are willing to stay here until Marcus is cleared to leave the clinic." The silence was loud before he continued. "Our challenge is his girlfriend. Although she will survive, she has no one here. If your mother, aunt, and son return to Seattle, will your doctor friend allow for her to travel with them?"

"When we get back on the ship, I'll find him and get an answer for you. I'll call you tomorrow." He finished a slice of pepperoni. "Dag, Regina, let's check the kids and get to the ship."

In the recovery area, Marcus jabbered about the kidnapping to a nurse as she checked his vitals. Delinda sat quietly listening, alert to the conversation. Marc stayed a moment watching the exchange, realizing his son had recovered. "Alright, Romeo, your girlfriend is right next to you. Stop flirting with the nurse." He strode in and stood by the bed. "Time for me to return to the ship and relieve the rest of the miscreants of their freedom." He glanced at Delinda. "You look to be recovered, as well. I'll let your father know."

Hugging his son for what he determined could be the last time for many days, he hesitated to let go. "It's good, Dad." He iterated his comment. "Delinda and I will play the role of dead zombies and eat their brains." He raised his arms and groaned. Delinda giggled.

"I leave the clinic with fear and trepidation as to the havoc you may raise in the next few hours. Be good for your grandmother and aunt."

In the Skylark Tashika rattled on about all her adventures in Skagway and how meeting the Jefferson clan had been the highlight. Dag and Regina smiled in the back seat, while Marc slumped in the front seat. "Your family is so exciting. So rad. Wow." Marc set a firm jaw line.

At the dock three intrepid investigators paused. "Someone wants me dead." Marc said. "I can't lose any members of my family."

"And yet, you're going to pretend one may be missing or dead." Dag said. "How's your head?"

"It hurts, but I'm okay."

Regina injected her own opinion. "Marc, what if the person or persons who want to cause you harm are unaware of my presence? I can keep an eye out for anyone who is acting weird near you."

"I suppose. The thing is; Dag arranged for you to be aboard. If someone is aware because they're privy to passenger lists and scan data, they'll know you've arrived."

Dag spoke next. "I can get the data scans canceled when you come on. My crew understands we are investigating. We rounded up the compromised scan crew and the replacements are loyal to me." They started the ascent to the ship showing their key cards and the authorization form from the main office in Seattle which allowed Regina passage.

At the gateway two scanners operated as passengers placed bundles on the conveyor belt along with all metal objects. The upright body scanners checked for any contraband or forgotten metallic items. The key cards were scanned to count the return of those who left to explore. Dag stopped at a gate and asked, "Do you have the proper materials for my assistant?"

"Yes sir, and as requested, her identity will remain with us."

Regina passed through the scanner which was temporarily switched off. An envelope with a key card was handed to her. Dag followed protocol, as did Marc.

"Let's head to my office and get oriented." Jarina watched the maneuver with a keen eye and greeted them with her usual glee.

In the security office Dag asked Marc about the revolver confiscated from the steward who attacked him in the cargo bay. "Yeah, I have it. It's in my suite."

"Good. Regina, you and he are both officers of the law and competent to use deadly force when needed. I have my Sig Sauer 320. As passengers, technically, you are not to be armed, but we are up against a murderous gang or what's left of them. Part of the paperwork handed you, Regina, is authorization for you and Marc to carry weapons. You are also unregistered as a passenger. Let's clean up this ship for Dalgaard and American Pacific. Marc, if you are correct about the people who want you dead, then we finish cleaning up your investigation in Everett and stop the drug flow."

"I'm going to find Joan and my kids." Marc left for the upper decks and his suite.

An empty suite raised a curious angst, but he let it go and headed to the Lido deck. What to say to Sarah and James? They would be left in the dark, a condition, not optimal but necessary. They needed genuine mourning to enforce the setting of the play. As he arrived at his destination, he scoured the field of passengers enjoying nightcaps and desserts.

Joan waved a hand and stood to gain acknowledgment from Marc. He raised his head and smiled, seeing her and two children. As he strolled toward them, a steward intercepted and handed him an envelope accompanying a short conversation. His vision followed the man as he returned to his station at the bar in the lounge. Sitting in a chair by his wife, he said, "A woman gave this to him to give to me. I asked him who she was and he said she was gone." He unsealed it tearing the end of the envelope. Pulling the paper out, a hint of jasmine tickled his nose. He placed it next to his face and inhaled a quick slight breath.

"What is it?" Joan asked.

"An aroma, a hint really, of something I sensed somewhere." He opened the folded sheet and read. An eyebrow rose as he ingested the words. A hint of a grin caught Joan's attention. He finished and transferred the note to her. "I guess it begins."

Rage filtered through her as she perused the message. "Does this person think you'll follow through with this?" Looking at Sarah and James, she began the first act. "Sarah. James. This note says your brother is in trouble and your father must do something evil to save Marcus." She returned the note to Marc. "We need to be diligent and watch for anyone who is acting oddly." Sarah stared at her mother. James watched his father.

"Mom, what are you talking about? Where's Marcus? And Dee? I thought you said they were here?" Puddles formed in her eyes. James remained silent.

"Joan, I'll respond to this and uncover what this person wants. Kids, I want you to stay with your mother. James, if I can't find your brother, you stay in our suite tonight. Sarah, sleep with your mother so James can have your bed. I'll stay in the boys' suite." He stood and hugged the two surprised offspring. Grasping Joan, he whispered, "I'll find Middlebury and let him know what's up." He released her, but she clung to his arm and pulled him to her lips.

"Be careful." Her plea played for her children.

Marc waved as he left. The note said to meet the young woman in the library. His son was kidnapped and she was forced to be the go between. If he did not meet her and do exactly as she said, then his son was dead. Curious about what needed executing, he climbed the aft staircase and entered the lounge area. Scanning the room, no one stood out. No brunette nor Hispanic person sat in the lounge. Marc ordered a beer. As he watched the library next to the bar a familiar face stared at him. Picking up his drink, he sauntered toward his quarry.

"I guess we are to meet." Marc extended his hand. She accepted and asked him to sit. For a person supposedly extorted to compromise another human, she acted nonchalant. He sat in a chair next to her and waited. Her move.

"I suppose you have some questions." Kaliana leaned forward. "What role do I have in freeing your son?" Marc waited. "When I was ashore, a man approached me and asked if I was a passenger on this ship. When I answered that I was, he asked about my sister."

Marc made his move, accepting the bait. "Your sister? Isn't she more like your twin?" Her move. He waited.

"Yes, but that isn't the important part. He said my sister was in danger if I didn't send you a note. He showed me a picture of her tied to a chair. She was bleeding and they had a gun pointed at her." Opening a purse, she removed a cell phone and clicked open a picture. Pointing the screen toward Marc, he frowned.

"When was this taken?"

"I received it this afternoon. Who are you that someone would kidnap my sister to get to you? What did you do to them?"

"I assure you. I have no enemies in Skagway. When I saw you in Juneau, I wondered who you were. Two of you. So alike. And when I thought you followed me to the hospital, I was suspicious. Now you have a curious note about my son being taken. I have no proof of what you say. Your note was cryptic. Why should I believe you?"

"Oh, I'm sorry." He waited for her next move. "Can we go to my suite? So we can finish this? I'm supposed to call them as soon as the ship leaves."

"And how do I get my son returned to me, if we leave Skagway?"

"My sister will be freed and can fly to Anchorage to meet us. Your son will be turned over to the police. That's all I know." His move.

"Alright then, let's see what your cabin looks like." He carried a set of restrains which Dag had given to him. Did she know Marcus was reported dead? Did she poison his son? Was she wanting to poison him? Middlebury had been his next stop, but Dag would be informing Randolph. "Before we go, let me finish my beer. I will meet you. What's your cabin number?"

"Don't you care about your son? We should finish this as soon as possible." Marc didn't want to tip his hand. A quick search of the aft lounge area revealed his tail. Regina sipping a soda, snapping pictures.

Marc decided to walk into the spider's web. Was she truly hoping to compromise him on camera and blackmail him? Well, then alright. This was police business. Joan understood what was needed to remove this threat to the family.

# CHAPTER

# 46

Randolph read the note again. "And the young woman who left this said nothing else?" Olivia wagged her head. He remembered what Marc had proposed. Pretend the children were returning until someone contacted them about a kidnapping.

"Liv, I'm going to follow up on this." He departed. As he rode the elevator to the lounge deck, he called Regina. After a few beeps she answered. "Where's Marc?"

"He's leaving the lounge with a woman about my age. I snapped a few pics of her. I've send them to you. I'll stay with him."

"Good. And I have a note to meet with someone about my daughter. The thought plickens."

"What?"

"Never mind. Stay in touch and out of sight." He trusted her to follow and remain a ghost. Jorgen had said she was the best. Dag once asked his son if he had any interest in her other than as a fellow Mountie. The answer uncovered his true intentions. The revelation of Marc's nephew finished any other possibility.

The bing of the elevator alerted his brain to focus. As he approached the lounge, no one attracted his attention. He sat at the bar and ordered an Alaskan Amber. A long draught didn't relieve his anxiety. A doctor was not an undercover detective. Fingers tapped the mahogany surface. Breathing quickened and heart played a kettle drum. Another swig tasted sweet and bitter together with a slight hint of hops.

"Is this seat taken?" The voice, soft and alluring, raised hackles. His note giver?

Turning to face the voice, a scent of jasmine teased his nostrils. Hispanic, young, beautiful. He fumbled words. "Ah, no. Please, join me."

Sitting, she said to the bartender, "I'll have the same as he has." She placed a hand on his leg. "You're the doctor on this ship, aren't you?"

He removed her hand. "Yes, I am. Did you leave a note for me in the infirmary?" She grinned and cocked her head. "So what's it all about?" She reached into her handbag and produced a written paper and thrust it toward him.

He unfolded it and read without looking at her. He held it as he stared out a window at the scenery. With a deliberate plan he rotated and locked eyes. She grimaced and asked, "Can we go to my suite and talk about what these people want from us?" Hesitating to compromise himself, he stayed seated. "We can't let them hurt our families. Please, if all they want is for us to enjoy time together, then why shouldn't we? Once it's over we send them the video and get our family members back."

"I'm not sure they will follow through. What's their aim, their goal? It makes no sense to me." He emptied his bottle and signaled for another. "I have no proof of my daughter being in trouble or your sister being kidnapped. Dee left this morning with a fine young man who would fight to keep her safe."

Kerrine hadn't wanted to issue the surprise in her purse, a picture of the comatose couple she had taken as she left. Resisting the temptation until Middlebury was isolated, she closed the area between them. "I have the proof. But if you do not come with me and my sister dies, I will haunt you to the end of your life. And I will be sure your time on this earth will be far shorter than expected."

Randolph place a hand around her neck and whispered in her right ear, his cheek against her cheek. "If my daughter dies, I will not care what happens to me. You could not do anything to me which would be worse than Delinda's death." He sniffed the jasmine behind her earlobe as his tongue laced her neck. "Now let's take this to a private place and finish it. Prove to me what you can."

⤝⚬⤜

Marc and Kaliana stood at the aft railing. His walking out of the lounge and to the open air confused her. What was his ploy? Did he know something about what transpired in Skagway? She slipped her arm in his. He made no move to stop her. He was a handsome older man. A shame he had to die for destroying her family, real and adopted. No doubt he was smart. Her charms and the pictures sent to her by Kerrine should seal the deal.

"Do you believe in Karma," she asked.

"You think this is Karma?" He unlocked arms and faced her. "I believe in truth. I don't know what your ploy is, but I will not let anything happen to my family. So, this isn't Karma or fate or predestination. But it is an attempt to harm."

"The harm's already happened. I have another picture to show you. I received it this afternoon." Opening the gallery app of her phone, the picture of two constrained naked teens elicited no reaction from Marc. She closed the app and asked, "Are you ready to save them now?" He smiled.

"Let's go do what they want." She reacquired his arm with both hands, as if she feared his abandoning her quest. They walked past a young woman who stirred a faint memory in Kalaina. She glanced at the couple, smiled, and returned to the e-book she was reading.

Marc tugged at his companion before any recognition of the Canadian Mountie.

"Mr. Jefferson, I do want to apologize for causing any problems between you and your wife. I do take marital vows seriously. But saving family is more important."

"Think nothing of it. Joan is an understanding person. She knows what I must do to finish this. You get your sister. I get my son."

At the suite she slid the key card from her pocket and laid it next to the door lock. He pushed the door open to let her enter. "Always the gentleman," she thought. The suite was smaller than the Elliot Bay by several dozen square feet. Twin beds seemed appropriate. "Have a seat. I'll make myself ready." Marc sat on a couch. He pulled out his phone and clicked a note to Dag. Another message to

Joan explained his present situation and that nothing was going to ruin their relationship. He closed the app and pocketed his phone.

The bathroom door opened. Kaliana joined him wearing a robe supplied by the cruise line. Marc scrutinized the attractiveness of her face and the cleavage exposure she made sure was present as an enticement. "Do want some tea? I have a wonderful blend which I can whip up in no time."

"Thanks. I'll be right back." She tensed but watched him disappear into the bathroom. Pouring a bottle of water into the coffee maker to heat it, she pulled a bag from the supply they brought aboard. A jar of honey sat by the cups.

⤐⧫⤏

Regina walked past the door into which Marc and the twin entered. The small monitor was placed above the picture hanging across the hall from the door. She returned to the main deck information desk and asked for Dag Ingersoll.

"Come back with me to my office." He led her through a maze of rooms. Indicating a place to sit, she did. "What have you found out?"

"He met with a good-looking Spanish girl about my age. They went to her cabin. I left the camera across from the door."

"I hope he's able to resist her. And I do hope he doesn't eat any of their poisoned honey." He picked up a folder which contained the history of the investigation. "Peruse this and tell me what you think. Another set of eyes on this case can only improve our odds of catching the culprits."

Regina opened it, scanned through the various papers, and stopped at a particular sheet. "This states the number of people captured at six, and one dead. How many more are suspected?"

"Good question. We know these twins are probably in on it, but we haven't any proof of their involvement with the drug trafficking. Delinda and Marcus testifying about the kidnapping, rape, and attempted murder will be enough to put them away for life. Someone got them credentials to get aboard in Juneau. And that person is still unknown, but only an officer or high ranking staff member could accomplish that feat."

Still flipping pages, Regina asked, "Could Captain Dalgaard be compromised?"

"I doubt it. He came to me about his suspicions. That does not exclude other officers and staff, though." Regina handed Dag the folder. "My best guess would be someone with financial needs which exceed salary."

"Does the captain know I'm here?"

"No. You're a ghost. I received all of the documents from Seattle and asked that Captain Dalgaard be left out for now. I trust him, but others he trusts may be less dependable than he expects."

Regina stood and turned to the door. Stopping, she faced him. "Who do you suspect?"

Dag raised eyebrows and grunted, "That's a difficult question. I've played the inept security man for a reason. Amazing how people ignore you when they think you aren't competent. I have some suspicions but nothing I can use to arrest them."

"You've observed someone acting, shall we say, differently?"

"As I said, not enough good evidence which would convict. I am glad to have met Marc Jefferson, though. That man has exceptional skills of evidence excavation. I can only imagine what pretzel he's twisting her into. And I don't mean that as some sexual position. More like she won't know when she hangs herself."

"When I met him and his father in Vancouver, I was acting as a clerk at a storage facility. His Uncle Jerry had deposited evidence which he requested we oversee. Since we knew the truth about the suicide, we obliged the request. Marc and Tiberius came looking for it and that began our destruction of the Vancouver and Everett drug cartels which have used this ship to transport product. Very clever on their part, but we still have the remnants to sweep up. These young twin ladies are more than likely associated. I'll keep an eye on them."

"And I have my targets. Let me follow up on the entry of our young ladies and that may give us a clearer understanding of the status of one person I have in mind."

"Do you trust the doctor?"

"He has not shown any inclination for illegal activity. With his daughter assaulted and poisoned, I doubt he's part of the group."

"How long has his nurse been a member of the crew?" Regina sat again.

"This is her first cruise, but she comes highly recommended by the head office."

"The officers?"

"As I said, Dalgaard is probably not compromised. Thorsen, his exec, has been observed with our cruise director, Jarina Camacho. Since he's married, it could be a ship romance with no other implications. Or he has been compromised. Camacho has plenty of opportunity to interact with crew and staff. I don't know about her being a member of the group."

Regina stood. "Well, back to being a ghost. I do hope Mr. Jefferson is getting the results he wants." She departed and caught an elevator to the deck with Marc and Kaliana.

CHAPTER

# 47

O livia arrived at the lounge and scanned for Jarina. The message
was clear. A report from Skagway, through her connection in
the police station, stated that two passengers of the Salish Sea
had failed to board the ship due to untimely deaths. The message
had to relate to Delinda Middlebury and Marcus Jefferson. The only
way for completing the mission as assigned to her was for Jarina to
surrender her position as the surviving head of the snake.

She was not present. Olivia proceeded to the auditorium. She had
two days to right the wrong which had occurred. Her secret, kept
from the many varied factions of the cartel and now the passengers
and crew, would unravel the last of the mystic tapestry woven by
Mr. Andrew Pepper. Killed by the Jefferson clan in a warehouse in
Washington state, Pepper's drug smuggling, prostitution, murder
for hire, and illegal trading, had hit a snag.

Jarina claimed his position and moved the operations to Seattle
from Everett. Although the drug flow and other parts dried up, the
remaining aspects of his legal businesses were intact and running.
Using the conduit of legitimacy, Camacho planned to restart the
other parts.

Revenge has a negative effect on the mind. Olivia understood.
Jarina had communicated with the killer-for-hire people and brought
them to Juneau. Somehow, she got them on board as legitimate

passengers and undertook an assault on the one person she hated the most.

As she neared the great hall, an idea crept through her brain. She turned and caught the nearest elevator to the veranda deck and the Elliot Bay Suite. Who better to divulge a long held secret than to the one person who could command the end of the bitter engagement. As the elevator door opened, she stepped out to find Jarina standing near the Elliot Bay, at a Puget Sound suite marked with yellow caution tape. She waited around the corner of the hallway as Camacho entered the author's vacated room. What was in there which she could possibly want?

Not wishing for discovery, Olivia played a patience game and pushed the elevator button to descend to the infirmary deck. She wondered about Randolph compromising himself with a woman not much older than Delinda, hoping to save his daughter now reportedly deceased. Was Marc Jefferson similarly constrained to betrayal of his wife and family for the sake of his dead son?

As the elevator dropped floor by floor and stopped for an occasional passenger, she changed her mind and pressed the button for deck 1 and the main concierge desk. Speaking with Dag Ingersoll about the information from Skagway could begin the final act of the bizarre melodrama started when James Blackthorne met death head on and lost. A murder gone awry when the Jefferson family traded suites with the tainted basket, and Marc Jefferson's elimination turned a freakish corner in the play.

At the desk she asked to see Ingersoll, so she could deliver her unexpected news. As she waited, an unexpected person appeared, Jarina. What had been her reason for entering the author's suite? Watching her hurried pace across the room to the far hallway, Olivia concluded the hunt in the suite was unsuccessful.

"Good evening, Doc." Dag's nickname caused no offense. Her degrees in anatomy, human biology, and medical nursing created an excellent medical personality. Her background attracted the attention of the one group she had not expected but delivered the path assigned her.

"Good evening. Do you have some time for me right now?"

"Sure, come into my lair and enlighten me." He led her into the depths of the operations center of the ship. Inside his office they sat in chairs around a small pedestal table. "So what you need?"

"You play the inept until quality is needed. I need quality now." She waited.

Dag grinned. "As an agent for shielding the passengers and crew from anomalies on this and any other cruise, I must play a role according to the group involved."

"We have the biggest anomaly I have ever seen on board right now."

"I agree. So what do you need from me right now. You're a medical person who understands the poisons which are being brought aboard. Probably within jars of honey."

"I have more than just an interest in understanding the poisons. I have a secret from Skagway that has implications for actions currently happening to two of our friends by the twins which are aboard. They have ulterior motives."

"What is the secret?"

"I have confidential information that Marcus Jefferson and Delinda Middlebury have met untimely early deaths due to poisoning."

"A secret I find hard to believe. Who told you this?" Dag sat back in his chair and turned his head a slight to his left. He listened, knowing the truth. Knowing the information was the plant instigated by the Jefferson's to diverge the plot to eliminate Marc.

"I have a contact in the police department. The report came into the station as a reported homicide." Olivia interlaced her fingers and planted them in the middle of the table. "What ruse have you and the Jefferson's concocted? And what role does Doctor Middlebury play? He's not a law enforcement officer. His skills at deception are as limited as a new born."

"I do not know of what you speak. The demise of these two youngsters is a surprise to me. I have just arrived from Juneau where my son is recovering from his wounds suffered in the attack by a madman. Explain what is happening?"

Olivia remained silent. She stared at the head of security as if he had sworn on a Bible to tell the truth, the whole truth, and nothing but the truth, and then lied.

She stood. "You are not incompetent, and you may have come from Juneau, but you met with them before coming aboard. They cooked up a story for someone on this ship to believe and you are part of it. If the children of our doctor and Detective and Mrs. Jefferson are in reality alive and well, where are they?"

"Conspiracies? I think maybe the deaths of the author and our steward, along with the unfortunate illness of young Mr. Jefferson, have altered your sense of reality. I checked the boarding logs and their key cards indicate they are on board. So your confidential source is either ill-informed or deluding you. Stick to medicine and let me do the detective work. It will work out much better for both of us." Dag stood as he spoke. He moved toward the door of his office to open it and release Breckenridge.

Placing a hand on it to prevent his opening the door, Olivia said, "I have observed the actions aboard this ship by you, Mr. Jefferson, his wife, and our doctor. The game is still being played and I want to be part of it."

"What game is it of which you speak? We play no games."

"The ship is used, or has been used, by smugglers to transport contraband between Canada and the United States. The crew members arrested and detained in Juneau were part of a larger cartel. You are hunting for the remaining members and do not know who they are. Am I getting warm? You want a deceptive action to unmask anyone who falls into your ill-conceived trap. Am I hot, yet? What you lack is solid evidence against the people who run the operations. How about now? Am I sizzling?"

Dag released the handle of the door. "You seem much more interested in this matter than I would think you should be. Maybe part of the problem is; you're here to end my involvement. Maybe you are here as a spy for the cartel. You just came aboard in Seattle. Maybe the fact that Marc Jefferson is aboard with his family is not a coincidence for you being part of the medical staff on this particular cruise. How am I doing? Am I warm?"

"Okay, let's say that I'm here because I have an interest in what happens on this ship, and particularly, this cruise. Why?"

"All I know from your file is that you worked for a research group in Bellevue and were released for unknown reasons. Did they downsize your job? Or just you for being ineffective?"

"Dag, I have a story for you which must not leave this room or people will be coming after you next." They sat at the table, again.

"I'm all ears."

Olivia Breckenridge began relating a tale as tall as any written by authors of the finest thrillers. She gave him background information about her start in life and the resulting transfer to a ship plying the waters of the Pacific Ocean in search of entertainment for thousands of adventurers. He listened with intensity, as his impregnation with unsuspected recognition of her truth collapsed stereotypical thoughts of her medical history. She was not who she played for them. She had to make him believe she was who she was.

# CHAPTER

# 48

Tiberius signed the necessary documents releasing Marcus and Delinda from the hospital. Randolph arranged for his daughter to be overseen by the Jefferson family before his return to the ship. Jerry helped pack the few articles of clothing the kids had. Gabby and Lydia arranging a shopping trip before flying to Juneau and on to Seattle.

"Thanks to all of you for assisting my grandson and his girlfriend through this horrific event. They are fortunate young people." The clerk simply smiled and accepted the clipboard from Ti. Two nurse assistants waited with wheelchairs to accommodate transfer from the clinic to the waiting Buick Skylark and Tashika.

"Well, let's go get them." Tiberius had contacted his son and left a message that all was commencing as planned. The ship had left Skagway on time at 8PM the previous night. Their next meeting would be in Anchorage in two days. After wheeling to the recovery room and picking up the teenagers, part of the family crammed into the Skylark for the ride to their hotel. Another night had been arranged with accommodations added for Marcus with his grandparents and Delinda with Jerry and Lydia.

Tiberius and Jerry waited at the clinic for Tashika's return. "Why does your son get into such perplexing situations?" Jerry asked, a hinting tone of sarcasm in his voice.

"I guess we're all guilty of running into the fire. His last investigation is your fault, though. Hiding all that evidence against Pepper and his cutthroats in Vancouver and faking your own death sure stirred a hornets' nest when Lydia contacted Marc."

"I never did uncover how they eluded the border patrol to get drugs into Everett. Now we know. As soon as we clean up the last of this mess, I want a real vacation." Jerry leaned against a door frame away from the automated front doors of the clinic.

"Gabby and Lydia have endured an awful lot from us over the years. We need to take them somewhere without any crime following us."

"Yeah, and just where is that Eden?"

They laughed a personal, quiet interplay. The doors opened and a smiling tall brunette with golden interwoven strands said. "Ready?"

The two Jefferson men pick up bags and followed her to the Buick. Ti said, "Tashika, I do hope you stay in contact with us. We've enjoyed getting to know you and look forward to seeing your success in the commercial world."

"Thank you. I'm so glad I was in the area to help your grandson and his girlfriend. You live extraordinary exciting lives. I do want to know the outcome of your son's investigation."

The short drive ramped up the anxiety of the men who were helpless to aid Marc. He was fighting a battle without his usual reinforcements.

⚬⚬⚬

Randolph waited for Kerrine as she opened a picture on her cell phone, taken before she left Delinda and Marcus. His cabin was not large but contained twin beds and enough room for he and his daughter. The conversation about blackmail and saving Delinda unnerved him.

"This is what was sent to me." She placed the image in his face. "It's not pretty." He winced at the nakedness. He had not seen her body since she was about five. She was much different as an eighteen-year-old.

He wanted nothing to do with this woman, and the truth could set him free. All he needed to do was explain he knew they were alive and safe. But what reaction might she have? So he played the part assigned.

"This doesn't look good for either of them. Why are they naked? And tied together? You're right, this isn't pretty." He turned away from the picture. What next?

"I have this note about what needs to be done. Your daughter will be returned only when you certify that the death of a particular passenger is from natural causes."

"Natural causes? Who? Who's going to die? This sounds like someone is going to be murdered and I'm to cover it up." He took two steps and turned. "I can't be a part of this. I can't certify something that isn't true."

Kerrine placed her hands on his shoulders. "I want my sister free and I'm sure you want your daughter back unharmed." Her hands slid along his back and pulled him close to her. His resistance created a forceful clasping as she placed her lips on his. He relented and remained in her embrace. His hands clutched her back and locked their bodies together.

Play the part roiled in his head. Act like her story is reality. Allay her doubts. When she ceased her kissing and slipped her hands to his face, she said, "I want you to make love to me." His arms slackened from her back.

"To what end? We're in a crisis and you want sex? I don't understand." He grabbed her hands and removed them from his cheeks. "What makes you think I want to engage in activities which are not going to solve our dilemma?"

She sat on one of the beds, her legs slightly apart. Her shorts were loose fitting. "When I get stressed, one of my releases is physical. I can think more clearly after I've done it. You know. The nasty." She loosened two of the six buttons that locked her blouse together. Her anatomy was a definite asset. Had she used it to lure others to an untimely end?

"So; to not have sex leaves you in an agitated state? I have medicines which can aid your condition." He fingered the small syringe in his pocket, a protective ally for impossible situations.

"I don't like artificial solutions when a wonderful natural one exists." She unhooked the last four buttons and removed her blouse. A lacy, revealing brassiere contained her assets. "To resist me is futile." She reached for his shirt and unbuttoned it, his resistance waning with each successive button. "I do believe we can calm our nerves. You agree to my request and slake our primal urges." She completed her mission and pressed the shirt from his shoulders until it fell. Her lips pressed his as she placed one of his hands on her breast.

Warmth spread through him and breathing slowed. He would lose control without an ending of her engagement. Randolph pushed her from him. "This is not right. I have a reputation to uphold and compromising my medical oath is not something I can do." He reached for his shirt but only managed to touch it before a foot kicked him to the floor.

"You are a hard person to convince. I will harm you if anything happens to my sister." As he lay on the carpet, his thought was how well she played her role. He could do no less.

"As I said in the lounge, if anything happens to Delinda, I won't care about me." He rose to his feet and kicked off his slip-ons and unbuckled his belt.

"Now you see the rationale for sharing your body with me. Her shorts slipped off as easily as his shoes. Her panties matched her bra. He lowered his pants abandoning the protection of the sedative for the moment.

"Now what? We stand here in undergarments determining whether one of us wants the other dead after our interplay? Or shall we be honest and admit a tall tale has been scripted for the entertainment of one and the humiliation of the other."

"Doctor, I believe you know more than I figured you did. What do you suspect?" She slipped the straps from her shoulders and released the front clasp of her garment. One hand grasped his boxers. "Shall I guess what you know? I figure you think I am responsible for your daughter's predicament. I think you figure she's already dead. I think you want this last action to be my death. What's in the syringe? Sedative or narcotic?"

His pants lay out of reach. He had no options. She was smart and resourceful.

She slipped his boxers to the floor. "Here's how this is going to commence." Pushing him on a bed, she grasped him in her hands and relished it with a strength which surprised him. "I am to have my pleasure and then I will be sure to have your spoiled bitch returned to you. If you want her alive, then follow instructions and declare Mr. Jefferson's death to be a suicide or naturally caused."

Her concentration occupied, he reached for pants which lay just outside his parameter. Her hand manipulated his erection pulling him away from his implement for sleep. "Oh Doctor Middlebury, we don't want to seduce me as an unconscious victim. That would be rape."

"And what are you about to do with me? It amounts to the same thing."

A glint filled her eyes. "But men can't be raped, can they?" A smirk enjoined her lips and tawny cheeks. Rage failed to soften any part of him as she continued a slow stroke.

"She's already dead, isn't she?" He wriggled, attempting to free himself. Her grip tightened.

"My dear doctor, why should she die so young? They are such a cute couple. I'm sure they enjoyed sharing bodies. Now we will, and you'll like it." He wanted nothing more than to disappoint her, but she slowed her pace as his body tensed. With her free hand she removed her panties and straddled his body. Randolph submitted to the situation. If she meant to kill him; it was soon. If not, he would have a victim in his infirmary with a death he must declare was from natural causes.

# CHAPTER

# 49

M arc cornered Kaliana and pressed her body against the wall. "What you propose is not going to happen. So now that we have a clear understanding of that, I want to know your connection with my past? Are you part of an organization that wants me dead?" Her breasts rose with each inhale, a hint of fear.

"I don't know what you're talking about. Please, get off me. I want my sister returned to me and denying our enemies their wretched voyeurism will not bode well for your son." She placed her hands on his waist and pushed. He allowed space between them.

"I'm quite sure the ruse being perpetrated is as false as the game you're playing with me." She picked up and tore her blouse and then scratched her face.

"Maybe this will convince you that others will not tolerate you holding me hostage and forcing yourself on me." Marc grinned and let a guffaw escape.

"I suppose editing the recording makes me look bad. But without any of my DNA on you, it will be hard to prove." His phone continued to record their conversation.

Kaliana collapsed onto her bed, a trickle of blood staining part of the sheets. The robe had opened exposing her body and she made no effort at modesty. Marc was suspicious of this display of defeat, but he made no move to close the terry cloth garment.

"I would like something to drink," she said as she stood and swept past him, her hand crossing his face in a tender seduction. She picked up the carafe for the coffee-maker. Turning to him, "Tea?" Without a response she entered the bathroom. He heard the water run. When she returned the robe lay open for his entertainment. The carafe filled with five cups of water.

Pouring the liquid into the reservoir and clicking the switch, she placed the carafe on the tray for the heated water to enter. She situated two cups next to the machine and opened a box containing teabags. She carefully extracted two and placed one in each cup. "This is a special blend I have made because of its unique flavor." A jar of honey sat with the bags in the box. "Would you care for some honey in your tea? I also have some sliced breads which go well with the honey."

"Thank you. I appreciate your change of attitude." She slipped off the robe and turned to him.

"You must have a very strong personality to reject this." Her hands swept the air around her. She cupped her breasts. "Others have not been so reluctant to sate their lust." He understood the attraction. Distract with a delightful body and poison with a friendly cup of tea. The pot filled with steaming water. Kaliana turned her attention to the cups and poured water into each. Careful to hand him the correct cup, she checked the imperceptible mark on the teabag's tag.

He accepted his beverage and said, "Please, cover your body." He set the cup on the small table near the couch.

She placed her cup next to his and picked up the robe. Handing it to him, she held out an arm for a sleeve. He obliged and drew the gown around her shoulders. Her arms clasp his face as she planted lips on his. He did not fight it, but waited for her to complete her attempted enticement. With one arm covered and the other exposed, she reeled back from the empty response.

"Have you nothing but ice running in your veins?" He finished draping the robe across her shoulders. She raised her other arm for the sleeve. Marc held the front of the robe closed and tied the belt. Completing the task, he rapped arms around her waist and pulled her to him. Lips locked and tongue explored. A moan transgressed vocal chords as wobbling legs hindered standing.

He held her up to regain her composure. "I have no ice. You ever experience true affection from a man? Or are you just using them for sex and then finishing them with your poisonous personality?" He picked up a cup of tea and drank it.

"I hate you." Words spilled from her like a raging volcano, venomous words from months of pilloried anger. Raising her hand to strike him, he stepped back and put the cup on the counter by the box. Nothing contained her riled psyche. Fists formed and arms straightened to her sides. She whispered. "I've hated you for a long time and now you will pay for what you have done to my family."

"And what might be the reason for this revenge? What did I do to you?" Defense training and raised adrenaline focused his attention to the environment. The suite was a Puget, like James and Marcus had. Enough room for sharing, but a battle was close quarters. A fight with her could be harmful.

Composure gained rule over her. Hands relaxed. She picked up a cup of tea and sipped. The flavor differed from her usual taste. "I am sorry for losing my temper. I've never met a man like you. I can't do to you what I wanted to do. You're not at all what I expected." She put the cup down on the table and opened another container of small loaves of pumpernickel and rye, neatly sliced. Removing several of each kind and using a knife on the counter, she put honey on the slices. "I suppose you want more tea."

Marc poured more water on the teabag in the cup from which he drank. He noticed the tiny felt tip ink mark on the tag. After consuming a second cup, he said, "I must go. You're not getting what you wanted from me. I don't have enough proof for an arrest, but I know what transpired this morning. My son almost died because of you or because of your sister. And Doctor Middlebury almost lost his daughter. As soon as I have the proper evidence in hand as to how you disabled and attempted terminating these young people, I will come for you. We will dance then and share our intentions, but not with any physical action other than to incarcerate you and your sister."

Kaliana acquiesced. "I had nothing to do with what happened to them." She handed him a piece of bread. "A peace offering." He took it, but did not bite. "You saved my life, once. I should be grateful instead of angry." She spread honey from another jar on a slice of pumpernickel and ate it. Marc put his slice of rye on the counter next to the cup. The honey leaked through the small holes, sticky and gooey.

"I saved you? When? I usually don't have such negative reactions from people being saved. People are usually pleased with being saved."

"I was part of a group of secretaries in Everett when you and several others raided the warehouse where I worked. You moved three of us from an office to another room away from the gunfire." The connection realized, he wondered what her employer had her do. Her rage, genuine and unabashed, hid a truth worth exploring.

Curious as to her involvement, Marc said, "I wanted no one hurt that day, but resistance cost several lives, including one cop. If you want to have the courts be lenient, assistance in cleaning up what is happening aboard this ship will go a long way to keeping any prison time short." He watched her pick up the cup he drank from and take the bag out of it.

"You knew. Didn't you?" His stoicism didn't surprise her. "Seduction was only part of the plan. I like sex, but you knew the rest of the plan. How did you guess I wanted you dead?"

"I'm a detective, remember? Telltale signs of your plot enlightened me. Where is your sister, right now? She's not being held captive, and I doubt she's alone. Is she compromising Middlebury or attempting to end his life? He knows Delinda is safe and not dead. He will not be a willing partner."

"He's supposed to certify your death as naturally occurring."

"That's not going to work now. So when your sister uncovers your failure, will she harm you? Maybe she has ice in her veins." Kaliana sat on the bed, the robe spread by legs held apart. Marc hid a grin at her last beguiling act.

"No. But you're not safe nor is anyone in your family. If you're willing, I can save you. I can change her heart if she thinks I have you in my clutches. I can convince her you're a dirty cop, like your uncle, although he faked it. You can be richly rewarded for helping us to rebuild our operations and we can share time together." He stared at her.

"Tempting as that may be to keep my family safe, I am more

interested in you and your safety. Why would you want me alive when you declared earlier you wanted me dead? You make no sense. Are you more caring and your sister more cold-hearted?" He figured her continuing the chess match of deception was as much a ruse as the kidnapping scenario.

The attempted murder of Marcus and Delinda was real. Harming his family was still possible. He had to return to them. "Think about what I said." The door to the suite opened before she answered.

# CHAPTER

# 50

D ag's jaw dropped as he sat listening. Olivia's story was a most intriguing tale of deception and false personality. He understood why she was assigned to the medical staff of the ship. Her mission was highly classified and coded. Her true employer, asked by the cruise line for help, was part of the ploy trailing killers and drug dealers.

Captain Dalgaard recruited him to act as chief of ship security and ferret out malfeasance, suspected but unproven. Marc Jefferson traveled as a passenger unaware of the problems aboard until an unexpected death of an author, James Blackthorne, who still resided in the ice chest of the ship morgue. Adding to the obfuscation, the original target had been the Kitsap County Sheriff Detective on vacation with his family.

Two deaths, three attempted murders, and a couple of assaults escalated the terror surrounding unsuspecting passengers enjoying a cruise through Alaskan waters.

Now another revelation unmasked for the sake of securing the remaining members of a large cartel, operational in British Columbia and Washington State. Hyperbole of an investigation far greater than he realized until today, now sat with him in his office.

Olivia spoke. "Please keep my information in here. I'm not ready to reveal who I am until I can connect the last of the dots."

"Your secret is safe with me. Are you sure you don't want to let Marc Jefferson in on it?"

"At the proper time. His plate is full. I suspect the idea of someone trying to kill his son will not sit well with him. Someone is going to pay for that mistake." She stood to leave. "Thank you for clarifying the note from Skagway announcing their deaths to be a ruse to reel in the bad guys."

"You go be one, too."

Olivia departed. A damn good nurse and now this revelation. Dag had kept secret Regina's presence as a hedge against anyone being harmed who was not part of the investigation. Another accidental death of an innocent traveler would shatter the resolve of Dalgaard regarding who was who on board.

What connection did Jarina have to the twins? Did her occasional trysts with Cayde Thorsen act as deterrent for him to look the other way when drugs were aboard in transit from Vancouver to Seattle? Had he authorized certain people's passage?

Now another person had been part of the plot against the cartel from early on. Marc had disrupted the sting she was running when the Snohomish County Sheriff's office and Everett Police, along with King and Kitsap police personnel, raided and destroyed the illegal businesses of Andrew Pepper. She transferred aboard to finish uncovering the head of the snake.

Dag turned to the computer screen and activated the recording of entries into Kaliana and Kerrine's suite. Current shots showed nothing. The door remained closed. Rewinding the video, he hoped to see any activity which was suspicious. He halted when a brunette person stopped by the door, hesitated, and then used a key card to enter.

Regina had said that Marc and Kaliana were alone in the Puget Suite. The other occupant was her twin sister, now entering the room. Dag reversed the feed to see if Marc had departed. Nothing showed until the beginning of the recording when he saw the stunning face of Regina McDonald.

Two against one. He hoped Marc was able to offer resistance or at lease survive an onslaught of unknown proportion. He made a fateful decision to open a channel of escape by leaving his office and attending to the rescue of his latest friend. He coursed the hallways and stairs of the ship skipping steps as he ascended. In the elevator area of the floor housing the notorious women, he met Regina.

"You seem in a bit of a hurry," she said. He halted his pursuit.

"Marc is in trouble. He's still in the suite with the one twin and the other just arrived."

"I know. I watched her get off the elevator. I figured it was the second one since they are so alike and Marc and his antagonist have not vacated the room."

Dag stared at her. "And you're just going to stay here?"

"You asked that I be a ghost and allow for whatever action to happen. If he is in trouble, he will alert me."

"And how can he do that, if he is in a compromised position in their room? Or maybe she's poisoned him and he lies dying." Dag peered around the corner and down the hallway. No one was there. He turned to Regina. "How? How can he alert you?"

She pulled an ear fob from her left ear. "I am listening to his conversation. He and I are connected by phone. The other twin just entered a few of minutes ago. Their interplay is quite intriguing. You might not know this about Marc, but he can handle himself." She replaced the tiny speaker.

Dad stood dumbfounded. Jorgen said she was the best of the best. He understood more with this interchange. She pointed a finger to the ceiling.

"He's leaving." She pulled the fob from her ear and clicked her phone, disconnecting from Marc. He rounded the corner and met them.

"Did you get it all?" Marc asked as he shook hands with a bewildered security chief.

"Every word. I can imagine the fault line you created between sisters with her failure to compromise you and then to live instead of dying." A passenger couple stepped off an elevator, glanced at the three detectives and disappeared down another hallway.

Marc pushed a button to summon another elevator. "Let's head to my room and see if my family is still intact. The hour is late and I hope they're sleeping. We can use the boys' suite to debrief." The bing indicated the arrival of a car. Several people vacated but an elder couple remained. Since the car was heading the correct direction, Marc entered and held the door for his companions.

As the doors closed the elderly woman asked, "Are you passengers on board?"

Dag answered her. "I'm head of ship security and these are two of my staff. I do hope you are enjoying the ambiance of our cruise." She smiled. Her husband stared at Regina, until a tap on his elbow alerted him to an infuriated wife's annoyance. The bing for their floor saved any additional questioning. The couple stepped out before Dag, Marc, and Regina.

In the Elliot Bay Suite Marc discovered Joan reading a book. Sarah slept in the king-sized bed in the separate room. James lay on the hide-a-bed sofa hopefully dreaming of better days.

Joan looked up as they entered. "Did you get what you wanted?" A verve in her voice made for a relaxation of Marc's mind. He had said he would do what was needed. He feared she might believe he was willing to engage in coitus to get it. He trusted her; she could trust him and her words conveyed that message.

"For now. I have a better understanding of what this is about." He explained the relationship to Andrew Pepper and the destruction of his organization. They knew he was aboard because someone who worked for American Pacific fed the information to shipboard cartel members and they plotted revenge. He ambushed the plot quite by accident when Sarah suggested the unsigned note card was more suited to the author, James Blackthorne. Amended plans still failed to accomplish the original goal. He lived.

"Are you staying here tonight? I can move Sarah to the sofa bed."

Marc approached her and kissed her. "We're heading next door to plot a conspiratorial counter punch and end this by the time we dock in Anchorage. I'll be back in a little while."

They left secure with the knowledge his family was safe. For how long depended on the deception they would devise in the adjoining suite.

# CHAPTER

# 51

"Tashika, can you take us to the house where you found our kids?" Tiberius asked as they waited for the plane to depart from Skagway to Juneau with precious cargo stowed. Gabby, Lydia, and two young people were returning home to Seattle.

"Sure," her Tennessee voice twanged. "Why, if I may be bold enough to ask?" Jerry chuckled.

"We need to see if anything of our kids was left behind." She thought it a reasonable request. "Are the police here going to investigate what happened?"

"I don't know. In the past they've called in the state when a murder occurs. Since you wanted it reported that your kids died, they might consider the house a homicide site."

"Then we need to get there asap." Tiberius and Jeremais bade good-bye to their families and departed for an investigation of their own. The ride was silent as two men contemplated what they might find. All energies were concentrated on helping figure out the attack.

As the car approached the house, a Skagway patrol car sat on the street out front of the building. A male officer stood on the porch examining the window next to the door.

"Am I going to be in trouble for smashing that window?" Tashika parked the car and stared at the scene.

"You rescued a dying person and saved her life. I doubt anyone wants to punish you for breaking a window," Jerry said.

Tiberius added, "You're a hero to us." She grinned with pride.

They exited her Skylark and approached the young officer on the front porch. He looked up when he heard them. "May I help you? Oh, hello again, Tashika." His eyes widened and a pink rose in his cheeks. He then stared at Tiberius and Jerry. "Who are you and why are you here?"

The two Washington state policemen displayed their badges as Jerry answered his queries. "My name is Jeremais Jefferson. This is Tiberius Jefferson. A relative of ours was found at this house by this young lady. She discovered another person inside and took them both to the clinic." They secured their identifications. "We would like to look around and see if we can be of any assistance in finding out who poisoned these young people."

Tiberius checked his name plate and asked, "Officer Harms, we're experienced investigators and will not disturb the crime scene. We are trailing a group of people who want to injure another relative who is aboard one of the cruise ships that left last night. It was his son who was poisoned here, along with the daughter of the ship's doctor."

"They were reported as deceased. We're here because of the homicides." He pointed a finger at them. "Wait here. I'll get my supervisor." He entered the house.

"I guess your ruse worked. If the message got back to the ship, then Marc and Dag can poison the plot of the perps." Tiberius then said to Tashika, "You did well when reporting this to the police and explaining where you found them." She smiled.

The door opened and another older man with a bar on his shoulder appeared. "I understand you are related to the two young victims found here yesterday. I am sorry for your loss." He folded his arms. "Harms tells me you are policemen from Washington State. What are you doing here?"

Tiberius answered him. "We're assisting another officer of the law who is aboard one of the cruise ships which left last night. He is part of an investigation which is dismantling a drug smuggling ring using the ships to transport contraband into the United States from Vancouver. One of the victims was his son, my grandson."

Jerry interceded, "We are interested in whether anyone aboard the ship contacted your department asking about what happened here?" The lieutenant turned to Harms then back to Jerry.

"I have a friend aboard the ship who is on the trail of a person she suspects of being the ringleader of your group. I contacted her when I found out about these kids dying. I haven't heard from her since then."

"Then all is hopefully going as we planned."

"I'm confused. Who are you?"

"I'm Jeremais Jefferson, the boy's uncle."

"And you're all police officers?" He placed hands on his hips. "We don't get much excitement like this in our small town, except when the ships arrive, but this is the first time we've had someone murdered in quite a long time."

Tiberius decided to ease the situation. "And you haven't had a murder, yet. We asked the doctor to report the deaths so we could unlock who the perpetrators of the attempt on the couple are. They were poisoned with what we think is the same material used to kill two aboard the ship and make the youngest Jefferson boy very sick. We suspect whoever the lady was who did this is on the ship along with her twin sister. We would like to see if there is anything we can convey to Detective Jefferson which might help take down these demons."

"Usually, I'd want you to stay here while my team processes the scene, but there are only three of us. More eyes and experience can help. We'll continue to treat this as an attempted homicide. Harms, see to our cabbie and what she knows." Three men entered the house.

⟡

Marc, Dag, and Regina sat in silence for several minutes. No one had an idea how things became so convoluted. Marc broke the dead air. "The sisters are not the only ones on this ship who are causing problems. Someone allowed them to come on board. They've been fed information about my family and me. Middlebury has suffered from his daughter being attacked."

"Where is the doctor?" Regina's question evoked gasps from Dag and Marc.

Dag said, "I must find him. His nurse has information for him."

"He's not with the other sister." Marc said. "But he may have been before she returned to her suite and caught me there with her twin." Shoulders rose and hands splayed out.

"We better go see if he's alright," Marc said. Putting their plot on hold, they departed the Puget suite to determine the condition of the ship's doctor.

In the infirmary Olivia sat at her desk reading a book. No patients made attending to duty a boring situation. She looked up with a gleam as if she expected a sick person or an injury to fix. Glee disappeared like a mist on a warm day. "Mr. Jefferson, I hear your son is alive and well. May I be of assistance?" A watchful eye glared at Dag. Secret kept for now?

"Doctor Middlebury around?" Marc expected nothing and received it.

"He's chasing down somebody who left him a note about his daughter. I suspect you're here to chase down the person who left the note."

A furrowed brow answered her. "Who left him a note? Do you know what it said?"

"A young lady came in looking for him, wrote a note, sealed it, and left. I gave him the note and he left to meet the lady." She noticed Regina lurking behind Dag. "Who are you?" A familiarity teased her brain. Everett? The raid. The sharpshooter. Yes. She remembered because the accuracy was amazing.

Dag asked, "Spanish looking? Late twenties? Exceptional looks?"

"Yeah, that's her. She had secrets like other people who keep them. For a good reason." He frowned away from Marc or Regina observing.

Regina extended her hand and introduced herself. "Regina McDonald. Official ghost. No one sees me unless I let them."

"Humor and deadly aim," thought Olivia. "Nice to meet you," she said aloud. "A ghost. I've never met a real live ghost. But then, nothing aboard this cruise surprises me anymore. How did you die?" Olivia embraced her offering of a hand and shook it. "Very real for a non-entity." She released the hand and continued. "Marc, how's your head? I'd like to take a look at it. I want to be sure nothing has infected it." He nodded a couple of times.

"Make it quick, I have a family to protect."

"Is someone still out to do you harm? I'd have thought they'd have given up by now."

As she examined her handiwork, he said, "I suppose all is well for now. They're on high alert and will stay in populated areas. Safety in numbers."

Olivia countered, "Danger from many sides and melting into the crowd can make it more difficult." She finished daubing at the wound now more a scab than an actual crevasse. "You need to change the bandage more regularly if you want your wound to heal with little scarring. Anything else?"

"Let Randolph know we're looking for him." Marc's voice pleaded with her. He worried because he imagined the man lying in an alley on a heap of rubble, bleeding from a knife wound. She nodded and the three law enforcers left for upper decks and a more conspicuous scrutiny.

# CHAPTER

# 52

Kerrine and Kaliana sat at the table in their suite. Kaliana had explained her encounter with Marc Jefferson, displeasing her sister. "How could you fail me so badly?" She stood stepping away and turning. "This complicates things. I have the video of my time with Middlebury, but it's not going to be useful if Jefferson's still alive."

"But he knew the kids were alive. He knew we lured them to the house. This guy is not going to be duped by beauty and naked bodies. He suspected the honey was poisoned."

"What aren't you telling me? I know you like I know myself. And don't hold back on me."

Kaliana squirmed. "I'm not hiding anything from you. He's crafty."

"Then a more direct approach is needed."

"What? What do you mean? Direct? I don't think we'll get close enough to him for a direct assault." Kerrine grimaced at Kaliana. Opening a drawer in the cabinet of the room, she removed a small caliber pistol and a box of bullets.

"Isolate the target and eliminate. We do it near a railing and over he goes." Cradling the weapon like a small animal, she smiled and continued. "He promised to help you, didn't he? He wants me for trying to off his kid. Middlebury is not going to be a problem. So that leaves the security team. What's the chief's name? Ingersoll?"

"Where did you get the gun? I don't remember you ever having a gun." A solid rap on the door interrupted the conversation. Kerrine opened the door to find a familiar face.

"Are you going to let me in?" Jarina pushed past into the suite. "You two have created a rather interesting conundrum with your botched attempts to finish off Jefferson. Now we need to plan a way to escape and fight another day."

"Escape?" Kerrine laughed. "We're on a ship which won't see a port for another day. How do you propose to leave the ship when it gets to Anchorage?"

"Have you no faith in me? I know this ship inside and out. I have ways to evacuate and disappear. No scanning. No reporting to anyone." Jarina sat on one of the beds. "What we must do is eliminate Mr. Jefferson in such a way, he isn't discovered before we can depart. I suggest taking one of the kids."

"How can we get to his kids when they aren't leaving their mother's side?"

Jarina stroked her chin and let out a guffaw. "The youngest has a crush on me. I can separate him from parents and get you to let Jefferson know he's in trouble. When he comes running, you kill him and get to a cargo area for offloading and conceal yourselves in a crate I have aboard which is designed for my escape. You use it and I'll stay aboard, since no one suspects me."

"Can you contact our people in Anchorage?" Kaliana asked.

"It's arranged already. I'll see you when I return to Seattle with the ship." She stood and moved toward the door. Before opening it, Jarina admonished the twins. "Don't screw this up or I'll see to it the crate is delivered to the incinerators." She left.

Kerrine snorted. "I don't like being threatened. If she thinks we're incompetent, then she can kill him." Kaliana whimpered, placing hands over her eyes. "Catch hold of yourself. You need ice water in your veins."

"That's what Marc asked me. If I had ice water instead of blood."

"So now he's Marc, huh. You need to remember; he's responsible for the demise of our uncle, Jorge, and the collapse of the cartel and a thriving business. We have been tasked with the revenge sought by all of us in the family." Kaliana nodded but kept her own council regarding Marc and a possible understanding for cooperative behavior.

><-••©-><

Middlebury rapped on the Elliot Bay suite glancing at the author's room. So much heartache. He wondered how the young business companions were faring back in Arizona. Blackthorne's body still resided in the morgue, one last task to do when the ship docked in Anchorage. Arrangements for a trip home had been made by radio and James would depart on his last flight before internment somewhere in his home state. His daughter was arriving to take command of the venture from Alaska to Arizona.

The door opened and Joan greeted her friend. "Come in. Marc's not here, but you're welcome to stay as long as you like." He glanced about the room. Seeing Sarah and James he hesitated.

"I'm sorry. I don't mean to intrude. Let Marc know I was here and have information for him regarding this afternoon's activities." He turned to leave.

"Wait, he needs to see you, too. Come in. He'll be back as soon as he and Dag formulate a plan to end the siege." He stared down the hallway and changed his mind.

"Sarah, go see if your father is still next door." James rose from his seat to accompany his sister. "Where are you going?" Joan asked him.

"I'm bored and my games are in there."

"Alright, but both of you come right back here." After they left, she offered coffee and cookies to Randolph.

"I have a confession," he mumbled. He stared out at the veranda into the evening twilight of a late northern night. "I let one of the twins do something I hope I don't regret." He faced Joan. "She tried to convince me that Delinda was in trouble and that sleeping with her was my only option for saving her."

"You knew, of course, that Dee was safe. So what happened?"

"I'm not very good at this detective thing. I played along because I am supposed to issue a death certificate for Marc that states he died naturally or by his own hand. I figured it best to find out what she planned, so I let her. I had a syringe with a sedative ready to knock her out, but I didn't get a chance to use it. She knew I had it and kept me away from it. So I had little recourse to assure my safety. So it happened. I left her and went off to be alone. I figured Marc should know since the other was going to seduce him and then kill him."

"He told me. He outfoxed her and left, very much alive. Your companion arrived to find him still breathing and was not pleased."

Randolph sat on a chair. "I'm glad to hear he's okay." The door opened. Sarah and James wandered in looking like lost sheep.

"Dad's not there." Sarah plopped down on the sofa and picked up her tablet to read. James fired up his game console and proceeded to attack animated enemies.

"Did our children make it out of Skagway?" Joan assured him with a smile and a nod. "Good. I'll miss her, but I know she's safe. I like your son. He seems a good friend for her."

Joan grinned, "I think they're more than friends. They were inseparable on board and in port. We may have to be understanding of their being a long term couple, regardless of their youth. Does Dee have plans for school this fall?"

"She's been accepted to the University of Minnesota and plans on pursuing a degree in biometric medical research. She wants to help solve diseases by studying what causes them and recording data to track natural cures. Her mother's death precipitated this choice."

"Are you doing okay?" Joan asked. "I can imagine you missing her, as well."

Clasping his fingers together in his lap, he said, "I do. And had Delinda died, I would break my oath as a doctor to do no harm." He stood to leave them.

"Be safe."

"I will." Turning at the door, he finished, "Marc will not be certified as having died of anything. He's too smart to become a victim of their plotting." He left for another part of the ship and to find his nurse.

# CHAPTER

# 53

Darkness enveloped the ship around midnight while Marc, Dag, and Regina searched lounges and entertainment venues for their doctor friend. After a quick meeting with Captain Dalgaard and Commodore Thorsen to reassure them all was well aboard the ship, the three embarked on the hunt for Middlebury. Regina had checked the recording device outside of the twins' suite and saw another woman enter. Her face had not been visible until she left.

Dag commented about the incident. "That's Jarina Camacho. I wonder what she's doing with them?" Marc froze the frame on the cell and stared at it.

"We have another of the conspirators. I wondered how those young ladies got aboard. We may have the answer."

"She doesn't have the same access to entry as I do." Dag reflected about the security clearances for officers and staff. "If she and Thorsen are having a fling, he may have allowed for them to board. I'll check the logs again."

Regina's remark surprised her male cohorts. "She's rather attractive. Does anyone on the ship have ugly as a requirement for hiring?"

"Below decks crew may be the ugly ones." Dag's comment brought laughter. "It is important for crew and staff who interact with the passengers to have a certain look. Those who don't must have certain skills."

Marc pointed out the skills of the crew incarcerated in Juneau. "I suppose a certain skill at obfuscation is a must when smuggling."

As they entered the Lido Lounge, Regina pointed at a soulful effigy of medical science clasping a stein with both hands. "He may not do well with his daughter off the ship." Marc's comment stirred nods from the other two.

Surrounding their prey, Dag said, "May we join you?"

"Oh, hi. Marc, I was looking for you."

"Not too hard, I see."

"Funny. I'm supposed to certify your death as an accident or natural causes or suicide. I forget which one. As long as you are dead, of course. Homicide is not an option but may well be the real reason for your demise." He swigged from the stein.

"When is this to occur?"

"Kerrine doesn't know Dee is safe in Juneau. She thinks she compromised me with a video of her and me having sex." He finished the drink and held the glass up for the bartender to refill. "Don't be crazy enough to actually get killed, please."

"Her sister wanted to do the same with me. She was not... successful. I do believe your dominatrix was surprised to see me still breathing when she entered their suite. She probably knows now that the kids are alive and safe." Marc clapped Randolph's shoulder and kept it there for a moment. "Are you okay?"

"This trip is not what I expected when it began with a simple heart failure caused by an unknown substance with deadly ingredients. I feel like I'm in a Greek tragedy and all the players are destined to die. I get to live and suffer the fate of Orestes."

"You haven't killed anyone. I'm not your father or brother and I doubt your daughter despises you." Marc sat in the seat next to Randolph. Catching the attention of the bartender, he held up two fingers. The man filled a second stein. Regina and Dag sat on the other side of Middlebury and ordered beers.

"Marc, thank you for keeping my girl safe. Well, except of course, from your son." A half grin materialized. "I like him. He has your level-headedness. And Delinda seems smitten with him."

"Not what I wanted for my son to discover at the tender age of eighteen. But she is smart and beautiful, so I can't complain." Marc sipped his beer.

"How are we going to survive this?" Middlebury's words sulked from his mouth.

Dag interjected, "We should get to a more private location and we'll fill you in." They grasped the glasses and moved to a table in the lounge away from other passengers. The band was on a break before their last set. It was the same band whose manager had met a fate close to terminating his life. He and other members of the entourage sat a few tables away from them. The manager rose from his seat and approached.

Each pair of eyes stared as he neared. "Doctor Middlebury, I just wanted to say thanks for helping me the other day when we were leaving Juneau. I don't know what happened, but I feel like you saved my life." He pressed his hand out for a reciprocal shake. Randolph obliged. "Again, thanks." He returned to the band group as the four players rose to run a last set.

"We've had too much disturbance on this voyage." Dag commented as he watched the band work the stage. "Marc, I'm sorry you had to deal with it." They sat and listened to music, a style Regina appreciated more than her male companions.

"Dealing with surprises is my history. When it looks like the end is near, the sky is clear, the air is calm, the water mirrored, then the storm approaches and disrupts the environments of all concerned. I do not trust people aboard this ship." Raising an eyebrow and crinkling his mouth, he said, "Present company excluded."

"Marc, we're farther along our path to success than they are along their path," Dag responded. "Besides, we're on a cruise. Aren't we supposed to have fun?"

Regina and Randolph glowered at the attempt at levity. Marc answered Dag's comment with his own humor. "Our game is moving along fine until some ref's call crushes our hopes. Which one of us is the referee?"

Regina added her repartee. "Hickory, dickory, dock, four mice ran up the clock. The clock struck one, but the rest got away with minor injuries. Too bad the clock was not on four."

Marc finished the comic-relief session. "Let's make the clock strike the rest." The band finished a song signaling a time for departing. Marc, Dag, and Regina stood. Randolph hesitated. "Are coming with us?" He stared up at the intrepid trio.

"How can you want me to be with you after what I've done? I let one of the twins use me."

"Randolph, what you told us may have indicated a slight crack in the solidarity of our young ladies. A bit of leverage and the crack may crumble the remaining walls of security the cartel feigns to have." The doctor rose from his seat and they walked from the lounge before another song started.

"Let's return to my suite," Marc directed, "to check on Joan, Sarah, and James. Then we can coordinate an assault which leads to their downfall and the end of this gang." He led the way to an elevator.

At the Elliot Bay Suite, he collected papers and memos about ship activities left in the message box and entered the room. Joan and Sarah slept in the large king bed. James was not in the fold-out bed. Marc, reluctant to disturb two peaceful bodies, asked for indulgence from his friends so he could check the Puget Suite for his son.

Joan awakened before he left. "Marc, are you alright?"

"We're fine. Where's James?"

"He wanted to be alone. He's next door. I had him put the privacy lock on. He's sleeping." Marc kissed her.

"Go back to sleep, then." She lay down and closed her eyes. He checked his watch. It showed 1:36. "Listen, gang, it is late... or rather early. Let's gather at 8 AM in the dining room, have a nice breakfast, and discuss this matter with rested brains and bodies." Each agreed to the arrangement. Dag had secured the suite previously occupied by Gabrielle Montoya and Paula Merino for Regina. She was to oversee the Jefferson clan. He and Randolph left for their crew cabins in the lower bowels of the great cruise ship.

"Regina," Marc said, "thanks for coming on this mission. Jorgen is a good man and I know the attack on him must have shocked you." They walked to the suite three doors away from the Elliot Bay. She removed a key card from her pocket and unlocked the door.

"Please come in. I want to check the camera feed and see if any other action has occupied our two ladies." He followed her in.

As the door closed, she turned to him. "Are you alright? I ask because I care for you and your family. I don't want anything bad to happen." Marc flicked his head and shrugged his shoulders.

"This was to be a vacation; time away from the vagaries of crime fighting. It seems my history follows me." She opened her laptop and logged on. He watched as the screen populated the space.

She reached for his hand. "Are you and Joan okay?" Regina's resignation of her hidden confession was not satisfactory to either of them.

"I can't." He pulled away from her. "I've made peace with Joan about my job, and I do love her. You need someone like JJ."

"Actions between you two hinted at a struggle. Communications appeared tense. I thought maybe you and she were drifting apart."

"We were moving in different directions, but Uncle Jerry's ruse demonstrated to me how much a couple can endure and survive. I decided I had to try and amend my personality to fit my family into my life. We had planned this trip and Joan and I are working together for each other and our children. JJ loves you. I'm sure of that. Go to him."

"I do care for you and what happens. You're one of the nicest, smartest people I know." She clicked on the keyboard of her laptop and said, "Let's check the camera and see if they've had any visitors."

Marc headed to the door. "I must get back to my family. Thanks for understanding." In his suite he thumbed through the papers which had been in the basket outside the suite door. An envelope attracted his attention. Opening it, he extracted a note, hand-written and exuding a hint of jasmine. He read, dropped the note, and fumbled around on the shelf for another key card. Picking it up, he raced to the suite next to them and opened the door. Clicking on the light to illuminate his worst fears, he noticed two empty beds. One neat and unrumpled. The other, messy and unoccupied. He checked the bathroom. Nothing. James was missing.

# CHAPTER

# 54

Olivia caught up to Dag and Randolph as they returned to the lower bowels and crew quarters. All of them dragged for lack of sleep. She invited them to enter her room. As they sat, she said, "Dag, this investigation has gone on long enough. I have the evidence needed to incarcerate all of the people involved in the drug trafficking, attempted murders, and the deaths of the author and the steward." Middlebury narrowed eyes and curled his lips. "What are you talking about? You sound like Jefferson on a case."

Dag voiced an ahem. "We have something to tell you." Palm up, his hand deferred to Olivia.

"I want you to know; I am a board certified pediatric and adolescent nurse with a real master's degree. I also have a degree in criminal science." She let the words sink in. "I work for the Federal Bureau of Investigation as a special agent. I'm undercover to gather evidence about the transportation of illegal drugs and other contraband from Vancouver to Seattle. Marc Jefferson and his father and uncle stumbled into my case and created a need to alter my investigation by coming aboard the ship. We suspected the cruise line's illicit activity, but I discovered the ships were being used and the cruise line was not directly involved."

Randolph sat slack-jawed and more alert than earlier. "Does Marc know?"

"Not yet, but he's to be informed when we meet at breakfast," Dag injected. "Olivia, you should be with us as we complete our roundup of the last of the culprits." She nodded.

"We have one other person we need to collect before we arrive. She is the head of this snake and the sooner we have her in custody, the better."

The two men leaned forward. Olivia continued her confession. "I worked with her in Everett before she came aboard and I followed as soon as the cartel was destroyed. I have been gathering a large body of material which will put her away for a long time. We need to get Jarina Camacho before the ship docks."

Dag spoke first. "I'm not surprised. She always knows what's happening on this ship. Do you think she suspects we know about her?"

"No, but she is aware that the twins are compromised. She's a chameleon and will disappear if we don't keep an eye on her."

Middlebury sat in quiet resignation of his indiscretion with Kerrine. Dag said, "She can't go anywhere until Anchorage. I brought a friend with me to replace Jorgen. She is a Mountie in Vancouver and knows the Jefferson family. Since she is unknown, I have her spying on our naughty girls. However, Jarina was present when we boarded. I'm not sure whether she can spy on our cruise director with effect."

"You let me take care of her. She and I are close and are plotting revenge for the collapse of Pepper's outfit. I can be close and nab her at the right time," Olivia said. "Right now, I want some sleep, so I'm kicking you boys out."

They left for cabins and sleep of their own.

><><

Marc woke Joan with a gentle touch and a kiss. Sarah squirmed but remained asleep.

"James is missing," he whispered as her eyes opened and awareness of his speaking aroused her brain. "He's not in the suite and this note was left for you and me."

She sat up and took the note in her hand. "This can't be. He was locked in. I had him put the safety on." Adrenaline finished alerting her mind.

"I just checked using the spare key card. His bed is not made but he's not in the room." Joan reread the note. "I have your son. If you want him back in one piece, you'll do exactly as I instruct. Any attempt to find him and parts of him will be sent to you."

Marc took the note and read the instructions. "Leave me and my sister alone until we dock in Anchorage. We will get off the ship and you are to remain on board and sail back to Seattle. Your son will be safe until departure. Any attempt to follow us will result in his death."

"Marc, they mean business. Desperate people do desperate things."

"Regina is checking the camera to see if anyone visited them. We should see if she has anything." He crumpled the note. "If they harm him, I promise you they will suffer the ultimate punishment. No court will see them." They moved quiet as mice so as to leave Sarah asleep.

A light rap on the door garnered a response from Regina. "Come in. I have some interesting video for you." They watched the pictures of a woman approach the door and knock. Her face was away from the camera. Marc sensed a familiarity, confirmed when she left the room and Jarina's face scanned the hallway. Marc cringed as he realized the cruise director was part of the cartel and probably its surviving leader. He smoothed the note and gave it to Regina.

"Where could they hide him? I'm not sure they're familiar enough with the ship."

"No, but our Cruise Director is." He balled his fists unconscious of the action. The ship was to arrive and dock in Anchorage in just under 30 hours. Hostages rarely lived that long.

"I have to get Dag and elicit his help. We can't wait for breakfast."

Joan said, "Go. I'll take care of Sarah. Find our boy." Quavering words led to tears. Regina touched her shoulder.

Marc iterated, "I promise you I'll find him." He and Regina exited. He pulled his cell out and checked for a signal. No bars. "Damn." Regina looked at her phone with similar results. "We'll have to get ship to shore. I need to contact Dad and let him know what's up. He and Uncle Jerry can monitor who gets off and stop those girls before they escape."

As they descended to the crew deck and Ingersoll's cabin, Marc's rage, fueled by his history with Pepper and the members of the gang, developed into a controlled determination to end this assault on his family. Regina stayed silent watching him.

He rapped on Dag's door with a ferocity to awaken the dead. He balled his fist and pounded again. "What the... Oh, Marc," Dag squinted as light from the hallway blazed at him.

"They took James." Marc let the words strike an understanding.

"Come in." Dag directed them to his couch. He sat on the bed. "Who took James?" Marc handed the note to him. "Well, this escalates our plans."

Regina injected her information. "Our camera feed showed the cruise director enter and exit the twin's suite. If she doesn't have the ability to get them on board, who does?"

"That is a good question. I suspect we need to have a strongly worded conversation with our second in command. He is spending off hours entertaining our entertainment leader. If she has her hooks in him, we need to know to what depth. Dalgaard will not be happy with his friend and fellow officer. They've been a team for over ten years. Let's get the doctor. He's as much a part of this as is Olivia Breckenridge. I'll be right back."

Regina assured Marc of a positive outcome. "We'll find him and arrest these people. You should contact your FBI since this is a high seas crime. They should be involved."

"I know. We kept them out of it so as not to scare off the entire cartel team. Dad, is contacting the local office when he gets to Anchorage, today." A yawn interrupted his thoughts. A door opened and three people entered. Torn from the arms of Morpheus, happiness was a distant companion.

Marc asked, "Where can a person be hidden from the crew and passengers? Our twins are not familiar with the ship's holds, cargo bays, or other exits not used by passengers. Camacho is the key. I think she set up the kidnapping and has James. He won't be happy unless he's sedated."

Randolph snapped to attention. "Uh... I may have inadvertently made that possible." He related his tale of a syringe in his pocket with a second dose in a vial. Kerrine confiscated it from him. "He can be silenced for the remainder of this leg of the cruise."

Marc and Dag looked at each other, while Regina stared at Randolph. Olivia smirked.

"Randolph, if my son is allergic to the sedative, what are his chances?" The concern showed in his face as eyes glared and lips were set straight. "Could the poison in the honey be conducive to causing a reaction to other drugs?"

Randolph glanced at Olivia and back at Marc. "I can't say nothing to worry about, but the chances the sedative will have negative affects is small. As to the poison, I don't have any clue what kind causes the type of reactions I witnessed."

"Marc", Dag said, "Olivia has something to tell you." He smiled.

Marc looked at her, frowning with the possibility of another unwanted surprise.

Olivia, sat down in a chair by the couch. "I haven't actually been truthful with you. I related this information to Dag and Randolph, but no one else on this ship. You and I crossed paths when you raided the warehouse in Everett and finished Andrew Pepper's illegal business. I was working as a medical technician keeping wounds out of the hands of public doctors." Marc folded arms and cocked his head. "I was working undercover for the FBI. I'm not only a certified nurse; I'm a special agent. I was assigned to keep an eye on Andrew Pepper. Your uncle's investigation had a leak which we knew not until you cracked the case and surprised us. Your uncle is a very clever man who understood the need for time. When the American Pacific Cruise Line contacted the Seattle office about suspicions of international smuggling, I was sent to be the nurse of the Salish Sea."

"So you knew about Camacho and her involvement."

"Yes."

"You knew the danger I faced."

"No. Your involvement was a surprise. I had no idea you and your family were on board until Blackthorne died. I put two and two together, but my work was not finished and I had to remain hidden from both sides of the war, appearing loyal to both in different ways. Now we need to conclude the investigation and arrest all of them."

"The question remains." Marc pointed at her. "Who else is part of the cartel?"

# CHAPTER

# 55

Jarina covered the sleeping body in a small wheeled box containing a mattress and blanket. James still wore the night clothing he donned when he went to bed. The syringe Kerrine acquired from the doctor had been administered while he slept. The three women used the key card obtained from his brother to gain entrance. Placing him in the box and covering him with blankets, sheets, and other bedding, they transferred him to an isolated hold.

"Did you place the note in his basket?"

Kaliana nodded.

Jarina raged at the failure to finish off the detective. This direct assault, an alternative to the original plan, now played the main stage. She had three shows to emcee and then a quick departure from the ship, never to return. One last chore needed to be completed, but her target was unaware of the imminent end of his extra-marital affair with her.

"Both of you need to be here after midnight so you can get off the boat with other cargo leaving here. You should bring only what you need. I'll take care of cleaning up the honey and tea from your room. I'll leave with other passengers and we'll meet up after the crate is delivered to the warehouse for disposal. Remember. This crate is equipped for me so space is tight with two of you. As soon as Jefferson comes to get his brat, I'll kill him and crate his body for transport to the incinerator."

Kerrine and Kaliana left her to finish sealing James in the box. She had no intention of killing him, but suffocation would finish the job. She locked the box sealing it with the tape provided for the job. Oxygen became a premium.

Checking the other crate, she closed and latched it to keep others out. Her crew had been the ones responsible for the small holding area. Now she controlled it since their removal from the ship in Juneau. Other crew members would handle things but she ordered them to stay out until she ordered the move.

Under a stack of towels, she placed a small caliber pistol and then left to lure Jefferson to his fate. He could join his son in the small box.

❦

Dag and Lars Dalgaard sat with Marc and Regina as Randolph and Olivia tended the infirmary. "Marc needs to contact his father in Anchorage and update him and his uncle about progress on the ship. They're to arrive this morning. We have a line on the remaining culprits and should wrap this up by the time we arrive in Anchorage tomorrow morning."

"I'll set him up with our ship to shore. I want to thank you, Mr. Jefferson, for involving yourself in our problems. I don't know how much longer we could have continued to function."

"I am sorry for the loss of the author. You handled his death professionally and with the passenger's feelings in the forefront. You have suffered enough."

"As have you. How is your head?"

"Doc says I should be fine."

Dag said, "Lars, we have one other piece of information which you need to have. The FBI has been aboard from the beginning of this voyage. Our nurse, Olivia Breckenridge, is an undercover special agent who has been trailing the cartel from Everett, Washington, to now. She has first-hand knowledge of the operations and has collected enough information to arrest Jarina Camacho and two passengers for conspiracy, attempted murder, and trafficking. When we dock, FBI and Alaska State Patrol will come aboard to seize them and any evidence which they have."

"I didn't realize the extent of this when I asked you to come aboard and be my security chief. You have done wonderful work."

"We have a question, though, about Thorsen. I know he's your friend, but rumor has it that he is sleeping with Camacho. If she has her talons in him, he may be aiding and abetting her and anyone else still working with the gang."

Dalgaard stroked his chin. "I find it hard to believe, but you may be right." Marc rose from his seat.

"I need to inspect the holds and empty cabins in this ship. My son is still missing. Middlebury's sedative is a problem as he won't be alert and fighting to escape. Dag, get one of your people to escort me. Regina, shadow Camacho, although this early in the morning she's probably hold up somewhere with my son."

Dag nodded and made a call. Regina opened her tablet and checked her camera feed. Nothing stirred in the hallway outside of the twins' suite. She left to search for Camacho.

Dag clicked off his phone. "Meet my guy at the main deck information desk. He'll stay with you as you examine the holds. Do have the gun the steward had when he shot you?"

"It's in my suite."

"I suggest you carry it with you. My staff doesn't carry anything other than Tasers." Marc departed to retrieve the weapon, which contained only five bullets, but that was better than none.

In his suite he watched his girls sleep, free of concerns for the moment. He opened the drawer with the gun and placed it in his waist and covered it with his shirt. As quiet as needed to keep sleep happening, he opened the door and left.

At the desk a young man dressed in casual clothes smiled. "Mr. Jefferson, my name is Aaron. Mr. Ingersoll has assigned me to accompany you in the bowels of the ship. I understand we're looking for your son."

"Thanks for coming along. I hope you have an understanding of the ship."

"Yes sir. I have a master for every door and cabin."

"Marc shook his hand. "Let's get to work."

Randolph sat at his desk as Olivia loaded her Glock and checked two added clips. "You played me." He rested his head in his hands with elbows propped on the desk. "FBI."

"I do apologize, but my field office in Seattle had me working to destroy what Marc Jefferson and his family succeeded in accomplishing."

"When you said you thought I was attractive and you wanted to get to know me more, was that just part of the game?"

"No, you are an attractive catch. When this is finished, I would be interested in exploring whether we have anything. You have a daughter safe in Seattle and I'm sure you want to get to her. So we stay in Seattle at my place and I show you around."

Standing, he stretched a hand to her. She clasped his offering and stood as well. They embraced and kissed. Randolph asked, "Do you want to leave here? I don't think anyone is needing our medical expertise at this time." She nodded.

Locking her pistol into the holster on her hip, an action which had not occurred until now, she followed him to his room. Closing and locking the door, Randolph collapsed on top of the bed. Olivia lay beside him. They embraced, kissed and held each other until sleep overcame other inclinations.

><====><

Thorsen shrieked, awakened from a sound sleep by a loud thunder at his door. Robing his naked body, and opening it, he groused, "What the hell... oh, it's you." He stepped aside to allow entrance. His early morning visitor strode past him and turned. He let the door close and reached a hand out.

"We're in trouble."

"What do you mean?"

"It's coming unraveled and I need to keep my interest in our business from disclosure. Can you maintain silence? They suspect you have a solid interest in what has occurred here and in Washington State."

Cayde folded his arms. "So? What can they prove? Our relationship is discrete. And as to what happened in Everett, I wasn't anywhere near there. I was on a cruise ship in Hawaii."

"Alright, I trust you. But if anything points to me, I want your plausible deny-ability. You go down with the ship. Your part won't cost you much jail time. Clear?"

"Clear." His guest departed without another word. His thoughts betrayed him "I'm not taking a fall for anyone." Out in the hallway, a slow nod to Jarina Camacho signaled for her to execute her assignment. When the person was gone, she knocked on Cayde's door.

He opened it and asked, "Do you trust me or not?" Jarina smiled.

"I do trust you. Let me in." He vacated the doorway. As it closed, she asked, "What was that about?" She placed a small flowered clutch on the table.

"Nothing. I thought you were someone else." She untied his robed and slipped it off his shoulders and let it drop to the floor. As he stood in front of her, she slipped off her blouse and skirt. He grasped her close and kissed her neck. Her hands explored his back. He picked her up and placed her on the bed.

Morning continued its crawl to dawn and completion of a mission. Jarina slid from the bed, not wanting to awaken her early morning exploitation. Cayde turned to his side but continued sleeping. She reached into the small flowery purse she carried with her. Picking up a pillow, she gently laid it over Cayde's head and pulled the trigger of the small caliber pistol. A muffled thud was the only noise made. Blood trickled from under the pillow. She dressed, checked the room for telltale signs of her presence and departed after checking the hallway for occupants.

# CHAPTER

# 56

Kerrine and Kaliana packed the few possessions they brought aboard. Jarina had said she would dispose of the honey and tea, but Kerrine obsessed with keeping her choice of weapon in her possession. Another day of avoiding contact with Jefferson or his family would be easy. Middlebury was another matter. He used her and she did not like being used. Delinda's escape meant he was not vulnerable and he knew it when she forced him into a compromise which melted like the glaciers of Alaska.

Revenge was the sweetness for righting a wrong. She wanted it. Kaliana stared at her when a pause in action signaled her sister's mind wandering. "Don't do whatever you think you want to do. We need a clean break from this ship." Kerrine grunted, but stopped packing the small valise.

"And what is it you think I want to do?"

"He used you and you don't like being taken advantage of. I could think the same thing about the detective. How he knew what I wanted and how he turned the situation against me. I'll get my revenge later, when he is less likely to know I'm after him." She continued placing clothing items into her small carry-on case.

A watchful eye and careful action played against the ones who wanted them locked up. Kerrine rebuked her comments. "I never get used. He was a plaything. Nothing more. When we get off tomorrow, I want to know he will never enjoy the company of a woman. I want his brat to live the life of an orphan. I want him to suffer before he dies." Kaliana understood the rage, but she did not proffer the same for Marc Jefferson.

In her mind the alliance with her sister was to suffer a slow, agonizing death. Her revenge would destroy his marriage and from the ashes build a different alliance. She laid with men who had little or no scruples. Her heart and veins did contain ice until last night when a man of integrity transfused her body with a warmth not experienced since childhood.

Jarina warned them of the dangers of the crate. Small and cramped. Designed for one person. And without proper crew to handle the disembarking, discovery of the contents meant arrest and confinement or at worst, death. Unlike young Mr. Jefferson who lay asleep in a sealed box, the twins had a small supply of air, insufficient for any lengthy journey but adequate for escape.

✕⊶⊷✕

Marc and his security escort, Aaron, plotted a methodical course from large to small. If Camacho remained with James to lure him to attempt a rescue, he would accommodate her wishes. Each room which contained shop stores frustrated Marc. Nothing worked in his favor.

As the two men closed another cargo hold door, Marc asked, "How does the trash get removed?"

"A barge on the outside of the ship is moved into place. It remains until we leave. No one usually sees it as it is opposite the passenger portal."

Checking his watch, he noticed that morning and sunlight had arrived. In the depths of the ship only light from the wall fixtures illuminated his trek. He needed an enlightenment of thought to provide clarity about what happened to James. Time crawled as slowly as a Washington slug.

"Show me the portal for the barge." They strode to a small room and discovered a lock added to the door. The security man shook it, despairing the impediment.

"This shouldn't be here." He removed a keyring from a pocket, checked the lock type, and picked keys to try. Nothing worked.

"Break it open," Marc said as a stern face stared at his companion.

"Let's get a bolt cutter from the supply office. It's one deck up." They left. Upon returning to the locked hold, the door stood open. Marc planted a hand on the young man who pushed at the door. Darkness greeted his sight.

"Wait," Marc whispered. "Is there a light switch near the entry?" He nodded but held a flashlight up for Marc to observe. Taking it from him, Marc shined the light into the room as he crouched. Nothing ominous threaten them. He entered, found the switch and flipped on the lights. Shelves and crates occupied the space. The cargo hatch was secured from the Pacific Ocean entering.

"Keep a watchful eye," he reminded the security officer. "I'll check these boxes and then we can leave to await whomever unlocked the door's protection.

"What are you doing?" The voice caught Marc unaware, as the security man turned from his observation of the search. They held identifications out for the crewman to see.

Marc asked, "Why is this room locked?"

"Orders." He answered.

"From whom?"

"I don't think I need to answer your question."

Marc's security companion interrupted. "As you saw on my badge, I'm ship security. So explain; who ordered the lock?"

He hesitated, unsure if an answer was appropriate. "Commander Thorsen. He said this room had special cargo to off-load in Anchorage." Marc knocked on boxes and crates hoping one would return the inquiry. A small one was wrapped with sealing tape, unlike any other in the room.

"Does anyone have a cutting device?" The crewman produced one from his pocket. Marc severed the seals and unlatched the clips. He opened it and removed towels and blankets until nothing remained but the bottom. "There has to be another area of the ship which has boxes large enough for a body."

The security member said to the crewman, "Which of the holds has been off-limits for this journey?" The crewman shook his head and shrugged.

"I don't know of any which aren't occupied with something."

Marc interrupted, "Enough, I don't care what room has what in it, unless one of the rooms has my son. This note says I am to come to the lower deck and get my son. This note says I'm to find a locked partition and wait for a person to bring a key." He rolled his arms around each other and stared at the crewman.

Eyes flitted from one man to another searching for an exit. "Most of these rooms are unlocked. There are more small rooms aft which are slated for clearing in Anchorage."

"Take me there." Marc encouraged the crewman when he pushed him toward the door. His security companion stepped between them.

"Do as he asked before the boy is harmed, or you are." They began the trek to supply rooms which led to collection areas of the ship. A muffled sound echoed in a cavernous main holding space. Ears training on the sound until Marc pointed to a corner and a room. As they approached the noise increased in volume. Inside the room he discovered the box from which the sound emanated. As they inspected the carton, a fourth person stood from behind another crate and reached for the pistol under some towels. She raised it when the three male backs were targets.

As the pistol aimed at one of the backs, a kicking noise drew attention to the crate. "This is the end of the line." She thought. Jarina had not planned on a small army, so each shot had to make its mark. If she missed and exhausted her initial missiles, reloading was not an option.

Her first victim, the crewman, burned in his upper chest as the bullet lodged near his aorta, nicking it as it entered. He slumped to the flooring as red stained the back of his shirt. A second bullet struck the security person within a few seconds of the first shot. He collapsed as blood escaped from his lower abdomen. Marc raised his hands in surrender.

Marc turned to confront his adversary. "Jarina, before you shoot me, let my son go. You have me, which is why he was kidnapped. He's an innocent bystander in this war you wage against me."

"He's your son. Innocence is nothing to me." She waved the gun away from targeting Marc and continued, "You have meddled in affairs long enough." Marc spied the tape around the joints of the box, realizing that time was critical.

She stepped away from her hiding buttress and allowed Marc to cut open the tape sealing in the fouled air and unlatch the cart. Opening the box in what seemed an eternity, James was wrapped up like a graduation present from an office staff affair. Wide eyes penetrated the brightness as son and father reunited. As she raised her weapon to complete her mission, a flash of a muzzle behind her disrupted the reunion. She lowered the pistol and turned to a ghost. A pain in her spine stopped her legs from functioning. Jarina melted onto the floor. Marc returned to the box, finished lifting a groggy James from the mass of bedding which had muffled sounds.

Regina checked the two males and shook her head with the crewman. Aaron's wound was not mortal. She tended to it with pressure.

Jarina lay in a spreading pool of red. She raised the pistol, took aim and pulled the trigger. The reverberation of another explosion raised awareness. She was still a threat.

# CHAPTER

# 57

Middlebury tended to the Aaron's wound, while Olivia attached a plasma bag to the intravenous line in Jarina's arm. Her unconscious body lay with her back exposed, a gaping hole scabbing over where Regina's bullet entered.

Marc stood nearby with James at his side. Dag lamented, "I'm sorry about the crewman. Olivia, is she going to make it?" Marc glanced her way. She shrugged.

Regina had returned to her suite to inform Joan of the results of the search. "We're not finished yet," Marc frowned. "Someone on this boat is hiding from us. I don't mean the twins. Someone else. I suspect Jarina knows who this person is. I hope she survives long enough for us to uncover her co-conspirator."

Middlebury joined the conversation. "What are you talking about?"

Marc asked, "How's our man?"

"He'll be fine. But you said something about another person. Who do you suspect?"

Standing with James, Marc stared a moment, then answered, "Jarina has been seen with Thorsen. She knows if he is part of the problem. Keep her alive." He departed for the Elliot Bay and his girls.

Olivia followed him. "Marc, may I speak with you?" He turned and waited. "She's not in very good shape and may not be walking again. I've known her for a while and she's not a bad person, but her life was closely tied to Everett and your actions destroyed her world."

"Maybe, but she perpetrated this war and attacked my family without honor. If she survives, a court of law will determine her future." He turned and walked away holding James hand to keep him close.

At the suite Joan hugged her youngest child desperate with a fear she had lost him. "Marc, I want to go home. I can't bear staying on this ship any longer. Too much has happened and tainted any enjoyment." Marc agreed.

"I have one last task to complete before the ship arrives in port. Two young women must atone for the attack on Marcus and Delinda. And I have a call to make to Dad and Uncle Jerry." He gathered his family close to him and let tears fall.

A knock on the door interrupted them. Sarah opened it to find Regina. She entered and received an encompassing squeeze from Joan. "Thank you for saving him for me."

Regina reacted with a hug of her own. "He loves you very much. I couldn't see her winning and not try to prevent it." They relinquished their holds. "Our ladies are on the move."

"Let's get them in custody and find out what else they know. Dag will be interested in Thorsen, as well." Marc and Regina bade goodbye and left. Checking his watch, he lamented the lack of sleep. Time had passed to nearly ten in the morning. Passengers carried on as if nothing had disrupted the sailing. Fear and panic remained hidden transgressions.

"Where were they heading?" Marc placed a hand on her arm.

"Breakfast. At least one of them said that was what she wanted. I'm guessing they think the crowd will deter any action on our part to detain them."

An idea sprinted into his head. He explained it to Regina who grimaced. "It will throw them off their game. They are not running away and we can gather them before the gangways are put in place."

In the Lido restaurant area, they found Kerrine and Kaliana sitting by a window eating pancakes, eggs, and meats. Marc approached with a plate of his own. "May I join you?" Regina stayed a couple of tables away having entered after Marc.

Kerrine held out a hand, pointing at a chair. "Please do. I must say, you are an intriguing person. To what do we owe this pleasantry?"

"One must be a fool to think you are done attempting to end my life. So I wish to make a deal with you. You're friends with Jarina Camacho. I know from your sister's conversation with me last night that you are acquainted with the raid which destroyed Andrew Pepper's operations in Everett. Since Jarina is in my custody, I'm asking for a truce for the rest of today and tonight. I will come and get you in the morning and turn you over to the authorities in Anchorage. Since you have no way off the ship, and Alaska State Patrol people will be waiting for you on the dock, it will be best to cooperate. Do we have deal?"

Kerrine stared at him like his sanity had vanished. "You are nuts. How is your son? I understand he's missing. Wouldn't your time be better serviced by locating him?"

Kaliana remained silent. Her intuition indicated that Marc was not being as honest or fair as he sounded.

Kerrine continued. "Had I been with you last night, I do believe our time together would have been quite stimulating and that today you would be visited by our esteemed doctor to be declared dead from natural causes."

"Interesting that you would say that. I figured you for the cold hearted one. Did you kill Mr. Blackthorne? You weren't aboard at the time, but did you have some activity which involved your supplying the poison?"

"Plausibility manifests in many ways. To what poison are you referring?"

Marc took a bite of eggs and chewed. He picked up a cup of tea and drank. "What did my son have in Skagway? You certainly gave him something to knock him out. Then you poisoned him and Delinda. Seems to me your actions have a pattern. You been in Edmonds recently?"

"Poison?" Kerrine smiled, her eyes sparkled as she attended to his questions. "Why, Mr. Jefferson, I do believe you are as creative in writing as that author I heard about. As for Edmonds, my sister and I live in Lake Forest Park. So I can say yes to having been in

Edmonds. Why? Someone there get poisoned?" She sipped from a cup of coffee.

"Kaliana, I want to thank you for such an entertaining evening attempting to compromise me. If your sister hadn't come in when she did, there's no telling what fun we could have had avoiding each other."

She surprised him with her response, "Why don't you invite your shadow to join us."

"Excuse me?"

"Your sharpshooter. I finally figured out why I recognized her. She covered your ass during the raid." Marc signaled to his ghost. Regina stood and walked toward the antagonists.

Kaliana moved a chair out from the table. "Have a seat." Regina scrunched eyebrows as she sat. "I remember you from the raid in Everett. You have quite a dead-eye shot." Regina just stared.

Kerrine rocked her head. "Now that we are all becoming besties, maybe we can forgive each other for the bad behavior you have exhibited."

Marc grinned and glanced at Regina and then directed his words at the twins. "You have the right to remain silent. Anything you say can be used against you in a court of law. You have the right to an attorney. If you cannot afford one, an attorney will be appointed for you. Do you understand these rights as they have been given to you?"

Kerrine said, "Are you arresting us? I'm guessing you think we have done some illegal activity which has clouded your judgment of us. Or is it just me because my sister has cut a deal with you?" Marc remained quiet. Kaliana leaned forward to Marc.

"You're missing out on the opportunity of a lifetime." Turning to Regina she continued. "And Miss RCMP, how do you think it looks for you in your future?"

Marc signaled Dag and three of his agents to come forward. "We have arranged for you to complete your journey with us in your suite. Food will be available to you as you request. Entertainment shall consist of watching TV, listening to music, sleeping, I don't know, just being under house, or suite, arrest. These gentlemen will escort you to your room. Be good girls for once and cooperate."

"Don't you want to use handcuffs on us? We might escape."

Kaliana held out her arms.

Kerrine stood. "Let's go."

Dag sat with Regina and Marc after the twins departed with their guards. "I hope your men are resistant to sex, drugs, and rock and roll." Marc laughed at Regina's comment. Dag assured her the men would be capable of handling these two sex-kittens.

"We still need to talk with Jarina about her contact aboard this ship. Has anyone seen Thorsen?" Marc asked.

Dag responded with a shake of his head. "I'll talk with Dalgaard. Aren't you supposed to call your dad about now? Marc glanced at his watch and nodded.

"I'll let him know what has transpired and find out if he can get the results for Middlebury's samples." He stared a moment at nothing, and then said, "I still find it hard to believe Breckenridge is FBI." He finished his breakfast and the three officers left to meet with Captain Dalgaard and make a ship to shore call.

Near an elevator, Marc changed his mind. "I have to let Joan and the kids know the end of our vacation is close, and they are safe to roam the ship again. Regina smiled and agreed. Dag stated that he would be in his office on deck one. What else could go wrong?

# CHAPTER

# 58

Sitting by the pool Joan, Sarah, James and Marc relaxed for the first time since the death of James Blackthorne. Marc had finished eating a club sandwich for lunch. Joan consumed a Cobb Salad while hamburgers sated the children. Regina ate pizza with Alaskan salmon.

"I contacted Dad to have him arrange for the Alaska State Patrol and FBI be present at the dock. He's picking up the results of the tissue samples this afternoon."

Joan asked, "How's Camacho?"

"Middlebury thinks she could make it but won't be ambulatory without surgery to remove the bullet next to her spine. It's pinching a nerve or something. She hasn't awakened, yet. The security guy is back in his room recuperating."

"I want to fly home as soon as possible from Anchorage."

"Dag says the ship will not return to Seattle until a full investigation is complete. I'm guessing the cruise line will be refunding passengers for the lost part of the trip."

The silence of the small crowd eased minds. Other passengers enjoyed the sunshine and warm air of the pool deck. The water invited children, mostly.

Middlebury and Ingersoll arrived with Breckenridge. "Who's minding the store?" Marc quipped.

Dag spoke first. "Can I speak with you alone." Marc stepped away with him and Breckenridge. "One of my agents just found Thorsen in his cabin. He's dead of a gunshot to the head."

Marc's jaw dropped. "Any ideas who did it? Or was it suicide?"

"Not self-inflicted. He had a pillow on his head which had a bullet hole and GSR on it. Someone murdered him." Jarina came into Marc's head. "The final agent of the cartel and someone was tying up loose ends."

"That must be the end, then." Marc didn't doubt his words, but he reserved any finality to them. "Beyond the fact that we had nothing on the captain's friend to assume the worst, his death does add one other factor. Which one of them was the head of the snake? Jarina or Cayde?"

⊰⊱

Tiberius and Jerry approached the Scientific Crime Detection Laboratory, entered, and asked to see the superintendent or person in charge for the day. "Just a moment, please." The young woman picked up a phone and punched buttons on a console. "Yes, ma'am, I have two Washington State police officers who requested time with you." She listened to instructions, well trained for fending away interlopers who wanted something for nothing.

"She will be with you in about fifteen minutes." She pointed to chairs for sitting.

Tiberius and Jeremais sat and watched her retrace her path to the desk. "I guess Alaska is in good hands with people like her working for them." She glanced at them as though she heard what was said. Jerry remained stoic. Magazines about exploring the wilderness regions of Alaska displayed places such as Denali and the Aleutian Islands. Tiberius thumbed through one.

Punctuality showed when a middle aged woman emerged from behind doors. The receptionist pointed at them and the lady approached.

"Good morning. I'm Director Renae Shannon. How may I be of help to you?" Tiberius and Jerry shook hands and revealed badges.

"A relative of ours is aboard a cruise ship which is to arrive early tomorrow morning. He is a Washington State Kitsap County

Sheriff's detective on vacation with his family." After supplying the circumstances of the situation, Shannon motioned for them to follow her. They trailed her through the door from which she had emerged. She walked through an efficient, sterile white hallway to an equally efficient office.

"We normally return results to the department from which they arrived. If instructions were left for you to pick them up, then there shouldn't be a problem. I assume these deaths were suspicious in nature and the results of the blood work and other samples will aid in the investigation of what happened." She picked up a phone and asked for another person. After listening she directed them to again follow her. "The fact you have the case number is an advantage. As I stated, we would be sending results back to Juneau."

Jerry said, "We appreciate the odd nature of this request. We had not expected to be part of any investigation until my nephew contacted his father and we came north." In a laboratory area which fostered strange scents of chemical elements, Shannon introduced a member of the testing team. He wore the usual white lab coat which reminded Tiberius of the times he visited the forensics lab in Seattle.

"Dr. Zacharias is one of the finest forensics specialists anywhere. I'll leave you with him to uncover the results of your test requests." Director Shannon departed for tasks undisclosed.

The three men exchanged pleasantries and delved into the necessary questions and investigation of paperwork. "First, I'd like to say the test requests from Dr. Middlebury were standard for poison discovery. The follow-up we did, to answer his other inquiries regarding heart related diseases and possible pathogens, gave mixed results."

Tiberius asked, "What poisoned James Blackthorne and the young steward?" He was handed a sheet of paper. He scanned the information. "No poisons?"

Jerry took the paper and read it. "If no poisons, how did they die?"

Dr. Zacharias said in a clinical manner, "Without a complete autopsy I cannot say for sure, but I can confirm that an agent of some sort paralyzed both of them so that heart tissue samples indicated myocardial infarction occurred. Their hearts quit beating.

Trauma associated with the condition was also indicated." The policemen remained silent knowing more information was coming. "I concluded they had died from heart failure of an unknown reason. Since both indicated the same condition and the age differential was significant, I ruled these deaths to be homicides. I have alerted the State Patrol and FBI, as I understand you have as well."

"We expect to collect at least four members of a group involved in smuggling drugs into the United States from Vancouver, B.C. by way of the Salish Sea, an American Pacific cruise ship." Jerry's answer received an understanding nod.

Tiberius continued, "I spoke with my son, a passenger on the ship. He revealed that an FBI special agent has been undercover aboard the ship since Seattle."

"Very good," Dr. Zacharias said, "but I need to inform you about the remaining results of my testing." He produced another sheet of paper. "The tea samples which came in showed the usual blends of tea leaves expected in morning breakfast and Earl Grey teas. What was not expected was the inclusion of another substance which is very common in this part of the world as it is in Asia and the middle east, especially Turkey." He handed the paper to Tiberius who read it and then gave it to Jerry.

"I don't understand. How can this substance produce these kinds of responses?" Tiberuis said with an incredulous tone to his voice. Jerry handed the paper to the doctor, who placed it in the folder with the other test results. "Can we take a copy of your results and conclusions with us? We want to contact those aboard the ship and let them know." Dr. Zacharias handed the folder to Tiberius.

After leaving the Scientific Crime Detection Laboratory, Tiberius and Jerry returned to their hotel room to discuss their next plan of action. Marc had to receive the news that his sons were both attacked with the end result to have been death. "Ti, contact Marc while I read some research about what this material can do." Tiberius extracted his cell from his pocket and clicked the preset button to call the ship to shore and have Marc informed of the need to return his call.

"Do you think the death of that guy found in the Edmonds hotel might be connected?" Ti asked.

Jeremais answered, "I'm not totally sure, but what happened to him sounds like the resulting deaths aboard the ship."

"We need to pull other odd cases which remain open because a poisoning agent was not discovered. There may a serial killer on the loose or someone who supplies materials to otherwise normal people interested in offing an enemy or supposed enemy." Jerry did not respond. He was on his cell phone waiting for an answer from a friend in the King County Forensic Laboratory.

# CHAPTER

# <u>59</u>

Randolph Middlebury, Olivia Breckenridge, and Dag Ingersoll stood by the bed in which Jarina Camacho lay recuperating from the bullet Regina McDonald planted in her back. Her wound pinched a nerve bundle which prevented leg movement. Consciousness wavered as medications to keep her calm were withdrawn. Dag had questions for her and Miranda Rights to administer. Olivia's friendship meant cradling anxiety for an uncertain future. Being on the wrong side of the attacks against the Jefferson family and the miscalculated death of James Blackthorne necessitated a friend, even one who was law enforcement.

"She will be fully awake within the next half hour," Randolph said. "Do treat her with care. If she moves inadvertently and repositions that bullet, it could render irreparable harm to her spine and possibly death."

Olivia placed a cup of water and a small anti-inflammatory pill, along with a syringe for a local sedative in her back for pain, on the nearby table. Dag sat as still as a cat stalking prey.

A groan alerted them to their patient returning to another momentary conscious condition. Randolph listened with a stethoscope for her heart rhythm, took a pulse measure and stepped aside so Olivia could read blood pressure.

"Get off me, bitch," streamed from a slurring mouth. Eyes opened and closed. Olivia finished reading without paying attention to the interruption and recorded the numbers. She wagged her head side to side, as she handed Randolph the chart. He read and concurred with a nod.

"How is she?" Dag's worrying strained his voice.

Randolph pulled him out of the room. "The entry angle is high and the nerve damage and loss of blood have made her weak. Don't be surprised if she dies."

"She needs to tell us who runs the operation on this ship."

Olivia signaled them to return. "She's awake. I gave her the pill and the syringe is in the intravenous line." Dag closed the space to her side.

Jarina groaned, "He's still alive, isn't he?"

Dag attempted to hold her hand. She pulled away. He answered her question. "Yes." Her eyes closed. "I need you to listen to me. You have done some serious damage to your future. I'm placing you under arrest for the death of one of the crew and critically wounding one of my security men. You intended to kill a passenger, until stopped by Officer McDonald."

"I should have succeeded..."

"Stop talking." He instructed her regarding the Miranda code.

"There doesn't seem to be an attorney present." A sneer crossed her face as the pain subsided with the drip of the sedative.

Olivia approached. "Jarina, you..."

"I need nothing from you. If you're not under arrest, then your complicity tells me you are not who you pretended to be."

"I'm with the FBI. I was undercover to break the back of Pepper's operation. Jefferson and his family changed my role."

"You were my friend." Olivia remained quiet. "You played your part well. Am I going to live? Or has the end come early?"

"You will not walk again."

"Doctor, is this true?"

Randolph said, "You have a bullet pinching a nerve bundle which will prevent your motion. Unless you have a surgery to remove it, recovery is unlikely."

"And my life?"

"It's at risk."

Jarina quieted and turned her head. "Ingersoll, you're not the imbecile you portray. I might want to help your reputation."

～◦◦～

The security guard stood outside the door of the suite ignoring the strange looks from passengers whose awareness of the odd behaviors of crew and officers created an angst which needed addressing. Captain Dalgaard walked the halls and passageways of the ship, speaking with passengers. People who chose to sequester in cabins and suites for the few remaining hours were provided food and drink by the crew.

At the doorway to the twins' suite, the guard received an order to take a break and send a replacement. In the few minutes of unsupervised time a knock on the door provided the opportunity for freedom. Kaliana and Kerrine left everything behind and followed their savior to the small room where Jarina had instructed them about the escape box. After being assured of transport to shore within a short time after docking and secured inside, the savior left to resume duties.

～◦◦～

Marc received a note from the ship's office of the call from his father. He left the Elliot Bay Suite and Joan, Sarah, and James. As he approached the desk, Dag Ingersoll intercepted him. "I have some startling news for you. Jarina admitted to killing Thorsen on the order of the one person who oversaw the entire operation for Pepper." The explanation astonished Marc. "My men are heading to his suite to detain him. Control of the ship is now in the third mate's hands. Dalgaard ordered Thorsen's death to eliminate a perceived weak link."

"Well, then let's find out what the sample results are." They entered the radio room and placed the call. The arrival time was still several hours away. Daylight was not fading in the summer evening of the northern latitudes.

When connection was made Tiberius gave the shocking results. No poison was found in the honey or the tea. Tissues did indicate something triggered a negative cardiac response, and testing of the tea samples presented traces of rhododendron leaves.

"The lab evaluated the honey for any toxicity and discovered grayanotoxin and arbutin glucoside. The honey itself was the murder agent, and tea increased the severity of the reactions. It seems whoever makes this brand has created a hybrid which is many times more potent than regular rhodies honey."

"Thanks, Dad. I knew rhododendrons were poisonous to animals and could make a human sick. I didn't realize a person could be killed with its honey."

"I researched a story of a Greek army decimated by Turks after consuming honey from the luteum azalea. It's called the Golden Comet."

"Is everything ready when we dock?"

"Yes, and how are your prisoners?" Marc clarified the situation and the fact that the ring leader was now known.

"Jarina gave testament to Dag Ingersoll with Olivia Breckenridge regarding her role. The twins are secured in their suite with an armed guard. For the most part passengers are remaining in cabins and being supplied food and water by the stewards and crew. We'll round up the girls as the ship ties up. Passengers will be escorted ashore to be debriefed and the FBI will be in charge of the investigation."

"I do hope Joan hasn't decided to finish you off."

Marc growled, "Dad, that's not as funny as you want it to be. Joan encouraged me to become part of this, especially when James ate the honey and became sick. When we concluded I had been the target, she pressed for me to work with security and medical to end the assault."

He ended the call with a promise to stay ashore with them and tour the area before returning to Seattle. Joan might recant and a broken promise to his father was easier to endure than a broken relationship with her.

The Salish Sea eased into the pier with the experienced crews of three tugs. As lines were cast, Dag said to Marc, "Let's go get them." Tension escaped as quickly as the darkness of night. Elated to have survived, he wanted nothing more than to please Joan with some rest and peace. The enemies were vanquished. Cargo doors opened for removal of all luggage as ordered the evening before following usual protocols for departure. Passengers accepted the instructions for remaining aboard until escorted by State Patrol and FBI.

As the holds were emptied of collected trash and food supplies no longer needed, Marc and Dag arrived at the suite and had the guard knock and then open the door. An inspection determined the accomplishment of their vanishing act.

Dag inquired of the guard, "Has anyone opened this door?"

"Not while I've been here."

"How long have you been on duty?" Dag asked as his mind calculated the time needed to get to the shore and find his quarry.

"I was asked to come here about three hours ago. I replaced Burdette."

"Asked by whom?" Dag's anxiety rose with the timber of his voice.

"Burdette came and got me. He was relieved by Captain Dalgaard. When I got here nothing seemed out the ordinary. The tape still remained on the frame untampered."

"You didn't check inside?"

"I didn't think I needed to." Dag turned from the room with Marc and the security man following. He scurried to an elevator as he pulled a radio from his waist. A call to the passenger departure ramp arranged for the detention of Kerrine and Kaliana.

Dag released the guard from current duties so he could aid in the capture of the fugitives. Marc and he returned to the infirmary to get updates on the security man and Jarina.

"How's little Ms. Priss doing?" Marc's words splashed syrup around the room.

Randolph shook his head. "She passed away about half an hour ago. She reiterated that Captain Dalgaard had control of the smuggling and oversaw everything which was occurring aboard. Dag, you were the one person he worried about. He knew of your skills and once Marc was dead, he would have felt more at ease. Blackthorne's death screwed up the entire plan. He played clean-up to keep his identity secret."

Marc asked, "So he ordered the shooting of Thorsen."

"Yes, Jarina used her advantage with Thorsen to get him relaxed and asleep. She then did the deed."

Dag pulled his radio out to call his office for staff to detain Dalgaard. Marc intercepted. "Are ship radios on the same frequency?"

"I think so. Why?" Before Marc answered his eyes widened and awareness awakened. "He can hear everything when we make calls. Good catch, Marc." He left to gather forces and arrest his captain before a departure from the ship.

"How's the security man?" Marc asked Randolph.

"He's fine. I called the hospital. They're sending transportation."

"By the way, where's Olivia?"

"She's heading to the gangway to assist her FBI special agents in the dismissal of the passengers. Since she's privy to who is staff and who paid their way aboard, she can sort out who gets to leave and who stays. Orders are that only passengers will disembark."

"I guess I need to be there with Joan and the kids." Vacation adventures were more insidious than planned. As they departed the ship with a promise to stop at the FBI office to make a report, they met Tiberius and Jeremais.

An empty cargo box with evidence of human content was discovered in a warehouse owned by the shipping line for the removal of waste product and transfer to recycling and disposal.

The return to Seattle became a primary goal and any further traveling by Marc and Joan Jefferson would be to their home in Kitsap County. Dalgaard remained a fugitive until he was discovered sulking in his cabin, a Mauser by his side. Surrender was not an option.

## ACKNOWLEDGMENTS

*Creating a book can be a daunting task for any writer to accomplish. The seed of an idea, planted in the mind of the author, germinates as words begin migrating from head to manuscript. The journey is not done alone.*

*'Death Stalks Mr. Blackthorne' is no exception to my pattern. Rhododendrons are toxic to humans, as well as to other animals. Stories abound as to the negative effect which eating the leaves and flowers has on animals. The creation of honey, primarily by bumblebees, gives humans a food which has a history of illness and death associated with it.*

*As with any project, research becomes a paramount duty to uncover and discover information which relates to the tale's creation. I have relied on several people to provide for me the essence of the core materials providing the twist to the weaponization of a common food. My first investigation uncloaked the poisonous nature of rhododendrons and azaleas when I read Book of Poisons, A Guide for Writers, by Serita Stevens and Anne Bannon. I had relied on the book for two other manuscripts, Motive and Jerry's Motives, to enhance the stories using common drugs and medicines in uncommon ways. My pharmaceutical friend, David Smith, researched the grayanotoxin which the plants produce. He provided a detailed printout of information. I asked a friend, who produces honey, for guidance about bees. Barbara Stedman of Stedman Bee Supplies, Inc. directed me to her store manager, Sheyanne Ricicar. Sheyanne and I discussed the processes of beekeeping and honey production. It became clear that bumblebees had the best chance of surviving a hive which processed the nectar of rhodies and azaleas.*

*I visited the Rhododendron Species Botanical Garden in Federal Way, Washington, and spoke with Steve Hootman, the executive director. He offered advice regarding the cultivation of rhodies and azaleas and how to create plant starts from cuttings. I purchased a luteum azalea which now grows in my garden. I wanted to be sure the next book in my series, 'In the Garden of Eden', had a plausible premise for the manufacture of a pure rhododendron honey which had the increased toxicity to become a method of seeking revenge and other nefarious activities.*

*The setting for this story was told in 'Jerry's Motives', when Joan raged at Marc for opening an investigation of his uncle's death. She feared it interfering with their vacation cruise. To help me with the finer points of larceny aboard a cruise ship, I contacted a well-known cruise company located in Seattle, Washington. I contacted the public relations office to make an appointment to speak with the director about protocols when a death occurs, and it is suspicious. When the office contacted me, I discovered the director was a former student of mine. We had a great reunion and over a two-and-half hour meeting I picked up the procedures followed by security and medical aboard a cruise ship. I am honoring a request by the director to not name him or the cruise line as a courtesy to them.*

*My wife, Sandy, and I undertook a research project with a week-long cruise to Alaska in October of 2016. I met and spoke with a nurse who was a staff member of the ship. I also met the security people. These members of the ship's crew provided invaluable information about the tasks undertaken by crew and staff.*

*No book is released to public consumptions without first being vetted by eyes other than my own. I gave a manuscript to Susan Wall who returned it filled with corrections and suggestions. Other beta readers, Pat Ryan and Elizabeth Moorhead, pointed out the changes which improved the book immensely. RJ Bauer edited the book finding the necessary changes.*

*I sat with Tim Meikle of Kitsap Printing, reviewing the interior design he did for me, and we corrected the mistakes in the book. He reformatted the book for a better look and the result is what you see. The cover had several changes to it before the final version. I had designed it, but it needed some modifications of title and back cover. Tim helped with that process, so the cover would be acceptable for printing.*

*Now onto the next book, 'In the Garden of Eden' which continues the Jefferson family saga of crime investigations and crises. Thanks for continuing your support in my career as an author who wants nothing more than to satisfy an insatiable reading public.*

CPSIA information can be obtained
at www.ICGtesting.com
Printed in the USA
JSHW021557261122
33766JS00002B/10

9 780988 647152